Black Gold

***By:* Mike Rollin**

"BLACK GOLD" is a work of fiction. This novel is a product of the author's imagination. The characters, incidents and dialogues, organizations and events portrayed here are not to be construed as real.

Credits:
Publisher: MRL Productions, LLC
Cover Photo: Mercedes-Brandxpictures / Coal-Creatas
Author Photo: Tiffany Studio
American / English Edit: The Glades Group
Partner: Gary L. Marvel

ISBN 978-0-9797677-3-9
LOC Number: 2007941738

For information on other mystery novels by Mike Rollin, visit the web site: **mrlproductions.net**

Black Gold

From the Author

As a young man I would often sit and look around me, wondering just what life had in store for little old me.

Much further down the road, I now know that life holds exactly what you want from it. The only proviso is that you have to use plenty of imagination and then go out and grab it with both hands, as it won't come to you.

If you can't imagine it, you'll never get there.

Black Gold starts in the bomb craters of war-torn London and moves to a castle across the German border. This mystery, though fictional, is interspersed with some of my own early life experiences, with lashings of imagination thrown in.

Take your time getting to know the characters, then let your own imagination run free, climb aboard this exciting journey, taste the sheer terror in the bowels of the earth. Then join in a wild chase across Europe, ending in a climax that will have your adrenaline running, surprising and shocking you right up to the very end.

In life, the journey should always be as exciting as reaching the destination.

Mike Rollin

Black Gold

By: Mike Rollin

Preface

I sit here at my desk, at the ripe old age of sixteen and a half. As I look out of the open windows of my bedroom, I am reminded of how much has been packed into such a short time, and indeed how fortunate, I am to be sitting here, in this vast Yorkshire mansion in the North of England.

It is a rare hot summer day; the view is one that has stirred many a literary scholar to wax lyrical. Reminding me of one such; William Blake 1804, whose poem turned hymn, 'Jerusalem,' was sung at my school's morning assembly on many rousing occasions:

'I will not cease from mental fight. Nor shall my sword sleep in my hand.
Til we have built Jerusalem; in England's green and pleasant land.'

As far as the eye can see there is nature's woven patchwork quilt of multi-colored fields; the birds, they too are singing their appreciation, and much like we humans, they're pushing to the back of their minds the extremes that this same view will surely reflect, in but a few short months.

As I look down into the courtyard below, and across from the stable block, the doors to the garages are open. There I see the front of my latest trophy, a 1936 model Mercedes Benz convertible, the deep red bonnet, gleaming as it is caught by the afternoon sun. Tied to the front bumper bar is a white plate bearing an equally bright red letter 'L', reminding me that next week I have the daunting task of taking my driving test.

On the desk in front of me is possibly the most important letter of my life to-date. It bears the credentials of the Bursar of Oxford University, confirming the commencement of my further education at this most revered seat of learning.

I have not always lived in this kind of luxury. The mansion is the property of a wealthy mill owner: my guardian, mentor, and great friend Harold White.

I share the home with Harold and his son David, along with the household staff.

A grunting noise from behind me interrupts my train of thought, as my closest canine friend Titch is disturbed in his sleep by a summer fly buzzing around his ear. He turns over noisily on my bed. As I walk over and sit next to him, I hear a tractor in the distant fields, as the unique smell of new-mown hay wafts through the room, taking me back over the recent past months. I relax back on the pillow, my hand resting on Titch's head.

A butterfly flutters to the open window, pausing in flight but for a brief moment, then moving on. I'm reminded of Harold's wisdom, when he'd said that there are no rehearsals in life; when a moment passes, it's gone forever, so each should be relished, as one savors a fine cognac. Only memories remain; they too will fade with time.

I feel my eyelids begin to get a little heavier; as I drift off into a welcome siesta my thoughts give way to vivid dreams…

There was much feverish activity around the delivery room at the Salvation Army home for unmarried mothers in The Royal Borough of Hackney at London's East End. The busy nursing staff prepared themselves to witness the greatest miracle; another new life was about to enter this harsh world.

A senior midwife held aloft a minute figure, smartly slapping the rump in the time-honored fashion.

Instantly this latest male addition to the poorest area of the capitol began to yell and scream his head off, heralding his arrival to all, at the same time clearing the vital passages to his lungs.

Quickly bathed then wrapped tightly in a blanket, he lay on his side as yet unable to focus his eyes on this new world.

Had he been able to do so, he would have witnessed the saddened downcast faces of the medical staff. For just as he had taken his first breath, the mother who'd brought him into this world had taken her last.

This young orphan's eyes would eventually see quite a number of foster homes, before finally being sent to the North of the country where he was taken into the home of more permanent guardians.

We follow the earlier life of this very fortunate young boy Matt. Maybe he'd had a less lucky start in life than most? Then he is taken in by good people, given family love, guidance and a good education. Born inquisitive with a very imaginative nature, this bright young lad becomes involved in a whole series of unbelievable, exciting and gripping circumstances.

Black Gold is set near to and sometimes deep down a Yorkshire coalmine during the last few years of World War II. Matt finds himself in the midst of foreign agents, intrigue, espionage, government agents and even murder.

This daunting experience takes him and his cohorts' half-way across Europe before the mystery is finally solved. But not before producing a most shocking turn of events!

Though still in his last year at school, and later at university, Matt goes on to become quite the young detective, getting involved in many more thrilling and exciting mysteries.

The Coalmine

Water poured down profusely from above. I remember looking up into that cavernous space some twenty feet above towards my only avenue of escape; I could see nothing but a daunting wall of rocks in front of me.

I began, somewhat frantically at first, to scramble up there, pulling at the large stones from the escape side of the rock fall as I went up, throwing them behind me from where I'd just climbed. Twenty or thirty more of them slid down again. I hadn't even begun to scratch the surface; despair took over my mind and distorted my judgment, it prefaced my every thought.

I know that I should try not to panic, I should attempt to keep calm, but I'm lonely, scared and I think that I'm going to die.

Then fine sand started to trickle from above, like an hour glass. *Time's running out?* At first a mere sprinkling of dust, then two small pieces of rock fell as a prelude, then much larger ones began to crash down next to me; it was too late for me to get back to the bottom.

Suddenly with a roar reminiscent of a prehistoric monster, the whole world seemed to shake and tremble as it crashed down on top of me. I felt a searing pain in my left arm, then a blow to my head, as if I'd been hit by a steam hammer. Then, just like that day on the football field, nothing, just a floating, fluffy blackness!

I regained my senses sometime later; I wasn't sure how long I'd been unconscious, or even if I had been. There followed what must have been an hour or so of abject loneliness, sheer terror; a feeling of involuntary submission, of hopeless defeat.

At first it was like a nightmare, I wasn't sure whether it was real or just a dream. If real, then I was both blinded and paralyzed, for I could neither see nor move.

Slowly I began to remember what had happened and where I was. The stale rancid air hung heavily, the total darkness was indescribable, so thick it felt as though I could reach out and actually touch it; and then everything felt so final. I knew that I was actually buried alive. Apart from the sound of dripping water, the silence was deafening.

It's so hard to adequately describe the feeling of finality then, like a man buried to the neck in the sand, hands bound, in front of an oncoming tide. There seemed to be no escape.

I blinked my eyes tentatively, the only part of me that I could move. God, I was blind, for if my eyelids were actually functioning, then closed or open, I saw nothing. Then as I tried again to move, slowly my fingers began to operate, my toes too. I pulled frantically with my right arm which very slowly came free; my left arm was now giving me a great deal of pain, still trapped, as indeed were both of my legs.

O dear God, help me please………

Chapter One

The Village of Casleton

It was the winter of 1948: the war had been over now for three years, celebrations concluded and long since forgotten.

The euphoria of victory had long since been replaced by an overwhelming loss of direction. But life had to carry on in the small Yorkshire village of Casleton. Many young men had gone to war never to return.

Some of the so called *"lucky ones*" returned wounded, limbless, blinded, some with lungs damaged by mustard gas, crippled for life, most of them physically afflicted, others mentally. Some were so shell- shocked they were doomed to spend the rest of their lives in a suspended state of emptiness, what thoughts if any went on behind their vacant stares.

Widowed and fatherless were words too often employed. It was all well and good for those wealthy politicians to give their rousing speeches in the Houses of Parliament, sure we beat the Hun, but at what cost?

The powerful speeches of the acclaimed victor Winston Churchill resounded daily in the Houses of Parliament. Throughout the world the airwaves vibrated with his eloquent exuberance.

"Never in the history of human endeavor has so much been owed to so few, by so many." Sure his leadership had lifted British spirits to the highest peaks, but now what?

"Why did we fight? What has been gained? Where to next?" Those were the real questions on the minds of the poor people of Casleton, and of all British people, as the likes of Winston Churchill retired for the day to the luxury of an elegant Knightsbridge house, able to relax with a large cognac and cigar, attended hand, foot and finger by servants.

Or alternately at the country estate in Surrey in front of a roaring coal fire surrounded by family and loved ones.

The winds of change were sweeping the country. The Labor Party led by Clement Atlee had won a historic victory in the General Election of 1945. The voting populous had decided that his views on socialism and nationalization should be put into legislation.

As a result in January that year, the coal industry was nationalized and became the N.C.B. (National Coal Board). This was much to the delight of the working people of Casleton, socialists to a man. The gas and electricity companies were next, to be followed shortly by the railways.

Most of the village male population worked down the coal mine, or at the railway repair yard. Though some were employed by the mill, the main work force there were the women of the village,

As coal mining was a deferred occupation, the miners had not been allowed to do military service. Although some volunteered, they'd been forced to continue producing valuable coal for the war effort.

The majority of the young men who'd worked at White's Mill had been conscripted into the forces, leaving the factory staffed by the women and older men of the village, who'd proved to be a formidable work force.

The White family, as they were known locally, owned the mill, which had produced rope, twine, string and Hessian for almost a century. Harold White lived in the only local mansion, along with his son David.

The property was built at the turn of the century, constructed of local Yorkshire stone, forming part of a vast rambling estate consisting of some fifty acres of land. The ravages of time, the inclement northern weather along with the ever-present coal dusts from the adjacent mine had turned the exterior into a dark dreary forbidding vista. It sat at the top of the hill overlooking the whole community like a feudal castle of old. Although the exterior appeared dull and grim, the fifty roomed interior was luxurious.

The property even had a banquet hall with minstrel's gallery. The stables were vast and could accommodate up to thirty horses, above which were living rooms for stable staff and grounds-men.

The mansion employed some thirty-five villagers. Unbeknown to the Whites, its herd of cattle, dairy and beef, as well as sizeable herd of pigs and a large poultry farm, had kept the black market supplied with valuable produce. There had been amazingly high estimates of chickens eaten by the local fox populous!

Harold White was 56 years of age. His wife Margaret had died in 1930 of tuberculosis.

His only son David had returned home from the war, a beaten worn- out shadow of the young man who had left eight years before to join the military.

He'd held a commission in the Kings Own Yorkshire Light Infantry where he had been badly wounded, now having to rely on the support of a walking stick. David returned from the war decorated with the Military Cross, awarded for extreme bravery in the face of the enemy. Mr. Harold White, also the local magistrate or JP (Justice Of The Peace), was extremely proud of Captain David White M.C. (retired). David had just celebrated his twenty-seventh birthday.

At the opposite end of the village, there was another large dwelling, home of the Armitage family who until last year had been the owners of the village coal mine. Nationalization had meant compulsory purchase and early retirement for George Armitage. His son Carl continued to manage the operation pro-tem, pending the installation of a new NCB appointee, the new breed of management.

Their house, built in 1920 was by standards a more modern piece of architecture constructed of red brick with expansive lawns including a tennis court; by proportion not as grand as the mansion, and far less forbidding.

George Armitage and his wife Eve, along with daughter Cheryl and son Carl, had lived in the house since it was built.

Unlike David White, Carl had not served in the military. Instead he had worked alongside his father at the mine.

Carl had not been allowed to fight in the war, even though against his father's wishes he had tried to volunteer.

Before the outbreak of war David and Carl were very close friends to the point of being inseparable. They had attended the same school and shared the same interests. They were both fine horsemen, and as athletes they had competed at county level. Carl was invariably the trophy winner, David taking a place.

During the three years David had been back from Europe, a strange rift seemed to have come between them. David had made numerous attempts to contact Carl but to no avail.

Carl's sister Cheryl, at the outbreak of war had put aside her medical studies at Leeds University and joined the Royal Army Medical Corps. She too had returned home after serving in the desert with Field Marshall Montgomery's forces. Cheryl had also been decorated for extreme bravery under fire; before the war she had been romantically involved with David.

After resuming her medical studies, she had gained a scholarship to Oxford University obtaining her doctorate with Honors, and then went into research, losing herself in her work.

As a result David White hadn't seen Cheryl in two years, with the exception of one brief encounter at a party the previous Christmas. He well remembered her parting comment accompanied by a consolatory peck on the cheek.

"See you soon darling, don't work to hard, and do take it easy on that leg of yours," she'd said in a patronizing, doctor-like fashion.

Before the war it had been generally accepted that the couple would eventually marry. During the war their contact was reduced to mail only, even that had become infrequent as time went by.

Carl's continued refusal to make contact with him began to prey on David's mind; he wondered what was so serious that such good friends couldn't discuss it?

Thinking back across the years, David vividly remembered their parting at Leeds City Rail Station, the day he left to enlist. Cheryl had stood there, looking forlorn with tears streaming down her cheeks as scores of uniformed soldiers pushed and scurried past them in every direction carrying loaded kit bags.

Railway guards' whistles screeched, as the noisy PA system issued its final message like a hanging judge passing final sentence.

"The London Express is leaving platform three, all aboard, stand clear of the doors," announced a female voice almost drowned by the powerful hissing, rising steam from the massive express engine. Then the shrill screech of its steam whistle reverberating throughout the station was accompanied by the final banging of many doors.

Carl had grabbed David's shoulders as the train started to pull slowly away from the platform, giving him a farewell hug. He shook David's hand with their secret handshake, the schooldays sworn oath, 'friends forever.' Though they wouldn't know it at the time, it was to be their last gesture of youth and innocence.

David hung out of the carriage window, an unfamiliar lump forming in his throat, his eyes straining through the blur of the uncontrollable tears that flowed involuntarily down his cheeks, as though washing away the pictures of his youth and then baptizing his eyes in preparation of sights that were to scar his memories forever.

He saw that Carl was already walking away from the platform, Cheryl stood with arms by her side and head bowed. David found himself saying aloud "God bless you my darling, and you Carl, my best friend in the world." He was just eighteen years of age, with not the vaguest idea of what lay before him; Carl was his senior by six months.

The Mill, East Casleton 1948

If David ever needed to catch up on local gossip, he didn't need to buy the local newspaper; he only needed to visit the canteen at the mill during morning tea break or at lunchtime. He would often take a seat off in the corner and listen for a complete update. It was the nerve center of gossip and information, not just for Casleton but also for the entire county.

During one such visit he overheard two of the more eligible young women of the village discussing the lack of available and eligible young men nowadays. They were so engrossed in their conversation that they had failed to see David take a seat at the table next to them. He sipped his tea and feigned reading the daily newspaper. The pretty little blonde whose mother by all accounts cleaned the offices at the neighboring coal mine said;

"What a damn shame about Carl Armitage; Mum was saying how he's lost so much weight, he hardly ever goes out and spends all of his time at the mine. Mum said he had a fearful argument yesterday with one of them German prisoners of war, you know the one that didn't go home with all the others."

At that point the canteen radio burst out the introduction of the popular daily BBC program 'Workers Playtime.' David was irked to have missed the remainder of the conversation; the girls collected up their belongings, as the second girl said,

"What a waste, he's such a dishy bloke too, that Carl Armitage." As they rushed back to their work, the blonde turned around quickly, and looked across at David, saying:

"Hello Master David, I didn't see you over there. How about you taking me to the dance one Saturday eh?" She ran to catch up with her friend, giggling as she went, and then turned again at the door:

"I'm not joking you know, I'm serious," she added, turning towards him as she walked giggling.

Recently David had thrown himself into helping his father to modernize operations at the mill; he was now managing director, his functions being split between manufacturing and personnel.

Across the country the unions under the Labor Government gained strength daily; their continued demands were putting a great strain on both the management and financial resources of most privately owned companies.

That evening David sat in the quiet of his room, the silence being broken only by the strains of Tchaikovsky and the BBC radio orchestra.

Those powerful and emotive compositions transported him from the surrounding hum-drum of normal life, relaxing him completely.

His mind began to wander back to those dreadful recent years, even though it was three years now since the end of the war. He could not rid his mind of those vivid memories, which continually came back to him like the Pathe news reels at the cinema: Scenes of screaming soldiers, the dreadful smell of burning human flesh, and the sight of body parts squandered amongst mud and debris everywhere.

He could almost smell the cordite and hear the never-ending thump of heavy artillery and nerve-piercing sporadic rifle fire. He looked down at his hands, rubbing them, as he still remembered the feeling of the warm blood that had dripped there, as he had held one of his dying men back in those killing fields. A loud knocking at the door brought him quickly back to reality with a jolt.

"Master David, please come quickly, there's an urgent phone call for you."

The nearest telephone was downstairs, either in the main entrance hall or in his father's study.

He left his room in such a blind hurry; he'd forgotten his old army issue walking stick. For the first time since his return, he realized he was a cripple as he staggered, his ungainly gait almost sending him headlong down the wide staircase.

He clutched frantically at the handrail that he'd so often slid down as a youngster. He eventually made the bottom step painfully, limping with difficulty across the marble hallway.

His father stood there holding the phone with a drawn and worried expression on his lined face.

"Son, I'm sorry but there's been a terrible accident. Carl White has been hurt, he's in the hospital."

Chapter Two

My name is Matthew Harper: 'Matt' to most. I'm a bit of a foreigner really. You see, I wasn't actually born here in the village; in fact I wasn't even born in Yorkshire, though I do class myself as a native of these parts.

My birthplace was an orphanage in the east end of London, in the winter of 1930. Obviously I have no recollection of the Salvation Army mother's hospital and orphanage, in the Royal borough of Hackney. I suppose I'm a sort of a 'Cockney Yorkie!' But don't let the London Cockneys hear that.

In the first couple of years I was shipped around to a number of foster homes in London; I never stayed very long at any of them for one reason or another. I still get a birthday card and a small present from one of those families. Auntie Claire remembers my birthday religiously each year.

Due to the German bombing on London, I was sent to my current foster home, in the village of Casleton Yorkshire. Though many miles from the devastating blitz of Adolph Hitler's bombs, it was a cold, bleak and very tough corner of the world.

It was a working class environment with no frills, just hard working God-fearing survivors.

I remember once back then, a well meaning lady said how lucky I was to be away from that awful bombing. I'd wondered at the time, which was worse, to be hit by a bomb or frozen to death up here?

That's the memory I've retained of those unusual, undemanding people, never complaining, working like horses fifty weeks a year, taking two weeks mandatory holiday, everyone at the same time.

They mostly lived frugally, balancing on the very edge of poverty, existing on the bare essentials, then illness, then death, unwittingly passing on the same legacy to their unfortunate successors.

Many years later I thank God often for the innumerable blessings bestowed upon me and mine.

I wish that these tough survivors could have experienced some of life's pleasures that too often we all take for granted, but they would have been incredible and unforgettable luxuries.

One of my earliest and most vivid memories of those days was seeing busloads of children arriving outside the local senior school one evening. There must have been two hundred of them, standing around looking lost with name cards around their necks. Their few personal possessions clutched in their hands, contained in string-handled brown paper bag. Each child carried a box containing a gas mask held by a strap hanging across its shoulders and chest.

Names were being called out as the children were allocated to the families of Casleton. More mouths to feed on an already meager budget.

These were some of the many thousands of children who were evacuated from London when Mr. Hitler stepped up his devastating blitz on the capitol, which included those infamous doodlebugs, or flying bombs. I clearly recall the total chaos that night.

Why is it that an emergency or disaster never takes place on a balmy spring evening, instead of happening on a dark bitterly cold night? I distinctly remember thinking to myself, as a bitter North wind was blowing the freezing cold rains, rapidly turning them to sleet, heralding the coming snow that night.

My own nose and ears almost numb to the touch, or was it my finger tips that were numbed?

My foster mother, who was holding an official looking piece of paper as she moved along a sea of frightened, homesick, but somewhat expectant faces, read labeled chests as she progressed.

At the same time the local policeman, helped by volunteers, was carrying folding military issue camp beds into the school building, for use by those children who were not on the Casleton list and who would be traveling on to the next port of call the following day.

Maybe some of them would have been better off taking their chances back home in London, rather than coming into this God- forsaken, bleak, poverty-stricken, freezing environment, I thought ungraciously.

That night The Salvation Army was serving hot tea and sandwiches from a mobile canteen. I saw the smiles on the faces of the grateful kids as steam rose from the chipped enamel mugs, faces aglow, breath forming little frozen clouds, noses running profusely from the heat of the tea. A little girl wandered off crying.

"I want me mum, where's me mum," she screamed. Another boy rushed to take her by the hand in an attempt to console her. The young boy around my own age went up to my foster mum.

"Is there any sugar for mi sister's tea Missis?" he asked her in his cockney accent. I was detailed to the tea truck to ask. On requesting I was quickly told:

"Young lad, unless you hadn't noticed there's a war on and sugar's rationed," said a lady standing behind the counter, when a jolly-faced man winked at me, reaching across the counter and pressing a sugar lump surreptitiously into my hand.

"Ere you are sun, but mek it go rownd," he said in a strong Yorkshire brogue, grinning as he spoke. I returned to find my step mum holding the hands of the same boy and his sweet-toothed sister, who had by now stopped screaming for her Mother.

"Matt, I want you to meet John and Anne. They'll be staying with us for a while or at least until this awful bombing stops. Say hello!"

My foster dad arrived with his van, a small boxy 1936 Morris seven. We left that hectic sad scene for a comparably quiet ride home, that's if you can call a Morris seven van quiet!

During the trip home, a matter of a mile or so, no one said a word. I sat on the floor alongside the new arrivals, wondering what life had in store for us all. I'd already been taken halfway across the country, from an orphanage in London to a poor mining community in the North of England. It was 1941, at nearly twelve years of age, my whole life ahead of me, and nothing in my pocket but a sugar cube!

The village has a population of around eight hundred, built on the side of a hill or small mountain. The half at the top called West Casleton, the other part at the bottom 'Fall Hill.'

East Casleton, colloquially referred to as down the falls, consisted of rows and rows of terrace houses, a small playing field called, 'The Paddock,' three or four shops, including my foster mum's haberdashery, and of course the mill.

Further down was the main railway line separating us from the next village. There was a large rail yard and some vast sheds where repairs were carried out on all the great steam locomotives of the Northern Region of the L.N.E.R. London, North Eastern Railway. My foster father was employed there as a fitter; he worked on alternating shifts, days, afternoons and nights. Changing shifts each week allowed him time to run his own firewood supplies business on the side.

One of my great treats was to accompany him on some weekends and stand next to those massive towering iron giants, then unusually cold and quiet. I would often stand on the footplate, or sit on the driver's seat with my arm leaning out the side, imagining the countryside and wind rushing past my ears. Sometimes I would climb into the cavernous fireboxes with their special linings burned white from the intense heat of fire. At one time or another all of the locomotives came there, from the stubby tanker engines used mainly for shunting goods and commuting, to the pride of the fleet, the sleek futuristic streamlined "Bluebird".

The village was very old; the houses had stood for many years and consisted mainly of two types. All were terraced and consisted of long endless rows joined together, thirty to forty on each side of the street. The houses that were built back-to-back had passageways called 'ginnels' leading through the building every four houses or so; each house had one room on the ground floor, and two bedrooms upstairs.

The other varieties were much larger with two rooms downstairs and three bedrooms up, a front entrance and one at the rear. The extra sitting room called the front room was used only on special occasions. In our case the front room was Mum's drapery store.

The vast majority of these houses had no toilets inside the building. All of the back-to-backs had theirs outside built in blocks of four. None of these houses were originally built with bathrooms.

Usually a zinc bathtub was set in front of the fireplace and filled with hot water from the boiler built into the chimneybreast behind the fire. The whole family, occasionally being topped up with hot water boiled on the stove, would use the bath water. Only the better off could afford a proper enameled bath piped to the water supply, although they were becoming more commonly used

The village boasted three pubs: The White Horse, The Bedford Arms, and The Bay Horse Inn. There was also a workingmen's club at the top of the hill, a non profit-making association, having a bar, clubhouse, dance hall, and recreation room. Children allowed, but not in the bar.

A dance was held most Friday nights, tambala (Bingo) on Wednesdays and a "turn" every Saturday, meaning a comedian, singer, or some form of entertainment.

There were all of the usual kind of shops including the bakery, post office and cobbler. The cinema was known as the bug. There was the Church, or *Church of England*, and the Methodist Chapel. Add our drapery or haberdashery, and dad's coal and the firewood from disused railway ties, the large logs on which sat the rails. Of course not to forget the "local Chippie," fish and chips to the un-initiated.

There were two school buildings, infants and juniors, from 4 to 10 years, and seniors, to age 14. If pupils passed the entrance exam, they could go to either grammar school or technical college; there they went until seventeen years of age, then possibly on to University. *The next one would be the first!*

East Casleton 1941

Following the packed, cold van ride home we arrived at the house, the new arrivals looking lost and afraid, not quite knowing what to expect. I knew that feeling well.

"Well ere we are, ome sweet ome," said dad, in his Northern brogue.

"Lets take those silly name tags off, I think we know who you are by now, we aren't going to need these gas masks either," mum said, pulling the shoulder strap over Anne's head.

"At least let's hope not," she added. John stood near the door clutching his carrier bag, as though ready to leg it.

The room was warm; before leaving Dad had banked up the fire. One commodity not in short supply here was coal. The fire glowed red hot. Cocoa was made, and then we were escorted upstairs to bed by foster mum.

Then my first disappointment came. My bedroom had been the one next to my foster parents, the one with the fitted bath in the far corner. Anne was being shown into it. I was taken into the normally empty front bedroom over the shop, now housing metal bunk beds. I remember seeing this as a retrograde step. *Who was to have the bottom bunk?* I remembered thinking to myself.

That night was one of the most sleepless that I have ever experienced, not being used to sleeping on that side of the house. Rain and snow battered the windows endlessly and the wind howled mercilessly, I began to think that they would smash right into the room. There was a draft getting through a crack in the glass, fit to blow me right out of bed. But that was only the half of it. John who was in the top bunk, I *won that discussion*, was sobbing heavily non-stop.

"What's the matter John?" I asked cautiously.

"I miss's me Mum and Dad, I'm worried that somefing might appen to 'em, ye know what I mean, all them bombs and everyfink" he said sobbing even louder.

You should try it without having parents at all! I thought to myself. Maybe that was somewhat unkind though, he was only nine years of age, his sister one year younger.

"Come on John at least you're in a warm bed in a nice home where people care; you could still be wandering around freezing Yorkshire in that awful bus or worse still in London." The last comment unfortunately really brought on the water works.

"At least you have your sister with you." At which point the door burst open and as if on cue, his sister rushed across the room, her bare feet slapping noisily on the cold linoleum floor.

"Where are you John, I'm frightened, and I want me Mum," then she too burst into an uncontrollable bout of crying. I was on the bottom bunk now sitting on the edge; I stood and put my arm around her shoulder in a gesture of consolation. *Wow*. The next thing I knew John literally flew through the air, landed right next to me, pushing me the full length of the room across the slippery linoleum floor.

"Git yer ands orf me sis, and don't yer ever touch er agin," his broad cockney accent pierced the air. My reaction was automatic and instantaneous. I dived back across the floor and in an instant I had him pinned down on the floor by his throat.

"I was only trying to be helpful you stupid ungrateful little git," I yelled as I shook him.

At which point I felt myself being hoisted through the air and slammed into the corner of the room, still standing upright.

"If anybody lays down the law in this ouse, it'll be me my lad, does tha understand?" My foster dad's face was an inch from mine. I was left in no doubt as to what he meant, and have never since that day ever seen him so annoyed.

"Yes," I replied.

"You don't understa...." I cut myself short realizing that it would have been futile to try and explain how badly I felt at that moment.

"Matt, don't you think these kids have gone through enough for one day, without your bully boy tactics?" my foster mother interjected.

Anne stayed in that room with John for the night. I was sent in ignominy back to my old room, my arms hurting like hell from my father's strong grip. I could hardly move them. But worst of all, I had displeased my new foster parents, who had taken me in by choice; I liked them so much too.

As for John, he knew the truth; he also knew now not to mess with me. I was going to have to keep a close eye on him.

I woke early the next morning, not aware of the time. It was still dark outside; my ears and the tip of my nose were cold, being the only parts of my anatomy outside the bedclothes, the remainder of me as warm as toast. Turning over, the pain in my arms brought back last night's happenings; it gave me a jittery worried feeling in the pit of my stomach.

Am I going to be on the move again? I wonder what I have to face this morning," I thought to myself as I prepared for the worst.

Downstairs the radio was playing; my temporary new brother and sister were both seated at the table eating porridge, good old Quaker Oats. Foster Dad had left early for work, or was at his smallholding; he seemed to work somewhere every hour that God sent. I glared across at John, neither of us spoke.

"Say good morning to John and Anne, Matt," mum said.

"Why don't they say good morning to me?" I asked.

"Don't answer back," then:

"Mornin, Matt," John said.

"Morning," I muttered begrudgingly. This lad was getting me into trouble twice now.

School that day was total chaos and for many weeks to come. There was at least double the amount of pupils in our classroom, and for some reason the new kids didn't integrate into the class easily. Regular pupils sat at the front and the evacuees at the back. This was to be the cause of much friction before very long, creating a "them" and "us" situation.

The most commonly used phrase from the back of the class was:

"But sir, we don't do it that way in London." Some weeks later a number of evacs, as the locals called them, were taken away. I remember feeling a little peeved because ours weren't among those leaving; nevertheless, life did become a lot more bearable at school.

One day during the morning playtime recess. I spotted four or five evacs standing in a circle; they included George Biggs. He was in our class, and was either very large for his age, or had not been sure of his age when asked, prior to coming North. The latter would have come as no surprise to me. 'Biggsie' was as thick as two short planks and, unfortunately, just as hard. He was big and strong, and a thoroughly ignorant, ill-educated bully.

To carry on: in the center of this group was our John being pushed from one kid to another.

"Yer not a real Cockney, yer a Yorkie lover ain't yer."

"I'm not."

"OK then cum wiv us at dinner time, yer scared to ain't yer."

"No I ain't, I just don't like nickin fings." I heard John reply. *They evidently stole candy from the local shop*.

Just then John was pushed again. He ran straight at the boy who had shoved him, both of his fists flailing. Two other lads grabbed John and held him as 'Biggsie' started punching him in the face.

I looked around the playground, not a teacher in sight. *That's typical*, I thought. *When you try to get away with something there is always somebody watching, but when you need help, it's sod's law!!*

I took off as fast as my legs would carry me, hitting Biggsie full tilt with all my might. My right shoulder landed smack in the middle of his back and he was pitched forward onto his knees. I distinctly heard the air rush from his mouth as he turned still on his hands and knees. He groaned audibly as I hit him full on the nose.

The other kids stood back, the looks on their faces a mixture of surprise and horror, but nothing compared to the feeling in the pit of my stomach right then - a sensation somewhere between total fear and panic.

"Ere e's hit Biggsie," said one of his surprised cohorts.

"Shit, Biggsie's going to kill him," said another. *Dead right!* I thought.

I looked down at the big lout, still on his hands and knees and gasping for air, blood flowing freely from his nose. I began to wish that I was somewhere else right then.

Biggsie lifted himself onto one knee, the color returning to his whitened face.

"I'll blady kill yer, ye norven git," he said as he started to rise to his feet. I wasn't quite sure what to do next; I'd learned at the orphanage and at some of those other foster places that the best form of defense is to attack, and so, *in for a penny in for a pound,* as we say. I launched myself right at the brute again and hit him in the right eye.

At that precise moment an ear-piercing blast from a whistle broke the silence. I was about to make my second attack when I was stopped in mid-launch by a strong hand grabbing the collar of my jacket and was hauled off to the side

"Alright you lot break it up, come on move yourselves, move it now." Mr. Wilson the P.E. teacher had never, and would never again present such a pleasant sight.

"Harper, go to the headmaster's office immediately," he said to me.

"You go as well Biggs." He was by now standing against the wall with a bloody handkerchief to his nose.

"Now what's this all about?" I heard him ask the group.

"How did you get blood over your face, Sykes?" his hand held firmly on the top of John's head.

"It's nothing sir," replied John.

"To the teachers' room my lad, let's clean this mess up." John was led off by the arm protesting.

Meanwhile I was standing outside the headmaster's office next to Biggs.

"I'll break yer bleed'n neck see if I don't," he said poking me very hard in the chest with his forefinger.

"Nobody messes wiv a Biggs, you arsk me bruvers if they does, I'll get yer wen we gits art'v ere, yer beta believe I will Yorkie." I was about to tell him that I was as much a Cockney as he was, maybe even more so.

To be a true Cockney one has to have been born within the sound of Bow Bells, the bells of the church in the London Borough of Bow. I had been. I wondered if he had.

The door to the headmaster's office opened.

"Inside you two, stand over there and hold out both of your hands Harper, and if you as much move them you get double, got that?" He took a long thin cane from a hook on the wall; the first stroke was extremely painful but numbed the hand for the following five.

The same agonizing performance on the other hand, during which time I kept my eyes on the headmaster's eyes, rather than anticipate each stroke; it certainly didn't seem to bother him one little bit. He gritted his teeth together on every stroke. I was tempted to move my hand, but managed to heed his earlier warning. I had to fight hard to keep back the tears, and to stifle the yells.

Not so with Biggsie, who yelled at every stroke and earned two extra lashes for moving his hand. I also noted the tears trickling down his cheeks.

After a brief lecture ensued on the follies of not keeping the school rules, the most serious of which was fighting, we were finally sent out of the office. My hands were completely without feeling and remained that way for a good hour or so.

Outside the office John and Anne had waited for me, a group of Biggsie followers gathered round him.

"What happened, did yer get the cane Biggsie?" asked one of them. He didn't answer, just glared across at me. I didn't think that he wanted more trouble that day, I was sure that I didn't, but I knew that I certainly hadn't heard the last of the class dunce, not by a long shot!

"Fanks for yer elp today, Matt, you was mad to stand up to that lunatic, but fanks, Mate." John put his arm round my shoulder; Anne held my numbed hand as we walked down Fall Hill towards home. I could now cope with the extra pain that came as the feelings returned to my hands for it looked as if I had two new friends at last.

Can't all be bad? I wondered what Biggsie had in store for me. I didn't like the answers that slipped readily to mind.

Chapter Three

Casleton Two Months Later

The passenger train had the usual musty smell, somewhere between damp dust and dirty cigarette ashtrays. The journey to the City of Leeds usually takes 30 minutes, although that depends on how many times the train has to stop for signals; at that moment we were waiting for one at the exit of the station. Then the London express came screaming through. Whoosh, it was traveling at such speed that it made the windows rattle in our little commuter train; the carriage actually seemed to move a few inches sideways.

Foster mum and I were on our way to the child welfare offices; she had received a letter regarding my legal adoption from the welfare officer in charge of my case.

So far in my life I actually seemed to have spent most of it as a case number.

The welfare officer was called Miss Turner, quite a pleasant change from the usual frumpy matrons I'd met in some of the London offices. She was younger and quite pretty, she smelled of scented soap.

She had visited the house last week and looked at my bedroom; she even went to the school and spoke with the teachers, asked a ton of questions around the village too. As the train pulled into Leeds City station, my hair was duly combed and my tie was pulled and straightened.

"Look at your shoes, nobody would believe I cleaned them for you last night," said a concerned foster mum. I had a feeling that she was worried about something, but if so she never said.

As usual Dad was conspicuous by his absence, *what's new?* The station was the usual busy, bustling, pushing packed mass of humanity. I have oft since wondered why people don't slow down a little. What do they say, *"More haste less speed,"* whatever.

I was pushed from pillar to post, eventually was knocked clean off my feet, losing my guardian in the crowd. So I sat down on a station trolley filled with mailbags waiting for the stampede to subside.

There was an over-powering smell of fish everywhere; large puddles of water had collected where the platform had been hosed down after the fish train had delivered its cargo from the coast much earlier that morning.

I sat enjoying the respite when I heard a voice across the other end of the cart. I'd heard it before somewhere, speaking in a strange language, quite harsh:

"Ja so, Ja vul," or something like that.

A number of foreigners worked at the village, two at the local farm, another who repaired the roads, and others worked at the mine.

"Keep away from those men, they're bad, they're *prisoners* of war," I'd been told. Later I'd learned that the two working at the farm were Germans, the one on the road work was Italian and the one at the mine was also a German.

They all wore yellow patches on their clothes so they could be easily recognized.

Most of the kids in the village had patches on their trousers, though not yellow ones, but theirs were badges of poverty.

As I followed the direction of the voices, I recognized one of the men; he worked at the mine. He wore a normal pair of trousers with no patches and an open-necked shirt under a knitted woolen sweater, the kind that I'd seen fishermen wearing on our rare trips to the coast.

I didn't recognize the other man; he wore a suit and carried an attaché case. He seemed quite irritated, and though I had no way of understanding what he was saying, his posture and tone of voice were that of master not underdog.

His hair was cropped close to his head; he was young, quite big and looked very fit. I wondered what the mineworker was doing here and why he wasn't wearing his prisoner's patches, but now my main concern was to find my missing foster parent.

"Ticket please, young man." I looked at the uniformed man on the barrier as I approached.

"I've lost my mother, and she has my ticket" That was the first time that I had ever used those words, *"My mother."* It really felt good, *Mother!*

"Well, well, well, I should officially take your particulars and make out a report but I don't think a fine young man like you would lie, now would you?"

I couldn't give him an argument to that.

"Stand over there, when I get these passengers out I'll direct you to the station-master's office," said the kindly man with a smile.

"Matt, where have you been? I looked everywhere for you!" came the voice of my foster mum.

"You found him then Mrs.?"

"Yes, thank you, constable." A towering policeman stood with a smile on his face, hands on hips, his gaze following us as we left the platform.

"Come on Matt, we're late for our appointment. We can't keep Miss Turner waiting. What will she think of us?"

"Excuse me Mrs., do you have this young man's ticket?"

For the first time I saw annoyance on her face. She glared at the official, rummaged in her bag and thrust the ticket at him, which was duly clipped.

"Thank you Mrs. Try and keep your eye on him now won't you!"

After an uneventful journey across Leeds on foot and bus, followed by two hours of questions and a thorough exam by a doctor, a stern-faced nurse had drawn blood from my arm. I'd taken one tentative step backwards as she'd produced an enormous hypodermic.

"Come on now you're a big boy, this is not going to hurt." *Why do they all lie, it always hurts, whether you're big or little, I hate it!*

Later that day we made our way back across Leeds to the station. We were sitting in the station cafeteria drinking a cup of railway tea, and eating a sticky bun. Railway tea has a flavor all its own, defying description by the most lucid among us. The train back home was due to leave shortly.

"Are you happy living with us Matt?" asked Mum. I nodded, not quite knowing what she wanted me to say.

"It must have been hard for you luv, being moved from one place to another, not knowing where you will end up next." She got up from her side of the table as she spoke, came round to me, took my face in both hands and kissed me on the forehead as tears welled up in her eyes.

"We love you and we want you to stay with us forever. Matt I want you to call me Mum, and to call Jack, Dad." She went back to her seat, took out her handkerchief and wiped the tears from her eyes.

"We can't have children you know, your Dad and I both had tests, and they say that it's me."

I looked at her and began to realize just how lucky I was. Isabelle Harper to me was the nicest person in the whole wide world, and she was going to be my mum forever!

Just a few years later when she became ill, she'd said to me one day:

"Matt, you must never feel ashamed about being adopted. I've overheard some of the other young kids saying cruel things to you but always remember when they were born, their parents had no choice in the matter.

We picked you above all of the others at the orphanage and you are very special to us."

Mum told me later on the train that a date had been set for the official court hearing to finalize my adoption within the next few weeks.

As we got off the train that late afternoon, for some reason the streets of Casleton seemed different as mum put her arm round my shoulder and gave me a big hug.

"Come on my man, let's go home." For the first time in my life, I experienced the feeling of truly belonging.

Lots of people with blood relations never really appreciate that feeling, as they have never known the opposite.

Everyone should belong to someone, somewhere; it's what a life is built upon. It's the very foundation of our being.

Chapter Four

The piano and I never really hit it off. Perhaps it was because I was forced to play it at an early stage in our family relationship. Mum, who played very well, insisted that I take lessons. We had an upright piano in the living room, *cum family room, cum dining room, the only room*!

I had to practice solidly for forty-five minutes every evening come rain or shine, when all of the other boys were out and about. I was tied to my sonatas, preludes, chromatic scales, etc. Not only did I miss a few impromptu games of soccer and cricket, dependent on the time of year, but I became the subject of some ridicule from the village boys.

Once a week I had to go to my piano lesson, a two to three mile walk across country fields to Miss Marshall's house, a stern-faced spinster who had hair on her top lip. She lived with her brother a railway engine driver.

When I set out on my weekly trek I had to pass the football field behind the White Horse pub, where most of the lads would be playing soccer; there the ridicule began.

"Can't come to play soccer, mummy says he has to play the piano, thinks he's too good for the likes of us." So far only words but I knew only too well that sooner or later I would have to put the record straight. Maybe put those words to some different kind of music that they would clearly understand!

My story really begins on such an evening, one of those rare pleasant late summer days; prolific buttercups and daisies in the fields, the smell of fresh mown hay, birds singing their evensong.

Mum had taken Anne to some dress-making class at the village club. John, who decided to walk with me to my punishing piano lesson, said he'd pick some wild blackberries while waiting for me.

He went for a stroll as I went into the Marshall's home. I'd completely forgotten I had an extra half hour lesson that night as I was to take an exam the following week.

When I got out it was already getting dusk and John was nowhere to be seen. I shouted for him I even went into the fields either side of the road. Eventually I decided that he must have become fed up waiting and gone on ahead.

Tonight was fish and chips night, my favorite meal of the week.

It was getting darker by the minute as I set off for home. Just then I heard labored footsteps coming up the lane behind me; someone was running quite hard.

"Matt, Matt," it was John.

"Come quick and see what's going on over there." He was breathless, it took him a good two minutes to gulp air enough to calm down and speak clearly.

"Follow me." Before I could question him he was gone, with me in close pursuit. We crossed at least three big fields where I could hear cattle moving around in the semi-darkness. *Hope the bull's not out here tonight.* John had slowed down now and was gesturing for me to keep down.

We both approached a hedge, and then he cautiously crept along the perimeter until we found a clearing in the bushes and in the barbed wire fence. Somebody had cut a hole big enough to crawl through. It was a little more difficult getting through the hole than anticipated so I left my music case behind, then crawled through.

I lay on my front waiting for him. I heard an oath:

"Shit!" followed by a ripping sound.

"Be quiet John they'll hear us."

"I ripped my bloody trousers, your Mum'll bloody kill me when we get back," he whispered.

"Over there in the middle of the field. Can you see them two blokes? They've put some white cloff on the grass. It looked like they were goin ter put up a tent." Though John's accent was now much improved and he was pronouncing his vowels like a Northerner, he still used 'ff' for 'th'.

As my eyes became more accustomed to the dark I followed the direction of John's finger.

I could just about distinguish the shapes of two figures moving around and I faintly heard voices. From the occasional reflection of their flashlight beam I could just make out a white object on the grass. Nighttime blackout rules were very much in force; looking around I saw no houses or buildings in the immediate area.

"Can you see that lump of somefink between them and us Matt?" John asked. I could see what looked like a stack of hay or straw.

"Okay John, lets crawl over there, and then maybe we can get a closer look or hear more, but for god's sake don't make a sound, follow me," I said.

We crawled cautiously on our stomachs across the center of the field, like highly trained commandos. We quickly discovered that the haystack was a pile of cattle manure and that the wind was blowing straight in our direction, which did not help our noses or stomachs; it did assist in improving our hearing the voices of the two men, as their words carried towards us on the wind, foul as it was.

"I can't understand a soddin word," John whispered.

"That's because they're speaking German," I replied.

"Christ, ar do yer know that?" he asked.

At that moment one of the men strode directly towards our hiding place. My heart missing at least one beat, he stopped just the other side of the manure heap and placed something on the ground.

He then seemed to pace out a distance at right angles, repeating the procedure until he'd delineated quite a large square. I crawled forward out of the shelter of the manure but still couldn't make out the object since it was pitch dark.

I thought that I could smell paraffin.

"Pst, pst, Matt where are you? Can you hear that noise, sarnds like a motor bike engine or sumfink?" Sure enough I could hear the distant sound of a light engine, very faintly at first.

Suddenly I thought of the time. How long had we been here? I didn't possess a watch; in fact I had secretly hoped that my birthday benefactor, dear old Auntie Claire might send me one for my next birthday present. *There's no law against hoping!*

I was just about to suggest to John that we go home. I was hungry, and the smell of that manure was becoming nauseating to put it mildly. Just then a second man came running in our direction, stopping just before the object on the ground.

He lit a match and, whoooof, there was an explosion of light temporarily blinding us both, and at the same time other flames were lit until the center of the field was ablaze with light. Though my vision had become somewhat impaired when he'd lit the paraffin lamp, I'd got a quick glimpse of his face. He was the same German that I'd seen at the railway station that day in Leeds.

Everything then seemed to happen at once, the noise of the engine became increasingly louder.

"Matt what's going on, what are all those lights for?" John stuttered as he asked.

"I don't know but there's something odd happening here." A voice close by yelled something in German. Looking up I spotted something in the sky, which was where the engine noise was coming from, an airplane!

It came directly overhead, then it seemed to fly away, and then it returned yet again, this time a little higher. One of the two Germans was kneeling on the ground, shouting into what seemed like a radio. Just as quickly as it had started, it all went silent again; the plane was gone, nothing more than faint buzzes in the distance now.

All of the flames had been extinguished. The second German came dangerously close to us then moved away again, now nothing, not a sound, absolute and complete silence.

"Matt.....?" " Shh. John," I said, my forefinger to my lips indicating for him to be totally quiet.

"Where did those blokes go?" he questioned in a whisper.

"Look Matt, up there, look, what is it?"

I followed the direction of his hand and saw that something was floating out of the sky: It looked like a box, no two, three, yes there were three of them carried by billowing greenish parachutes.

The first one landed with a loud crash at the other side of the field, the second into the next field. Horror of horrors the third was coming straight at us!

"Let's get out of here, it's going to hit us."

I moved as fast as I could on my stomach, with John close behind. At that moment a large box, followed by masses of billowing green cloth, smashed into the fence no more than twenty feet from where we lay petrified.

We had to get out of there; I saw by the expression on John's face that he would need no prompting. Just then a farm tractor drove through a gate at the other side of the field. Judging by the sounds of grunting and shouting, the men were struggling to lift the other boxes onto the back of the farm vehicle.

One does not have to understand a language to perceive anger, irritation and bad temper.

"Come on John let's get out of here before they come for this other box here."

As anticipated he was out and through that hole in the fence like a greyhound out of the gate. I quickly followed him across the two fields. As we neared the final hedge, I thought I heard voices out in the lane.

I struggled through the hole in the fence, leaving my music case on the ground behind. I walked tentatively towards the voices in the darkness, not knowing who, or what to expect next.

Fifty feet further up the lane we walked slap bang into Constable Ellis, the village policeman, who had just bid a passer-by good evening. For some inexplicable reason, I wanted to get him away from that area, *don't ask me why.*

"What are you lads doing out at this time?"

I answered first. "I came down to Miss Marshall's for a piano lesson, then John and I took our ferret into the fields to try to get some rabbits," I blurted out as I walked further away from the field.

"Hey, don't be in such a hurry, what's the big rush?"

"We lost the ferret and spent too much time looking, it's late my mum will kill us." By now we were a good fifty yards from the field as I kept creeping further away. Constable Ellis shone his powerful light on the side of my face.

"Stop!" he roared, "I'm not in the habit of talking to the back of people's heads."

"Now, get here, the pair of you." his voice bellowed as he leaned his bicycle against the fence.

I looked back towards the field. There was no sound of the tractor and everything was quiet. Maybe the Germans had seen the light, the tables were turned and they were at this very moment watching us?

"You're Jack Harper's lad aren't you? Matthew isn't it?" the irritated constable asked.

"Lost your tongue have you lad?" he snapped.

"Yes, er no I mean, yes I am Matthew Harper and no I haven't lost my tongue."

"No need to be cheeky my lad, and who might you be?" he asked glaring down at John, who still had a look of sheer fright on his face.

"John Sykes, Sir, I lives wiv mi sister at Johns house, we're evacuee's sir," he spluttered.

"All right you two, on your way, hurry home before they send out the search party. I'll have a word about this with your dad the next time I see him." With that he threw his long leg over his cycle, then peddled off. I watched as he passed the field, then he continued into the night.

As if by telepathy we both started to run, not stopping for breath until we had put a couple of miles between us and what we'd just seen. When we got home mum was out and of course dad was working.

"She went out looking for you, you two ain't arf goin to cop it when she finds you," said Anne frowning.

"Thanks Anne, thanks for nothing," I said resignedly.

I won't go into the details of the next half hour. Summary: no fish and chips, no going out evenings for a week, and an extra half hour's piano practice for a week!

In bed later that night I lay awake, the events of that evening turning over and over in my mind. What was in those boxes that was so secret they had to be sneaked into a remote field by parachute and by Germans?

Why hadn't I told the police about it when I had the chance, and what was I to do next? Maybe I ought to go straight to the police tomorrow?

"Matt, you awake?" I near jumped out of my skin as John crept onto the end of my bed.

"Matt why didn't yer tell that copper what we saw tonight?" *I had not so long ago asked myself the very same question*. I knew he was right.

"That's a good question. Wish I had the answer for you. Maybe there were a few other questions that needed answering too. Off you go to bed, John. It's late and I'm tired; don't know about you."

"He tiptoed across the room and then he paused with his hand on the door knob.

"Matt, one fing I fink you forgot.".....

"What's that?"

"You left your music case next to the hole in the fence!"

The very next day I was given temporary reprieve from my enforced confinement. Mum sent me on some errands to West Casleton, quite a long walk. I had to take some cakes made by a number of the village women and deliver them to the church hall.

En route I was to collect some shoes from the cobblers. As I came out of the cobblers turning towards home, a familiar voice from behind said:

"The very man, just the man I'm looking for." It was the voice of Constable Ellis who walked towards me.

"I still don't know what to make of you lads last night. Did you two see anything odd down the fields, see any bright lights did you?

Two gypsies say they saw bright fires near to where I saw you lads."

"Sounds odd to me Mr. Ellis, it's usually them that have the fires. Did they see anything else?"

"Like what?" he asked me. *Come on now's your chance to tell all,* I thought.

"I have no idea sir. It seems odd that anyone would light fires when they know that there's a blackout on." Again I lied by omission, this time absolutely determined not to tell anything.

"I have a strange feeling that you're not telling me everything. Oh! And by the way lad, you'd better take this," he said holding out my music case. I nearly snatched his hand off. I'm sure that he'd noted the eagerness with which I reclaimed the case, and that I was more than a little pleased at its safe return.

"The post lady saw it in the hedgerow, read your name inside the flap, no address. She brought it to the station. It's your lucky day. Good job those gypsies never spotted it or that would have been the last you would have seen of your music case." I opened the case, everything seemed to be in order.

"Let's keep this matter our little secret," he winked a conspiratorial grin on his face.

"But remember if you see anything strange going on, tell me, you hear? We are at war, and it's your duty!"

I walked home with a bit more of a spring in my step than when I'd left earlier.

What was in those boxes, and where were they now? I asked myself. I would have to look, but where was I to start, the farm maybe? Deep down I knew that I should report the whole thing to the law, but I wanted to find some answers first, then be able to give them the full story.

Chapter Five

The Village 1948

The ear-piercing, shrill blast of a powerful steam whistle could be heard throughout the village. It came from the coalmine, announcing the end of the day shift. At the head of the mineshaft the Banksman who operated the cage from above rapped the red button three times, signaling to the engine room that the cage was to bring men back up to the surface, or more correctly, the corresponding cage at the bottom was ready to bring the men up.

With a loud hissing noise accompanied by the clanking and groaning of steel, the gears were engaged. The great steam engine began to roll, slowly at first, then gathering momentum. At the same time the massive wheels aloft began to turn in opposition as the cage made its descent to the bottom of the shaft some three hundred yards.

Simultaneously, the cage at the bottom began to ascend, carrying its cargo of tired men back up to God's welcome fresh air and precious daylight, after ten backbreaking hours down that black hole.

On the pit top, the cage slowly emerged into the view of the fresh clean-faced men of the afternoon shift, awaiting their turn to descend. Coming to a halt, the cage automatically lifted the retaining barrier, men spilled out, their metal clog irons clattering and scraping on the sheet metal floor and steps, as they hit the fresh air, like rabbits out of a warren.

Kneepads still strapped onto their legs, empty sandwich tins hanging from their belts, some with electric lamps attached to their caps still alight. All of them showing white teeth and the whites of eyes in contrast to the black of their coal dust-encrusted features.

Their lamps were handed in through the small window of the lamp room; simultaneously their time cards punched into the recording clock finishing the shift; another punishing day was over.

The relief to get away apparent on their faces as some climbed onto bicycles, others starting out on foot across the fields for home, a few to the pit canteen for a welcome cup of tea. Yet another day starts for the next shift, another backbreaking session about to begin.

Carl Armitage stood waiting for the return of the next cage. He climbed aboard alone, heard the usual three raps on the signal button and felt the cage drop beneath his feet on its nine hundred foot descent.

Even after all these years, he still had that uncomfortable feeling as if he'd left his stomach behind. The engine controller seemed to know when he was in the cage, he thought to himself, as the cage gathered speed.

He listened to the echoing twang each time the guides on the corners of the cage passed over a joint in the thick steel hawsers. He could see from the light of his lamp the surface water pouring down the rounded brick walls of the shaft into the sump way below.

Because the six steel hawsers that form the guides to each cage are fixed only at the top and bottom of the shaft, the cage has a tendency to sway from side to side. The faster the ride, the more it sways.

It is always a pleasure to get out of this bloody contraption, Carl thought to himself, *and preferably at the top*!

During the times when coal and supplies are being carried, the cages travel at twice the speed. To differentiate between men and cargo the engine room receives different bell signals from the Banksman on the surface and the On-setter down below, the two controllers on either end of the shaft.

Absent-mindedness or forgetfulness on their behalf can give you a bad ride.

Carl stepped out onto the pit bottom to a hive of activity as men were being allocated their jobs for that day's shift. The senior man below ground is the Overman, who in turn reports to the under- manager. A man called a deputy controls each coalface zone.

The 'pit bottom,' as this area is known, is a large open area finished out in brickwork and brightly whitewashed. In one part there is a small office used by the Overman or by senior management, leading off to a fully equipped first aid room.

In a separate part there is a long stable accommodating some thirty ponies.

The large open area with four sets of rail tracks is for shunting the small trucks, or 'tubs' as they are called, prior to them being taken up to the top. These are the metal rail trucks three feet by four feet and three feet deep. The tubs run on the rails carrying materials on the way in, and coal on the way out. They hold over a ton of coal each.

Behind the shaft is an engine room that houses the powerful electric motor that drives the steel haulage ropes that run on pulleys on the ground all the way to the workings, pulling the valuable coal-filled tubs back to the pit bottom.

The main tunnel called the Main Road has smaller tunnels called gates leading off to the coalfaces.

Each coalface is around 200 yards long and has a smaller tail gate on the left end and a larger main gate on the right. Miners enter by either gate; when they reach the face they crawl under and along the three foot high face and begin work digging out the coal. The coalface progresses further out each day.

A conveyer belt runs along the floor of the coalface into the main gate, which spills onto a bigger conveyor belt set on rollers, taking it out to the main road, where it eventually spills into the tubs.

Initially workings were very close to the bottom, but after years of taking out coal progressively, the nearest ones are now three to four miles underground, quite a long trek.

Mostly, the miners are able to ride in to the workings on a paddy train; this is a number of trolleys with fitted wooden seats, pulled along the Main Road rail tracks by the endless steel haulage rope, which runs on pulleys in the centre of the rail road.

Normally this hauls the coal tubs out to the bottom, but is reversed for men traveling, and also for taking in materials inbound.

At the other end they still have a good half mile to walk to their coalfaces.

Air is pumped through large ducts along Main Road into the tail gate and regulated by a series of air doors as it circulates to the coalface, then along and returning out of the main gate.

Each collier works underneath there kneeling all day.

He has around 10 yards of the coal to remove, called a 'stint,' approximately two tons to each yard, which he shovels onto the conveyor belt running along the floor behind him. He erects supports where the coal has been removed.

When more supports and supplies are needed on the face, verbal requests are relayed along the face to the timber boy in the tail gate, who puts the material on the conveyor belt under the face.

On the day shift, tubs full of roof supports and materials needed at the face are taken to the end of the haulage rope, and then the tubs are pulled by ponies along into the tailgate. Supplies are then emptied and stacked at the coalface by the pony drivers.

The empty tub is then returned to Main Road, where it is filled with coal from the conveyor belt, then pulled by the steel haulage rope to the pit bottom.

Usually there are twenty or so tubs linked together in a train, then connected to the haulage rope. They are accompanied by a young lad called a Bevin boy. In case of derailment, he can stop the haulage rope by using electric signal wires running alongside the track.

Not so many years earlier, similar but smaller tubs were actually pushed underneath the coalface, the coal physically hacked out, shoveled and filled by hand.

Now mechanization is taking over: conveyor belts, coal cutting machines, shot firing explosives to break up the coal, instead of hand picks; nevertheless, still extremely perilous, soul-destroying, backbreaking hard work, which I once heard aptly described by an old retired collier as being worse than a prison sentence of hard labor.

Carl waited until the bottom had cleared of men then sat down with the Overman.

"What brings you down today, Master Carl?" the Overman asked quite casually. "We don't normally have the pleasure of your company of an afternoon."

"Yes that's perfectly true Ralph, but the day that I've to explain my movements to you, I think would be my last one down this bloody hole. Now if you're through with the questions, perhaps you would like to get out of here and let me have a spot of privacy. I'm sure there's plenty of work to be done."

"Yes, Master Carl, well I'll be off then." As he walked away he thought to himself how much Carl had changed, and wondered what it was that seemed to be eating away at him.

Carl watched as the Overman walked off along the main road, the glow from his cap lamp disappearing into the distance. He went through to the stables; seeing the stableman bending over a gray pony he said:

"How are things with our four-legged staff today?"

"Oh, hello, Master Carl, you gave me quite a turn, didn't hear you come in," said Ben the stableman. Ben had lost an eye in an accident years ago as a young miner.

"Things are OK. This little chap has a nasty leg, a tub turned over and scraped his shin badly, a full tub at that. The vet just left; he reckons he'll be just fine but he'll be off work for a week. Thought I might as well get him up top, a bit of fresh grass and sunshine works wonders you know."

"Well, Ben, if anyone can put him right you can," Carl said as he walked along the never-ending row of stalls.

Towards the end he spotted a toolbox on the floor outside one of the stalls; the farrier was re-shoeing one of the ponies.

"Gutten Tag Mein Herr, Oh, I'm sorry, you don't vish me to shpeak in ze mutter tongue ja!" the ex-prisoner of war said flippantly in his broken English accent.

"I got your message, what do you want?" Carl snapped as the farrier threw a tool noisily into his box.

"Our friend, he dit ask me to ask you, ven you intend to pay some of ze money you owe, unt he vishes you to meet mit him at ze club in Leeds tomorrow evenink. Is zere a message you vish to send him, mein friend?"

"No, there is not and don't call me friend. If I had my way you would be in prison where all you wartime krauts belong." Carl walked away with a look of anger on his face.

"Zen can I assume zat you vill be zere tomorrow?" he shouted.

Carl turned his face puce with anger.

"You can assume just what the bloody hell you like you kraut bastard." Carl snarled as he spoke.

"Everything alright, Master Carl?" Ben asked, as he came out of a nearby stall. "No, everything is not alright. Now you get on with your work and stop being so damned nosey," snapped Carl marching out of the stables. Ben walked along to where the farrier was working.

"Did you say anything to Master Carl just then?"

"Nein, not me sir. Not vun verd!"

Carl stood by the shaft picking up the battery telephone handset. He had wound the handle three times but got no reply. Eventually he heard:

"Pit top, who is it?"

"Armitage here. Are you asleep on the job up there or what? Get that damn cage down here, get me out of here, and do it right now."

"Sorry, Master Carl," but Carl had already hung up the phone. He spoke to the On-setter standing next to him as the cage arrived at the bottom.

"Sweep that lot up, some poor bugger slogged his guts out to get that here today," said Carl pointing to coal that had spilled around the entrance to the cage. The cage went up the shaft with Carl inside.

"Yes, Master Carl, three bags full Master Carl, screw you Master Carl," the On-setter said in a loud voice. "What's chewing your balls lately?" *I wish his father could hear him talking to people like that,* he thought. *It won't be too long now before he's replaced by the new breed of N.C.B. managers already being trained and schooled for the job,* he thought to himself, smiling smugly.

Carl came out of the cage scowling at the employee who lifted the swing door out of its catch.

"It's pouring down out there Master Carl. Watch your step on those stairs, they're treacherous in the wet."

Carl gave no answer, ignoring the employee's warning. He went over to the lamp room handing in both his battery lamp and the old Davy lamp, a brass kerosene lamp carried by all officials down a mine. It is used for detecting the presence of the deadly gases that form underground and hang around in the roof spaces.

The rain was pouring down as Carl crossed the pit yard towards his parked car. Black mud had churned up into furrows by the heavy coal transporters, which seemed to troop endlessly towards the lane that led to the road. He took off his boots, caked with mud, placing them on newspaper in the trunk of the car.

Carl then drove home thinking about his conversation with the German and the meeting that he knew he would have to attend. As his car crunched up the gravel drive to the big house, he felt sick in the pit of his stomach.

Chapter Six

East Casleton 1940

In the summer of 1940 Hitler was dominating Europe from the North Cape to The Pyrenees. His two remaining enemies were Britain and Russia. Prime Minister Winston Churchill vowed to continue fighting.

After the fall of France, the news had so shocked the Americans that they had begun conscription, or draft as they say, for the first time in American history since their Civil War. I spent as much time as I could with my ear glued to the wireless.

"I'm surprised that you aren't permanently joined to that wireless Matt," Mum said to me one day, as I listened intently to the latest news.

Hitler's ambition was to conquer Britain by crossing the English Channel, though he wasn't yet prepared to take that risk until the Royal Air Force could be put down, or at least neutralized. That is why the battle of Britain was fought in the air and not here on our shores.

At the same time, The Battle of the Atlantic was waged, the Germans continually blockading us with submarines from bases in France and Norway in an effort to cut our overseas lifelines, and starve us into submission.

At that time intelligence reported Germany had only twenty-eight U-Boats, but it was still sufficient to keep us in constant danger until the spring of 1943. The war correspondents went on to tell us that during the last year the Germans had been carrying out daytime raids in an attempt to bring our fighters out. But they had not reckoned with our new invention called 'Radar.'

They went on to say that between August of last year and May of this year, the Luftwaffe had made seventy-one nighttime raids on London and fifty-six on other of our Cities.

"It is believed that Hitler will now postpone any invasion of Britain after his defeat in the Battle of Britain!" came the welcome news that day.

"Thank God for those fantastic Spitfires and those brave Airmen," Mum said, her heartfelt vote of thanks to be immortalized later, and somewhat more eloquently by Mr. Churchill. There was also talk of London's evacuees returning home in the near future.

That week I was legally adopted. After all of the meetings, interviews and weekly visits to Leeds, the event came as quite an anticlimax. We spent more time sitting outside the courtroom than in it. Mum, Dad and me. Yes, Dad was there too!

The courthouse was a most strange and musty smelling building with gigantic ornate pillars, doors and shiny wooden benches worn by generations of posteriors over the years. Noisy feet clattered on highly polished marble floors with statues everywhere. There were busts of long dead and fearsome looking Judges from the past. I looked at one that seemed to glower directly down at me. *I'm glad he's not doing my case today. Maybe this will be the last time that I shall be referred to as a case!* I thought as I purposely scowled back at those white lifeless eyes.

People were rushing everywhere clutching pieces of paper, lots of men and women wearing gray wigs. I later learned that to walk around in such a busy area clutching papers, and looking resigned, is one way of becoming virtually invisible to the onlooker.

Eventually our names were called. The Judge was sitting at a table; no wig, no mallet, no one else there, with the exception of the court recorder. I assumed that's who she was as she kept tapping things down on a small quiet typewriter.

The Judge asked me the same old questions, talking to me as though I was a five-year-old simpleton; then he announced in a loud clear voice to no one:

"If there are no objections, this adoption will be legally entered into the court records as official." It was over.

Though my parents had the foresight to register me at school under the name of Harper, all other official documents had to be changed. I was now and forever officially Matthew Harper. I'll bet you there was not a happier person in the whole world, or a Mum and Dad more proud that day. I forgot to mention, my birthday had come and gone, and guess what? Good old Auntie Claire hadn't forgotten me; she'd sent me a watch. I have since wondered whether it was an act of divine providence, or perhaps the result of some subtle prompting by an erstwhile Mum. Either way, I was now the proud owner of a Kelton watch complete with leather band, luminous dial, and the latest sweep second hand.

By far the best present though, was the one from Mum and Dad: a Jack Russell Terrier who I named Titch. Apart from time spent at school, Titch and I were rarely separated from that day on.

One very memorable, earth-shattering day at school during morning assembly, the headmaster announced the impending return of the evacuees. bringing about much cheering from both sides of the fence. With that news and my adoption finalized, I felt ten feet tall.

Walking home that afternoon towards Fall Hill, passing the large stonewall surrounding the soccer field, I heard lots of laughter and shouting. I squeezed through a hole in the adjoining fence where a board had been strategically loosened. An impromptu game was being arranged, accompanied by the usual comments.

"I wanna be on that side, let me be goalie."

"Aw come on, all the big guys are on one team."

"It's not fair all the best players are on your side." These arguments could go on for ages. Then a voice was heard above the others.

"Ere, as they say we're all orf ome soon, let's ave a real match, Londoner's versus Yorkies."

It was the voice of Biggsie! After much bickering, it was all arranged. The following Saturday morning the game was to be played, not behind the Pub as usual, but up West Casleton at the "Reck", or recreation grounds.

They had a full sized field with proper goal posts instead of two sticks in the ground.

One of the older lads who was a pony driver at the pit had volunteered to be ref; kick off was scheduled for ten in the morning.

Saturday morning dawned, a damp and miserable vista; it had been raining during the night. The field had large puddles, seemingly strategically placed in both goalmouths. The largest mini-lake had formed slap bang in the center, where many feet had worn the sparse grass away.

Titch, my dog, was having the time of his life charging through puddles of the water, attempting to catch the birds who were trying to enjoy the luxury of a freshwater bath. Under normal circumstances such an event would have been postponed, but not on this momentous occasion. Only an earthquake or perhaps a monsoon could have derailed this match.

This was to be the biggest needle match of all time, the outcome a matter of the North-South divide.

I thought, at the time, to call this proposed game a grudge match would qualify as the understatement of the century. I remember thinking that perhaps battle or even war would better describe the coming events of that day.

The game was to last the usual ninety minutes, forty-five each way. On a normal field the customary change of ends at half-time can only be beneficial as regards strong wind or ·bright sunlight; though not in the case of the 'Reck.' The gradient here was so substantial that the ball would almost run from top to bottom un-aided; with a wind, it most definitely would.

At nine thirty, twenty-two players of all shapes and sizes were duly gathered dressed in a multiplicity of clothing, ranging from coveralls to old oversized trousers tied by string at the bottoms. Some wore oversized army issued shorts borrowed from dad.

Footwear ranged from clogs to heavy work boots to PE pumps. The only way of distinguishing one team from the other was by the colored bands strung diagonally across each chest. We had red and they had green.

The teams had already split into two groups either side of the field; there were a lot more spectators than I had anticipated as word travels fast in Castleton.

As it worked out, the teams were evenly matched. Earlier the evacs had been a couple of players short and after much arguing they had been allowed to import two evacs from the neighboring village of Middleton, one of whom was later to become a national soccer star.

We also had a budding star, actually two. One was to become a county school player and Robert Hodgson would go on to become a professional player.

The referee blew a shrill blast on his whistle, beckoning to the respective team captains to approach the center of the field. The customary coin was sent spinning into the air, sparkling as it began falling to the ground.

"Heads," yelled the evac's captain. It is customary for the visiting team to make the first call. Heads it was.

"We'll play uphill first half," said their captain. *Wise decision.* The teams took their designated positions. Mine was one of the defensive positions. Oh yes, I was going to play in this match. I wouldn't have missed it for the world. My position was fullback, one of the two defenders of the goal, along with the goalie.

The remaining nine players, a mix, were of midfield and halfbacks, or attackers, the two important wingers the sprinters who move along the outsides. Their job is to pass the ball across to the forwards. Usually the center half is taller than most, enabling him to get up into the air and head such passes above the defenders. Robert, our captain and center half, was thirteen years old but already over six feet tall; yours truly, five feet ten, and a 'lanky hundred twenty pounds' Mum often used to say.

"Matt, you eat like a horse, but never seem to put on any weight."

"A growing lad, Mum," was my usual retort. I think in those days I was built for speed and not comfort.

Having won the toss the evacs also had first possession of the ball. We lined up for the kick off; the referee looked at the church clock. I could see Titch pulling on his leash as John held onto him.

"Come on Casleton," shouted a number of the village girls.

"Let's give 'em what for," yelled our school mates.

At the same time I noticed a tall slim, rather well-dressed man standing on the sideline whose face I didn't recognize. I remember thinking that he looked uncomfortable, maybe a little out of place there. The whistle blew, the game was on.

I was wearing an old pair of grey flannel trousers and I'd taken the precaution of packing thick pieces of corrugated cardboard down the insides of my long socks to protect my shin bones.

A wise measure as it turned out. The first twenty minutes was comparatively uneventful, apart from a mud bath for those playing center field. A shrill blast on the whistle heralded a penalty kick; evidently an evac had touched the ball with his hands in the penalty zone. Our captain drove the ball into the back of the net, so to speak. It actually went a hundred yards into the park as there was no such luxury as a net. The first blood to us was demonstrated in the delight of our supporters judging by the tumultuous applause.

A defender never gets to see much detail beyond the half-way line. Then about twenty minutes from half time their right-winger broke loose as he sped down the wing, deftly sidestepping two of our men. He kicked the ball high into the air. As it soared towards our goal area I went up towards the rapidly descending ball, a soaking wet heavy ball made of stitched pieces of leather, a ball with a heavy laced cover, over the neck of the inflated inner bladder.

The laced area hit me on the temple. The force bent my neck backwards as a blinding flash set my world spinning. I heard a distant whistle and then, nothing else.

I awoke to the disgusting smell of ammonia, later to learn 'smelling salts.' I remember hearing the game still in progress and looking up into the face of the stranger that I had seen earlier.

"Don't try to get up just yet young man, that was a nasty bang you took on the head there," the stranger said.

"It was a good save though Matt," said one of our supporters peering down at me.

"I think I'm alright now," I said to the stranger, as Titch rushed across licking me all over my face. I sat up freeing myself from the support of the man. My whole body felt weak, the damp was striking up through my already soaked trousers. Suddenly I felt ill as though I would vomit; someone passed me a tin mug of water, which tasted like nectar.

"Here, take a sip of this, but just a small sip mind, don't gulp it down," he said, simultaneously screwing the top from a small flat silver container and putting it to my lips.

"Medical purposes only," he'd said as I experienced a most peculiar sensation. The liquid seemed to make my lips and mouth tingle like putting your tongue on a small battery.

"Just one more sip," the man said. The second sip was bigger than the first; as the fluid went down my throat it seemed to warm every part of my body and made me cough a little.

"Wow, what was that?" I asked, my throat still tingling pleasantly.

"Brandy he replied," it will do you good." Gingerly, I got to my feet still feeling a spot shaky.

"What's the score?" I enquired of no one in particular. I was informed that the evacs were in the lead two goals to one with five minutes left of the first half, and us to play uphill in the second.

Neither of the teams could afford the luxury of reserve players. They had lost one player who was dragged off the field by his irate guardian who evidently had sent him to the shops an hour ago. I just had to pull myself together, ready for the second half. Sadly the end of the game was to come quickly for me. After a five-minute break at half time, the game was resumed.

The evac's attackers made a concerted effort. Their forwards were on us before we were ready. One man broke away, passed the ball across the front of me.

I went to tackle the recipient who spun around hitting me viciously across the ear with his massive elbow. I looked into the face of Biggsie!

Out of the vision of the referee, he kicked me hard on the right shin, but thanks to my home-made shin pads, the force of his kick was reduced. I went for the ball with my right foot as he pushed me, most of my weight on the one leg. His 170 pounds had me crashing to the ground.

I heard the ref's whistle as the big lout dived on top of me, again out of sight. He drew back his right hand and hit me with an almighty blow to the ribs. I felt a sharp pain and heard a crack somewhere around my rib cage. I had never experienced such pain, it was excruciating. I somehow got to my feet, to see Biggsie still kneeling, a broad sickly grin showing his yellow teeth as it spread over his ugly spotty face.

"How dye feel now piano player? I owed yer that one!"

As he spoke gloating in that irritating accent, I looked at his ugly smirking spotty face and an uncontrollable anger welled up in my chest, accompanied by an enormous hatred. Grabbing a handful of his wiry hair, I drove my right knee with all of my might straight under the chin of the bully; I heard and felt a most satisfying crack reverberate down my leg. Simultaneously a searing pain from my own ribs seemed to shoot through my body like an electric shock, once again my senses left me completely.

I regained consciousness amid a sensation of moving and the strong smell of leather pervading my nostrils. I was half-sitting, half-reclining across the rear seat of a car. I groaned, sweating profusely from the continued pain in my rib cage and forehead. The car was pulled over to the side of the road.

"You were certainly in the wars today young man." It was the same stranger from the football field earlier on.

"My name is Harold White. I'm going to need yours for the people when we get to the hospital in Wakefield shortly," he said, leaning over the front seat

"I don't need the hospital," I exclaimed.

"I think so," he said as the car pulled away. That was a nasty blow you took to the head earlier. You could be concussed and I suspect the power punch you took from that lout could have fractured your ribs." He told me that he had a friend at the hospital, a doctor who would help.

I awoke the next morning in a hospital ward alongside twenty or so other patients in neatly lined beds. I often think that the word 'patient' is a very apt word, an admirable quality to possess, particularly useful when dealing with the national health service of Great Britain. Though I'm not wishing to sound ungrateful, for how else could I afford such excellent treatment?

I remembered sitting in the waiting room the previous day, outside the emergency room, for at least two hours, *trying to remain patient*!

Each time it appeared to be my turn next, some other emergency would arrive. At least they all looked worse off than I, most were deemed more deserving.

Harold White was standing by the bed positioning the only chair for my Mum to sit on.

"How did it all happen: why were you involved? Is there anything seriously wrong? Why do you have stitches in your head? They say that you broke three ribs. Matt, I've been so sick with worry!"

She had not stopped for a breath. "I'm alright Mum, really I am." Just then a nurse came over with some forms.

"Are you Matt's Mum?" There were forms to be filled out. *There are always plenty of forms*. Mum went off with the nurse.

"So how's the patient today," Harold White asked. I thanked my newfound benefactor for all his generous help.

"You remind me of someone that I used to know a long time ago," he said with little more explanation.

Afterwards he took us home in his car, refusing Mum's invitation to come in for a cup of tea, which left me with a lot of explaining to do.

They had x-rayed me at the hospital and put five stitches into my head.

"Take one of these tablets twice daily, try not to move around too much until your ribs heal." *Did you ever crack a rib?* Every movement, every cough, each sneeze and laugh becomes sheer agony and goes straight to the subject area. Secretly, I hoped Biggsie had as much pain.

I later learned that his jaw was broken, both sides, and that he'd lost two of his front teeth. I still bear the scar from those teeth on my knee to this day. Evidently he was taken to Leeds Infirmary for surgery and came home with his jaws wired together.

They never finished the game, the score, three to the reds, and three to the evacs; an acceptable draw given the circumstances.

Shortly after that day the evacuees returned to their respective homes in the South. We had a sort of a farewell party. The wireless had good news; the war should be over soon, though it was actually to last three more long years.

The final day of parting came. Mum and I took Anne and John on the train to Leeds Central station, where railway warrants had been issued by the government. We all walked sadly across the Leeds City Square to the main City Station, where they were to board the London Express.

What an emotional, upsetting day it was for us as they went to board the train amidst the usual hustle and bustle. Another group from the village came and joined them, relieving some of the tension.

John promised to write, which he did, twice, in reply to my letters. Anne started to cry, said that she loved me and would never forget us.

It was to be some time until I experienced such a feeling of loss and emptiness again. I'd been used to goodbyes before, lots of them, but not from such close and dear friends. You see, I'd never had permanent friends before.

There was little conversation between Mum and me on the return journey, we both understood each other well. The house seemed like a morgue for many weeks to come. I thanked God for Titch; he was always there when I needed him. After my ribs had healed, I returned to school and enjoyed a short-lived celebrity status from classmates and teachers alike. You know *The Dragon Slayer syndrome*.

I wasn't aware of it at the time, but as it worked out I wasn't going to be spending too much more time at Casleton school.

Chapter Seven

East Casleton 1948

David arrived home from the mill in the evening with mixed feelings. He had just spent the day with a young public school boy, who was selected to carry out a work-study program at the mill, prior to attending university.

The young man had a fresh and somewhat naive outlook, which had affected David. He wasn't ready to accept it, but he was actually envious of the young man's open and positive attitude.

It was years now since he'd spent any time thinking about anything or anyone, outside of his own rather small world. He began to realize that he was continuingly wallowing in self-pity.

Could it be that the meeting with this bright, but tough young lad had brought back memories, pleasant ones for a change? Perhaps his refreshing and most positive approach was making David take a closer look inwards.

He had left the door to his room slightly ajar; his father walked past the open door, and heard what he thought was:

"That's what I am going to do, I shall begin to live my life to the full."

"Is everything alright in there David?" Harold asked tentatively.

"Yes father, actually I feel better than I have for quite a long time." A broad grin had spread across his face as he came to the room door.

"Father, how would you fancy a complete change of venue this evening? Let's go to the Bedford Arms for a pint of ale. We'll walk across the green together; it's been a long time since we did that, don't you agree?"

Later that evening they sat in the cozy lounge to many nods of recognition accompanied by looks of surprise. David said to the landlord,

"Give everybody a drink on me, and get one for yourself, Teddy."

"No this round is on me," said Mr. White senior.

"How long has it been since you poured the last one for me, Teddy?"

"Good lord, it must be at least 5 years, Mr. White," the landlord replied cheerfully. Turning to David, Harold raised his glass.

"I don't know what has brought about this change in you son, maybe one day you'll tell me when you're good and ready." As their glasses clinked together, he said to himself, *"Thank you God; welcome home, my son, welcome back home at last."*

City of Leeds 1948

It was eight o'clock in the evening, the city traffic was still quite heavy. It had been raining most of the day; that fine drizzle, oppressive and miserable. As the rain had now stopped, Carl found it almost impossible to see through the mud and dirt that flew from the wheels of the vehicles in front. At the same, the inadequate wipers smeared the mess, turning the glass virtually opaque.

Carl had pulled over a couple of times, much to the annoyance of drivers behind, to wipe off the grime with his once white handkerchief. The traffic was now at a standstill so he decided to take the next left turn and attempt to cut across behind the large wholesale fruit and vegetable market. His chance came sooner than expected, as he turned between a gents outfitters and a large pub, only to come to a halt behind two horse drawn carts, apparently parked.

He saw that one of the horses had his nose into a feed-bag, munching away oblivious to the fact that he was holding up the traffic. *I'll bet his owner has his nose into a pint too,* Carl thought. There was nothing for him to do but to follow an old adage: 'If you can't beat 'em, join 'em.' He locked his car and walked into the side door of the pub.

"What can I get you sir?" the barman asked.

"Got any good scotch?"

"Sorry no, it's still difficult to get the good stuff in any quantity. We have some whisky and gin, but not labeled."

"I'll take a pint of best bitter."

"Sorry, we only have mild at the moment."

"Oh just give me a bottle of beer, anything will do." The barman poured a beer, Carl couldn't see his hand through the other side of the glass, the beer was so cloudy

"Well, well, well, fancy seeing you in here, if it isn't the great Carl Armitage himself. What brings you to these parts, amongst us lesser mortals then?" a voice across the bar shouted. Carl looked around to see one of his old-school chums, Bruce Bell.

"Hello Bruce, what a pleasant coincidence, let me get you a drink."

"No, let me do it. Get me two large Johnny Walker black label, and be quick about it." The barman looked embarrassingly at Carl, who'd just been refused a good whiskey

"Coming right up now, Bruce," the barman looked across at Carl and shrugged his shoulders apologetically.

"Sorry sir, we have to look after our regulars first, I'm sure you understand. But any friend of Bruce is a friend of ours, any time."

"Is your father still in the coal mining business?" Bruce asked.

"My father still owns half of this market" he said. Carl explained that nationalization had retired his father. They both then passed a few unsavory comments as regards the unions, seeming to share the same opinions.

"I heard that, Mr. Bell," shouted a large, fit-looking man who was leaning on the end of the bar, big red hands dwarfing a pint glass.

"You shouldn't be saying things like that about us God-fearing, hard-working, union men. I've half a mind to report you to the shop steward," he said with a look of anger on his face.

"Those would be the last words you utter before you see the inside of the infirmary," Bruce replied.

The big man put his mug down on the bar with a crash and as he started to walk aggressively towards them, the whole bar fell silent. Carl moved quickly to Bruce's side, as the big man came closer.

Then suddenly, he roared with laughter, putting both of his massive hands on Bruce's shoulders as he asked:

"Who's your crazy friend? I guess he thought we were serious." The whole bar was in an uproar.

"Carl, this is Gerald Steel, he's been with us for years. He's a sort of market supervisor. We don't need City Police assistance here. We have our own unwritten laws, don't we Gerald? Carl's an old mate from school, keep your eye on him though, he's a tough little bugger," Bruce said as the big man shook hands with Carl.

"You never answered my question, what brings you here? It's not the market air, that's for sure" Bruce said, grinning.

"I'm on my way up to Meanwood Road where I go to a club. It is sort of a gambling establishment. I got stuck in the traffic so came here quite by chance," Carl replied.

"I've heard about that club. Isn't it called the Queen of Hearts or something like that?"

"It's the Ace of Spades actually."

"Do they serve food? If they do it's ten to one that we supply the vegetables. Why don't I have a ride up there with you; it'll make a change for me. Any talent there, you get married yet?" he threw in the last question as an afterthought. It appeared that they were both still unattached.

"Well that's settled then, two more Black Market, Black Labels," said Bruce to the barman with a grin.

"Is the Woolsey outside the door your car?"

"It's actually the old mans," Carl replied. As they left the bar, two smutty faced kids were standing next to the car.

"Clean your windshield for two pence boss?"

"Hey, what's going on here?" shouted Bruce.

"You'd better clean it for nothing or I'll want to know why."

"Sorry, Bruce," said the scruffy little urchin grinning all over his face as they threw clean water over the windscreen, cleaning it to a shine. Carl put his hand into his pocket and took out a shiny shilling, giving it to the young boy who looked up in total amazement as he gave a similar coin to the other kid.

"Bloody 'ell boss, Ta very much," they said in unison as they walked away, staring in disbelief at the shiny coins in the palms of their hands. They would normally have to sweep the whole market all day for that much.

"You always were a soft touch, Carl."

"There but for the grace of God go any one of us," said Carl. He drove off down the street towards the Ace of Spades to his meeting with a man that he had no wish to see.

East Casleton Village back in 1941

It was the weekend once again. I do love my week-ends. I had taken some letters to be mailed and while in the post office, bought myself a Mars bar. Mum had given me a couple of coupons from the ration book.

"Take these and get yourself some chocolate with the change from the postage stamps," she'd said with a smile. I leaned against the fence looking across the tall grass and weeds, towards the railway sheds, relishing the rare luxury of this Saturday treat, passing little pieces to Titch who licked his chops with relish, jumping up at my leg excitedly, asking for more.

"Chocolate will give that dog worms," Dad would say.

Suddenly, and for no apparent reason, floating boxes came back into my mind, *if you'll pardon the pun*. That evening in the fields seemed so long ago that I began to wonder if the events of that night were just a figment of my imagination.

"You come across anything? It's your duty to tell me. Don't forget there is a war on," the words of PC Ellis, still fresh in my mind.

Titch and I walked back up the steep hill. As I got to the house, dad was just getting into his van.

"I'm off to the wood yard, fancy coming round for an hour son? You can do some chopping for me, earn some pocket money, we're short handed today." *Keep me out of mischief, why not?* I thought.

"Sure Dad, but you don't have to pay me."

"A laborer is worthy of his hire," he smiled.

"Let's be off then, before your Mum finds something else for you to do." Titch jumped onto my knee as I climbed into the front seat next to Dad.

The yard had to be the most interesting place for miles around; he owned about three acres in the middle of a lot of smaller allotments. *Small plots of land rented from the city, here a villager could grow his own vegetables and flowers*. A refuge from domesticity, relaxation after a day down the mine, or a day in the noisy twisting sheds at the mill. Dad's yard had large stacks of sleepers (rail ties). You could see the holes where the bolts had been removed. Some still remained as did some of the shoes that had held the rails in place, they were thrown into a pile.

Dad always returned them to the railway company.

"Waste not, want not," he would often say. His vocabulary was rather limited, therefore somewhat repetitive, hence his collection of well used clichés.

He employed one old man full-time, and a number of other young men part time. As we approached, two men were driving metal wedges into the sleepers, splitting the lumber full length into more manageable widths. They would then be cross cut by the big circular saw into blocks of eight inches long.

Two other men were sitting down inside the building, initially chopping them into one-inch slices, then into finger-thick chips. These chips were then put into a bundling vice, around twenty each time, compressed together by pulling a handle down, then tied with thin wire twisted around them.

As all railway sleepers are pre-soaked in creosote, a good preservative but also inflammable, they became the ideal firelighters and were sold to the home owners. That morning I had been appointed head bundler.

Across the other side of the building was the huge circular saw. The noisy paraffin engine had a large flywheel on the side with the broad belt that drove the saw blade.

Last year one of Dad's helpers cut his finger clean off, so now as a precaution only Dad operated the device.

Outside, the back of the building was the more interesting area. Here there were a number of other buildings; the stable with two stalls and tack room, the pig sty, a long building housing ten pens holding up to one hundred pigs, then the hen hut housing ten dozen chickens. We had two horses, well, ponies actually a mare called Dolly, a gentle Welsh cross and a black Cobb named Bob. He was a stocky character, with an extremely volatile disposition, quite nasty.

Dad said he was a Rig, which meant when he was gelded only one piece of manhood was removed, the other remained up inside.

"He thinks he's a stallion, but he's not," Dad used to say. On some occasions Bob was right in his thinking.

I have seen him almost kick the bottom out of a cart. Everybody walked past his stall with great reverence, including Titch. At the one end a kick, at the other a spiteful bite, a very unsavory chap, our Bob, but a very hard worker for all that.

Dad also kept a number of cats, much to the disdain of Titch, who now kept well away from the feline species, a lesson well-learned. He would spend most of his time rooting around the pigpens for rats; he had already killed a number of rodents and bore the scars from one that he hadn't.

Back in the wood shop, two men were working, their axes industriously producing vast mountains of chips for the bundler, yours truly.

"Is the wife still making a bit of money with that sewing machine of hers? She's good with her hands, that one," said one of the men to the other.

"Yea she keeps busy," was the reply.

"She's just made some fantastic women's blouses. A bloke from Wakefield bought 'em all to sell in his shop and she's still got some material left over. She was going to talk to Matt's mum about it," he said nodding in my direction.

"See if she could sell it in her shop, but she reckons silk won't sell in Casleton; she says it's a bit too posh."

"Where'd she get silk from anyway? It must have cost a bloody fortune!" exclaimed the other chopper.

"Funny you should ask, but it was me that got it, not her."

"How did you manage that?"

"I was in the bar up at the club a couple of weeks ago and one of them prisoners of war came up to me. To be honest I don't like them bloody krauts around me, but he asked me if I wanted to buy some silk.

"How much is it?" I asked. We went outside to his bike where he had a whole load of the bloody stuff. It was sort of a green color, but there was so much of it I said to him, 'I'll never be able to afford that lot, most I can afford is a couple o' quid.' I walked back inside the club," he said, taking another expert down-stroke with axe.

I was just pulling down the lever to compact another bundle of wood chips and paying only partial attention to what he was saying. Hearing the comment about green material, I spun round in surprise and the lever shot out of my hand, springing back to the bench, crashing onto a plate that had contained food for the cats. Pieces of porcelain flew in every direction.

"Look out Matt, what ye doing over there, yer tryin' to wreck the bloody place?"

"Sorry, I wasn't paying attention. Did I hit you?" I asked.

"No but you were close," he said, with a broad grin across his face.

"I'm bloody glad you broke that and not me. Wait till yer Mum gets here, that's her plate you just smashed, you'll be in for it lad."

"So what did the Kraut say next?" the other wood-chopper asked.

"Well that's the strange part. I thought he would've told me to bugger off. Instead he walked up to the bar, told me to buy him a beer and just take the cloth. He said I would certainly owe him a favor some day." Then silence fell.

"Well, go on then, don't keep us all in suspense. Did ye take it?" asked the other man.

"Bloody dead right I took it, but ere's the funny part. I get the stuff home and as the wife and I opened it right up it, it was round. I thought it were a tent or something, and that's not all, it had some sort of foreign writing on it and lots of thick string.

The wife said the strings were made of silk too and she should know as she works at the mill. She's better educated than me, says the writing on it could be German!"

"How many blouses did she make then?" the other guy asked.

"About a dozen, but there's still lots of stuff left over," came the reply.

"You lot must be rolling in soddin' money," he said. "Bloody lucky, I'd say," he added enviously.

I couldn't believe my ears; excitement coursed through my body. So the parachutes are still around. How about the boxes, I wondered.

"Are those prisoners allowed to wander around at will?" I asked.

"I always had the idea that prisoners were locked up," I added.

"I guess there are too many of 'em in the country. It costs too much to keep 'em locked up," replied the one with the silk.

"Besides which, they have to work," the other replied. Fishing for more information, I asked:

"Where do they live then, at the police station?"

"No, the one I'm talking about lives with an old widow down Pit Lane. The government pays her a grant and she gets extra ration coupons," he said.

"Why don't they run away, and try to get home?" I asked.

"Well the cops check 'em every day. Besides, who the hell would want to be in Germany now with our lads pounding buggery out of 'em every night? Anyway they've got it too good here."

"I suppose you're right. Where do you think that silk came from?" I asked him.

"I don't know, and I don't bloody care," replied the man. "By the way, you mention just one bloody word of this to anybody young Harper, it won't just be broken ribs you'll get my lad, you understand?"

"Yes, sir," I snapped to attention giving a facetious military salute.

Dad was busy feeding the pigs as I shouted cheerio. I could see the old man bending down brushing Bob. It was now one thirty; the other two men had gone to the pub for a lunchtime pint.

"Tell ye Dad we left at one, and there's another two hundred bundles in the shelves. I'm sure he counts 'em anyway but you tell him just in case, and remember you... not a bloody word," he frowned tapping the side of his nose with his forefinger. I wanted to ask the name of the widow in Pit Lane but I would just have to go and find out for myself.

When I returned home from the wood yard that afternoon, it was a little after two-thirty. Nearing the house I saw Harold White's car, the black Rover parked outside.

He was sitting on the couch talking with Mum.

"Ah, there you are Matt. Mr. White came round to see how you were getting on."

"Please call me Harold. 'Mr.' makes me feel so old," he smiled as he spoke.

"Alright, Harold," replied Mum smiling.

"Matt, Harold came by to see if you would like to go fishing with him tomorrow." Harold explained that he had hired a boat and a captain to fish at Bridlington, about sixty miles away.

"Can I go Mum, what about Church, it's Sunday tomorrow?" I hated church. It always seemed that everyone was there under sufferance.

"Of course you must go," she said. It was all fixed; we had to leave at five-thirty in the morning! A bit of a setback but missing church plus a trip to the coast, then add on a boat trip, it seemed well worth missing a little shuteye.

Harold left the house, arranging to be outside at five-thirty the following morning.

Mum went to the chippies and we had a pleasant lunch, no sign of Dad still busy working.

I decided to go for a walk. Whistling for Titch, off we went up the hill and across the fields towards Pit Lane.

About a half mile from the entrance to the mine in Pit Lane was a collection of older dwellings. These were cottages that had been owned by the Armitage family and rented out to miners. They were now similarly owned by the coal board and rented out to their employees. There must have been twenty of them in all.

I spoke to one or two people, then passed the time of day with an old man who was sitting on a bench at the roadside.

I could see that he was a miner from the blue scars on his face, caused by coal dust getting into wounds. Sadly, his only topic of conversation was his lifetime occupation.

As it seems with the majority of older people, they become lonely and love to talk, usually about old times. I learned in later years the part of the memory that stores short-term events seems to deteriorate first. Leaving those older and earlier memories, I suppose in most cases is a blessing; The old man went on:

"Modernization is an incredible thing lad. Do you know that they have installed a new-fangled engine down there that operates a steel rope all the way from the pit bottom to the very end of the main road? Tubs are clipped to it; it pulls them all the way to the pit bottom without the use of one pony. They call it an endless rope," said the old man.

At that time I didn't have the vaguest idea what he was taking about. It must be awful to get old. I carefully steered him onto the topic of the war and was subjected to a tirade about the trenches in the Crimean First World War. He was totally un-stoppable.

As I listened, bored to tears, I noticed a black police car pulled up at one of the cottages. A man in plain clothes wearing a brown trilby hat opened the gate and knocked on the door of the house second from the end, in the usual officious manner.

The old man came up for air looking across towards the car.

"That's the police checking, she has one of those prisoners of war staying there you know. Prisoners of war I ask you, in my day we would have bloody shot 'em." I caught him mid-breath, wished him a good afternoon and went on my merry way, a little tender around the hearing department.

After my close shave from death by boredom, Titch and I went into the fields behind Pit Lane, coming up to the rear of the properties behind the cottage second from the end. There was a large shed in the rear yard, the garden was well kept. I looked over the fence but everything seemed to be locked away; there were no windows to the shed and quite a formidable lock on the door.

I did however notice that two of the boards had come away from the frame at the rear. The real reason I'd spotted them was because Titch had shot through a hole in the fence in hot pursuit of a cat, disappeared through that very hiatus, and into the shed.

"Oi, is zat your dog?" I was looking straight into the eyes of the man from the railway station and also from that night in the fields.

"Yes he is," I replied.

"Zen get him avay he vill kill mine cat." I shouted for Titch who for once obeyed and we both went quickly on our way. I went away with a smile on my lips and quite a spring in my step, for now I knew where the purveyor of silk parachute cloth lived!

It was still dark as night as I opened the door, just as Harold pulled up outside our house. I'd hardly slept a wink that night.

Mum was up too. She made sandwiches of cheese and pickle, wrapped them up in greaseproof paper and put them into a carrier bag along with an apple and some of my favorite digestive chocolate biscuits. As we drove out of the village heading towards the East coast, the Rover literally purred along eating up the miles as we went.

"How fast will she go?"

"Oh she's good for over ninety," replied Harold. Rover was one of the better cars available, though at that time in short supply due to the war. They were very well-made with lots and lots of wood and leather, the smell brought back memories of my recent trip to the hospital. I think my ribs twitched a little in recognition.

It was such a pleasure to have a change of scenery; we were coming to the town of Tadcaster, not far from the City of York.

Yorkshire is the largest county in England and split into four Ridings. Casleton is in the West Riding. We drove along past the famous racecourse and through the gates of that ancient walled City of York; it was like entering a bygone age. Harold said that the City along with its Cathedral was built in the fourteenth century. He said the Germans had bombed there only a few weeks ago.

"We'll have a quick spot of breakfast here, then speed on to the coast," said Harold as we pulled in front of a quaint old café.

The street was called Wipma-wopma-gate, so narrow that people in the upstairs rooms could open their windows and shake hands with those on the opposite side. I ate a breakfast of poached egg on toast, a steaming hot mug of tea, then more toast with preserve and margarine. *No butter in those days*. Later as we sped along the coast road, Harold asked me:

"Are you happy living in Casleton?" I remember thinking at the time, what an odd question to ask. *Where else would I live?* But I replied that I was indeed happy there.

Next I saw the sign telling us that we had entered the coastal town of Bridlington, it coming up to seven-thirty by my watch. Suddenly as we turned the next corner there it was, sparkling under a slight mist, the mighty ocean.

It's hard to explain the feeling that I had that day, and indeed have had ever since. Whenever I visit the ocean after a period of absence, I always experience feelings somewhere between excitement and fear, awe and respect. One minute it's calm tranquil and relaxing, another, ferocious powerful and destructive. That morning, it was flat calm.

The populous of Bridlington lives on and from the harvest of the sea: cod, haddock, mackerel, sole, and plaice, along with the crustaceans, winkles, whelks, mussels and crabs.

We drove around the edge of this pretty, but bustling hive of industry. Harold parked the Rover on the old cobblestone along the harbor wall facing toward the water. Taking a small box from the trunk, he took my sandwiches and placed them in the box next to his own. We walked along the harbor; I had climbed up and was walking along the top of the sea wall. I could see in the distance the lighthouse at Flamborough Head, then I heard a deep voice shouting from the harbor below:

"I don't believe it, that is you, Harold, isn't it?"

I saw the ruddy, wrinkled face of a short stocky man, an obvious man of the sea. A knitted hat on his head, his big red hands on his hips, he wore a specked polo-necked sweater and large rubber boots up to the knees. He reminded me of some of the pictures I had seen of pirates.

"As I live and breathe." *Why not shiver mi timbers, aarrr*? I thought.

"It is you Harold, come on down; this must be the scallywag you told me about on the phone. We'll see if we can't make a fisherman of him today."

The boat was a small trawler made of wood, 'Clinker built' to the aficionados amongst us. She was called 'Yorkie Lass'. I climbed aboard my first boat and to this day could still describe that boat in the minutest of detail, that memory is so vividly and indelibly impressed on my mind and senses.

There was a distinct smell of the engine as it spluttered and splashed, ropes were freed off as she began to reverse slowly, then she turned to the right, or should I say starboard, then gathered momentum as we passed the harbor entrance and out to sea.

Instantly the motion of the boat changed. I was standing facing towards the front; Harold was inside the small wheelhouse behind me with Pete, the captain.

The front of the boat was now hitting waves, which began to splash over the bow, sort of gently at first.

"Hold on young un," Pete shouted with his head hanging out of the side of the wheelhouse as the engine roared into life.

At the same time a large amount of water hit me square in the face and chest. I was thrown backwards landing on a pile of fishnets, hardly able to catch my breath.

I could hear the roars of laughter from behind me as I swallowed the salty sea.

I went rather quickly into the small cabin, pretending to share in their mirth though somewhat half-heartedly, the taste of brine on my lips, my eyes smarting.

By the time we reached our designated fishing spot, I was dry and ready for anything. I did however begin to wonder at the time, how one could find a fishing spot when all the water looked the same to me. My question was soon answered.

We began to approach a small ball in the water. The boat engine slowed down, the Captain moved to the side of the boat, then with a boat hook he pulled the small floating sphere, *called a buoy* alongside. It was about the size of a soccer ball attached to a rope anchored to the bottom. The boat was then tied to this buoy, her engine cut, and then absolute silence reigned.

The next question that came to mind, *but how did he find the buoy in all that water?* I looked around and could see no others. I never did get an answer to that one mainly because I never asked.

That day I learned how to put bait on the hook and how to select the correct weight (sinker), depending on the depth and strength of the current, how to feel the lead weight touch the bottom: it was one of the most formative and informative days of my life. I fell in love with the sea that very day. We sat in that healthy, relaxing but bracing atmosphere, talking and eating our sandwiches. Harold and Pete discussed old times, Pete asked him

"How's your son and his good friend Carl? We all used to have some fun out here, didn't we?"

Harold seemed to change the subject abruptly, so unlike him I thought. I felt that the captain noticed it too.

Just at that moment I had my first fish sensation on the rod, just like when Anne used to tug on my jacket to gain my attention, only maybe a little softer. Then the tugging on my line became less frequent, but stronger. Then, whoosh! The reel screamed as the line began to fly off my reel; I looked down in absolute amazement and Harold came over to me.

"Here we go! We've got one on here!" he yelled, "let him run a little." To be honest, I wasn't quite sure what other avenues were open to me. The fish felt so strong, it seemed to have taken miles of line, then Harold leaned over pointing to the lever on the side of the reel.

"Increase the drag just a little, move that lever forward just a little, it puts the brakes on a bit," he said.

"Not too much though or the line will break." I did as he suggested and sure enough the reel slowed down, until it came to a stand still.

"Good," Pete said in a contented voice.

"Now lift the tip of your rod up into the air." As I did so I looked up at Pete a little concerned as the reel started to go again. He put his hand on the rod and pulled it up along with me.

"A little slower than that," he said smiling.

"Now as you bring the tip down, lower it back down steadily and wind the line back in at the same time.... good that's the way, gently does it. Now move the line from side to side with your left thumb so it goes back onto the reel evenly and doesn't peak in the center."

It seemed an age before Harold who was leaning over the side of the boat shouted:

"Here he is Pete." By which time my arms were really feeling the strain. By now Pete was by my side.

"Matt, keep winding slowly. Stop only when I tell you," said Pete.

"Step back toward the wheel house so I can grab the line, that's good, here we go."

With that he leaned over the side, took the line in his left hand and put the handle of the net in his right hand into the water, then both hands on the net.

What a sight, what an indescribable sensation. I'll never forget the splashing, jumping, bashing, thrashing, as the big silver fish was dropped with a loud slap right next to me, still tangled in the net. It was such a sleek looking creature with a thin black stripe along the length of his sides.

"Haddock" yelled both Pete and Harold in unison.

"And it's a beauty," said Pete.

"He must be all of ten pounds. Congratulations Matt, well done."

"Well done," said Harold clapping his hands in applause.

"Not bad at all for a first effort," said Pete in a jocular tone of voice. We fished all day; Harold caught two codling, the boat turned round twice that day.

"She turns with the tide," Pete said." The tide is coming in now so let's cast off and drift in on the current, see if we can get a few mackerel for tea." As we drifted slowly towards the shore, the earlier bait of lugworms had been changed to mackerel feathers.

Within minutes we had caught around a dozen, and it looked as though it would go on forever. Once I had three on at a time, the boat seemed to be covered by jumping mackerel. Then suddenly Pete stood bolt upright, holding up his hand.

"Did you here that, Harold?" Pete shouted

"Hear what?" Harold replied, looking up.

"I thought I heard a siren coming off shore."

"No, I heard nothing," Harold replied. Then from the cabin the sound of the radio crackled lots of static and squelch, as Pete moved into the wheelhouse and turned up the volume.

"Attention all craft, attention all vessels offshore," came the crackling sound from the squeaky radio.

"This is an air raid warning, repeat this is an air raid warning. All shipping on mid-segment off northeast coastline, take shelter where possible. A large concentration of unidentified aircraft reported last seen twenty miles due east of Yorkshire coastline, take cover where possible Attention At..." The radio was cut off. I leaned into the wheelhouse.

"I thought I heard a faint siren ashore," shouted Pete.

"Get those lines in and make sure everything is fastened down. Put the rest of those fish in the box Matt and let's make ourselves scarce, let's get the hell out of here."

All of the lines were in, everything was stowed away. Pete gunned the engine as we sped off towards the shore; after a few minutes I could see the high cliffs in the distance. Suddenly the otherwise loud noise of our engine was drowned by a thunderous, throbbing roar from above and the sky literally became darkened.

We all looked to the sky at the same time and gazed in awe at the spectacle above us. The prevailing setting sun coming out of the west reflected from the fuselages of thirty to fifty aircraft approaching from the east. In a way the vision was magnificent, but it was also an overwhelming and intimidating sight.

The sensation from the vibration of so much mechanical airborne horsepower was captivating yet spine-chilling. The little boat sped towards land and relative safety; we heard the scream of smaller engines. Then as I looked up I saw a spectacle that will remain with me to my dying day.

Coming from the shore, much higher than the incoming bombers, were masses of small airplanes in formations of fours.

"Spitfires," shouted Pete, as the small angry fighters attacked with the unmistakable chatter of machine gun fire. The bomber pilots had the setting sun in their eyes. As the fighters attacked, the formation of the bombers fragmented at first and then broke up completely, some turning around, others moving off towards the North and South.

We motored into the relative calm of the harbor as the action above seemed to be heading southeast. We saw three bombers go down in flames another blown up into oblivion, and then another one went screaming into the sea, flaming and smoking as it hit the water, sending up a great fountain of water and steam. We saw others dropping their deadly cargo into the sea before turning tail.

We heard over the news the following day that three German crewmembers were taken prisoner. The remainder of the task force was kept out over the ocean, eventually driven back, dropping their lethal cargo into the waters of the North Sea.

"Well that was a nice little bit of excitement to round off the day," said Pete, which must have been the understatement of the year.

"Let's see if we can't clean that haddock for you, so that you can take some home for your Mum. I think we'll make a fisherman out of this fellow. What do you say Harold?"

"No doubt in my mind whatsoever," replied Harold.

It seemed hard to believe that from the time we first saw the German aircraft until we got into the car had taken no more than forty minutes, during which time an historic air battle had taken place.

During the journey home we had a very interesting conversation. Harold told me of his son David who was away fighting in the war. He also said that one day he would like us to meet.

"You are so much like a very close friend of David's," he said.

"A young man called Carl Armitage, his father owns the coal mine. I remember taking him and David fishing in Bridlington, which was their first time too. All we got that day was mackerel."

As I walked into the house Dad was sitting with Mum, as usual she was knitting.

"Oh, thank God you're safe, we heard the news; did you see any planes?"

"Yes, Mum they were directly above us at sea. Look what I caught for us," I replied.

I dropped the packet into her lap. She jumped up and kissed me on the cheek, so pleased to see me!

A few weeks after our fishing escapade, Mum told me that we had been invited to the mansion to have supper with Harold White the following evening. There was a strange reticent tone in her voice and I had the oddest feeling. My instincts told me that some big changes were to take place, don't ask me why; it's being intuitive that seems to get me into the oddest of situations.

We arrived at the mansion that following evening, my first visit and what an awesome building. Just how one person could live there in all that space alone was totally beyond my comprehension.

After supper, where we were served by an old man wearing a black suite and bow tie, we went into another room, the sitting room.

"Matt there is something that both Mr..er, Harold and I want to talk to you about," said Mum.

"Your Dad and I, though we are comfortable financially, we don't have the finances to give you the education that you really ought to have."

"Mum, I'm quite happy where I am; I consider myself extremely fortunate," I replied sincerely.

Then Harold entered the conversation.

"Matt, please don't think for one moment that I wish to interfere. You are a very bright and intelligent young man. I have watched you for some time now and have had conversations with your parents over a prolonged period.

I am a very wealthy man with more money than I can ever use. If you were to agree to allow me to set up a trust fund for your future education, I would consider it a great honor to pay for your schooling.

I only offer this because I can see that you have the intelligence to benefit from such an opportunity. There are no strings attached. I donate to many charities where the trusts are spread far and wide. I rarely have the chance to see any results directly.

It would be rewarding to see someone like you benefit directly. Come on, Matt, give yourself a great chance and at the same time indulge an old man. What do you say?" Harold looked sincere and most convincing as he spoke.

I looked at Mum, as she looked back at me.

"You owe it to yourself, what do you have to lose?"

"What does Dad think, Mum?"

"You know your Dad, if you and I are happy with the arrangement, so is he."

"If you agree Matt, though there are no strings, there are couple of ground rules that I would like to lay down, both of them in your own interest," said Harold with a look of genuine pleasure on his face.

When I left the mansion that night, I felt somewhat puppet-like, as though I was operating on strings, but I knew that in the end it was all in my best interests.

It has always struck me as rather odd, why in England we call a private school a public school. Nevertheless, such is the case. Public schools were originally instituted for the education of the upper classes. They have since become the norm for middle and upper classes, including nobility and royalty.

These establishments, sometimes referred to as boarding schools, are usually tough on discipline and morals; they are dedicated to developing strong leadership qualities.

I was to attend such an institution starting next term, assuming that after initial interviews, both parties were of the same opinion.

The ground rules to which my benefactor had referred earlier were indeed all beneficial to me. The only people privy to the arrangement was Harold himself, Mum, Dad, and yours truly.

It was never to be discussed with another living soul, including Harold's son David. I was to report to Harold on my progress, and he would receive term reports sent to 'The Trustees.'

Even the school was not in possession of the full facts. I was sorry that I would have to leave Mum and Dad. I knew that Mum was doing this for me at great sacrifice to herself, one minute gaining a son, the next letting him go. As she'd said, it was only for a short while.

It was the winter of 1943. Now thirteen years of age and soon to be fourteen, I had quite a lot more than just a sugar lump in my pocket, parents who loved me, a public school education in front of me and the rest of my life ahead, a lucky young man wouldn't you say?

Shortly after that meeting, I sat for my current school exams, passing with an A grade, which qualified me to go on to either the grammar school or the technical college.

Mum went to see the headmaster, explaining that I was leaving the state school system and would be attending a public school next term, adding that she would be appreciative if this could be kept from both pupils and teaching staff alike, so as not to create any bad feelings in the remaining weeks.

Later, a small party was held to say goodbye to some of my friends, and a special dinner was given in my honor at the mansion. Dad came too this time, wonders never cease.

Off we go again, another move! This time not from pillar to post, not from one foster family to another, I belong to a family now, and I'm really going to make them proud of me.

For some of the other new boys it was hard the first time away from home without a mother to run around cleaning up behind them, no one to think for them. Not so for an ex-orphan.

I knew the routine, as the dormitory had twenty beds. I knew to select the bed furthest away from authority but nearest to the heat source, a smoky old coal stove. The first bed inside the dormitory doorway always got the full thunder of authority. That bed space usually housed a regular but reluctant delegated volunteer, for anything and everything going.

I settled into boarding school life like a duck to water, although I had to admit that I did miss home dearly. Mum, Dad and of course my closest and loyalist friend Titch.

Chapter Eight

Leeds City 1948

As Carl and Bruce headed across town towards the Ace of Spades, Carl wasn't looking forward to the prospect of telling the German that he was washing his hands of the whole damned business. They approached the club, but the parking lot was busy and it took quite some time to find a spot.

"Good evening, Mr. Armitage, and how are you on this fine evening?" the receptionist asked politely.

"Let me take your coats. Perhaps you would like to sign your guest in as I check your things." They went into the bar, which was surprisingly busy.

"What can I get you?" Bruce asked Carl.

"My club, my invitation, I order the drinks, the treat is on me." Carl replied.

"I think that I rather invited myself along really," Bruce grinned, shrugging nonchalantly.

"No, it's my turn, after all you did pull some influence in the last bar. If you hadn't arrived, I may still have been trying to drink that cloudy beer!" Carl added, smiling.

"Gut evenink, Herr Armitage," Carl turned around quickly and looked into the face of the big shorthaired German whose grimace looked more like a mask than a smile.

"Let me get you a drink, mine friend." Carl winced as the man finished speaking.

"Excuse me, will you Bruce, I won't be a minute." Carl scowled as he walked away from the bar, at the same time beckoning to the German to follow him.

"Now let's you and I get one or two things straight; I am most definitely not your bloody friend, in fact quite the contrary and furthermore, I do not wish to be seen, nor indeed associated with you, do I make myself clear?"

"OK, Mr. Armitage, I think it's time for me to make a few things clear to you. Unless you wish us to go to your father and explain very clearly a few things to him, you had better pay attention to me, and don't ever treat me as you just did in front of anyone again, never again, do you understand?" He now spoke in perfect English.

"I will not tolerate your pomposity, also you will settle your gambling debts with this club, and I mean within the next twenty-four hours. If not, then I will have to send some of my public relations people, who will most certainly convince you that I mean business.

There is however another way that you can clear your indebtedness to us, that's if you wish to listen!" The big German went on to explain his demands.

Carl glanced across at Bruce, who was looking in his direction.

"Sorry, I'm not interested in your skullduggery. I suggest you send your people as I can't pay the debt at this time. I want no more involvement with you whatsoever. By the way, what is your position in this club?" Carl asked the German.

"I own this establishment, and have done from the word go."

"I notice that your German accent seems to disappear when you get annoyed."

"Yes, that is only used for the benefit of the likes of you. I was born in the Fatherland but educated and brought up here." The German sneered as Bruce walked towards them.

"Is everything all right over here, you don't look too happy Carl. Need any help?" Bruce asked.

"I'm fine, just someone I met during the war, there's no problem."

Bruce eyed the German with suspicion, looking as though he didn't really believed what Carl had just said. They both walked back towards the bar.

"Don't forget what I said now, twenty-four hours, you know how to reach me," said the German, smiling with his countenance, though his eyes were as cold as ice.

"What was that all about, Carl?" Bruce asked, turning to look at his friend.

"Nothing I can't take care of," Carl replied unconvincingly. The evening passed without further incident and they both had a great time discussing the old days, as they gambled and drank the night away.

When they left the club in the early hours of the next day, Bruce noticed the man with the short hair was standing in the doorway of an office, arms folded across his chest, a look of complete arrogance written across his Aryan face.

I have a pocket full of your money that I've won, which should make *me happy, but instead I feel distinctly uneasy,* Bruce thought to himself. He looked back at the club, fingering the wad of notes in his jacket pocket, sensing that all was not well with his friend Carl.

Bruce decided he would look into the people at this club, what was going on with a man who spoke with a foreign accent one minute, then shouted in flawless English the next. Why was he able to speak to his friend with such obvious disrespect and insolence, with no sign of anger from Carl, certainly not the behavior of his old school chum? Bruce was quite intrigued and somewhat mystified by the events that he'd just witnessed.

Carl had not been quite so lucky at the tables. He dropped Bruce back at his car which was parked at the market. Then he drove on home as the first signs of daybreak crept across the cloud-covered sky. He knew that things would now definitely be coming to a head.

"God, get me out of this mess," he yelled aloud, as his mind raced to find a solution to his self-inflicted dilemma.

The market started to come to life at around three in the morning. But one could buy breakfast at almost anytime after the bars had closed around ten-thirty PM, and then right through to a civilized daytime hour.

It was four o'clock. Bruce knew full well that even a look at his bed could mean trouble; he'd never get up in time for work. His father had a small bathroom with shower over the office, which Bruce had utilized before on such occasions. He always kept a change of clothes in the car, should he get lucky, as the saying goes!

He walked into the same local bar where he'd met his old pal the previous evening; the place was still swinging, the occupants a total cross section of people:

Long distance truck drivers delivering their loads, market porters, and hotel and store buyers. A smattering of tuxedos here and there, some with shirt collars undone, bleary booze-soaked eyes, a local cop sat browsing the early issue of the Daily Herald. All this was accompanied by the unmistakable aroma of fresh coffee, tea, bacon, eggs, sausage, black pudding and fresh toast.

"A full house, and one without beans," yelled a voice from behind the bar for the second time.

"Come on and don't blame me if the eggs have gone hard!" shouted the cook, as he passed two hot plates to a staggering vacant-eyed man, still drunk from the night before.

"Hey, Bruce, usual for you, is it?" the cook smiled as Bruce walked into the bar.

"Yep, that'll be great," he replied.

"Have you seen Gerald Steel around yet?"

"Yes, he was in earlier" the cook replied.

"But there was a spot of bother down on the truck park. His breakfast will be cold by now, somebody's going to cop it, no doubt."

"Cook him a fresh one when he gets back will you, put it on my bill; if you see him before I do tell him I want to see him when he gets through eating,"

"Sure Bruce, yours will be up in a minute," the cook replied.

Half an hour later as Bruce was getting out of the shower and starting to feel just a little more human, he heard Gerald shouting up the stairs,

"Be right down Gerald, go through to the office."

Five minutes later they sat together, Bruce in his father's chair.

"I need you to do a little job for me Gerald; what do you know about the Ace of Spades night club?

"It's funny you should ask, there's been a lot of strange goings on around that place of late. We supply them, so naturally some of the gossip comes back via the delivery men. What's the problem?

"I'm not sure just yet but find out all you can: who owns it, who the main members are, get me the full lowdown. We'll make a call there when you have the info. Get me a membership application while you're at it."

"Sure, Bruce, leave it to me." The phone on the desk rang.

"Bruce, the buyer is here from the Grand Hotel, says he needs to talk to either your Dad or you," said the voice on the phone.

"I'm coming down right now. Tell him I'll be with him in two minutes."

Green Cotes School 1948

School was going fine; my grades were acceptable but nothing to write home about. Harold had passed some sharp derogatory comments about my apparent lack of commitment to studies, in particular my weaker areas, especially math.

During the last visit home we met at a hotel in Leeds because his son David had now returned home from his service in the army.

The war had been over some time now, it seemed like only yesterday that the whole country had celebrated VE day. Hitler had committed suicide in his bunker in Berlin back on 30 May 1945. His appointed successor, Grand Admiral Doenitz, was left with no choice but to surrender. He had sent his representative General Jodie, to sign the unconditional surrender at General Eisenhower's headquarters, in Rheims early on May 7.

Both the British and United States Governments declared May 8, VE day (Victory over Europe). Winston Churchill spoke to the nation saying:

"This moment is a signal for the greatest outburst of joy in the history of mankind."

School broke up for a week of celebrations. The lights came back on across the country, there were celebrations in every village and town, street parties were held, fireworks were displayed, the whole of the country celebrated.

The village of Casleton was to be no exception and had a number of celebrations, the largest one being down the Falls, and financed almost totally by the White and the Armitage families.

It was a sumptuous affair, lasting into the early hours.

At the height of the celebrations I sat apart from the crowds, on a beer crate outside of the gate of our home. I watched people dance and sing, Titch sitting on my lap, a picture of Mum in my hand.

At first I felt butterflies in my gut, then a lump in my throat, then tears poured down my face, sobbing so badly that I almost lost control.

"If only Mum could be here today," I said to Titch, who looked up and whined, as I looked into his kind eyes. I asked him a question as my lips quivered in the sadness of the moment.

"Titch, if there is a God why would he let such a nice person die, when all of those other hateful people are allowed to live. Why, Titch, tell me why?" I felt a strong hand rest on my shoulder and looked up into the face of my Dad. He too had tears streaming down his lined face.

"Now come on Matt, lad, your Mum wouldn't want to see either of us like this, now would she?" his bottom lip shook as he bit into it with his teeth.

"She loved you, and she was so proud of you," his voice began to break as he tried to continue.

"Just thank God that we had her as long as we did, I do all the time, it's the only thing that keeps me going!" he said now shaking as he sobbed.

"You and I should be proud to have known her." Those few moments were the closest that I ever got to my Dad. Mum's death had changed him almost into a recluse.

I had now been away at school for close to five years; Mum had died almost three years ago when I was fifteen. Since her passing I really didn't want to come home at term breaks. I had often gone to stay with school pals. During that time Dad and I had grown even further apart. One day, he said to me, looking me straight in the eye:

"You and I live in two different worlds now Matt. You get on with living, you have the whole world in front of you and that's what Bella would have wanted."

Each time that I hear the learned religious expounding their philosophies on the goodness, wisdom, and kindness of God I go back to a question that I have never to this day been given a satisfactory answer to; it hangs out there permanently, between religion and me, and I suspect will remain there for the rest of my days:

Maybe God made a mistake when he made me an orphan; accidents can happen. But why would he then take away my adoptive Mother, after such a short time?

I do however count myself fortunate to have been a part of her life, no matter how short.

Dad was never a philosopher, but his words on VE day gave me some solace. After all, only God really knows where else I could have been right now! I shudder when I think back to those early foster homes and the abject poverty that surrounded them. Thanks, Mum. Thanks, God!

I remember once reading a banner painted across the rear wall of a Salvation Army Hall: Always be thankful for small mercies!

Admittedly my outlook is much improved since that black endless day when I stood by Mum's graveside. Such feelings are beyond description. Time is a great healer, (until you visit the memories) thanks to school pals, schoolmasters and the wise counseling of Harold White, dear old Harold, and of course, Dad.

After my second to final term and just before I returned to school, Harold came round to the house and confirmed what I had already heard at school. I was to take a sabbatical and complete two work-study programs prior to attending university, assuming that I passed the entrance exam, that is.

The big surprise was that the two work-studies were to be at Casleton colliery and White's Mill. No prizes for guessing who set that up. I would be back at home for six weeks in total and would start at the mine in just two weeks time. Again, Harold had asked me not to discuss our arrangement with anyone.

"When the time is right maybe, but not yet," he'd said with a smile on his face.

In the next few weeks, during your contact with my son and Carl Armitage, it is even more important that our secret remains between the two of us" he added.

The Mansion a Week Later

David looked out of the sitting room window, across the surrounding fields of the mansion, thinking how things had changed over the past few years. Technology was moving so fast. It seemed that the moment a new product was designed, another outdated it. The unions were making suggestions that were totally impractical; generally life was becoming very tiresome and most difficult.

Now his father had just announced over dinner that a young man was coming to the mill on a work program to further his pre-university studies and would be around for some weeks.

Evidently the same young man originally came from the village. David thought at the time that he didn't remember such a lad. But he'd been away during the war and many things had happened during that time.

The next morning David had just left his office and was walking towards the twisting sheds when he heard his name on the public address system.

"Will Mr. David please come to the office?"

David made his way across the floor. On arrival, he saw through the glass partition that his father had a guest, a young stranger. *Funny, they seem to be chatting like old friends! David thought to himself*, noting the pleased expression on his father's face, and the relaxed posture of the younger man who sat opposite to him.

I had spent the weekend at home prior to starting my first days as a worker. I wondered whether work-studies meant my actually working, or my studying others working. Somehow I guessed that it would be the former; tomorrow was my time to find out. Saturday had been spent sitting around the house, though I did try to tidy up the place a bit. Mum certainly would not have liked the sight that met my eyes on my return home from school; the house was a total mess. Dad had agreed to get a woman in a few times a week to keep the place clean and tidy. The sooner the better, were my thoughts on the matter.

On Sunday afternoon I decided to go for a stroll. I went across the fields with Titch at my heels and found myself walking past Miss Marshall's, my old piano teacher. I turned off into the fields, my mind returning to the events of that evening during the war. The hole was no longer in the fence but the field still contained newer generations of cattle, chewing away at the cud.

I looked into the hedge, where I assessed that the last box had landed and saw a fragment of cloth hanging underneath an old broken keep out sign that threatened prosecution to trespassers. Pulling it from where it hung on the hawthorn branch, I examined the material. Sure enough it was silk, though slightly weather-beaten. The sign had preserved the texture, it was definitely part of the parachute that we had seen in the field that night, of that there was no doubt.

Standing there, I smiled remembering John's face, and could still see him as he had shot out of the hole in the fence that night; I wondered what he was doing now!

I walked to the top of Pit Lane, went down the hill and came around the back of the cottages looking for the shed.

Moving closer I saw that the door was open. I could hear sounds coming from inside. As usual Titch had gone through an opening, now pedestrian size; I followed and popped my head inside the door.

"Is anyone at home?" I shouted. The shed was typical of a garden store. Not being sure what I was looking for, I came face-to-face with my friend the German, or a somewhat older version. Growing up is so strange, the man looked positively small to me now.

"Who are you, what do you want?" came the retort.

"Just looking for my dog, do you have a problem with that?" I snapped at him as he looked me in the eyes.

"Don't I know you from somewhere?"

"I don't think so." There was no mention of any cat, so I assumed that the poor moggie had passed on, or maybe my presence was more formidable than the last time we met, and he didn't wish to offend a six-footer weighing a good 185 lbs. He actually seemed more friendly, maybe more subservient. I took another quick glance around the shed but saw nothing out of the ordinary, no packages of silk. Then I spotted a ball of green cord. Pointing to it I said,

"I wonder if I could scrounge a bit of that cord. I lost my dog's leash on my way across the fields today, that'll keep him out of other people's yards."

"Of course, help yourself, take it all, I have no further use for it, it's good strong stuff." Taking hold of the cord I did a pretend stress test.

"Wow, this stuff is strong, what's it made of?" Giving the best portrayal of innocence I could muster.

"Silk," he said emphatically, as though there were no other material.

"100% pure silk," he added. I thanked him and went on my way.

I was now more than ever determined to get to the bottom of this old mystery!

The work-study program being at home would be an ideal time to seize the opportunity, kill two birds with one stone. *Could there still be any trace of those boxes five years after the event? Would anyone have the answers to my questions? Where was I to start?*

Those cases had been too large to go through any normal house doorway; that narrowed down my search to some place with large doors wide enough to drive a farm tractor through the entrance. A barn maybe or a garage, a factory, a mill, somewhere close enough to those fields, so as not to draw too much attention, but then it had been wartime blackout.

So who would have seen anything on those dark nights anyway? These and a million other questions coursed through my mind as I walked back home, holding the silk parachute cord in my hands.

My thoughts turned immediately to my meetings tomorrow with Carl Armitage and David White. I was really nervous at the prospect of these meetings, as my last formal interview had been five years ago with the head of the school.

David was rather different. He felt more special to me, as if we were family, and after all, we sort of shared the same father in all but blood that is. I had heard quite a lot about Mr. Armitage, Junior too. He was said to keep to himself and could be rather officious and distant. Anticipation of the whole scenario filled me with excitement and trepidation at the same time.

I had heard so much about coalmines over the years, some good some not. The prospect of going so deep underground was sort of scary; of course the opportunity of meeting with the sons of the two wealthy families of Casleton remained equally daunting.

They had both attended my school. Carl Armitage had excelled in all areas of sports and athletics, whilst David White had been the more studious of the two. David's name was on the Old Boys honors board having earned one of the highest wartime decorations. He had been presented to His Royal Highness King George, himself.

I had noticed that the name Armitage seemed to appear on every rose bowl and shield in the school trophy room. The language master told me that when they attended the school, the two of them had been inseparable. It struck me as rather odd that Harold had not mentioned Carl's name that often, though I do remember him saying the day we went fishing that I reminded him of a friend of David's. I wondered if he had meant Carl. I also remembered the way that he had rapidly changed the subject when Captain Pete had asked after Carl's welfare.

Chapter Nine

The Armitage Household

The morning after his night out with Bruce, Carl awoke with a start as a result of a particularly nasty dream. Though he couldn't remember the content, he knew it was bad because he was sweating profusely; he had slept fitfully for only three hours, his conversation with the German the previous evening foremost in his mind.

Today was one of his days off which rather pleased him. Apart from the nagging worry, he also had a well-earned hangover. After he'd showered, shaved and dressed, he went down for breakfast. His father was sitting at the breakfast table reading the Daily Telegraph; he peered piously over his glasses as Carl walked into the room.

"Morning Carl, you must have come in late last night. I went to bed around midnight and the car was still out," said Carl's father.

"I am over twenty-one you know, Father."

"Quite so, but I worry about you staying out until the hours that you do; it's neither healthy nor normal. While you live in this house, I would like you to show a little more consideration, is that clear?"

"Yes father, very!"

"By the way, there is a young man coming to the office today; he is just completing his final year at school. It seems that they now send selected students out into the big wide world before they go onto university, and those selected are required to complete a job evaluation project.

"This young man is to work with you for a few weeks, I'd like you to see him at noon today. His name is Matthew Harper. He comes from the village and is also doing a similar exercise at the mill."

"Hell, Dad! Today's my day off, I have other things planned."

"Then may I suggest that you un-plan them," his father snapped in reply, folding his newspaper, and striding purposefully out of the room. As he reached the door, he turned.

"By the way, you look damn ghastly." Carl nodded sullenly. He helped himself to cornflakes and coffee, browsed the Daily Herald, and then went back upstairs to change into a suit in preparation for his un-planned, unwanted meeting with this Matthew Harper youth.

I arrived at the mine offices for my first interview ten minutes early. I'd been past the place so many times over the years but never actually been on the premises, what a depressing place! All the buildings were dirty, covered with a thick film of coal dust crusted to their structure by the never-ending rains. Stepping off the concrete walkways was not a good idea. The remainder of the area was a sea of thick black mud, being constantly churned by the wheels of heavy trucks, which were taking their loads of coal to the gas works. Most of the area was stacked with supplies waiting to be taken underground. Towering above was the main superstructure, holding the massive pulley wheels over the mineshaft.

I walked into the small reception area with its heavy Hessian mat underfoot. Knocking tentatively on the small frosted glass window, a bit like going to the doctor's less the medical smells, the window slid silently open to reveal a cheerful grey-haired man.

"Yes, young man, and what can we do for you today?"

"I have an appointment with Mr. Carl Armitage."

"Not today you don't my lad, today is his day off." I couldn't believe my ears. I was just about to protest when the door opened and in walked a smartly dressed, pleasant-looking younger man.

"Morning, Mr. Carl, I thought it was your day off today."

"Me too Fred, so did I!" he repeated himself ominously, looking at me quizzically as he spoke.

"You must be Matt Harper?"

"That's right, Sir."

"I was only told of this appointment first thing this morning," he said totally removing any feelings of self-importance on my behalf.

"Put Mr. Harper, here, in the waiting room, give him an application form, get me a cup of strong tea from the canteen, and give me today's underground roster. Any calls for me?" Then he was gone through the door into the office.

This is a good start, I thought to myself as I sat down and attempted to complete a form that appeared to be an application for employment, and bore no relationship to a work-study position. Eventually the grey- haired man Fred took it away.

"Come on in, he'll see you now. Hey aren't you Jack Harper's lad?" he asked, looking at the partially completed form. I nodded.

"How's your dad keeping these days? We were all so sorry about your mother. I haven't seen Jack for such a long time. I suppose you're doing well at that posh school they sent you to. Good luck to you lad, that's what I say."

"Take a seat, pull up that chair over here."

I stood up and offered my hand as Carl entered the office. He had a hand shake like a vice, a handsome man, about my own height, square chin, piercing blue eyes, though he looked very tired. As he read through my application he seemed un-interested, resigned, bored, then he looked up with a start.

"Well here's a coincidence, we both went to the same school," his eyes seemed to light up.

"How is the old place?" Before I could answer, his many questions were coming at me thick and fast. He asked after the head master, also many of the other masters, some of whom I didn't know. A conversation ensued for at least ten minutes, all about the old days, and then the door opened.

"Your tea, Master Carl, sorry it took so long, you know that canteen."

By the end of the meeting, Carl had told me most of the history of the mine, and the ongoing modernizations. How he was really holding the fort, pending the appointment of a National Coal Board-trained manager. Finally, he pushed back his chair.

"Well, young Harper, when are you able to start? There's no time like the present. I wasn't intending to go down today, but I'll take you down for a quick initiation if you like."

"Er, well that will be a little difficult," I smiled apologetically.

"How so?" he asked.

"I have another appointment in twenty minutes time at the mill," feeling rather un-gracious after his offer, and the way we had seemed to get on together.

"Oh, and who are you seeing there?" he asked

"David White, he's seeing me when the mill closes at one."

"Well we mustn't keep the Captain waiting then, must we?" he said in rather a curt and final tone. There seemed to be a complete change in his attitude.

I wasn't sure whether it was towards me, or due to my mention of the mill and David White, but a marked change had most certainly occurred. If only I'd been able to accompany him, we would really have got off on the right foot.

After some short words of welcome and his promise to have a full program laid on, I was ushered out of the offices, heading to the other end of the village to my next appointment.

Chapter Ten

The Market, Leeds City

Bruce was just about to leave the office for his usual lunchtime beer and sandwich. The market was relatively quiet, the usual mixture of the general public and wholesale buyers shopping; he picked up the ringing phone.

"Yes, Gerald what's up? I'm just on my way over there right now. I'll see you in the bar, five minutes; order my usual, will you?"

It was a busy afternoon in the bar. At first Bruce couldn't see Gerald but then he spotted him sitting down at a table.

Some years before Gerald had been a member of the City Police force; he had risen from the rank of constable and became a detective sergeant in the C.I.D. Some years later he had left the force, a subject which he rarely discussed with anyone.

"So what's going on, big feller?"

"This and that, I got some of the info on that club for you. Why are you so interested in the place anyway?"

"Okay I'll tell you, although I'm not exactly sure myself. You remember meeting my old school pal Carl in here Friday evening?" Gerald nodded.

"Seems like a pleasant kind of bloke to me," he added.

"One of the best," said Bruce.

"We left here and went to that club, he's a member there. When we got in there he spoke with a character, a nasty looking piece of work, who I didn't like at all.

"At first he spoke with an accent, German I think, but later the man spoke in perfect English. That's not what's bothering me; he spoke to Carl like he was rubbish, and Carl just took it. I know my old pal very well, I can tell you; normally he would either have taken the man apart verbally, or beaten the hell out of him. He did neither, in fact he seemed scared. I don't like it and I want to know what's going on, so give." As they spoke a woman brought a toasted sandwich to the table, along with a couple of beers.

"I have an old friend who's a detective here on the City Force," said Gerald.

"He owes me a couple of favors, here and there," he said nonchalantly.

"I know that club was never short of the best stuff, right throughout the war. The police never once raided it, I can tell you that. On one occasion a visit was planned, but got canceled from above, if you know what I mean. There are a lot of influential names on the membership list, the club is owned by a sort of consortium.

"From what I've learned the front man has no record on file, clean as a whistle, a bit of a mystery man. He seems to have taken over control in the last few months.

"One of our drivers said that there was evidently a problem one night with a few rowdies. It appears this man went out into the car park after them. By all accounts, he hospitalized two of them, one nearly died."

"What does this guy look like?" Bruce interjected.

"Over six feet, a good two hundred fifty pounds, not an ounce of fat, well-dressed, close-cropped hair, the kind of person that I like to play with," replied Gerald with a big grin.

"You and me both," Bruce added with a smirk.

"Did you get the application forms?"

"Forms? You only asked for one," said the big man, an evil grin crossing his battle-scarred face, and then he passed two forms across to his friend.

"You'll see that they have already been signed by appropriate sponsors. Remind me to tell you who proposed you, just in case someone should ask!"

"Tonight's Saturday, seems like a good time to inaugurate our new membership, wouldn't you say Gerald?" Bruce said with a look of anticipation across his beaming face.

"What time and where, my leader?" he asked Bruce.

They arranged to meet back at the market bar at ten o'clock that evening.

"Put on a suit and tie," Bruce shouted as he left the bar for his office a spring in his step; he was looking forward to his evening out. On occasions like this he usually felt a bit more comfortable with Gerald by side, but this time he felt uneasy in general. Perhaps tonight would allow him to find out what was bothering his old friend and what lay behind the inferred threat he'd heard earlier.

The Mill 1948

I left my meeting with Carl Armitage, a little despondent. I had to walk at quite a brisk pace if I was to keep my next interview on time. Up the steep Pit Lane, once past the old school, it was easy and down all the way. I got there with two minutes to spare, though somewhat hot and bothered. On arrival at the mill, I was ushered directly into the office of Harold White

"Hello, there Matt, how nice to see you again. How's everything?"

"Fine Harold, I just had a most interesting meeting at the colliery earlier, I'm to start there on Monday morning."

"How did you get along with Carl Armitage?" I told him about the meeting in detail, how the tenor of the conversation had changed at the mention of my coming to the mill. Harold listened with interest, then picked up the telephone and asked his secretary to put out a call for Mr. David. Shortly after, a tall younger man entered the office walking with the aid of a stick.

"David, I'd like you to meet Matthew Harper. You remember I told you he is from your old school, and is to come here for a few weeks of work study."

"Yes, Father, though you did forget to mention he was attending the old school," said David looking surprised. By now I was standing, and David turned to me shaking me by the hand.

"Well Matthew, it's a great pleasure to meet you, you really must bring me up-to-date, and tell me how things are at the old school. Let's go along to my office and see if we can't work out a program to suit your needs."

"Please, call me Matt," I smiled. "Everybody does," I added.

I liked David from the first moment we met; he didn't have the tension in his posture that Carl had displayed earlier. He seemed a lot like his father, with a sort of quiet inner strength that created confidence.

Two hours later it was agreed that if the plan met with the approval of the colliery, I would come to the mill on the fourth week, and so it was arranged.

That Saturday evening I decided, as a potential working person, that I'd take myself out for a bit of a treat, so at around seven-thirty I donned a jacket and tie, put on some Christmas-present cologne, gave my shoes a quick rub over, and then walked up the hill to West Casleton.

I arrived at the village club around eight-thirty. I'd been there a couple of times before but on special social occasions and outside of normal operating hours. I walked into the crowded bar for the first time; it was packed with villagers who all seemed to be talking at the same time in competition, with loud music coming from a stage in the corner. The air was thick with the smoke from cigarettes and pipes.

"Well, if it's not young Harper! And what brings you here tonight, slumming, are we?" asked a facetious and familiar voice. It was one of my father's wood-chopping men leaning at the bar.

"Let me get you a drink, I assume that you're old enough to have one, what's it to be then young 'un?"

He grinned. I really didn't know what to order, for apart from a couple of glasses of sherry, which had been consumed illegally in the school dorm, and a couple of shandies (half beer half lemonade) on a weekend visit to a school chum's home, I had no experience or indeed preference.

"Let's make a man of you and get you a pint of the best," said the woodchopper.

The bartender duly poured a mug of beer with a white foamy head and beer running down the glass onto my shoes. My first sip was not exactly a pleasure; in fact it was quite the contrary.

I have since heard many an unpalatable experience described as an acquired taste. I was sure at the time, acquiring *this* taste would be an uphill grind.

After five minutes or so of small talk, him cracking a few jokes at my father's expense, the donor of my pint went off to play darts. I wondered if his wife had used up all of the silk by now.

"Fancy ze game of dominos?" someone said to me, with a slight German accent.

"Do you know how to play?" he asked. It was the man from Pit Lane cottages, the railway station, and the night of the parachutes.

"I would *very* much like to have a game," I replied walking over to where he sat and joining him at his table. He shuffled the pieces (for some reason they call them cards), then dealt mine to me.

"You are not from zese parts are you?" he asked. I was not certain whether his use of rhetoric was a result of his ignorance of our language, or spoken intentionally.

"Yes, I most certainly am. I would think if anyone here is a stranger it's *you*, you're an ex-prisoner of war, are you not?" I added indignantly, surprising myself at my own apparent truculence, as he too seemed a little taken aback by my abrupt reply.

"Vell, ja, I am but all zat's ofer, I didn't start ze var unt had no choice but to fight, as many of your men dit. In fact, I shpent nearly all of ze var 'ere in Casleton, unt as you vill see, I'm shtill here."

"What do you do for a living?" I asked him.

"I'm ze blackshmitt, at ze coal mine, amongst utter sings. I shoe ze ponies in ze unterground shtables." I had one double six left to finish the current game.

"Thanks for the string," I said, he looked a little puzzled.

"Shtring?" he paused, "Ah, ja, I remember now, ze dog leash."

"That was most kind of you, whoops, here we go," I said placing down my last domino ending the game.

"Where did you say that string came from?" He looked at me curiously, then down shuffling the pieces for the next game.

"I don't qvite remember," he said.

"I sink zat maybe ze olt vuman, had it in her housen, I lodge zere, you know."

"Did most of the other prisoners go back to Germany at the end of the war?"

"Ja, zere iss only little olt me left in zese parts."

"How are you getting on with that pint young'en," interjected the voice of the woodchopper.

"Don't listen to a word old Adolf here tells you either. Let me top that beer up, your old man will have my guts for garters if I don't look after you."

"No, I think it's my turn, let *me* get *you* a drink," I replied. I walked up to the bar and asked for the same again for my friend, and ordered a vodka and tonic for myself. "Aren't you Jack Harper's lad?" the barman asked. I nodded my head.

"You were in the same school class as my lad, nice to see you again." I thanked him, paid for the drinks, and then went back to the game. My partner had just returned from the men's room.

"What's your name? Mine's Matt." I smiled as I pulled up my chair, tasting my first ever vodka.

"Kurt, my name is Kurt," he replied.

"Does he always call you Adolf? Is that some kind of joke?" I asked, inclining my head towards the dart player.

"You ask a lot of qvestions young Mista Matt, a *lot* of qvestions." he said, looking skeptically at me. *I know that you lied about the string; I know that you were in the field that night and I intend to get to the bottom of this affair,* I thought to myself as I returned the stare.

There was now no doubt in my mind, that something illegal went on that night back in 1942, possibly to do with the war, *but what was so important that our friend Kurt would still be here so long after the war was over and were there other people involved?* I've always had an inquisitive mind, if you don't ask questions you will never learn. He reshuffled the pieces. I selected mine.

"If you vill put your finger into ze fire, you vill get burned," he said, in no more than a whisper.

"I am sorry I didn't quite catch that," I replied.

"No matter, it vas not important," he concluded.

"Ve'll play ze next game for ze drink, ze loser pays," he said looking me straight in the eyes. At that moment it was announced that the Saturday night entertainment was about to begin. He won the last game, I still had four dominos left, so that cost me another pint of beer.

I still had some of my drink left so I sat down and listened to a female singer, followed by a comedian who was a little bit rude, but absolutely hilarious. After the show, people started to dance. I looked around for my friend *Adolf*, or Kurt, but he was nowhere to be seen. I had finished my drink and was about to leave for home when someone tapped me on the shoulder. I looked round into the face of a very pretty young girl of about my own age.

"This is a lady's excuse me," she said with such a sweet smile on her extremely pretty face.

"But I'm not dancing," I said somewhat taken aback, shrugging my shoulders. She took me by the arm leading me reluctantly to the dance floor area. I can still remember the smell of her perfume.

"Now you're dancing! I've been watching you since you came into the club," she said.

"I knew your face but couldn't remember the name," she said into my ear. "You don't remember me, do you?" she asked, giggling as she spoke.

"I'm sorry, no I don't, should I?" She smelled of roses and danced *so* well; the only dancing I'd done previously was practice at school, under duress, in the gymnasium with classmates as partners, looked upon then as a sissy's pastime.

"You dance well," she said.

"But relax, you are all uptight, you don't have to squeeze my hand so tightly, there, that's better," she said as I visibly relaxed.

It was one of the most pleasant evenings I had spent for as long as I could remember. Her name was Joan, her Dad owned the local joiners and undertakers, and she had been at the local school the same time as me. She remembered the soccer match.

After the last waltz I walked her home and we agreed to meet again soon, maybe go to the cinema. I floated on air the rest of the way home, a combination of vodka, beer, happiness, and that lingering heady perfume on my hands and on the lapels of my jacket.

The City of Leeds that Same Evening

Carl was driving round the center of the city heading towards the nightclub. He had given his predicament a lot of thought. He alone had allowed the debts to accrue, he must sort it out, if possible without anyone else knowing or being involved.

The amount owed was far more than he possessed so he had no way of clearing the total. He could offer some now, and pay off the remainder over a period of time. He didn't like to beg favors, but yes, that's what he'd have to do. As he pulled into the car park the front section was full, the only spaces appeared to be way at the rear. After carefully maneuvering his car into the limited space available, he thought he saw a car pull across the rear of his. Thinking no more of it, he parked, then locked the car. The space was so tight he had to squeeze out of his driver door, banging his knee on the neighboring car and uttering an oath as he slid out of the confined space and into the darkness.

Reaching the rear of the car, he was completely taken by surprise as a gloved fist smashed hard into his face. He felt a searing pain, as it caught him just to the side of his mouth. He tasted blood. Staggering round the rear of the car, he caught another savage blow to the solar plexus, followed by a kick to his left leg.

He could barely make out the two shapes in the darkness; he half knelt on one knee, struggling to regain valuable breath as they both moved in again. He saw the foot of the nearest one coming at him for the second time.

Carl moved to his left to avoid the oncoming kick. He grabbed the flying ankle as it was aimed at his head, then leaped to his feet still holding the ankle; he delivered a forceful right foot up into to the owner's groin and testicles.

The man screamed in pain, retching violently, then he began to vomit. The second assailant came in stooping forwards, holding some kind of weapon in his right hand. Carl had been on the school boxing team and had trained with the Army Cadet force; he'd also spent some time learning this newfangled, oriental Ju-Jitsu. Now one-on-one he was good and ready for whatever came next.

"Come on you scum, put the weapon down and fight like a man," he yelled into the darkness. The first assailant continued to moan as he lay on the ground. Carl couldn't make out the features of his attacker, but he could see in the reflection of the distant streetlights the occasional flash of the open razor that was held in his hand.

The man made his move and as he did so Carl faked a blow with his left hand towards the weapon, moved his weight over to his right foot, then as his assailant moved forward he grabbed the wrist holding the razor, in his left hand. At the same time he brought his right knee hard into the thigh muscle of his assailant who dropped the weapon, cursing as his left leg went numb. Carl then spun the man around. From behind, his left hand around the man's throat, he delivered a well-timed fist to the kidneys. His injured opponent folded and hit the ground like an empty sack.

A blinding flash was all that Carl saw next, he heard the crack to his skull, blackness came as his senses began to leave him, the ground rushed up to his face, his hands slid down the back of his car as he fell unconscious to the ground.

"Leave him there; pick up that weapon, you, get up and stop complaining, you're not dead *yet*, now come on, *move*. What a bunch of incompetent fools you are." At the same time, the man with the short cropped hair kicked Carl viciously twice to the ribs.

"Get into the car *now,* and *go*!" he yelled at Carl's assailants. A few minutes later the big man stood by the main reception desk, phone in hand.

"Yes, officer I was just checking the parking lot when I saw the body of a man laying on the ground; it looks as though there's been a fight, yes, I have called the ambulance. Of course I will be here to answer further questions. No there were no other witnesses, or at least we've heard nothing here. Thank *you,* officer." The big man put down the telephone receiver with a grin on his face,

"You will eventually do things my way, Mr. Armitage," he said out loud.

"*You will see,*" he thought to himself, as he heard the noise of the departing ambulance siren, rushing off into the night.

"That sounded close to here," Bruce said to Gerald.

"It was," said a man standing next to them at the bar.

"As I was coming in just now I heard that big guy over there talking to the cops, said he found a body in the parking lot." He nodded in the direction of the big man standing near the bar who had spoken to Carl the other night. Bruce walked over to the man.

"You in charge here?" he asked the big man.

"Why do you ask?" Gerald stepped forward.

"He asked, because he wants an answer, so don't be so bloody insolent. *Now* are *you* in charge here or *not?*"

"*Yes,* I am."

"That's better, good manners don't cost anything, as my old mum used to say. We just a moment ago gave two application forms along with money to your girl out there. We *would* like a temporary membership card, now.

"I'm sorry," but you can't have a card until your membership has been approved. Also you can't use the club's facilities until your membership is approved either," explained the man.

"Membership approved; can't! There's no such word as can't, and you soon bloody well will be afraid if I start," Gerald snarled as he stepped forward to get hold of the man. Bruce stepped in between the two men.

"Hang on a second, we don't want to hurt the man just yet!" Bruce said to Gerald. What's this that we hear about a body in the parking lot?" he asked.

"That's a matter for the police and is none of your business." snapped the big German.

"That's it," roared Gerald as he shot forward. Grabbing the big man by the lapels of his jacket, he lifted him off the ground slamming him onto a vacant barstool with a thud.

"Is this the git you were talking about?" Bruce nodded.

"Let's get out of this place before I really start on this Kraut piece of rubbish." He poked the shorthaired man hard in the chest.

"Remember my face, Kraut," his large forefinger stabbing the air. "When I come back be sure to have my membership cards ready or you will need to be very afraid, that I promise you!" At that point two of the club's burly bouncers came rushing towards the scene.

"Hey Gerald, what's up," one of the policemen asked.

"I was just giving your boss here some friendly advice lads. Tell him what happens to people who aren't good boys and don't behave themselves," he said with a grin.

"Come on Bruce, we can find better places to spend our money."

"I'll be looking *at you*," Gerald glowered at the big man. As he left he picked up a drink and poured it over the bar. "Remember that."

As they went across the parking lot, there were two policemen searching the ground with flashlights.

"Problem constable?" asked Gerald to one of the policemen.

"Hello Gerald, some guy got into a fight earlier, as usual no witnesses, he seems pretty badly hurt, and this is his car here."

"Wait a minute, that looks like Carl's car. See all the black coal mud on the tires," exclaimed Bruce

"What's the name of the injured man?" asked Gerald. The officer took out his notebook; searching the pages he shone the flashlight.

"Armitage, Carl Armitage, according to his driving license. He was taken to the infirmary, head and rib injuries. He's still unconscious, or he was when he left here so we can't question him yet. You know him then Gerald?" asked the constable.

"Yes I do."

They drove hurriedly towards the infirmary as Bruce broke the silence.

"We need to find out what all this is about, and then perhaps we can have a real talk with that bastard at the club." As they pulled past the emergency room entrance, Bruce spotted Carl's father walking into the foyer. He then told Gerald he would rather wait until the old man had left, and so they had to wait a few minutes before trying to see his friend.

Back at the Village

Sunday mornings always seem to take a long time to get moving. I hadn't seen Dad the night before, so I assumed that he'd worked the night shift. I moved around the house as quietly as possible so as not to wake him. I ate a light breakfast, and then decided to take a nice *long* walk.

Titch by my side, we made a complete circumference of the village, taking the best part of three hours. As we approached the back of the mine property I noticed in the distance a large pall of smoke as we approached; I saw the coal board fire engines at work.

Most, if not all coalmines have to separate the coal from the dross. This procedure, carried out on the surface, leaves thousands upon thousands of tons of waste, which is piled high forming mini-mountains called slag heaps. Some of them stretched a half-mile or more. Frequently they catch on fire due to spontaneous internal-combustion; such was the case on this day. One of the firemen told me that these things are permanently alight deep down, no vegetation can ever grow; these slag heaps form black, depressingly ugly scars across the countryside

I checked my watch, it was just after eleven. I looked down from the slag heap towards the mine and surrounding area. The place seemed tranquil, the colliery was still and peaceful, just a couple of the mine's ponies eating grass in the adjoining field, obviously injured or resting.

During the summer the mine closes completely for two weeks. As well as all the miners taking a holiday, the ponies are brought out and let loose into the fields, a pleasant but pitiful sight. These poor creatures only get out into daylight for two weeks each year unless they become sick or injured, or dead!

Looking over towards the cottages in Pit Lane, I noticed a large black car parked near the end of the terrace, where two men were talking at the gate of a cottage. Out of curiosity I walked across the field next to the lane; we neared the hedge when I noticed that the man leaning on the gate was none other than my domino-playing friend Kurt. I couldn't yet identify the other man, as his back was towards me.

I climbed the fence as Titch went underneath and we walked down the opposite side of the road just as the other man turned round towards me.

Like a bolt from the blue, the look on my face must have shown my shock. It was the missing link, the man from the station, the shorthaired German with the brief case, also from that night in the fields.

In an attempt to hear what they were saying, I stooped down pretending to fasten my shoelaces. A noisy motor-bike came between me and my target interest.

"Let's find some place where we can talk. I didn't drive this far to stand outside on the street." With that, friend Kurt came out of the gate speaking too quietly for me to hear a word that was said. They both got into the car and drove off up the hill; my first reaction was to run after them. Instead I stood there wondering how on earth I could find them again as the car disappeared out of sight, over the brow of the hill.

Pit Lane was always quite a climb, particularly after already having walked for three hours, even for a young man such as me.

By the time we hit the top, my legs were beginning to feel the strain.

As we approached the 'T' junction, opposite the Bed-ford Afms Pub, I could see only one car in the parking lot and it wasn't one of theirs.

Damn! I thought. Should I turn right to West Casleton or left toward home? Right was in the direction of the village club, which I now knew was a haunt of the erstwhile Kurt.

As I stood cogitating, Titch took off on another of his futile pursuits, chasing the pub cat.

They disappeared round behind the building; I waited knowing that my silly canine friend would soon re-appear, empty-handed, as it were!

I waited for a couple of minutes. *No dog.* Then I walked down the side of the pub whistling for him, there he was looking up at the cat sitting on a high wall staring down at him. As I rounded the corner, bingo! There was the car parked at the rear; they were in the bar.

I walked into a small bare looking room. With the exception of an old man smoking a pipe, it was totally deserted. The sign on the door read, 'Tap Room.' A rotund man with a handlebar moustache appeared behind the bar, hands on hips.

"Sorry young man, no dogs allowed in here," smiling, he said.

"There is a leash fastened to the down pipe outside, tie him to that. He'll be ok I'm sure." I thanked him and moved towards the door calling for Titch to follow.

"I assume that you're over the age of eighteen, and you did come here for a drink," said the bartender, as an afterthought.

"I am and I would like a half of mild please," I replied.

Man's best friend gave a look of utter disgust at being tethered like some horse outside a western saloon. Back inside I paid for the beer. I'd heard someone order mild in the club last evening; actually it tasted quite good, especially in my dehydrated state. I must say it went down rather well.

Now I know that in the average northern pub there are two bar areas: The Tap room has a basic stone floor, scrubbed tables, hard seats, brass foot rails, dartboard, and usually men only; The Lounge bar is usually quite the reverse with carpets, rugs, curtains, copper-topped tables, open fireplace, flowers and piano. Drinks in there are a little more expensive; beer one penny a pint more.

Picking up my beer and pushing open the dividing swing door, I went through to the lounge bar. This room was a total contrast and packed with regulars. Sunday lunchtime is historically a short period, open 12:00 noon, close 2:00 PM; just the two hours. Looking around the bar I spotted the men sitting at a table for two in a corner of the room. The nearest seat was a bar stool at the end of the bar, a piano lay between that stool and them. I sat down.

"Same again young fellow?" said the barman. I had failed to notice, due to a massive thirst and my preoccupation, the glass was empty.

"Yes please."

"I should by rights charge you extra for bringing your first drink through here, but I won't. Stranger in these parts are you?" I told him who I was, of course he knows Dad. We were all so sorry when your Mum died, such a nice person. Your Dad's never been a drinking man, can't say as I've ever seen him in here."

I tried to hone in on the conversation in the corner, but a lady was playing the piano and eavesdropping seemed out of the question. The barman leaned across holding a drink.

"Pass this drink to the lady who is playing the piano there."

I walked across, pleased to have a genuine reason to get over there. Picking up an empty glass and putting the full one down on the coaster, I strained to hear the conversation between the two men, again to no avail.

"Matthew Harper, what brings you here, what a pleasant surprise?" I recognized the voice instantly; it was Miss Marshall my old piano teacher.

There followed a tirade of questions: where was I living now, how was boarding school, was I still keeping up my playing, wasn't it awful about your Mum, more condolences. The frustration must have shown on my face, for she said "I must go and powder my nose. Why don't you play a little something for us, whilst I am away? That would be nice Matthew."

I sat down eagerly at the piano stool, not in eagerness to play; I was now close to my ever-increasing source of interest. I turned over the sheets of music slowly and heard the big German say, "Things are coming to a head a little quicker than was anticipated… there are complications…we have to make arrangements to move the stuff sooner. It must be done in one operation. It will have to be done at night and must look like a normal activity."

"Come on then lad, let's hear you, Miss Marshall tells us you were one of her star pupils," shouted the bartender.

"Come on it's worth a free beer to you," he said. *God, dammit!* I thought, *just as I was about to discover the details of Kurt's meeting.*

I started playing an old standby, one that I could almost play in my sleep: The Blue Danube by Strauss.

Over the years since, I have practiced the technique of listening to someone with one ear, whilst pretending to hear something else with the other. This I attempted now. Playing and listening was by far easier. I quickly tuned back into the conversation.

"We have just had a bit of a hick-up, but don't you worry about that, I have your management well under control. Your little man will not be a problem, he will not get in your way for a long time," said the big blonde man.

"I want this whole matter over and done with by..." His conversation was cut short by the return of Miss Marshall.

"That sounded fine, you still have a nice touch Matt, but I feel sure that if Herr Strauss would have wanted those twiddley bits, he would have written them in himself, you always were an improviser," said Miss Marshall, looking as stern as she ever did, then she laughed.

"Come on let's give them a duet or two."

Just then the two men stood up to leave as the big man gripped my shoulder.

"I think that Herr Strauss would have been perfectly delighted with your rendition, here, buy yourself a drink," he said placing five shillings on the piano top.

The bar man waved me to collect my free drink. I pocketed the money! *One back on all those games of football that I missed for piano lessons!* I was going to say it out loud, but didn't think that Mrs. Marshall would see the funny side.

She and I played until the pub closed at two and towards the end the whole of the pub were singing. I don't think that some of the wartime songs would have pleased the Germans quite so much as Herr Strauss had done.

I un-hitched a very sullen, not so much man's best friend. Walking home, I went over the day's events. The largest question mark in my mind: Kurt had still spoken with a Germanic accent after all these years, yet the big man spoke in perfect English as though he had taken elocution lessons.

In fact, his accent was educated English. I assumed the stuff to be moved was the content of the boxes, though it was such a long time ago. Move them from where to where and which management did he have under control? At least it seemed that the stuff could still be around. I promised myself that I would do some close surveillance work on friend Kurt the Kraut.

My top priority now was tomorrow morning, an early start at six o'clock. I felt quite excited about going down the mine for the first time after all these years in the North.

When I arrived home Dad was sitting down in his chair with a cup of tea.

"Aren't you going down the pit tomorrow, son?"

"Yes, it's a sort of work experience; I have to write a thesis on my impressions."

"Make sure that's all it is, down that hole is no place to be, you'll see what it does to a man, and be careful, it can be very dangerous.

"Listen to what people tell you, and keep your eyes open. I don't want to see you get hurt."

"I'll be OK, Dad, you worry too much."

"My father was killed down that pit," he said sadly.

The Previous Night at the Hospital

Carl came to his senses with a cocktail of strong smells of disinfectant, ether and medication in his nostrils. He heard the dull squeak of rubber shoes on a waxed floor, felt the over-emphasized silence as the shape of a nurse who seemed to float came towards him, and then became clearer in his continued blurred vision.

"There you are, back with us at last."

"How long have I been here?" he whispered, looking around him and trying hard to focus. As he spoke he felt pain from his mouth, he felt a very large swollen lip with the tip of his tongue and the prickly ends of stitches hanging out like elongated whiskers. His head felt as though it had been split open by a steam train. As he tried to move, a searing pain shot across his rib cage causing him to wince loudly.

"Now don't try to move, keep as still as you can and I'll get the doctor to give you something for the pain now that you're awake.

"Where am I, how long have I been here, what time is it?" He slurred his speech as the side of his mouth refused to move in unison with his mind.

"My, my, what a lot of questions you have."

"You are in Leeds City Infirmary, you have been involved in an accident, and you are going to be just fine." The nurse stood holding a note pad and pencil.

"Where is Leeds infirmary?"

"Let me ask a few questions now, how do you spell your name?" Carl paused for quite some time. Then at first the nurse thought that Carl had dropped off to sleep again.

"I err, it's er. I can't remember my name, nurse! I can't damn well remember!" He tried to get up but the punishing pain shot across his rib-cage putting a stop to any action or idea of any further movement.

"Doctor this is the nurse on ITU, you were right. The patient Carl Armitage, admitted with head and rib injuries *is* suffering from amnesia. I think a pain killer may be in order." she replaced the phone and walked across to Carl.

Later, Bruce walked into the private room just off the men's ward. He had been warned by the nurse that Carl was suffering from memory loss, which he was told is not out of the ordinary in such cases and that a friend's face could maybe speed up the process of its return. Carl looked up as he entered, showing no signs of recognition whatsoever.

"You another policeman? If you are I still can't remember a damn thing," he said in a weak voice, paying little if any attention to the new arrival.

"You look as though you've been in the wars," said Bruce as he took hold of Carl's hand and shook it firmly. It became obvious that his amnesia was total at this stage and that only rest would help bring back his memory.

Bruce said his farewells and left his friend in the capable hands of the caring experts. Gerald was waiting outside the ward and walked with Bruce; they stopped at the nurse's station where a detective was taking notes.

"Hey, my old friend what are *you* doing here?" The cop looked up as he spoke to Gerald.

"I'm just visiting an old friend with a head injury. Carl Armitage is an old school pal of my friend here," Gerald said to the detective.

"How are things with you these days?" Gerald asked the detective.

"Nothing much has changed since you left the job Gerald, same stuff, different faces, how long since you left the force?"

"Five years to the day, near enough," Gerald replied.

The detective said that the injuries were not accidental, and that a severe blow to the head with a blunt instrument had caused unconsciousness, followed by a nasty kick or two to the ribs. "Nice people," said Gerald.

"We are keeping an eye on the club where it happened as there's been some strange goings-on there."

"I just took out a membership there myself. I'll keep my eyes open too, let you know if I spot anything out of place," said Gerald.

"What is it that's bothering you boys?"

"Frankly we're not supposed to talk on this one. It's right from the top. Special branch and MI5 have been sniffing round, we're told to keep up surveillance, but outside and low profile; you didn't hear that from me," said the detective looking over each of his shoulders as he spoke. Gerald thanked his old partner, he and Bruce left for home as it was getting very late.

As they drove along the deserted city streets, Bruce broke the silence.

"What do you reckon of this lot, Gerald?" he asked his friend and colleague. "If you ask me, that German is up to his neck in this and from what we just heard he is no small-fry either. I can't understand how your friend could be involved with these types. We should really try and get to the bottom of this, for his sake, if for no other reason.

"One thing's for sure, someone hurt your pal for some reason or another and they weren't playing games. When he gets his memory back we need to ask him a few straight questions before he gets himself killed. It looks as though he is messing with people a little above your average villain." Bruce nodded in agreement.

"So what's our next move going to be?" Bruce asked.

"Let me think about it. That German won't talk, neither will he scare easily, we need to get some inside info on the club. I think I know where to get that so you leave it to me. Do nothing but visit your friend, let me know the minute his memory returns.

"Maybe you should go and see his parents find out what they know, ask a few questions around where he lives, someone must know him well, a girlfriend or close pal. Just ask around at the coal mine, find out where he used to drink in the village."

Chapter Eleven

Monday Morning

I hardly slept a wink that night. I woke up thinking about the whole mysterious affair. My mind was filled with a combination of un-answered questions plus the anticipation, or rather trepidation of the morrow's coming events. I got up and made myself a cup of tea, looked at my watch, it was already five o'clock. On the table was a parcel accompanied by a short note.

"I made you some sandwiches; take care of yourself, Dad." I put the note in my pocket, got dressed, and turned out the lights; it was still dark out. I went to open the door, Titch was at my heels.

"Sorry chum but you can't come today." I left the house, it was five-thirty Monday morning. I began my walk across the fields as other men were making the same journey. *Imagine having to do this every day for the rest of your life*, I thought.

I could see the lights of cycles being ridden up the hill as I surmounted the top; below me the twinkling lights of the pit. The smell of the sulphur hung on the early morning air from the smoldering slag heap, which hissed sharply as the light rain turned to steam on the surface of the drab warm grey rocks. I jumped as two larger pieces slid down the side of the bank, disturbed by either an animal or the increasing rains. I ran down towards the shelter of the pit yard, standing there under the cycle shed. The rain had reached torrential proportions. I was instructed to report to the office, but it was in darkness and the door was locked.

Cycles were arriving thick and fast; men covered in large canvass hoods, cursing the weather.

"At least it won't be raining where we're going," said one miner with water pouring off the back of his hat.

Looking around me at the drab scene that morning I felt absolutely lost and out of place there. I didn't belong in this strange place; I really felt like turning around and going home.

The lights were on in the office now so I ran across the yard, my feet squelching in the thick black mud, I opened the door.

"Wipe your feet on the mat before you come in here lad," yelled a voice, its owner unseen somewhere inside the office. The frosted glass window slid back, it was the grey-haired man Fred.

"Good morning young man, you've brought some lovely weather with you haven't you?" he said smiling.

I returned the smile with difficulty, nodding my head, as water ran freely off the end my nose.

"There's been a bit of a problem, Master Carl had an accident in Leeds on Saturday night, I am afraid he's still in hospital," said Fred.

"Is he alright? I asked.

"Well you could hardly say that, him being in the hospital and all," he answered facetiously. *On reflection it was bit of a silly question*. "They say he should be OK, he is suffering loss of memory right now."

"What do I have to do?"

"Good question," he replied. "I don't have a clue, sit there for minute; I'll see what I can find out."

I don't really fancy this lot anyway, maybe it will be canceled and I can go straight to the mill, I thought.

"What's up Fred?" a deep voice asked. Fred began to explain the situation, then closed the sliding window shut. I could only hear their mumbled voices through the glass.

"Come on through," said Fred pointing towards the door, I went into the general office and was greeted by a large friendly looking man. *Here we go, I'm going to be sent home.* I thought positively.

"Mornin', lad, my name's Ralph, I'm the pit Overman. Our under manager is also off sick so you'll just have to make do with me for the time being." He looked like a kindly sort, I felt at ease right away.

"You're Jack Harper's lad aren't you?" I nodded my head.

"I worked under his dad for years. You've grown a bit since I last set eyes on you, didn't you go away to school?" He was the only person recently who had not used the preface "*posh*" in reference to my school.

"Bloody good thing, education,you can't get enough of a good thing," said Ralph, saying that he had gone to night school to get his certificates. It was arranged that I would accompany Ralph on his rounds; first he had to clear it with regional office, as they could not find Carl's paperwork. Ralph said he had to be at the pit bottom to start the day shift off, and had to leave right away.

"Fred here will clear your permission to come down; he'll take care of it, kit you out and send you down. He will call me when you are ready."

I began to feel a little better about the whole ordeal. I watched Ralph walk out of the office and across to the lamp room. As Fred was on the phone I watched Ralph climb an iron staircase up into the building under those big wheels.

Send me down he had said, *sounds a bit ominous,* I thought to myself. It seemed like an age, sitting reading mining magazines, none of them for beginners, so unintelligible to this reader.

"Right, that's all done," evidently clearance had been found; it was on Carl's desk all the time unopened.

I was fitted out: new coveralls, issued a safety hat, then taken to the lamp room where my belt was threaded through the lugs of a battery that hung from my waist behind me, a cable leading up my back to the lamp that clipped to my hard hat. I was told to go down to Ralph!

The Mansion the Previous Day

After hearing the news of Carl's accident from his father, David returned to his room and sat down collecting his thoughts. Carl was in the hospital suffering loss of memory. He really must go and see his old friend but so many things were happening at once. Another of his ex-school pals, Bruce Bell, had made contact and wanted to talk to him. How had he found out about Carl?

There had been a note of innuendo and mystery in Bruce's voice; he really must go to Leeds and find out what the hell was going on.

He would call Bruce right back and meet him as soon as possible, and then another thought crossed his mind. Young Matt Harper was meant to be working with Carl tomorrow. He assumed rightly or wrongly that due to Carl's incapacity, the mine would want to make other arrangements. Maybe they would re-schedule and send the young man to the mill first.

On second thought, he decided to call the mine and find out what was to be done, and then decided to call on his return from seeing Carl. On third thought, he would call them right away.

Monday Morning Leeds

David drove through the busy rush hour traffic. He hadn't been into Leeds more than a couple of times since the end of the war. As he sat in a solid traffic jam, he found himself looking up at the massive statue of the Black Prince on horseback. He'd often wondered as a child who the subject was, as the bronze was so soiled by ages and pigeon decorations that the inscription was illegible.

After what seemed an age, the traffic started to move slowly. He drove down the main thoroughfare of the City Center, past Lewis's department store, with headless mannequins in its windows dressed in the latest fashions of the day. At the bottom of the Headrow he turned right at the traffic island and round into the busy market.

The whole place was like World War III, strewn with handcarts, horse-drawn carts, motor vans, and people everywhere. Paper mixed with cabbage leaves scattered amongst empty tomato boxes lay on the floor.

Salesmen shouting the quality and prices of their wares, it was impossible to drive an inch further. Then a truck behind him started to sound its horn, another vehicle behind that one did the same. The driver of the truck was shouting expletives at David, who was already out of his car, trying amid the entire din to explain why he could not drive one inch further.

The scene was reaching riotous proportions when Gerald came through the milling people pointing his finger. He spoke severely at the man in the truck behind David as all became quiet.

"Now sir, did we take the wrong turn? Driving in here is a bit of a joke unless you are delivering or picking up, even then... "

"No," said David, cutting the big man short.

"I'm trying to find the offices of a Bruce Bell." He limped toward his car door, which was still wide open.

"Here, allow me," said the big man, bending down to retrieve David's walking stick from the front passenger seat, handing it across to David. He turned to a nearby teenager, "Sammy, see that this car is put behind Mr. Bruce's office. Are the keys in there?"

"Yes, but err..."

"Don't worry; your car will be perfectly safe. Now come along with me and we'll take the short cut," he gestured; turning to David as they walked together, he said:

"You must be David from Casleton, I'm Gerald, Gerald Steel," he smiled holding out his hand to David. "I work with Bruce."

"I'm pleased to meet you Gerald, more than you'll appreciate under the circumstances." David felt an extremely firm handshake, and then they took off, weaving in and out of the masses of humanity.

"Mind you don't slip on all this vegetation on the floor," said David's guide, kicking a half cabbage across the road.

They soon reached an area where a large number of vans were parked, all of them bearing the name of his old school pal. Passing into a large warehouse packed to the ceiling with box after box of fruit, he saw his ex-school chum, standing at the top of a stairway, beckoning him up.

"Great to see you David, after all these years I'm glad you could come." Bruce shook David's hand warmly as he spoke.

"What happened to the leg?" he asked David.

"Got wounded in the war unfortunately, but others got far worse than me."

Bruce noticed the embarrassment in his voice, quickly getting off the subject.

"So how's life in Casleton these days?" he asked David.

"Pretty much the same as ever," David replied. Then Bruce went on to explain the situation regarding Carl's predicament, right up to the current moment. After some discussion and questions, David asked,

"Where do we go from here? I can't tell you any more than I have already. Carl hasn't spoken a word to me since I came back from the war; I worry about it every day." David looked down at his hands embarrassed at having to explain to Bruce as he spoke.

"The first priority is to find out if he will recognize you, it's important that he gets his memory back; otherwise everything that can be done will be based on pure guess work.

Bruce did not mention anything about the club or his suspicions in any way. He then suggested that they go immediately to the hospital, without further delay. As they climbed into a car, Gerald getting into the driving seat, David noticed that his car was neatly parked next to others within the fenced compound.

They arrived at the hospital and went past reception straight on up to the entrance of a ward. A nurse spoke to Bruce, then they were shown into a private single room.

There on the bed was his friend Carl, his face swollen at one side, stitches lined across his lips, looking a lot thinner than he last remembered, his eyes seemed sunken and tired. There wasn't a flicker of recognition on his face; in fact he seemed totally indifferent to the two as though a couple of total strangers walked across the room towards him.

"Some of your friends came to see you," said the nurse with a smile. Carl looked them both over.

"I don't recognize any of these people," he said tentatively, a worried look on his face.

"Should I?"

David reached across to take Carl's hand.

"Surely you remember me Carl. David, David White." As he spoke he shook Carl's hand using their old schoolboy hand shake. David felt sure that he noticed a slight glimmer in the eyes of his old friend, but if so there was no apparent reaction.

They left the hospital, the three of them had lunch together back at the market. They discussed old times, then David left for his drive back to the mill. As he climbed into the seat, he looked sad and confused. He shook hands with both men then drove off. Gerald shrugged his shoulders.

"Well, we didn't learn a lot there, did we?"

"I'm not so sure about that," replied Bruce looking pensively at the ground. He remembered that at school Carl and David were like Siamese twins. Now for some strange reason, Carl had never spoken to his friend since he returned from the war; maybe there was something that he was ashamed of or that he had to hide.

The doctor had said to Bruce earlier that in some cases involving memory loss, deep down in his subconscious the patient may not really want to remember.

"We need to know what he's hiding if anything" Bruce said aloud.

"Beg your pardon," said Gerald. Bruce looked up suddenly.

"Oh! Sorry mate, I was just thinking out loud," he said slowly and pensively.

Chapter Twelve

Back at the Mine Early Monday Morning

I took my first steps across the muddy pit yard tentatively with extremely mixed feelings. As I climbed the steep iron stairway, I appeared to be the only person around. I could see the cage just below me as men unloaded the metal cars filled to the brim with shiny black coal.

Materials and coal were loaded and taken off the cage, at ground level below where I stood. It continued to rain steadily as I spoke to the only other man I saw there; he was speaking on a metal phone.

"I'm to report to Ralph the Overman," I said with as much confidence as I could muster.

"He asked if you could call him first."

"Sure lad, what's your name?"

"Matthew Harper," I replied. I moved towards the Iron Gate across the entrance of what I assumed to be the mineshaft. Peering down, my loins tingled at the thought of the great void. I saw nothing, nothing but blackness. I looked up at the big pulley wheels turning overhead, as the incessant rain poured down through the opening.

"Long way down there, lad," said the cage operator, as though reading my mind. He walked over to the white-washed wall as he spoke, taking the earpiece from a strange looking phone; he wound a handle some five times, then spoke into a mouthpiece of the wall unit.

"Is Ralph there pleased? Well, tell him there's a Matthew Harper here for him... OK will do." He turned to me, a smile on his face.

"Don't look so worried, there's someone coming up on the next cage who'll take you back down. The look of sheer relief must have shown on my face at the thought of not having to disappear down that seemingly bottomless black hole alone. It seemed for the first time to lend a real live picture to the words of some of those fearsome preachers I'd heard.

"Condemned to the very depths of hell and damnation," I shuddered, as my thoughts were broken by the voice of the man next to me.

"First time down is it?" said the Banksman.

"Well, yes it is," I seemed to stutter as I spoke.

"Don't worry; I'll signal the engine room to go slowly." I thanked him, not quite knowing what slowly meant or faster, for that matter. Just then the right hand cage came to the surface, lifting the heavy Iron Gate to the shaft automatically as it came to a halt. The Banksman then lifted a second gate to the cage, pulling it open as three men got out. Two were carrying tripods and measuring instruments, the other came over to where I stood. He did not carry a lamp and wore only a soft flat cap, not the safety version that perched uncomfortably, digging into my own forehead.

"Hello there, lad, I'm Ben the stable man. Ralph asked me to take you down. I need to nip over quickly to the first aid room and get some rubbing liniment for one of my horses. Hang on here, I won't be a minute," he said as he went down the stairs. "Those ponies get better looked after than some folks I know," the Banksman said. Suddenly a bell sounded; its shrill ringing made me jump.

"They can bloody well wait a minute until Ben gets back. I'm not sending an empty cage down for the sake of a couple of minutes."

He scowled at the noisy bell, as Ben climbed the iron stairs he came back holding a small bottle.

"Ok let's go young man, hop in then," he said, slightly out of breath. I walked into the cage; it wobbled and swayed precariously at the weight of Ben and me. I could feel the eerie movement underfoot, picturing the endless blackness below it turned the butterflies in my stomach into full blown birds. The Banksman closed the inner gate with a resounding clang and I could smell the tainted air coming up the shaft.

I can't find words to describe the feeling of knowing that only half an inch of steel plate beneath your feet, along with a metal cable tied on above, are all that separates you from around a thousand feet of nothing. Then the cage began its descent.

"First ride then?" asked Ben. I nodded as the cage gathered speed.

"Scared?" he asked.

"A bit," I said trying to sound as nonchalant as possible in the circumstances, my knuckles lily white as I gripped the side rail.

"You should be; these cages put the fear of God into me, they always have, even after all these years." He'd really filled me with confidence.

The cage gathered speed and started to sway from side to side. I began to get a nauseous feeling like riding on a fairground, when suddenly I heard talking and laughter, then saw lights as the opposite cage came up past us full of men on their way out. *That must be half way* I thought. I jumped nervously as the cage shook and rattled and twanged as the guides went over joints in the cables, gripping even more tightly to the handrail as we continued down on what seemed like a ride to hell.

I jumped yet again as we hit another lump.

"Don't panic lad, that's only a joint in the cable." I could see the brick structure of the circular shaft, wet from the rain reflecting from my cap lamp as we plummeted and swayed towards the bottom. *I wondered what fast was like if this was supposed to be slower,* remembering the Banksman's offer to request a slower ride

I looked across and caught a glimpse of Ben in the glow of my lamp; he was leaning against the side of the cage, both feet spread apart, hands in his pockets. His chin lolled on his chest. From the glow of my lamp, I could see clearly that his eyes were closed; he was nodding off, not a care in the world. He must have been joking with me when he said he was scared, *maybe he just wanted to make me feel better*, I thought.

I smiled with relief at seeing the glimmer of lights as our transport began to slow nearing the bottom. We came to a halt slowly and I looked out into a strange new world. The Onsetter opened the gate, and I walked out onto firm ground, though be it a thousand feet below the earth's surface.

"Get what you wanted, Ben?" the man asked.

"Yes, thanks, mate," replied Ben. I followed him across this strange whitewashed grotto, a surreal atmosphere, everything seemed tidy and in its place. I could see rows and rows of small rail trucks lined up, filled with coal, others chock-full of supplies which were strange to me.

Railway lines disappeared into the dark forbidding distance and men moved in every direction; ponies were led towards the darkness by their drivers, their harnesses tinkling as they walked, cap lamps flickering into the distance.

No uninitiated person could ever believe that such a place existed; it was another world that seemed to be so far removed from reality. Strange sounds, in fact every sound seemed exaggerated, strange smells with a kind of dulled eeriness hanging over the place.

The loud noise of some sort of big engine roared into life, this was a complete factory underground; it seemed so far away from everyday life.

Just then and ever since, it felt like no other sensation I'd ever had, unreal, a world that most people will never see, understand, or appreciate until they've actually worked down there for a period of time, and as I discovered later a quick visit is just a novelty. Whenever I hear of a mine accident, my stomach churns and memories best forgotten are revived.

To this day, I have the deepest respect for the men and boys of the coal industry in any country of the world; when I hear people criticizing requests of miners for pay increases, I say to all who criticize and denigrate:

"Go sit in front of your warm cozy fire, try to imagine the work and pain it took to get the coal there, you have no conception."

I turned around the next corner to see Ralph sitting in a small white- washed office. He was at a desk completing some papers wearing reading glasses clipped to the end of his nose. This Dickensian pose reminded me of Ebenezer Scrooge. I sat down at the crude wooden bench next to his desk.

"You made it all right then, young man? Did you like your first ride down then?"

"A bit scary, it felt like there was nothing underneath me."

"Well, lad, apart from a bit of metal sheet, there wasn't," he answered as his large stomach shook with laughter. I managed a wry smirk, but couldn't share enthusiastically in his mirth, I looked up as two men entered the office.

"Gentlemen, this ere, is Matthew Harper, he's here to carry out an industry study, prior to going on to university. He's also going to do the same at White's Mill; *this* is not big brother checking up on us, he has no connection with the coal board, though he has their blessing.

"Please give him all the help you can. Matt, these two characters are my underground deputies, though that doesn't mean they wear a star and carry a gun; they deputize for me and for management generally. They also directly control a complete coal face each."

I took a seat in the office, paying attention to the procedures and routines that were carried out, and then the two deputies set off on their routine rounds.

When all of the reports were done and logs of the exact location of every man down the mine completed (*in the event of serious accidents, or disasters, these facts were vital*), we left the office, passing a door with a red cross emblazoned on it and past massive electric turbine engines surrounded by safety fencing; the noise was ear-splitting.

We passed through an arch into the stable area where the smell of ponies was quite apparent. Most were out working by now, only those from the previous shift were there, along with those needed for the afternoon shift.

Ralph was busy talking with Ben, checking and countersigning his reports; I walked along the never-ending line of stalls, all, without exception, immaculately clean and smelling of disinfectant. I walked past those stalls that were occupied, with caution, having learned my lesson from Bob, my Dad's horse.

The remainder of the day went by very quickly. It was very clear from day one of my work-study, how incredibly hard miners worked for a living, to retrieve this valuable Black Gold from so far into the very bowels of the earth.

Saturday Morning, Two Weeks Later

I had been at the mine now for two weeks, my third just about to commence. The first week had been spent on the day shift, the second on afternoons, the third and final week was to be on the night shift.

A longer weekend was ahead as I didn't have to commence work until Monday evening, reporting in at ten o'clock that night. It was Saturday lunchtime. I had completed a few spells of actual work on both day shifts; not being used to manual labor, I had discovered muscles that I never knew existed. I'd created blisters on my hands the size of my thumbnails which were covered in band aids.

I had left my notebooks at the mine office and needed to complete some observations. Dad was going over to the wood yard and offered to drop me at the mine.

When I got there the office was empty, an ideal time to do some quiet work. I thanked Dad and said that I would make my own way home. Just before he closed the van door, Titch jumped out, ran off behind some buildings and I decided to look for him later. I had never really taken a good look around the offices; curiosity got the better of me. I bumped into one of the clerks and told him that I had to catch up on my report; then I looked around the surveyor's office, the wages department, the ambulance and first-aid room and finally the Manager's Office where I'd been interviewed earlier by Carl Armitage.

His father had obviously set up this office originally because it had photographs of younger families on the walls. In one picture I recognized a younger Carl, along with an equally youthful David. Finally I sat at the large old mahogany desk, trying to imagine some of the conversations that had taken place across it over the years. I accidentally knocked a pencil to the floor which had rolled underneath its darkened foot well.

I was on my hands and knees searching for it when I spotted a crack in a side panel. I pushed my finger into the crack, the panel moved slightly, and as I pulled, it slid back to reveal a small secret cupboard which had obviously not been closed properly. Inside were a number of items, including three leather-bound notebooks.

I took out the books and opened the first one, it was written in careful handwriting; Carl Armitage's name and the date were inscribed on the inside cover. The other two also bore the same inscription, it seemed they spanned across a number of years.

Though it felt wrong, somehow I was compelled to read these notes which formed part of a private diary by Carl. I was startled by the sound of the office door being opened. I sat perfectly still.

"He must have left, he was certainly here earlier, Fred," said one of the office staff.

"I saw him myself. He said he was catching up on some paper work."

"You go on and I'll lock up," I heard Fred say; then I heard them leave, the front door closed with a definitive bang, the lock turned, I was alone, locked inside!

I took out the remaining contents of the cupboard: some photographs, another book smaller than the others, a bunch of unopened letters, postmarked via the War Office, on the rear some of them bore the name of *Lieutenant*

David White, others Captain David White. There was also a larger photograph of Carl, David and a pretty young woman together.

My attention was drawn to the smaller book; I saw written there amounts of money with a date by the side of each of entry, these amounts ranged from fifty, to fifteen hundred pounds. There were no indications as to whether these were amounts spent, or collected, or banked and meant little or nothing to me.

Earlier that day I'd heard there was little improvement in Carl's condition as regards the return of his memory. I wondered if any of these items might stir some thoughts, but if so how could I possibly explain how they had got to be in my possession.

With that thought in mind I hurriedly put them back as carefully as I could, trying to remember how they had been left there. As I was about to put back the smaller book, I took one last flip through it, when a piece of paper fell to the floor; on it was written the address of some place called the Ace of Spades. I took one last look at the list of amounts again, and noticed that by the side of each entry, was either a small letter L or the letter W.

I found a scrap of paper and transferred the address, all of the amounts and dates along with the Ls and Ws.

I took one last look around to make sure that everything was just as I had found it and then left closing the door behind me.

On reaching the front door I tried the handle; I was well and truly locked in. I looked towards the back door where I found two keys hanging on the wall labeled *men's toilet* and *rear door.* I took the rear door key off the ring and let myself out of the building, intending to return the key tomorrow morning. As I left the colliery, Titch fell in behind, covered in coal dust and looking like he needed a good bath.

When I arrived home in the late afternoon Dad was sitting in his arm chair, his hands across his chest, waiting for me with a look on his face like the cat that got the cream.

"Come through here, Matt," he led the way through to Mum's long-since deserted shop. He walked across to something in the center covered by a blanket, then he whipped off the cloth with the flair of a magician, and there was a gleaming bike! He'd bought it for me to save me *masses* of time, he'd said.

"Dad, you're a gem," I said.

"It's not new, but it will do the job; it has 5 gears, so should help on the hills," he said. Here's a new pump for the tires," he smiled magnanimously, throwing it across to me.

I went for my first ride on the new bike, *well new to me that was*. I rode straight back down to the colliery, my faithful Jack Russell running behind. I intended to return the office key, hopefully before its disappearance was discovered, then tidy up some of my paper work and go on to the village club in the hope of meeting up with my new dancing partner Joan.

As I neared the mine, I noticed that the pithead wheels were turning, wondering who was going down at this time on a Sunday then remembering that some of the area engineers were extending the haulage rope in the main road.

I went to the front door of the office, which as expected, was locked. Just checking that nobody was there I slipped around to the rear door and entered the building. I re-threaded the key back onto the key ring and returned both keys to their designated hooks behind the door.

I looked at the office time card clock, noting that there was a good two hours before the club was due to open its doors.

To fill in time, I decided to go down the mine, to see what progress the engineers were making.

It was all good stuff for my observation report. So I donned my coveralls, put on my hat and reported to the lamp room, requested a lamp along with a Davy lamp. Though usually only carried by officials, Ralph had said, that I should carry one for safety at all times.

These lamps are used for the detection of dangerous gases, which can collect in restricted areas. Gases are the main cause of fatal explosions below ground; normally the lamp flame burns bright yellow, but in the presence of lethal gas it burns with a blue aura.

"Are there many down today?" I asked the lamp man.

"Just the area engineers and the usual weekend water pump men and skeleton staff," he replied.

"The sensible ones will be getting ready to go to the pub, that's where I'm headed shortly," he said with a grin. *Me too,* I thought. As I walked away he said:

"Oh, yes, I forgot, the German blacksmith went down as well a few minutes ago," he added as an afterthought.

Once down the pit I got out of the cage, no assistance supplied on a weekend. I looked into the stables to see Ben's opposite number talking with the German blacksmith, then went on my way.

The silence at the bottom was actually eerie to those who spent time down there; the turbine engine was silent as the engineers were extending the rope. This is steel cable about two inches in diameter; it's wrapped round a drum on the engine and extends two miles or so to the workings. It returns around a very large pulley and runs along guides in the center of the rail track.

The small trucks, called tubs, are connected to the cable, back and front by means of a locking clip, going inbound with men and supplies and returning filled with coal. The engine was reversed outbound.

I had walked some of the way inwards where the fitters were working extending the haulage rope, when without warning and for no apparent reason, my cap lamp went out. The only illumination left was the very dim glow from the kerosene lamp as the center cable was not in its usual position I stumbled over it cursing as the safety lamp fell from my grasp, its flame extinguished too.

Darkness descended, I mean darkness; black, total and absolute darkness, so dense it felt like I could crash into it. Believe me, moving was not an option. I stooped down cautiously feeling for the wooden sleepers, then sat down on the rail and thought.

There was nothing left to do but wait until the engineers came back towards the bottom, but they were there for the day. Fortunately, Ralph had shown me how to re-light the kerosene lamp, naked flames being absolutely and completely taboo, as well as being potentially fatal. I remembered that somewhere on the side of the lamp was a plunger that one withdrew, and then simply pushed it back in against an internal flint like an internal cigarette lighter. There was, however, one major problem, I couldn't find the lamp in the dark! I groped around hopelessly for minutes in the stone dust on the ground, but to no avail.

Eventually I thought I saw the flicker of a lamp in the distance; then, sure enough the light became brighter. I resisted the urge to shout, *that sort of thing is frowned upon underground*.

I guessed that the person was about three hundred yards away. Then I spotted my Davy lamp in the glow of the distant illumination, it had bounced way over the other side at the foot of one of the steel girders.

I crawled over, knee-deep in the white stone dust, which was spread on floors and walls to keep inflammable and heath-hazardous coal dust down. It also acted as a good light reflector.

I retrieved possession of my lamp just as the oncoming light went out. It seemed to have disappeared completely, black darkness again.

I wasn't sure whether my eyes were playing tricks on me, or whether the owner of the other light had suffered a similar fate. Frowned upon or not, I shouted a number of times, but got no reply.

I heard the rope on the ground move as the engineers began to tighten it up. Returning my attention to the matter at hand, I groped around the case of the safety lamp for all of five minutes, trying to locate the igniter. I thought at the time, how is it that a blind person can distinguish between differing denominations of paper monies and here am I unable to find a simple little knob?

I cast my mind back, concentrated on my memory of the structure of the lamp, then carefully exploring the device, got it, but this one wasn't pulled. This one had to be turned.

Two quick turns, a flash of the flint, then light, heavenly light. Not bright, but sufficient to see by. I began to walk slowly and carefully, striding the rail sleepers, taking care not to trip over the loose cable again. I had traveled about three or four hundred yards, when I thought I saw light out of the corner of my eye off to the left. *Can't be, it's the shadows playing tricks on your eyes,* I thought. Nevertheless, I paused but saw nothing, then in the faint glow of my lamp, I noticed that I was at the entrance to some old workings leading off to an area where a long time before coal had been obtained, now disused and derelict.

I walked carefully only a few feet into the disused road. **Danger! Keep out! Danger! Gas**!

Big red signs everywhere. I turned to leave when I saw a flicker of light again. I put my Davy lamp behind my back and looked again; sure enough, through the crossed planks of the barrier forbidding entry there was most definitely someone coming out of there. That must have been the light I'd seen disappear moments earlier.

Any miner worth his salt knows that old workings do not have air pumped in, therefore gas can and will collect. Breathe it, you die, one spark from a piece of metal and everybody dies!

It is part of safety law that any coal mine roadway where trucks or tubs are operated must have a refuge from potential runaway vehicles; they are called manholes, which are big enough to hold a couple of men standing up. They are spaced at regular intervals on either side of the roadway or gate.

It was into one such refuge that I crept in order to see who was coming out of the disused road and hopefully not be seen myself. Knowing full well that whoever was coming out of the tunnel shouldn't be in there, and was therefore up to no good.

Taking a great risk, I shook my lamp until it went out again with a silent prayer that it would re-ignite later; I waited with baited breath. I froze rigidly to the spot as a mouse ran across the back of my neck, not the most pleasant of creatures, but prolific down most mines, doubly unpleasant in the dark.

Eventually the light became brighter; the noise of someone clambering and struggling through the barricade became obvious, as heavy breathing and some cursing continued.

I chose to stay put, anticipating that whoever this was would come out hopefully turning towards the pit bottom, not the other way; if so, they would pass my refuge place.

A man came out onto the main road turning towards the pit bottom. From the glow of his lamp I saw only a silhouette casting confusing shadows, all indistinguishable to me without my lamp.

Then I heard the rope in the center of the rail track begin to move; as it did so, the man turned around in my direction, with his electric lamp swinging loosely around his neck the beam seemed to hit me full in the face, and I felt sure that he must have seen me. As he took hold of his lamp to fix it to his cap, the light shone briefly into his face. It was the German blacksmith Kurt. He strode off purposefully towards the bottom.

I was just about to despair after three unsuccessful attempts at re-igniting my kerosene lamp, when two engineers came down the road behind me, evidently checking all guides before starting the big motor. I returned safely to the bottom by kind courtesy of the engineers' cap lamps.

I rode the cage back to the surface alone; suddenly my stomach sank right down to my boots and not just because of vertigo. When I'd decided to go down the mine earlier, I'd totally forgotten that I'd left Titch running around outside. Where on earth would he be? He would have been looking everywhere for me.

I returned my lamps, offering some totally un-constructive suggestions regarding the future of the electric one. There was a different lamp man on duty; he said he hadn't seen Titch. I looked everywhere, eventually leaving my coveralls and hat in the lamp room, and then rather dejectedly I cycled, worried, towards home. God, what if he was hurt? All thoughts of anything outside of Titch's disappearance faded into insignificance. I almost flew down Fall Hill, turned into our street and pulled up at the gate. There he was sitting on the doorstep, looking very indignant. I picked him up and got a salutary licking on the cheeks. He didn't carry a grudge for long.

When I eventually got to the club, Joan was there. She said that she'd hoped to see me, as her parents wanted to invite me to Sunday lunch.

Her Dad was there at the club and I was duly introduced.

Mr. Waters knew Dad really well; they went to school together. Though I felt there was an air of sympathy toward me, you know, *the poor boy doesn't have a mother* attitude. I still had the most fantastic lunch eaten in recent living memory.

I really liked Joan Waters; I wanted to see a lot more of her.

Chapter Thirteen

Monday Morning

The next morning I had a visit from David White who said that he wanted to meet me for lunch; there were things that he needed to discuss. There seemed to be an air of mystery in his voice and his manner. We arranged to meet at the mill around noontime.

There were a number of things that I needed to do at home first so I resigned myself to tackling these chores, like it or not. I really hated housework. I walked across irritably to answer another knock at the door to be greeted by a smiling jolly lady who introduced herself as Mrs. Mary Newbold.

"I'm here to start work: cleaning, washing and cooking. The arrangement with your father is that I'm to live in and take the spare front room," she blurted out in her jolly way, almost laughing as she spoke. Though somewhat of a surprise as Dad hadn't said a word, this lady did not realize it, but she was actually a real gift from heaven, I couldn't believe my ears.

"Come on in, please do come in," I said, my grin must have relayed my delight.

"I take it you've been here before." It appeared that she was a close friend of Mum's sister, Aunt Emily, who lived in Leeds. She said she hadn't seen the house previously.

Mary Newbold was recently widowed and seemed ideal for the job. There was a man waiting outside with a small van, who promptly proceeded to bring her belongings into the house. I carried box after box upstairs, putting them into the spare bedroom, which was twice the size of the other two. What a welcome sight, *thanks to Good old Aunt Emily*, I thought. Ten minutes later, Dad arrived from the wood yard and re-acquainted himself with Mary.

Evidently they'd met briefly some weeks before, Dad said he'd forgotten. Then she disappeared upstairs, but not before making a cup of tea for us all, including the van driver.

I was enjoying the remainder of the day off, well until the night shift, that is. I rode my bike up to west Casleton to collect Dad's work boots from repair. I then went into the hardware store and found a number of things that I needed. I had a plan in mind and I had created a list of requirements. As I was leaving the store a conversation was going on between the proprietor and a stranger.

"Do you see many new faces here, then?" the stranger asked.

"Some but not that often, why do you ask?"

"I'm trying to find an old friend who I haven't seen since the war, here's his picture, do you recognize him?"

"Never set eyes on him before."

"Well, thanks for your time anyway, good morning." The stranger got into a car, and drove away.

I couldn't help noticing the long swaying antenna protruding from the car's roof, the plate was not a local one, and the man had an air of authority about him. I went to the cash desk to pay for my purchases, the owner asked after Dad.

"Who was that, a policeman?" I asked as casually as I could.

"Not sure, but if he is, he's not local."

This place is like the local information center. I had that German from Pit Lane in here a while ago, asking the times of buses to Leeds: the way business is going, I think that we shall have to start selling information soon." he said with a grin.

My ears shot up at the mention of Kurt.

"What's he doing, going to the sales?" I asked, still fishing.

"I don't have the faintest idea, Matt, but he'll be on the twelve fifteen, arriving Leeds bus station at one zero five." he said sarcastically, sounding like a train station announcer.

When I got back home, I shouted upstairs to Mrs. Newbold, asking her permission to take some odds and ends from the closet in the corner of her new room that had been left there for years since John and Anne's days there.

"Come on up, Matt," she shouted. As I walked into the room I was completely flabbergasted by the transformation that had taken place, it was absolutely incredible; the room looked great and so tidy too. Seeing the look on my face, she said, "Wait till I get stuck into the rest of this place." *I can't wait, the house will end up looking like a palace,* I thought to myself as I took my stuff from the closet and transferred it to my room.

Then after putting a few things into an old army rucksack ready for going to the mine tonight, I slipped into a fresh shirt, threw on my jacket and shouted 'cheerio' to Mrs. Newbold, and off I went to meet David. As was I closing the gate:

"Matt, what time do you intend to be home today?" Mary called from the doorway.

"I have to be at the mine by ten tonight, I'm working nights this week," I replied.

"I was only thinking about food," she said.

"See you later," as she waved, smiling. *This seems pretty good,* I though grinning from ear to ear. *Can't be bad! All of this care and attention, what a life, eh?*

When I arrived at the mill, David was already waiting for me in reception,

"Afternoon Matt, let's go if you're ready."

"I'm ready when you are." He gestured towards the door.

"I have a call to make in Leeds. I thought maybe we could get some lunch there, and talk on the way over."

"Sounds fine to me," I replied. I wondered how I could get him to go past the bus station. As we drove off, David told me that Carl Armitage and he had been friends for many years, how he'd learned from another school pal, Bruce, in Leeds, that Carl had been badly hurt.

Reading between the lines, he felt that the whole affair was no accident at all and that someone had hurt Carl purposely, judging by his wounds. Also, he felt that Bruce wasn't telling him everything so he meant to confront him today.

First, he'd wanted to meet me to see whether I'd heard any kind of news about Carl from the mine. I told him that I knew no more than he did.

"I still don't understand what's really going on," said David.

"Particularly why someone would want to harm Carl, if such is the case." *I think that maybe I do,* I thought, remembering the contents of those notebooks.

We drove down the main thoroughfare, heading towards the big open fruit and vegetable market. I could see the bus station just behind and to the right of the traffic island. He pulled over to the side of the road.

"I'm going to talk to Bruce, you may come along if you wish." He got out of the car, then leaned back in to retrieve his stick.

"If it's alright with you I'll hang around here and find something to amuse myself with."

It was now twelve forty-five, David left saying that he would be back in about a half hour or so and if I needed him before, I was to find the offices of Frank Bell and Son, in the market.

The bus from West Casleton was due to arrive around one o'clock; *buses were never as punctual as trains, far less reliable.* With fifteen minutes to spare I went for a stroll around the market. Monday is always a quieter day, more a tidy-up and restock day, hence the many trucks and horse-drawn vehicles there. Organized chaos is the only phrase that readily springs to mind.

Walking along, I spotted the offices of David's friend. Then I saw it. The car with the long antenna, the one I'd seen at the hardware store in the village earlier. It also had the same man sitting in the driver seat; he appeared to be watching Bell's offices very intently.

A couple of days earlier I had found an old empty school note pad and written down every conceivable thought or piece of information that I could bring to mind or that had come my way regarding the parachute affair. Its contents were now stretching to some eighteen to twenty pages.

For no other reason than the book was in my pocket, I added the tag number of this car along with a brief description of its occupant. I entered the small cafeteria at the bus station; if I was to be seen, it would seem perfectly normal for me to be waiting for a bus. I bought a cup of tea and waited; the Casleton bus had not arrived yet. Ten minutes and a second glass of milk later, the bus finally arrived.

I walked across as though I was going to board for the return journey, looking around for Kurt but he wasn't there, the bus was totally empty. Feeling somewhat thwarted I walked past the rows of parked buses. *Damn it,* I thought. *What a waste of time!*

Then I spotted him climbing aboard a Leeds City Transport electric tramcar on the other side of the street. He must have got off the bus as it slowed down to turn.

This area was also the terminus for the electric trams.

Snap decisions were the order of the day; I decided to take a ride with Kurt on the tramcar.

He had gone upstairs, *no smoking allowed on the bottom deck.* Moving along to the very front seat downstairs, I sat behind the driver's cab. The vehicle rumbled to a start when the bell rang twice.

I always hated trams with those wooden seats; you could feel every bump and bend in the track along the metal rails set into the road surface. Each time we reached a stop, I looked into the reflection of the glass window in front of me, to see if my quarry got off.

"Fares please, have you bought your ticket, young man?" I looked up into the face of the ticket collector.

"Er, no I haven't," I replied passing him a coin. At that same moment, the bell rang once and the tram came to a halt. I looked around to see Kurt alighting from the rear platform of the tram.

"That'll be one more penny please, young man," said the collector. I rummaged into my pocket but could only find a three-penny piece, which I gave to him. Literally snatching the change from his hand I ran from the tram, no sign of the German. I looked around the left hand corner; he wasn't there, then to the right. Gone, nothing, he'd disappeared into thin air.

After standing for a while, I crossed the road and decided to catch the next tram back into town. I'd boarded the next town-bound tram and was about two blocks down the road when on the right I saw a sign over the door of a building, it had the picture of a playing card and it read 'Ace of Spades Nightclub.'

I ran along the length of the tramcar and leapt off whilst the vehicle was still in motion, accompanied by shouts of admonition from the conductor. The building looked deserted.

I took out my notebook and saw it was the correct address, but I wasn't quite sure what to look for or indeed what to expect.

I went around the rear of the building, a number of cars were parked back there but none that looked familiar to me. There were no windows, but then I suppose one wouldn't expect them at a nightclub. Out back the usual scene expected of licensed premises: rows of empty wooden beer barrels, stacks of empty beer bottle cases and that unmistakable smell of stale beer.

There was a truck parked with its rear doors open, a man carried sacks of potatoes and boxes of vegetables into the kitchen entrance, the truck bore the name Frank Bell and Son.

The driver was big and tossed the sacks around as though they were full of feathers, then went in carrying a box of cauliflowers. I followed cautiously at a safe distance; he was wearing a knitted cap pulled down over his ears. I hid behind a stack of boxes; it was then I noticed that there were two men.

"Gerald, you go through, I'll keep an eye on the back door," said a voice in a gruff whisper.

"Fine, replied the man with the knitted hat. He disappeared through the swing doors, the other one stayed outside the back door, I heard the minor explosion of a match igniting as he lit a cigarette. I tiptoed gingerly to the swing doors, peering cautiously through its round glass windows, when my vision disappeared as a pain shot across my nose when the door hit me full in the face, knocking me to the ground.

"What the...who the bloody hell are you?" said knitted cap.

Knitted cap grabbed me, lifting me to my feet with such ease that it scared me half to death.

But definitely not so much as when he held me with his left hand, whilst his right drew back, I waited for the inevitable.

"No, Gerald, no," whispered the other man, swinging on the big man's right arm.

"He doesn't work here."

"That right?" asked knitted hat rhetorically, I nodded frantically.

"Yes, I mean no, I don't."

"Get him out of here," he snarled throwing me out of the door, just as another big man came into the kitchen.

"What's going on in here, what the hell is all the noise about?"

"Sorry boss, we just dropped a couple of boxes, no problem."

"Did someone just come through to the office area?" asked the ferocious looking bloke, as he stuck his head out of the door looking directly at me and the other man who now had hold of my arm.

"Who are these two out here, they with you?" he asked as he turned back into the kitchen.

"Yes, they are," I heard knitted cap say.

"Seems like a lot of bloody people to deliver a few spuds, anyway what were you doing in the office?"

"Just dropping off the bill boss," he replied with a shrug.

"Sign here, will you" he said holding out the delivery note.

"I'm not signing for anything; you'd better wait for the chef."

With that he walked out, leaving the doors swinging squeakily too and fro.

"Get into the van," said the big man to me, again lifting me up and throwing me, all six feet and one hundred eighty pounds. I landed with a thud in the back, amongst a wide selection of fruits and vegetables.

"You wait for the signature and I'll see who the mystery man here is," he added as he turned in the front seat looking me directly in the eyes. *Go on, undo the rear door and make a run for it*, I thought to myself, *sit right where you are, if you've got any common sense at all!* The sensible side of me took over.

"Well I'm waiting, what were you doing in there?" I told him that I was looking for work, while waiting to enter university. With that he seemed to calm down somewhat, saying that I should not creep up on people, I could end up getting hurt.

"Besides that is no place for a decent looking young man like you. What's your name, lad?"

"What's yours?" I asked cheekily, knowing full well that I was really pushing my luck.

"Okay," he laughed, "point taken." The other man jumped into the driving seat.

"Let's get the hell out of here," he cut short as he saw me sitting in the back.

"Who's he, then?" he asked.

"I'm Gerald," said the big man to me, "I'll settle for your first name." he turned to face me.

"Matt," I replied.

"Sorry about the door, and the man-handling."

I looked through the rear window across the street and caught a glimpse of what I thought was a long antenna atop a black car.

"Is there any chance that you can drop me off in Leeds?" I asked.

"Sure," replied Gerald, "Why the hell not?"

When I got back to David's car, he was sitting on the fender as I walked up.

"Ah, there you are," he said with a smile. It was two o'clock, my little escapade had taken one hour fifteen minutes, as indeed he told me so had his meeting.

"Let's get lunch."

"What an excellent idea," I said enthusiastically. I was famished.

"I could eat a horse," I added speaking metaphorically of course!

We ate a very pleasant lunch at a fish restaurant. Grilled haddock on the menu brought back memories of my fishing trip with David's father. The restaurant was just off City Square and by all accounts was one of his father's favorites.

David told me his news: Bruce, his friend, was still a little backward in coming forward, meaning that David felt he was not telling all; however, Bruce did believe that Carl had been maliciously attacked. He was looking into the whole affair and would keep David up-to-date with any progress.

In all, David really hadn't learned a lot, he said that he would visit Carl tomorrow. Bruce had told him he had an ex-police friend called Gerald who was looking into the matter. *I'll bet I know him,* I thought, *almost grinning visibly.*

I'd decided to say no more to David or indeed to anyone until I was a little better informed, which meant a lot more ground work and much more information.

I still didn't know where my German friend had gone today, there was nothing tying him to that club, but he certainly ended up in that vicinity.

Had I imagined seeing that car with the same antenna as the one at the hardware store and later at the market? *Duly noted into my book.*

As I sat at the table opposite David I had the distinct feeling that we were being watched. I looked up to see a man sitting alone, and as I caught his eye he quickly looked back to the newspaper in his hand. Maybe I was becoming paranoid.

Chapter Fourteen

That Same Evening at Leeds Infirmary

The foyer of the hospital was a hive of activity. The outpatient's clinic was packed with people waiting their turn to find out those all important results; whispered conversations, wondering whether the test was clear, did the x-ray show anything, long silent faces of those who had their worst fears and suspicions confirmed.

Dr. Cheryl Armitage sat with her mother Eve and father George as they awaited the arrival of the specialist, Mr. Whitman. Here's another inexplicable foible of the English hierarchy of the medical profession. Once a doctor reaches the position of specialist in a chosen field of medicine, he is no longer addressed as Doctor, but becomes Mr.

"Dr. Armitage, will you come this way please, Mr. Whitman will see you now." The three of them followed the nurse along the long corridor into a consulting room, where a bald-headed man stood up from behind a desk in the center of the office. He extended his hand towards Cheryl.

"Doctor Armitage," Cheryl nodded shaking his hand.

"Mr. Whitman," she replied formally.

"Please take a seat," he shook hands with Mr. and Mrs. Armitage as they also sat down.

"As you are all aware, it is now a little over two weeks since we admitted Carl into the hospital; he was suffering from injuries consistent with those one would expect from a violent attack.

The head injury was particularly bad causing a concave fracture to the base of the skull; there was evidence of internal bleeding, fortunately, no pressure on the brain itself. From the most recent x-rays we can see no further complications. Doctor, if you would care to take a look," he gestured towards the ultraviolet glow behind a series of x-ray exposures.

Cheryl walked across looking closely at the skeletal depiction of her brother's cranium. It gave her a strange feeling to be looking at her own brother in this way.

"The fracture seems to be healing very well, there's only a hairline crack now," she told her parents.

"These are his rib fractures?" she asked rhetorically, pointing to further x-rays of the rib cage.

"Yes, that's correct," he replied.

"Here again they were done with great force, another fraction and this one could well have perforated his lung," he said pointing to the rib.

"Doctor, Mr. and Mrs. Armitage, our problem here is not really a mechanical one, if you'll pardon the pun," he said smiling.

"Carl seems to be a very robust person physically; however, we are not getting any breaks as far as the amnesia is concerned. His memory loss is still total, our resident psychiatrist shows concern that there is something deeper which stops him from cooperating. It's as though he doesn't wish to remember. This is where you, the family, can be of valuable assistance."

"Doctor, I want you to visit your brother now as planned, then I would like you all to go home and think of anything however great or small that may be putting pressure on Carl. Any worries that he may have from the past or present, anything at all that may be preying on his mind.

"Within the next few days he will be released from hospital, home surroundings are either going to help the situation or hinder it altogether. If there is some mental block, those surroundings could have quite a profound effect, unfortunately for the better or the contrary.

If I can be of any further assistance, please do not hesitate to call me." He rose to his feet and shook hands with all three, nodding his head as he said, "Mr. Armitage, Mrs. Armitage, Doctor Armitage," then walked stiffly out of the room.

Stuffy old twit, Cheryl thought to herself as she remembered her own training; all of those specialists seem to come from the same mold, she thought. *They are so knowledgeable and the epitome of professionalism, why do they appear to be so stereotypically stuffy*? Cheryl thought to herself as they left to see her brother.

The visit to see Carl was less traumatic for Cheryl than it was for her mother, though Carl seemed perfectly well physically; he showed no signs of recognition, which caused anxiety, tension and discomfort amongst the group, especially with Eve.

As they chatted away each tried to include a topic that might jolt Carl's memory back into action, but without any success. After about an hour, they said their farewells and left for home.

Crossing the hospital foyer Cheryl heard her name called, she recognized the voice instantly.

Turning, she saw David standing there.

"Oh, David," she exclaimed out loud, pausing where she stood for seconds, then strode across to greet him. She threw both her arms around his neck; he reciprocated as his walking stick clattered noisily to the floor. A young boy picked it up.

"Hey, mister, look out, you dropped your stick," he exclaimed, but he may as well have been talking to the man in the moon, they were in a world of their own!

Cheryl broke into tears, sobbing emotionally on David's shoulder.

"There, there, come on it's not that bad," he whispered, trying as best he could to console her. Quickly regaining her composure, she took a handkerchief from her purse, drying her eyes.

"Seeing you standing there, soon after being with Carl brought memories flooding back, you looked so lost and alone," she said, tears welling up in her eyes.

"Look, you two must have so much to talk about, why don't Mother and I make our own way home, we'll see you both later," Cheryl's father smiled conspiratorially.

"Your Mother and I will drive on home, you take your time and come back in David's car."

Back Home at the Village

After my lunch with David, he'd dropped me back home and gone on to the mill. I was just about to enter the house when I saw an unoccupied van parked on the other side of the street. It was a vehicle I hadn't seen around before, just a small plain black van. I entered the house to find Mrs. Newbold sitting talking to a complete stranger.

"Ah there you are, Matt, this gentleman here called to see you. I told him you were out, but he was most insistent that he wait until you returned. He sat out there for ages, so I invited him in for a cup of tea. I felt sure that you wouldn't mind, he does have identification on him."

The man, about twenty to twenty-two years of age at a guess, pleasant looking, blonde hair, stocky build, looked rather athletic, stood up and offered his hand to me.

"Macgregor, Sergeant Donald Macgregor, British Military Special Investigations Branch," he introduced himself in a broad Scottish accent, as he produced his I.D. in that suave, sweeping way that plain clothed officials do.

"What can the British SIB possibly want with me?" I asked.

"Let me get straight to the point. Have you seen, or do you recognize, any of these people?"

He proceeded to show me a number of basic mug shots and some photos of a series of people, including two women.

"No I can't say that I have," I replied.

"I think that maybe you owe me some kind of explanation, before asking any more questions. I looked him straight in the eyes as I spoke.

"Aye, perhaps you're right, laddie," he nodded in agreement.

Sergeant MacGregor looked across at Mrs. Newbold.

"I dinna suppose there's chance o a wee drop more tea, Mary?" he smiled as he spoke.

"How can I refuse such a good-looking young man. I wish I was thirty years younger. I'd show you a thing or two" she smiled suggestively, re-filling his cup.

I had misled the sergeant, as one of the men in the pictures, not a mug shot, but a snap taken of three German S.S. officers sitting outside a French café, was none other than our short-haired German friend from the fields.

The sergeant went on to tell me that he was engaged in an enquiry so sensitive that not even the investigating officers were in possession of the full facts. He told me the size of the operation was not restricted to this area only, but was countrywide.

He went on to say it was suspected that a foreign network of agents may have been infiltrated into England and had continued to operate throughout the war, possibly Nazis.

Mary was in the throes of beating a tactful retreat to her room whilst this conversation continued.

"There's plenty that I can be doing, I can see that you two would prefer to talk in private," she said making her exit.

"If you want more tea, there's plenty left in the teapot."

I liked the sergeant; he wasn't a great deal older than me. I was tempted to tell him what information I had but I thought better of it. I realized by the very fact of his presence there, he or someone had been following me, *for how long* I wondered. Suddenly he answered that question. He leaned right into my face:

"What were you doing at the Ace of Spades night club today in Leeds?" he said looking hard into my eyes. I reeled back a little at the force of the question and the intimidation of his posture.

"I'm doing a work-study program set up by my school."

"Yes we know, Green Cotes School, just outside of Sheffield, I believe," he interjected.

"Barnsley, to be precise," I added sarcastically, correcting his error.

"Please continue." He said not perturbed by my interjection.

"There really doesn't seem to be any point, you seem to have all the answers," I snapped back at him, feeling genuine annoyance and anger at his apparent trespass into my privacy.

"I understand that your work program applies only to the local colliery along with the rope factory, is that correct?" the harshness of the Scottish accent, lending a forceful edge to his statement, and question.

Realizing that I needed to give a reasonable answer, I told him that I had gone to Leeds with a friend, who was an 'Old boy,' ex-pupil from my school; we had gone to meet another ex-school mate of his, who owns a fruit and vegetable business in Leeds.

I wondered if I could find kind some employment after my work projects were over. I'm not paid during this period, by the mine or by the mill and during the long break before university, one has to eat.

I wasn't sure whether or not he knew of my allowance from Harold White. I also wondered if he'd seen me arrive separately at the club.

"I went along to the club to see if there were any vacancies. I'd been told that the money was good there."

"So you were looking for work?" he asked hesitantly with a note of some disbelief left hanging in his voice. I gave a shrug with upturned hands, and a look on my face of, *yep that's right*, trying best to avoid the bare-faced lie.

"Did you get a job?" he asked.

"No, I didn't. These people stay open until around four o'clock in the morning so I'd have to live in Leeds to be able to get home at that time, besides I don't drive." He seemed to accept my explanation, as he relaxed back in his chair, though one can never be certain with these highly trained investigators.

Changing the subject, he asked me how I got on working at the mine, telling me that he'd started his working life down in the Scottish coalmines.

"It must be more pleasant at the mill surrounded by all those girls," he smiled.

"I have one more week to go before I start at the mill." I told him. He was starting to make me feel a little uncomfortable with all these questions. I think he too felt my growing antipathy to the whole scene.

"Well, I suppose I'd better be getting along, remember what I told you, my investigations are of a most serious nature. They come right from the top of the British government, so if you hear or see anything that seems out of the ordinary, call me. Here's my card, you can leave a message with the office at any time of the day or night."

He held out a photograph again; the one of the short-haired German.

"If you see anyone resembling this man, remember it's your duty to inform me." He thanked me for the tea, then left.

"Remember, young Harper, we are at war, and it's your duty!" Those earlier words from the village policeman re-echoed in my mind as I heard the van drive off down the street. Mary walked into the room as if on cue:

"Now, both your Dad and you are working the night shift this week, which makes catering a little easier for me," said Mrs. Newbold.

"Its liver and onions tonight, you both have to be at work by ten, right? Food will be on the table at seven-thirty sharp." *I've never seen Dad get home for a meal on time yet,* I thought.

"I told your Dad the same, he says he will be on time," she added with a twinkle in her eye, as though she'd read my thoughts.

I went up to my room and flopped down on my bed. Titch jumped up beside me as my mind started to go back over the last few days' events. I made notes in my book as I went, now convinced that there was a definite connection between the Germans and the coalmine. There had to be some sort of association between Carl Armitage and the nightclub, hence the piece of paper I'd copied from his diaries.

I assumed, rightly or wrongly, that the figures entered in Carl's book were some sort of debts. Also the meeting at the pub between the two Germans could quite easily be connected to the much earlier night of the parachutes.

I still couldn't definitely put either German at the club on the night of the incident; there was no certain involvement on their part in the seemingly intentional injury of Carl Armitage, but then how would I know when I wasn't there?

Gerald was obviously no ordinary deliveryman; I now knew he was with Bruce, he'd been sent by Bruce, but why the club and again, what were they looking for? Also this matter was serious enough to warrant the attentions of the British Military and the government, maybe others. For instance, who was the man in the vehicle with the long antennas, part of Sergeant Macgregor's SIB maybe? If there really was an agent or spy network, where were the headquarters?

Going back to the eternal question, were those flying boxes still around? If so, where had they been hidden, and what did they contain?

They could be a million miles from here by now. The sergeant had said this was country-wide. I had a hunch that I knew where they might be and what's more, I intended to find out for certain in the not- too-distant future. From now on, I was going to have to keep a more careful look out and watch my back closely.

I had seen at least two different pictures of faces; according to MacGregor, these people are real experts, how many more I wondered?

If Carl's injuries were in any way connected, then these people were definitely not playing games either. They were playing for real.

"Matt, Matt. Are you awake up there? Come on, it's time to eat your supper!" It was Mary shouting up the stairs. I'd fallen asleep. I could see that it was now quite dark outside.

I could smell the most delicious aroma coming from downstairs so I followed my nose to see Dad already sitting at the table alongside Mary. He was about to dig into a well-stacked plate of liver and bacon. I sat at the vacant seat and was served an equally large plate of the same delights.

"This food is out of this world," I said making sure not to speak with my mouth full, but equally not wishing that it stay empty for too long.

"Why, thank you, kind sir," said Mary, her face full of smiles, obviously enjoying some genuine appreciation of her efforts.

"Nearly like old times," Dad interjected. The meal was unbelievable; a steamed treacle sponge with custard followed the main course. I left for the coalmine about an hour later, asking Mary to make sure that Titch didn't follow.

My cycle ride helped to move some of the food around, as it lay heavily on my stomach. I remember thinking how odd it seemed to be going off to work when most other folk were going to bed.

Chapter Fifteen

Earlier that Same Monday Evening

David had skipped his intended visit to see Carl; he was told that other visitors were there, already enough for one session. The nurse had said it was more than enough for Carl in his present state.

Shortly after he had met Cheryl, he'd been more than delighted at the tactful suggestion made by her father. It was getting quite dark outside as they left the hospital together, Cheryl with her arm linked through David's arm, as they walked towards the car. There was a lot of catching up to be done.

"Where would you like to eat?" David asked.

"Somewhere quiet will be just fine," she replied. David was pulling into the Grand Hotel car parking lot when Cheryl looked across at him, fear in her eyes.

"Oh, David, I'm so worried about Carl."

"Me too," he replied resignedly.

After such a long absence, she looked so beautiful to him at that moment, the lights of the hotel reflecting in her deep brown eyes. She was still the most attractive woman in the whole world to him; she was always the love of his life.

Suddenly he felt the urge to take her in his arms there in the car. Instead he turned off the engine, switched off the lights, and went round to her side of the car, holding open the car door. They made their way through to the main restaurant, where the head waiter escorted them to a quiet table, as requested.

Both ordered a cocktail, Cheryl preferring a very dry sherry, whilst David asked for a large scotch on the rocks.

"Tell me all about yourself, what's happened in your life since we last met?" said David taking a deep swallow from his scotch.

"There really isn't a lot to tell you, I am still deeply involved. In research." she added.

He had thought then, for one awful moment, she was going to say she was deeply involved with someone else. The look of negative anticipation must have shown on his face.

"Are you alright, David?"

"Sure. I'm fine" he said taking another sizable slug of his whiskey, leaving little but ice spinning round in his glass as he waved for the waiter.

"You seem to have gone a little pale, are you certain you're ok?" The attentive waiter brought another scotch.

"Never felt better, doctor." They ate their starters in relative silence; she had ordered smoked salmon, chopped shallots, and capers, while he enjoyed a pleasant Pate'de foie gras, apparently the Chef's own specialty.

After a leisurely meal, they sat drinking coffee and sipping at two particularly large cognacs, the pianist playing in the background.

"David, what do you think about this business with Carl, I can't make head nor tail of it?"

"Me neither, I can't make any of the pieces fit," he replied, as he warmed the Cognac, swirling the liquid around the glass bowl between both hands.

"None of it makes sense to me either," she added.

"Do you think he was actually beaten up?" asked Cheryl.

"Almost certainly, the police and the doctors are convinced it was no accident," David Replied.

"I know, I was shown the x-rays this evening," she sighed as she spoke.

"David, who would have done such a terrible thing?" she asked.

"We don't know yet, but we're looking into the whole affair."

"We, who are we?" asked Cheryl. David proceeded to tell her of the involvement of Bruce Bell.

Cheryl vaguely remembered him from some of Carl's sporting events at school.

He tried to reassure her that the police were doing everything possible to solve the mystery.

"If only Carl's memory would return, it would obviously speed up the process of finding his attackers and putting them behind bars," said David.

He leaned across the table, taking both of Cheryl's hands in his own, looking deep into her eyes, the alcohol having an effect.

"I have a serious question to ask you, darling Cheryl, can you think of any reason for Carl's refusing to see or talk to me? Since I came back from the war he's never spoken one word to my father or to me. It's as though he's trying to blank out our friendship and the memory of it completely. Everyone says he's been acting very strange, as though he has something to hide, not at all like the old Carl we knew and loved."

"I think I may know some reasons for his recent behavior, I don't have all of the answers, but I may have some. I'd prefer to wait a bit longer until he's a little better," Cheryl said.

"He really should answer these questions himself; I feel he'd rather explain himself than for me to second guess him."

"The most important thing at the moment is to find out what happened to him that night and of course why, and more importantly; who.

"I don't have any answers that will help find his attackers. I wish to God that I did."

"David, let's change the subject. I think it's about time we talked about us. I've been doing a lot of thinking of late and I have an important question to ask you."

Since you went away to the war, and since I have been out of your life for such a long time, has there been anyone else in your life, someone serious I mean?"

David stared into his empty brandy bowl for what seemed an age.

"No, Cheryl, there has never been and never will be anyone else for me."

She gripped his hands tightly, bending her head, she kissed his hands gently; he felt her hot tears running through his fingers.

"I love you, David White. What fools we've been wasting all this precious time."

He felt exhilaration, as though a heavy weight had been lifted from his heart, he really couldn't believe what he was hearing. Could everything turn out right in their relationship after all?

They left the restaurant and walked across the parking lot towards the car, suddenly Cheryl stopped and looked up into his face.

"Hold me, David, hold me tight, and this time don't let me go." An indescribable incandescence swept through his body, he felt as though he were eighteen again, he wanted to tell the whole world how happy he was. Throwing both of his arms around her they just stood there, holding each other for what seemed an age. They kissed gently then walked towards the car. They didn't have eyes for anyone but themselves at that moment in time.

So intent were they on each other that they didn't see the black car across the lot, or the driver wearing the trilby hat pulled down over his eyes. As David drove off towards Casleton, he failed to notice the black car following him at a discreet distance.

As they sat on the couch at the mansion, Cheryl turned towards him putting her left arm around his neck and they kissed; as the embrace turned from one of tenderness to passion, she bit his bottom lip, her tongue forcing its way between his teeth.

He felt the pressure as his erection began to swell inside his pants. It seemed a lifetime ago since he had felt this way.

He let his hand wander from the back of her neck to her shoulder, touching the bare flesh above her strapless top, as goose pimples covered his whole body. He felt the cleavage between her firm breasts. He was sure that he was going to explode as Cheryl's hand stroked along the inside of his thigh.

David eased his hand up into the top of her blouse, as it fell away exposing her exquisitely sculptured breasts, they were exactly as he had remembered them from before.

"Let's go upstairs darling, let's go now," she said breathlessly.

Once upstairs they hurriedly undressed each other, then began making love for hours. She took him to heights of ecstasy beyond his wildest dreams, she too had almost screamed with satisfaction and pleasure.

Afterwards they lay in each other's arms, totally satiated and relaxed. *This bed has been my prison of misery and sleepless nights for far too long,* he thought.

"Not any more," he said aloud.

"What did you say, darling?"

"Nothing. I was just thinking out loud."

"I shall have to be making tracks for home in a minute," she said.

"Stay the night," he replied.

"Not now, not just yet," she whispered as she took his car keys from the night stand.

"I'll get the car back to you tomorrow darling, sweet dreams." David heard the click of the door as she left.

Later that night as David lay in his bed, he knew that he had never felt happier in his entire life; he prayed that nothing would happen to burst the bubble.

The only blot on the horizon was this terrible tragedy that had happened to Carl; he hoped he would recover soon, regain his memory and at the same time erase whatever was causing the rift between the two of them.

This was the final obstacle to his complete happiness.

As the lights to David's bedroom where extinguished the driver of the black car who had watched Cheryl leave seconds before drove off into the night, noticed only by constable Ellis on his bike, who was completing his final tour of the village before handing over to the night shift.

He made a note of the event, time, color, model and tag number of the unknown car.

Earlier, I was cycling toward the top of Pit Lane on my way to the mine to begin my shift. Quite a pleasant night, lots of stars. *A full moon out here, but not where I'm going,* I thought.

I saw headlights coming towards me and then recognized David's car, as it drew near I waved, but he didn't stop. He had a companion, a young lady in the front passenger seat.

Some way behind another vehicle came by, it was driving on running lights only, as it drew level I spotted the large antenna, but the vehicle was traveling so fast I wasn't able to distinguish the face of the driver. I didn't have time to follow them either; I had to be on the night shift within the next thirty minutes.

What the hell was this motor doing in the village at this time of night? Why was he driving without headlamps?

Hoping not to be seen, I guessed. He must have been following David! Why David now?

As I freewheeled down Pit Lane towards the lights of the mine, I was certainly a little puzzled if not downright confused. Finally, I arrived at the pit yard, looking around carefully to make sure there wasn't a black vehicle following me.

After the usual formalities in the office, I duly collected my equipment from the lamp room, and made my way over to the mineshaft where the assistant manager and the night deputy were just ahead of me.

"Looks like you brought a lot of sandwiches," laughed the deputy pointing towards the bulging rucksack slung over my shoulder.

"Yes, we have a new housekeeper at home; she really believes in fattening us up," was my flippant reply.

The night shift is a completely different operation than the other two, though you can't tell night from day once you're down there; the atmosphere is much quieter and laid back, almost totally maintenance work. The only productive function is coal cutting.

During the last decade, the old-fashioned method of obtaining coal by hand pick had been replaced with more mechanization, indeed much more safety, too.

At night a team of men drive a cutting machine the full length of the face, making a cut six feet deep underneath the coal, removing about four inches of rock, not coal; the seam is three-feet high.

Above in the coal face, holes are drilled six feet long into the coal; they are about an inch and a half in diameter, placed at three feet intervals about a foot from the roof. Wooden blocks are placed at six feet intervals into the void where the cutter has left the coal suspended, to avoid any possible downward movement.

Explosive charges are then placed into the drilled holes and fired, breaking up the coal. A conveyor belt runs the length of the face, from the tailgate to the main gate. The daytime colliers shovel the coal onto it.

All of the above are descriptions of an ideal world where nothing goes wrong.

In reality the belt on the face breaks apart at least four times a shift, each repair taking anywhere from a half hour to two, as each collier has to take coal back off the belt. The roof often has faults, or slips as they are known; these are irregularities or veins of soft slime running between the hard rock.

On such occasions after a collier has removed coal and erected supports, the shot firer is called to loosen more coal and may accidentally blow out the newly erected supports, causing the roof to cave in. On occasion, these falls as they are known, can hold up production for a day or more.

Sadly, sometimes men are hurt or buried, even worse, they are killed! This night in particular, I was to observe the coal cutting procedure.

Cutting is an extremely dusty process; even though water is normally sprayed continuously on the cutting jib, one learns to stay behind the machine as it always cuts downwind.

The machine weighs some five tons and is about ten feet in length, two feet high and two feet wide. When the multi-toothed jib, which looks like an enormous sawfish, has cut under the coal to its six foot limit, a length of steel rope is released from inside the machine, tied ahead to a steel derrick forced up against the roof, the powerful machine then hauls itself along by retrieving the rope, the diamond teeth cutting as it goes.

Problems of one sort or another can make coal cutting a long laborious job. This night, by my calculations, they were currently taking up to ten minutes per foot. I began to get thoroughly bored, the noise was unbearable, the stone dust so thick I was eating the damn stuff, it was impossible to see more than two feet in front. Yet again the machine stopped. I indicated to the nearest worker that I was going out into the tail gate for a drink of my water; the head man nodded his assent.

I had already made some plans of my own for that night so I crawled out into the tail gate, standing up for the first time in about two hours. I took out my sandwiches and water bottle from my jacket hanging nearby, sat down on a pile of wooden props or 'supports,' then went over my plan of action.

Checking my Davy lamp, I put my rucksack over my shoulder, left my jacket hanging from the steel girder and set off down the tail gate, the welcome, comparatively fresh air blowing in my face.

As I arrived back at the junction of the main road, all was quiet, so much more than the daytime. The haulage rope was still, no traffic, deathly silence.

Turning right I headed in the direction of the pit bottom, passing many disused workings, both to the left and right, which all looked pretty much the same.

I must have walked a couple of miles when I came across an old road on my left; all of these disused workings were from the old hand- pick-getting days.

This was where I'd seen the German on Sunday, now I couldn't see anyone around.

Knowing that the under-manager would have completed his rounds and gone home, but the deputy could be anywhere, I had to be very careful not to be discovered in a prohibited area.

Danger! Keep out! Gas! The signs read. Large planks of wood criss-crossed the entrance prohibitively. I carefully slid one of the white dusted boards to one side and created a space large enough for me to crawl through. Squeezing into the space, then dragging my rucksack behind me, I reached back and secured my Davy lamp. Pulling the board back into place I picked up a handful of stone dust and sprinkled it on the part where my hand had been.

I had barely made it through when a bright light flashed along the main road.

I spotted a manhole just a few feet further into the disused gate.

Getting inside the alcove as fast as I could, I quickly switched off the light from my cap lamp and put the Davy lamp as far into the corner as possible.

All officials down a mine use a much brighter cap lamp than the ordinary worker. This is because they are usually traveling around and therefore need more distance vision, the reflectors are highly chromed. If men working together in close proximity used them, they would be blinded by the glare.

The big disadvantage to management and officials alike is that they can be seen from far off, giving a pre-warning of the approach of officialdom, which was exactly what was happening at that precise moment. I held my breath as the bright beam shone through the barrier, then I heard "Funny, I could swear I saw a light."

As there was no answer, I assumed whoever was talking was indeed talking to himself. I heard him adjusting the barrier, *I wonder if he'll see my footprints in the stone dust*, I thought to myself. The light seemed to stay for an age and then disappeared. I waited a while longer, then came out of my hiding place.

Turning on my electric light I went further into the gate, hoping for a bend in the road's direction. Sure enough, it veered off to the left a little further along allowing me to make a few safety adjustments without my lights being seen by any by-passers, a bit of a catch twenty-two; I didn't want to venture too much further without these precautions.

Rounding the bend, I took a seat on an old overturned one-sided flat truck; opening my rucksack, I took out a gas mask. In fact, it was the one left behind by my old cockney friend and evacuee John. I'd packed it that evening just in case. Placing it over my head, making sure that the glass was clean, I tightened the straps and began making my way further into the unknown.

I turned to check once more that I was not being watched, holding my lamp to my chest, all was clear, so off I went.

The lamp now fixed to my cap was perched uncomfortably on top of the mask straps. I walked slowly along, holding the special safety lamp aloft, looking carefully for any slight change of color in the yellow flame. I continued along like this for about a quarter of a mile, the gas mask smelled terribly of old perished rubber, the glass was beginning to steam up, my own heavy breathing echoing eerily in my ears, I could barely see a thing.

Suddenly I stood bolt upright with shock, I heard a very loud crashing noise close behind me and I nearly jumped out of my skin. Sharp creaking and snapping sounds followed it, the whole place seemed to shake and erupt into mayhem.

I looked around to see tons of rock and shale falling from the roof of the tunnel behind me, steel girders twisted and danced as though electrified, they fell down like rows of bowling pins.

When work had ceased previously, I had been told it was the practice of the demolition teams to take out every other steel arch girder the length of the gate.

This was done for economy as they were re-used, but of course by design which means that the place will eventually cave in. I turned to go back in that direction, it being the only exit, my sole means of escape.

I stood frozen to the spot as the eruption abated, a few small pieces of debris slithered down the side of the avalanche, then a deathly silence fell on the place broken only by the constant dripping of water.

Of course I immediately lost all interest in whatever may, or may not lay further along this road, my natural instinct of survival took over the controls, shifting into top gear!

The Davy lamp still showed a healthy yellow flame as I pulled off the gas mask, the air smelled stale as no fresh air is pumped down a disused gate.

The dripping water was becoming more of a torrent now as water was beginning to run down the rocks, which appeared to have totally blocked any means of my escape. There were further creaks and groans as the weight settled onto the ageing supports. *How am I going to get out, nobody even knows that I'm here*. For the first time in my life, an intense feeling of fear came over me.

I had broken into a cold sweat, knowing that what little air had been coming along the road was now blocked off almost completely. Venturing to the edge of a large pile of wet slippery rocks, I shone my lamp above, I could see through a gap, some thirty or forty feet up into a large cavern caused by the fall. Normally these old roads are about ten feet by eight feet.

I hung the Davy lamp on the last girder, its flame still bright yellow thank God. After a quick look around, I found an old shovel and a metal tie bar used to hold the girders in place. I proceeded to dislodge the larger rocks at the foot of the slope.

After moving some twenty or so, I had to run back for safety, as another avalanche cut loose. Tons of debris crashed down, knocking my safety lamp from the girder and burying it in the process.

After waiting a while for things to settle, I shone my lamp upwards, to discover a large hole leading up into the massive cavern above. I tried to clamber up, but immediately slid back down bringing with me another half ton of slippery rocks which grazed the whole left side of my face; I could feel the blood running down.

Again I picked up the metal tie bar and using it as a pick, I dug between the larger of the rocks and painstakingly hoisted myself up the side of the slope, trying hard not to cause another landslide.

Eventually, I emerged into the upper cavern; it was enormous. Standing on top of the fall, looking back down I must have been at least twenty feet off the ground, looking heavenwards another twenty feet above me.

Water cascaded down profusely from above. I remember looking up into that cavernous space some twenty feet above towards my only avenue of escape; I could see nothing but a daunting wall of rocks in front of me.

I began, somewhat frantically at first, to scramble up there, pulling at the large stones from the escape side of the rock fall as I went up, throwing them down behind me from where I'd just climbed. Twenty or thirty more of them slid down again. I hadn't even begun to scratch the surface; despair took over my mind and distorted my judgment, it prefaced my every thought.

I know that I should try not to panic, I should attempt to keep calm, but I'm lonely, scared and I think that I'm going to die.

Then fine sand started to trickle from above, like an hour glass. *Time's running out?* At first a mere sprinkling of dust, and then two small pieces of rock fell as a prelude, then much larger ones began to crash down next to me, it was too late for me to get back down to the bottom.

Suddenly with a roar reminiscent of a prehistoric monster the whole world seemed to shake and tremble as it crashed down on top of me. I felt a searing pain in my left arm, then a blow to my head, as if I'd been hit by a steam hammer. Then, just like that day on the football field, nothing, just a floating, fluffy blackness!

I regained my senses sometime later; I wasn't sure how long I'd been unconscious, or even if I had been. There followed what must have been an hour or so of abject loneliness, sheer terror, a feeling of involuntary submission, of hopeless defeat.

At first it was like a nightmare, I wasn't sure whether it was real or just a dream. If real, then I was both blinded and paralyzed, for I could neither see nor move.

Slowly I began to remember what had happened and where I was. The stale, rancid air hung heavily, the total darkness was indescribable, so thick it felt as though I could reach out and actually touch it; and then everything felt so final. I knew that I was actually buried alive. Apart from the sound of dripping water, the silence was deafening.

It's so hard to adequately describe the feeling of finality then, like a man buried to the neck in the sand, hands tied, in front of an oncoming tide. There seemed to be no escape.

I blinked my eyes tentatively, the only part of me that I could move. God, I was blind, for if my eyelids were actually functioning, then closed or open, I saw nothing. Then as I tried again to move, slowly my fingers began to operate, my toes too, I pulled frantically with my right arm which very slowly came free, my left arm was now giving me a great deal of pain, still trapped, as indeed were both of my legs.

O, dear God, help me please………

With a great tug, my right arm came free; I made a gargantuan effort to push a heavy weight from my chest as a large rock rolled to one side of me; my breathing improved considerably though there was an obvious lack of air. Sweat began pouring down my face and into my eyes. *Or was it blood,* I asked myself?

I reached for my left arm and touched the cold edge of a steel girder wedging my shoulder. It was obvious that I had been pushed down from the cavern by that further fall of rock, but was I on the outbound, or the inbound side of the fall? That answer was critical.

I'd no way of telling. The only glimmer of hope was that I thought I could feel a slight movement in the air, maybe just my imagination or perhaps wishful thinking. I pushed another large slippery rock from my right side, hearing a metallic sound as it moved. I groped around in the dark, my hand finding the metal tie bar that had helped me up into the cavern earlier.

As I pulled the bar loose, two things happened simultaneously. The cable from my lamp fell onto my arm and my sight returned in that instance; either the lens of the lamp had been buried in the dust or the switch had gotten turned off, then back on again. I didn't care; thank God, I could see now.

Looking around me, I pulled the cable gently along as the lamp came nearer to my right hand, then immediately all went dark again. I continued to feel my way down the cable as the lamp flickered again, then it stayed on as it fell into my hand. I grabbed it and shone the light all around me.

I was definitely trapped on my left side by a twisted steel girder, lying on the edge of a great pile of debris. I turned my right foot; it came out from under the rail track, which had protected it from the rocks.

My right side was almost freed; I put the cap clip of the lamp between my teeth, then I freed the tie bar, which I pushed under the girder that trapped my left hand using a rock below the bar as a fulcrum. I pulled down on the bar with all the strength I could muster.

The pressure began to release and I was able to pull my other arm free, the pain was excruciating. I shuddered physically as I heard movement above, looking up with the aid of the lamp, seeing a shower of fine sandy substance cascading down, previously the prelude to more rock fall.

I made one final Olympian effort and pulled with all my strength and my left leg came free at last. I crawled, dragging myself along the rails, clutching my lamp in time to avoid another sizeable tonnage of rocks which covered the spot where I had just lain trapped and helpless, putting away any ideas I had of getting to the other side; that's if I was actually on the wrong side of the fall.

A combination of sheer exhaustion and lack of air felled me again, as I drifted off into oblivion.

I came to my senses again: sweating and gasping for air, I struggled to my knees. The lamp was out again, but my movements must have made it flicker back to life once more, obviously a loose wire, understandable in the circumstances. I didn't possess the energy to stand up, so I continued to crawl along the railway. *Dear God, please let this road be leading to the main road and freedom, not back toward my certain death.*

The rails started to bend to the right; I hardly dared look as I dragged myself along, remembering that there had been a bend to the left on my way in earlier.

Each movement became more painful than the last one, dizziness began to take over again and negative thoughts began to eat at my brain as I dragged myself along the track.

I saw a picture of my Mum on her deathbed, I thought I could hear Titch barking; once again I was drifting towards oblivion! I saw the hideous grinning face of the school bully George Biggs.

I couldn't move another muscle. Just as my head was about to sag for the last time, I lifted it with one final energy-draining effort, lungs about to burst.

"Dear God, help me," I screamed aloud. In the halo of my blurring vision I saw the cross boards of the barrier at the end of the gate; an inner strength welled up inside of my chest which somehow carried me, not only to the barrier, but also through it.

I sat out on the main road, gulping the fresh air, God, it never tasted so good.

After quite some time I got to my feet and tentatively leaning against the side wall, I began to walk back, slowly at first, an agonizing mile or so, to where I'd left my jacket back in the tail gate.

I'd got into the habit of leaving my watch in the pocket, so as not to damage it. Until then, I had no idea of the time; it was four AM.

I had gone down at ten o'clock, spent two hours on the coalface, so I calculated that I'd been un-conscious for at least one and a half hours. I sat and drank all of my water: it tasted like nectar.

My arm was badly bruised but not broken, or at least I could move all of the joints and manipulate my fingers, though painful. They don't provide the luxury of restrooms down a mine, so I couldn't look at my face, but it did feel pretty sore.

Just then, a very welcome sight, the team of cutters crawled off the coalface and stood up in the tail gate. I'd never been so pleased to see anyone. I explained that I had taken a walk round to the main gate. I'd slipped and fallen near one of the big water drainage sumps, dropping my Davy lamp into its depths and grazing my face in the process

The senior man looked at my face and suggested that I go home right away. I couldn't find an argument to his suggestion, but I must make sure my mishap was entered in the incident book, before leaving the mine he'd had said to me.

As I almost staggered, towards the pit bottom, totally drained of energy but thankful to be alive, I began to wonder again what was in those boxes. There was more to all of this than met the eye: if the SIB knew who these people were, in this so called Nazi organization, or whatever it was, then why hadn't they arrested them by now, what were they waiting for?

I shuddered as I drew opposite the scene of my near demise. I walked into the entrance of the tunnel quickly checking that there was no evidence of my entry. As I covered my footprints I looked down that terrible gate and thought, *If there are any boxes in there, surely nobody will ever get to them now. They're entombed for posterity; their contents will never be known. Maybe that's an end to it?*

When I emerged from the cage later, I can only imagine what it would be like escaping the gates of hell, then walking freely into heaven. That's how I felt as I pushed my cycle home later that morning: tired, aching, and badly shaken. Feeling particularly cold, but glad to have been given a second lease on life that early beautiful morning, it was a little after five o'clock. Some would say that it was dark then. Not me, not when you've really been in the dark!

I sat on the couch, Titch on my knee, and fell asleep instantly.

"Matt, Matt!" I awoke with Mary leaning over me, Dad looking over her shoulder, two extremely concerned faces.

"I will go and get the doctor right away," she exclaimed as she looked at my face.

"No, no, that won't be necessary." I replied. After much ado, I agreed to visit the doctor later that morning. I drank a nice welcome cup of tea, swallowed a couple of aspirins, and then went upstairs accompanied by the ever-faithful dog. I slept fitfully for three hours or so, then lay in a hot bath for an hour, dressed and went on down to the doctor's surgery.

He agreed with me, the arm wasn't broken, just rather badly bruised. My face had two deep cuts and serious grazing. A very painful session followed, first getting the coal dust out of the wounds, then the stitches.

"You don't want blue scars on your face for the rest of your life from the coal dust," said the doctor.

"Come back in a week, and we will have those stitches out. Apart from a slight scar on your cheek, you'll be as good as new. Go to the pharmacy with this prescription, take the tablets three times daily and put the ointment on the grazed skin regularly.

"Thank you, Matt, that'll be all; try to exercise the arm. It may be painful at first, but you must keep the joints moving." he added as he scrubbed his hands.

"Next patient nurse, please."

Chapter Sixteen

Leeds City Later that Day

The grey-haired old man sat in a car opposite a terrace of Victorian houses; it was a cold misty morning. The houses built of brick with ornate stone arches over the front porches had stained glass windows surrounding the solid oak doors; they looked dreary and forbidding.

A newspaper delivery boy climbed the stone stairways leading to each house, pushing his wares through the letterboxes with a metallic clunk. Somewhere a dog barked as the milkman came past, leading his horse and cart to the musical jingle of harness and the clatter of glass bottles.

The horse stopped in front of the old man in the car, snorting as its breath froze in the crisp morning air, the animal temporarily blocking his view of the houses. A shrill whistle from the milkman, and the horse plodded lethargically further along the street. The steady clomp of metal shoes on the road surface heralded the start of yet another day as curtains were drawn back at bedroom windows, the normal daily routines began.

The door to the second house opened. A tall, broad man came out, standing at the top of the stairs, looking around like a fox in his lair, as though his suspicions had been aroused. Then he returned inside, closing the door behind him.

Looking at his watch, the old man resignedly settled back into his seat, watching the second house intently. Suddenly he sat bolt upright, started the engine of the car and pulled out into the street.

Turning left again, he came up behind the houses.

"God damn it," he shouted aloud, as he saw the rear of a big Austin sedan drive off down the road, crossing the main intersection as the lights turned to red. The old man drummed his fingers impatiently on the steering wheel, the red stop light from the car in front reflecting on his face.

Back in the same street, the black car with the long antenna was still parked on the opposite side, its occupant patiently watching the second house.

The old man had resigned himself to the fact that he was getting rusty, that he'd lost his chance, so he decided to call it a day.

He approached City Square, taking a short cut behind the railway station. He was just about to head off for home when he spotted the Austin sedan parked at the rear goods entrance of the station with its trunk open.

"The luck of the gods is with me today," he muttered to himself, as his large fist landed on the steering wheel with an enthusiastic thud. He parked in an adjacent street where he could see his quarry and could follow quickly without being obvious.

He didn't have long to wait to justify his perseverance. The big German came out carrying two heavy suitcases, followed by a small man wearing a long overcoat, a fedora hat and thick lenses in his steel-rimmed spectacles. To his right was a tall blonde woman, her hair pulled into a bun, high cheekbones and severe features.

They climbed into the rear of the car as the big man closed the trunk. He walked around to the front, then drove the short distance to the Grand Hotel with the old man following close behind.

The white-haired man parked his car outside the hotel; using a walking stick, he tottered with difficulty into the reception, stooping as he entered the revolving doors.

"Here, let me help you," smiled a young bellboy, taking him by the arm, leading him to a seat. Later he tottered across to the desk under the pretext of picking up a tariff, but really sneaking a peek at the guest register. He decided to wait just a while longer, watching the big man and his two companions and hoping for any signs to explain what they were doing and what was actually going on.

Casleton Village that Same Morning

When I returned from the doctor's surgery Mary was just on her way out to the shops; she made me a cup of tea. Then looking at the package from the pharmacy and reading the directions carefully, she took out a packet of cotton balls.

"Sit down at the table, Matt, I'll put some ointment on those nasty grazes. How did all this happen anyway?"

"I just tripped and fell."

"Keep still," she said. I winced at the touch of the stinging mixture. I went upstairs but couldn't sleep; trying to sleep in broad daylight is almost impossible.

I went back downstairs deciding I'd go for a ride on my bike up to West Casleton, taking the doctor's advice on exercise. I walked up Fall Hill choosing not to ride, mainly due to the arm. I was about half-way up when David pulled up beside me in the Rover; he looked on top of the world.

"Just want to confirm that you're starting with us as arranged on Monday. Good God, what have you done to your face? Shouldn't you be in bed?" I answered all three of his questions in rapid succession as well as accepting an invitation to dinner at the mansion, *to meet an old friend* the following Saturday evening.

Arriving, at last, in West Casleton, feeling like I had just gone three rounds with some heavy-weight boxer, I phoned the mill, fortunate to catch Harold who sounded, for some reason, very elated.

"Yes, that's fine, see you on Saturday, don't forget to keep our little secret intact." With that he rang off.

I had decided to ride further down to the main road and take a stroll around the cricket field. I was just about to cross the main Bradford road when I saw the German, Kurt; he was standing at the bus stop and looking a little smarter than usual.

Acting on absolute impulse, I turned left and cycled in the opposite direction, as my off-the-cuff intention was to catch the same bus as him but get on one stop before him. My theory was that if he saw me get onto the bus, then by some misfortune he saw me later on, his suspicions would be aroused.

I sped towards the previous stop and pushed my bike up the path to an adjacent house. I knocked on the door and asked the lady who answered if I could leave my bike in her yard for safety and collect it later on my return. She agreed, even let me put it in her shed.

I sprinted out of the gate just in time to see the bus approaching. The driver saw me just in time. I climbed aboard, selecting downstairs in the front, remembering that Kurt chose upstairs, smoking on the tramcar last time. *Keep your fingers crossed, here we go,* I thought to myself as we approached the next stop. I smiled inwardly as he came aboard and climbed upstairs, just as I'd assumed.

After an uneventful journey to Leeds, the bus pulled into City Square. Our German friend was standing on the rear platform and jumped off quickly and went straight into The Grand Hotel.

I got up as the vehicle restarted. When it slowed again for a traffic light I jumped clear of the rear platform, landing a few yards behind an older man. The older man had crossed and was just entering the Grand Hotel's revolving doors.

I crossed over, then went through the doors into the busy foyer. The hotel had an enormous reception hall and there were people everywhere, but no sign of Kurt. I went up to the desk and spoke to the young man.

"Excuse me, I am looking for a friend who just came in here a moment ago," I went on to describe the German.

"If you would take a seat for a moment sir, I will just book in these people, then I'm sure that I will be able to assist you," he pointed to a chair. Quite happy to rest the aching legs for a minute or two I sat down as requested. I jumped in surprise as an old man sitting next to me tapped me unexpectedly on the knee.

"Young fellow, I wonder if you could help me across the room, I could use a strong young arm to lean on." I stood up.

"Of course, sir, only too pleased to be of assistance." He walked very slowly, stopping a couple of times. He seemed to be looking around for someone. Then quick as a flash, he pulled me round past the elevators and restrooms into an area of public telephones. Without warning, he grabbed both of my arms *including the bruised one;* he slammed me up against the wall with such power that the wind left my body.

"Alright lad, I think it's about time that you leveled with me, I know your name's Matt, but who the hell are you and what are you doing here? You have precisely ten seconds to start talking before I personally break your neck, and for that matter every other bone in your body."

I recognized the voice first, then the face of Gerald from the club, the fruit and vegetable man. He was wearing a false hairpiece, moustache and bushy white eyebrows; on any other occasion he would have looked amusingly like Santa Claus. But now was certainly no time for mirth as the disguise was covering a very mean look on the face beneath. Without any doubt, I believed his threat was no idle one.

"I will tell you all I know, if you'll tell me what's going on," I said as he released my arms. The power of the man was phenomenal; he put his old hat straight, bent down into his stoop, put his walking stick into his left hand, and then took my left arm.

"Take me back to the seating area," he snapped abruptly. Once back at the reception area, he sat me with my back to the door so that he could see everything clearly, although there was no one close to us.

"Start talking," he said. "Make it brief and to the point."

I told him everything right from the start. He never reacted, nor did his eyes once stop surveying the reception area, then he turned his face towards me and looked me directly in the eyes.

"I believe you lad, now what am I to do with you?" Then:

"Here we go," he said. I saw from his eyes that something was happening.

"Don't you move, don't look around, I think your man is walking across the hall with some other people. When I tell you, look around slowly, casually. There may well be other people watching us too. Look toward the restaurant, look now," he said sharply.

I looked around slowly then moved my gaze to the hotel clock, then at my watch.

"That's him with the two men and the woman," I said.

"You did that very well there, we might make a detective out of you yet," he said, with hardly a movement of his lips.

They're going to eat so let's go somewhere and talk; we have a lot to cover whilst they're out. By the way, what does the other feller look like?" he said pointing to my battered face with a grin.

"There was no other feller, I had a small accident down the mine last night," I answered, and then realized that he was being flippant.

We left the hotel, got into Gerald's car and drove off. When he was satisfied that we weren't being followed he stopped at a roadside café. We took a table, and he debriefed me on every detail of my version of the Casleton affair, adding his own findings and opinions as we went.

It was then agreed that we would work together and exchange notes regularly. I was not to discuss this meeting with anybody, even David.

He in turn would discuss our meeting and agreement only with Bruce, his boss, who I was to meet in due course. Gerald added that he didn't want David knowing. The less people involved the better.

He then went on to tell me of his previous background in the Royal Marine commandos, and later the Police Force. Also he mentioned briefly he'd been told MI5 were sniffing around, so he was very interested in my meeting with MacGregor of the SIB.

We returned to the hotel, Gerald staying in the car whilst I sat in reception until the foursome went into the bar. I confirmed to myself that the big man was the man from the parachute fields; the other was his accomplice, Kurt from the coalmine. The other two were new faces to me.

After about an hour, Gerald went into the bar, disguised again as the old man It was getting late so I caught the bus back to Casleton. We agreed that Gerald would contact me at the mine or the mill. I would get in touch via Frank Bell's office. It was five-thirty when I got home, four and a half hours to another night shift.

I had collected my bike from the kind lady's shed and thanked her for her assistance. As my bike freewheeled down the street, I was confronted with the unwelcome sight of Sergeant Macgregor's vehicle parked outside our house again.

Chapter Seventeen

Frank Bell and Son, Leeds

Bruce sat in his office surrounded by paperwork, there were invoices strewn across the complete surface of his desk and on every other available surface.

"We seem to spend too much time shuffling paper around than selling goods," moaned his father, as he walked across the office.

"That's it," yelled Bruce. I've doubled the turnover of this place in the last twelve months, I only have one pair of hands, I can either sell or be a clerk, which do you want Father?"

His father looked dumbfounded as he'd never heard his son fly off the handle so quickly before.

"Furthermore, for your information Dad, I've arranged a meeting here tomorrow morning with a rep from Kalamazoo. They have just developed a new accounting system.

"Following that, there are four people to be interviewed for the new post of accounts manager and I'm not one of them. Unless you wish to lose touch with modernization completely, may I suggest that you make yourself available when the Kalamazoo guy arrives. The days of the quill pen are finished Dad, OK?"

With that he stormed out of the office, smiling as he went down the stairs two at a time.

"What are you looking so pleased about?" asked the head warehouseman. Bruce continued to smile and began to whistle as he climbed into his car.

Bruce arrived at his apartment near the entrance to Roundhay Park, a popular beauty spot in the area with acres of parkland, two large boating lakes, a sports arena for track events, and a large café with a bar.

He took a bath, a change of clothes and was just about to pour himself a nice cocktail, whistling as he screwed off the top of the whisky bottle, when the phone rang.

"Yep, who is it?"

"It's me Bruce."

"Hey, Gerald what's new?"

"Quite a lot actually, I need to talk to you soon, there have been quite a few interesting developments. When can we meet?"

"Come over to the apartment now, if that's ok with you.

"See you in half an hour."

Bruce was sitting, relaxing, sipping his drink as the buzzer to his door went off.

"Who is it?" shouted Bruce. There was no reply as he walked over to open the door, and he looked into the face of a grey-haired bespectacled old man. A very shaky voice coughed then:

"Excuse me sir, but is this the home of Mr. Bell?" then changing to his normal tone of voice.

"Any chance of a beer?" said the old man

"Gerald, you daft bugger, you really had me going there for awhile. What's this, Halloween practice night?" They both had a good laugh as Gerald got out of the disguise and changed into a sweater and slacks, which he'd carried in a hold-all, then said with a more serious look on his face, "I told you that a lot's been happening recently. I think I've kept my identity a secret, this disguise has helped me considerably."

"You'd better bring me up-to-date. Let's have a stroll across to the bar in the park."

Bruce slipped the latch on the door of his apartment, then they strolled through the park gates towards the café; on the way Gerald told Bruce everything that had happened to date.

"So how did this kid get involved in the first place?"

"Just a bunch of coincidences I think; I believe he's only met Carl once but knows David fairly well. By the sound of things it's highly probable that whatever was dropped during the war is down that mine.

"Carl is still sick, but this young lad does have access to the mine, which may prove very helpful. I don't speak German very well, but from what I overheard this evening, I believe the mine to be of great importance.

"One other thing, this Matt Harper kid learned German at school. Oh, and by the way, he attends your old school. He's just completing his last year prior to university."

"If he's at the old school, he must be a good guy. When do I get to meet him?"

"All in good time," Gerald said, "all in good time." Tapping the right side of his nose with his forefinger, he winked his left eye conspiratorially.

"You remember that first night at the hospital, one of my old cronies told me that Special Branch and MI5 were involved. Well, so is the military Special Investigations Branch; according to them, this German team is country-wide.

"They've interviewed young Harper at some length to find out what he knows. They believe the hub of the network is somewhere here in Leeds."

"Why don't we take a trip to the hospital and see how Carl is progressing, then maybe we should pop in and see if our membership cards have been prepared at the Ace of Spades. What say you?" asked Bruce.

"Sounds like a good idea to me, but maybe first we ought to offer this guy here another beer," Gerald added, as he strode across the bar, poking a stranger on the shoulder.

"Are you following us, or are you just normally a nosey bastard?" he asked the surprised man. "Because if you are, when we leave here, I'm going to throw you right into the middle of the bloody lake, got that?"

Gerald poked the man's shoulder one final time and then walked back to Bruce.

"Let's go then my old friend, maybe I was wrong about him after all," he winked and smiled, as he spoke to

Bruce. The two of them finished their drinks and then left the building, the stranger didn't follow them.

Gerald knew that he'd let his temper run away with him and made a big mistake in challenging the man.

Once a tail has been 'made' he'll be replaced: that means another new face. A nuisance, particularly when you don't know whose side he's on!

Leeds Infirmary

"Mr. Armitage, Carl, wake up, it's time for your injection." Carl woke up to the dulcet tones of nurse Moira. She was a good and dedicated nurse who'd looked after Carl on the night shift since his arrival. The natural cheeriness of her Jamaican heritage had helped keep Carl from sinking further into depression. He opened his eyes slowly, it was still dark outside, and he could hear rain beating heavily on the window panes.

"Go away with your needles Moira, I swear you get pleasure out of stabbing me with those damn things," he grimaced as he spoke.

"Now, Carl, you know you don't mean that." She began to roll up his pajama sleeves and started to rub his upper arm with alcohol.

He winced as the needle entered the flesh; Moira withdrew the hypodermic, putting pressure on the puncture with a cotton ball.

"Hold that a minute while I get the tape, that wasn't too bad was it?"

"I suppose it all depends which end of the needle you're on!"

He reached out and tried to slap her on the rump as she walked away, but missed by a mile.

"Naughty, naughty, missed again! You'll have to be quicker than that."

"I used to do the mile in four-fifty," he replied.

"Oh, you did, did you? And when was that prey tell?"

"It was at err… I'm not sure, oh God, Moira, I just can't remember."

"Carl you just said that you used to run the mile, that's fantastic, your memory is starting to come back. Don't try to rush things, nature will not be hurried, you seem to have forgotten something else though," she added, as she straightened his pillows.

"What might that be?" he asked taking hold of Moira's hand.

"Carl, you're going home today." Carl gripped her hand so tightly; she thought he would break it.

"What's wrong Carl, you're hurting me." He let go of her hand and turned away quickly, she didn't see the flash of fear in his eyes.

Carl lay silently in his bed for some time, his mind in a complete turmoil.

The feeling was as though he was in another person's body, looking at faces that meant nothing to him, though at the same time they seemed vaguely familiar somewhere deep down in his subconscious.

His head felt as though it were filled with cotton, like a nerve end injected with Novocain. He knew the answers were jumbled up in there; he just couldn't pull the bits together.

Several things that he did know were that the pain had gone from his head and his ribs were still very sore, his stitches had already been removed. He still had the prominent bald patch where they'd shaved his head.

One day he'd overheard medical and police personnel talking, they believed a particularly vicious person deliberately inflicted these injuries.

Just then his breakfast arrived: corn flakes, a boiled egg, toast, and a cup of tea. As he hit the egg with the spoon and peeled the shell away, he wondered how he could remember to do that, and yet couldn't remember his own name.

He knew that the cup he held in his hand contained tea, nobody had told him, he just knew.

"Morning, Carl," it was the voice of the day nurse. "You look better every day, you're the lucky one, going home today." This comment caused him to experience sudden fear. What was he frightened of he thought; he began to perspire and physically shook.

"Are you alright Carl?" asked the nurse.

"I don't feel too good at the moment, no," he pushed his unfinished breakfast to one side, threw his legs over the side off the bed. Putting on his robe, he slid his feet into his slippers and shuffled off to the bathroom, where he promptly wretched violently, relieving himself of what breakfast he had just eaten. He stood wiping his mouth with a piece of toilet paper.

"And what was that all about?" Carl looked round to see the nurse, hands on her hips.

"I don't know nurse, just came over-bilious and threw up." She took him by the arm.

"Come on, let's get you back into bed. I want the doctor to take another look at you. Maybe you are still concussed, in which case there'll be no going home for you just yet."

He walked slowly back into his room, holding onto her arm, not sure of what had made him ill, but happy in the knowledge that he wouldn't be leaving the hospital just yet. He felt safe again, *safe from what*? he asked himself.

The phone rang at the Armitage home; Cheryl picked up the receiver and answered by habit, "Doctor Armitage."

"Good morning doctor, this is the staff nurse at the Infirmary, I am calling about Carl Armitage."

"Is there a problem?" she asked.

"Yes, I'm afraid there is, Carl had a bit of a relapse this morning; the doctor will not release him just yet."

"Put me through to the doctor will you nurse, please?

"Certainly Doctor Armitage, hold the line please, I'm putting you through now."

Back Home, Casleton Village

When I got back home from Leeds, Sergeant MacGregor was there again, sitting in the house waiting for me to come home: he had more questions. He questioned my unseemly appearance, and then on hearing my explanation seemed satisfied and nodded, the expression on his face of one who knew the perils below ground.

When he asked me where I'd been during the day, I lied and told him that I'd slept most of the day, not knowing whether he had talked to Mary or Dad. I'm not normally this economical with the truth, but for some reason it seemed right in the given circumstances.

He concluded the conversation, telling me he'd not been to see me on two separate occasions for the good of his health, more for the good of my own. He'd said he believed that I was involved in something he should know about. If and when he proved it, I would be arrested for obstruction. He then added with a look of steel in his eyes:

"Obstructing any officer of the law is as serious an offence as actually committing the crime under investigation." His threat left me feeling very intimidated.

I arrived at the mine that evening feeling slightly second-hand, due to the last 24 hours hectic events. When I got into the office there was a message on the board for me:

"Please contact me ASAP. Gerald." It was scribbled in Fred's inimitable scrawl. I called the number immediately.

"Good evening, the Market Pub." I could hear the unmistakable sounds of a bar in full swing.

"Hey, Harry, keep it down will you, I can't hear a bloody word on this phone."

"I said, may I speak with Gerald Steel," I shouted louder myself the second time.

"Hang on a minute will you." After a minute I heard Gerald's voice.

"Who is it?"

"It's me, it's Matt."

"Are you at the mine?"

"Yes, I am."

"OK. I'll call you right back," with that he disconnected. The phone rang again almost immediately.

"That's better, I'm in the back office at the pub; now I can hear what you're saying, and it's more private here. Listen Matt, I want to get together with you and look through those notebooks, and also I want to get down that mine with you somehow. I've had a false I.D. made up which says I'm from the education board. I've already spoken with the under-manager there; he's cleared it for me to go down with you whenever we decide.

"There seems to be quite a lot of activity amongst our German friends; I've a tail on them right now. After they left the hotel, they went to the club where they were seen packing stuff into the trunk of a car. My man said that he saw coveralls and safety helmets going in the trunk.

"I believe that they are going to the mine. Check on the blacksmith at your end; I'll bet he is around there somewhere tonight! I'm on my way over to you right now. Make whatever arrangements necessary to get me down tonight; incidentally I have been down a mine before, once, during a disaster."

There was a definitive click of the phone. He was gone. I looked around the offices for whatever I could find to kit out Gerald to go below, eventually finding a large set of coveralls and a helmet in the surveyor's office. I checked with the winding room. The blacksmith was on duty and had made arrangements to take a large box below after all of the miners had gone down. Apparently he wanted to travel with the box; therefore, he wanted the ride classed as men going down, not just supplies.

I couldn't believe my ears, were we actually going to see those boxes after all these years! But why take them down the mine? I remembered the big German had said the stuff was to be moved at night, that it must look like a normal activity. How on earth were they going to achieve that?

I spoke to the lamp room attendant who cleared a lamp for Gerald, having spoken to the night deputy who didn't regard the request for Gerald to accompany me as being anything out of the ordinary.

During my wait for Gerald, I began to update my notes when the door opened and in walked Sergeant MacGregor.

"I was just having a wee ride around before going off duty, thought I'd stick my head in and see if you actually made it tonight. I was betting to myself that you would'na, but you proved me wrong, yer a tough wee Sassenach, I'll gi ye that much."

MacGregor turned as someone knocked on the office reception window; I half slid the panel back to see Gerald standing there.

"Oh, I won't be a minute, I'm just talking to Sergeant MacGregor, a friend of mine," motioning with my eyes for Gerald to make himself scarce. See you at the lamp room in about five minutes," closing the window as I spoke, and at the same time trying to appear as casually nonchalant as I could under the circumstances. After a couple minutes more, he finally made a move. I went to the door with him, watching as he got into his van and drove out onto the lane, his rear lights disappearing up the hill.

I locked the front door to the office as everybody who needed access had come and gone. I opened the rear door; Gerald was standing there looking a little irritated.

"What the hell was he doing here?" he asked as though inferring that in some way it was my fault.

"I don't have the faintest idea, I am pretty sure he didn't believe a word that I said to him though, he as much as said that earlier on this evening. I told you this guy is not going to go away easily."

Then I explained to him about the blacksmiths' intended trip down the mine that night.

"I knew that something was going on tonight," he said with a satisfied nod.

"Let's take a look into the blacksmith's shop, it can't be too far from here," said Gerald.

"It's about fifty yards from the mine shaft, has a direct rail link to the mine shaft, most heavy metal-made parts are taken down direct from the workshop," I replied.

"Let's go," said Gerald, as he walked to the door.

"Not so fast, put these coveralls on first, then try this hat for size, and by the way, you can't possibly go down a mine wearing those shoes."

He was wearing a lightweight pair of dress boots, more suited to dancing the quickstep than stepping quickly from one railway tie to another. I went back into the surveyor's office and drew a blank, same in the general office.

I was about to give up when I heard an exclamation from him.

"These will do just fine." He was walking out of Carl's office carrying a very large pair of gum boots. He took off his own boots and twisted the coverall bottoms around his ankles, slipping his feet into the rubber boots. Looking more like Captain Pete than a coal miner, but as he rightly said, he was there to get a job done, not to win a fashion parade.

"Let's get this show on the road, then hopefully we can all go home, young Matt!"

I looked across the pit yard; the blacksmith's shop was in darkness and as we walked across the yard, squelching in the thick swamp-like mud, it was impossible to walk quietly. I beckoned Gerald to move over to the center of the rail lines where the feet of the ponies had hardened the surface. The wide doors were open into the loading bay of the blacksmith's shop. There in the center of this area was a large packing case strapped firmly to a flat trolley. It was twice the size of the original boxes. I guessed at the time, it was six feet long, by four feet deep, by four feet wide A fair size to be moving around un-noticed.

The case lid seemed to be bolted down; as I looked closer it had holes drilled around the sides of about one inch in diameter. I bent down to take a closer look when I heard a voice coming from the doorway of the blacksmith's shop.

"Vot can ve do for ze domino champion?" It was Kurt, the blacksmith.

"You startled me there, Kurt; we were looking for some six-inch bolts for the cutting team. The ones that are used to secure the cutter rope to the derrick."

"We?" he asked, looking round the loading bay. Turning round, there was no sign of Gerald. I was alone.

"Oh, er yes, I meant we, the coal cutters and me, do you have the bolts?"

"One of the team took a whole bag of things, not ten minutes ago."

"Thanks Kurt, oh what's in the case here? Looks big enough to be a new cutting machine."

"You get on mitt your job unt mind your business, young man," he snapped quickly in reply.

"It is my business; I'm here to study all aspects of this mine." I emphasized the word 'all'.

"Do you want me to open it for you?" he asked, calling my bluff. "If so, you will need to get written authority first, I am only ze verker here," he said spreading the palms of his hands in a gesture of humility. He noticed I appeared to back down, I felt it was better not to challenge him at this stage.

"You always vere a vun for asking too many qvestions," he muttered as he walked back into the workshop. Outside, Gerald was waiting in the shadows.

"I wondered where the hell you'd disappeared to in there," I said.

"There's no need to have un-necessary confrontations," he replied. "I heard all that he had to say and that's quite sufficient for now. What's next?"

"To the lamp room then down the hole" I looked around carefully, seeing nothing unusual. I introduced Gerald to the Onsetter, explaining briefly his reason for being there.

A couple of the night water pump operatives and some of the coal cutters were standing waiting for the cage to arrive. I spoke loud enough, so all and sundry heard as the night Deputy arrived.

"So you're just here to observe then?" he asked. Gerald nodded, as the Deputy added, "That's a shame, we can always use big strong lads like you in a mine," he said as he walked away.

"Oh, by the way, there's some equipment coming down from the blacksmith's a bit later," he told the Onsetter.

"I hope he's not taking it too far in, we're doing repairs on the big engine below and the rope won't be running tonight!"

By the time the cage arrived, packed with the remnants of the previous afternoon shift, there were too many to ride legally, so I stood back, pulling Gerald by the arm.

"We'll catch the next one," I volunteered, after all we're observers, we don't want to stop the workers." There were a few jocular jeers as the gate banged shut and the cage descended.

I'd hoped that the packing case would arrive before the next ride, but no such luck. Up came the cage carrying the afternoon Deputy, holding his reports. We duly climbed aboard and away we went. I glanced at Gerald's face by the glow of my lamp as we shot down the shaft, a picture of sheer terror, and his big fist clutching his belt buckle, knuckles whitened from the pressure. I turned away so as not to embarrass him.

"Shit," he moaned.

"God, I'd forgotten what this felt like, when you think that people do this every day for a living!" *Life is a great leveler, even the toughest and most brave of men have their own Achilles heel.* I smiled as the thought came to mind.

The cage slowed down and then came gently to a halt; the Banksman threw up the outer barrier and then opened the hinged door. As I anticipated, Gerald was first out the door, his face ashen; he went immediately behind the quiet turbine engine. I heard the sounds of him throwing up.

"Some of 'em just can't take it," a mechanic sniggered as he worked on the engine.

"Maybe he had too many beers the night before," I interjected. Eventually Gerald returned with a sheepish grin on his face. We walked round into the stables. Ben's small office was empty; Gerald sat down, his hands visibly shaking.

"Not a word of this to a soul," he said, a mild threat lurking somewhere in his tone of voice.

"Here, drink this," I passed him my water bottle. He took a good slug then he replaced the top and passed the metal container back to me.

"You'll be alright in a minute or two, just sit there and relax. We have some time to kill." A head came round the door.

"Are you two going out to the coalface?" It was the mechanic who was working on the rope engine.

"Yes, we are."

"You'd better get a move on then, unless you want a bloody long walk. We're running only one paddy train before the motor is shut off for the night." Shortly after he left we heard the familiar roar of an engine.

"Come on Gerald, we need to leave now, unless you fancy a three- mile walk in your sea-going footwear!"

We walked out into the pit bottom and across to the paddy train. It was just about to be connected to the now moving rope. Gerald and I climbed aboard, taking the last two remaining seats at the rear of the train.

As our transport jolted into motion, Gerald's face still had a look of anticipation with a definite tinge of trepidation.

Chapter Eighteen

The Mansion that Same Night

Later after Cheryl had left, David began to drift off to sleep, but not before he had begun to wonder where Cheryl had gained all of the experience that she had shown earlier, then he dismissed the thought.

It really is none of my business, he thought, nevertheless the question was there at the back of his mind, sowing the seeds of doubt!

As Cheryl drove David's car home across the quiet village, her thoughts went to her married lover Derek, who she had not too long ago separated from. The pressures from his wife had been too great for him to handle.

I do hope that I am making the right decision, she thought. Deep down, she knew the answer; she could never love anyone but Derek. If she couldn't achieve her own happiness, maybe at least she could make David happy. *What a cruel, mixed up world we live in*, she thought.

At precisely the same time as the tires of the car crunched along the gravel driveway to her parent's home, deep below ground, the cast iron wheels of the paddy train rattled and clattered along the metal rails of the main roadway.

Meanwhile, Sergeant Donald Macgregor sat on the slagheap above the mine. He looked down through the service-issue binoculars wishing there was some way of seeing better in the dark. He smiled as he thought of his mother's promises that eating carrots would help him to see in the dark; so far it had amounted to nothing.

He'd watched young Harper and a colleague walk across the muddy yard and seen them enter the mineshaft. All seemed rather quiet, so he felt he could afford to drive a little nearer to the mine, park his van in the lane, and then go in to have a good look round the place.

He was just about to move when he saw a new car arrive on the scene across in the pit yard; a large black Austin sedan.

Three people emerged from the vehicle, looking like mine officials; all wore what looked like dark-colored coveralls and white safety helmets. They made their way into a building under the corrugated tin roof close to the mineshaft entrance.

The sergeant moved with alacrity, sliding, slipping and running at the same time as he sped down the slagheap. At the bottom, he rushed over to his van, literally falling through the doorway. The engine started at once; engaging the clutch he was hurtling down the cart track to Pit Lane. The large antenna swaying madly as he negotiated the potholes.

The Paddy Train Back Underground

The miner in the front seat of the paddy train jumped off as we moved along. He reached out grabbing the two wires that were fixed by rubber covered clips to the steel girders, running parallel all the way to the pit bottom. As he touched both wires together, the train came to a halt. *Two touches of the six-volt bell wire to start, one to stop, directional change, three rings outbound, four inbound.*

About a mile back I had pointed out to Gerald where the disused tunnel was, saying that we would no doubt be back there shortly. We walked along the tail gate another quarter of a mile or so until we reached the coalface. There we sat down on some logs of wood and talked for a while with some of the cutters as two others read newspapers by the light of their lamps.

Tonight, for Gerald's benefit, the team explained the principles of coal cutting then slipped over to the usual topics: sport and sex. We borrowed a couple of pairs of kneepads, and then I took Gerald under the face before the dust started to fly.

Judging by his reaction as he crawled along the two hundred yard face, he looked far from happy. I saw earlier in the shaft that his problem seemed to be more claustrophobic than vertiginous; however he was a tough man and offered no form of complaint. Though he did make one significant comment as he crawled out into the much larger main gate, standing up and taking off the kneepads:

"These people really earn their bloody money don't they? I certainly don't ever want to hear anybody say otherwise in my company. Now, young Harper, what other pleasures and untold delights have you got in store for me next?"

The reason that I brought us through to the main gate was that the phone was always situated there, usually a bit further back from the face, inexplicably it was the last thing that the electricians seemed to extend as the workings moved forward.

I wound the handle of the phone the requisite amount of times for the pit bottom and got the Onsetter, asking him if the blacksmith had come down with his cargo yet; he replied in the negative. Giving him my thanks, I sat down next to Gerald.

"Why the distorted voice?" asked Gerald.

"I didn't want him to know who was speaking, just in case he mentions the call to Kurt."

"Good thinking, you'd make a good cop, you know," he added, as he lifted his helmet, trying to find a more comfortable position on his head, *the only one being off your head*, I thought. The weight of the lamp leaves a permanent ring around the forehead after a while.

"So why did you leave the police force?" I asked, throwing a small rock at a mouse, as it scurried past the beam of my lamp.

"It's a long story; maybe I'll tell it to you one day, let it suffice to say, I wasn't thrown out, though I'm a bit of a ruffian sometimes. I learned that in the Marines earlier. Let's say the one thing I can't stomach is dishonesty, that's why I became a cop in the first place; read into that what you will."

A bit of a ruffian, *that must go down as the understatement of the year*. I smiled inwardly at the thought. We sat for a while longer. I'd brought some food, which we decided to save until later; I had re-filled my water bottle, also I'd borrowed another one from the stable, which I gave to Gerald.

We set off in the direction of the disused gate at a steady pace, me wondering what the hell was coming next. I knew if the packing case came down, it wasn't official. I'd read the reports. It hadn't been sanctioned by management!

Meanwhile back above ground, Donald MacGregor parked his van and was walking around the rear perimeter of the mine. Apart from a light in the medical offices and the building next to the shaft, all others were in total darkness, including the lamp room. He almost lost his balance as he fell over a large stack of steel supports when he came up behind the workshop with the corrugated metal roof.

The main structure was wood, in some areas the boards had warped, leaving uneven spaces; he could see rays of light shining through.

He went towards one of these small openings; as he came closer he could hear voices. He tried to peer through the small space but materials stacked inside blocked his vision.

Spotting another ray of light a little further around the side, he found an old door which obviously hadn't been used for years. Through the door, the voices were now much louder. but he couldn't quite make out what they were saying. After straining his ears, he realized that they were speaking in a foreign language; apart from schoolboy French, he was at a loss.

He thought what he was hearing was German, mainly from the harsh guttural tones he'd heard before from training films on interrogation courses he'd attended.

There was some kind of motor running inside the building, adding to his hearing difficulties.

He decided to try and open the door wide enough to see inside. He took out his penknife and began to lever the edge, he paused as the voices became louder.

"I think that we should conduct our conversations in English from now on," said a woman. For a second MacGregor was startled, he hadn't noticed the woman before, the next words he heard were in English.

"If anyone happens to be walking around, we will not attract attention to ourselves if we speak in English."

"I agree with Helga," said the big man.

"I vill find zis not qvite as easy as ze rest off you, but I vill do mine wery best," said a short bespectacled man.

"Good then that's settled," said the big man.

"Let's get things moving, we're scheduled to get this case down within the next thirty minutes. Kurt, is everything ready, have all of the necessary arrangements been made?"

"Ja vul.... sorry, yes, sir,"

"Good, but for my benefit let's go through it all again, to coin an English military phrase, time spent in preparation is seldom wasted."

"Do we have to listen to that noisy machine?"

"No, but it's a generator and it's usually left running most of the time," replied Kurt.

"Turn the damn thing off, it's driving me crazy," *I think that already happened a long time ago my Gestapo friend*, Kurt thought to himself.

He walked across the loading bay, threw the switch off irritably as comparative silence fell.

"That's much better now, is the top of the packing case undone?"

"No, I had to fasten it, or somebody vould certainly haff looked inside, ze young man on ze work-study program vas already asking qvestions zis evenink."

"Is he an official?" asked the big man.

"No, not exactly, he is a student."

"Is he going down the mine tonight?"

"Yes, but he is vorking mitt ze cutters vay up on ze coalface. He von't be any real problem to us." They all turned as a loud snapping noise came from the corner of the building.

"What the hell was that?" the big German asked.

"*Shit*," MacGregor said, half under his breath as the blade of his knife snapped clean in half.

Blood began to pour from the cut across his knuckle. A few seconds before the motor had stopped running, he was sure they must have heard him inside the building, so he kept perfectly still, hoping he was wrong. Then suddenly he heard a voice in English say,

"Kurt, take a look and see what that was, will you?"

"It vill be a rat, or vun of ze mines cats, zere are always noises around this place."

"Nevertheless, go and take a look, and that's an order." The big German snarled as his face began to redden. Kurt went over to the area where he thought he had heard the sound as the big man moved towards the door.

Sergeant MacGregor mentally went through his pockets, searching for some means of stemming the flow of blood from his finger. He noticed, a few feet away, a trailer containing very long steel rods. The longest one had a rag tied on the end of it, obviously it had been a warning to following traffic whilst on the road, but was just what Donald needed.

He turned his back to the building, took one step across, and then pulled the rag from the steel rod. Looking as closely as he could in the dark, he found the cleanest part of the rag and began to rip the cloth into strips; he felt a hard prod in the back of his neck.

"Keep perfectly still and you will not be hurt," said a voice close to his left ear. He was just about to take evasive action, when the hard object was slid from his neck around to the side of his face; he recognized the German military issue Lugar.

"In case you are thinking of doing anything stupid or heroic, this is real, it's loaded, and the safety catch is off. I will not hesitate to use it, if you doubt me, please go ahead. Now place your hands above your head, lean on the wall there, and then spread your legs wide."

MacGregor realized that this man was no amateur by the way he carried out the thorough search.

"Look what we have here," exclaimed the German, as he brought MacGregor's handcuffs from his belt.

"Just what the doctor ordered, as you English would say."

"Not so much of the English, if you don't mind," said MacGregor. The man snapped one cuff onto the sergeant's raised wrist, then pulled it down behind his back, ignoring the Scotsman's comment as the rains poured steadily down.

"The other one behind if you please, now put your hand through your legs."

As MacGregor stooped to carry out the instruction, he spun round quickly. Bringing his head up, and aiming it at where he assumed the gun would be. Unfortunately, his head flew up into emptiness, and he found himself looking directly down the barrel of the Lugar. He saw the sheer hate and fanaticism in the eyes of the man holding the gun: a sudden flash in the darkness, as the metal hammer hit the shell case, then for Sergeant Donald MacGregor, nothing. He'd felt no pain as he fell across the steel supports.

Blood had trickled from the hole in his forehead; it had welled into his wide open staring eyes, diluted by the continuing rain. The German quickly removed the dead man's ID from his inside pocket and then leaned over to put it under the ray of light.

"Well, well, SIB," he said in a resigned, superior fashion.

"You can't say that I didn't warn you, Sergeant," he said, pocketing the ID. Kurt came running at the sound of the shot; he looked down at the corpse as it started to rain heavily, diluting the sergeant's blood as it ran down his face.

"Mine Gott in Himmel," he exclaimed, as he looked around.

"Speak English, you fool!" the big man screamed as the other two arrived on the scene. The little man peered down through his thick lenses.

"Vo iss zis man?" he asked without any sign of compassion whatsoever.

"Your English is terrible, you mean who *was* this man? He was a Sergeant with the British Military Special Investigations Branch.

"Kurt, let's get this body into the building before anyone comes along; take his legs. Come on, stop staring and get a move on, you must have seen a dead body before."

The lamp room attendant was fast asleep, sitting in a chair with his feet supported by another seat, his head resting on his rolled-up jacket. He awoke with a start, he wasn't quite sure whether he'd heard a loud crack, or maybe dreamed it. The room was in complete darkness as he walked across and peered out of the window.

The only light outside came from lamps hanging over the main walkways, which cast a dim yellow glow as they swung to and fro, reflecting the driving rain in the drab light. Another stream of light came from inside the blacksmith's shop. He thought he saw two men carrying a sack, then he took his watch from his vest pocket. It was twelve-thirty.

The heavy rain beat down incessantly on the windows, washing away the recent dust. He decided to settle back into his chair, listening to the howling of the wind as it drove water under the door into the room.

Below ground, Gerald and I had walked quite some distance. Nearing the end of the main gate, the air began to thicken, dust was coming from the cutting machine, our faces were already beginning to blacken up.

"Christ I'm eating the soddin' stuff," Gerald coughed, clearing his throat as he spit out a black mouthful.

"They haven't noticed the water sprayer is turned off, that sometimes happens, they'll spot it soon or they'll have the Deputy on their tails," *said this very experienced, three weeks on the job, mining expert!*

As we approached the main return road, I held up my hand.

"Turn off your lamp and hang onto this, I'll be right back." I passed the Davy lamp to Gerald. I then took the lamp from my hat and turned it to the dim setting. I peered around the corner down the main road; seeing no other lights, I put the lamp back on my hat and beckoned for Gerald to come forward.

I remembered that the road from here to the disused tunnel entry was mostly straight, but past there, it had one or two slight curves, which worked in our favor.

If, indeed, the Germans did appear and the road had been perfectly straight, they would see us clearly way off in the distance.

The situation was still tricky, because it's impossible to travel without lights and we must travel on dimmed bulbs. They'd have less chance of seeing us. Their brighter lights would reflect back off the road, in front of them; that was my theory anyway, so off we set making very slow progress.

Meanwhile, back on the pit top the blacksmith and the Banksman pushed the trolley along the railway lines, onto the rails inside the cage at ground level.

"What you got in here Kurt, a dead body or something? It's bloody heavy, I'll tell you that!" gasped the other man, wiping the rain from his eyes as it poured from the peak of his cloth cap.

"Zere's no great mystery, it's just some parts for ze return end of ze rope, zere are lots of smaller parts, zat vould end up all over ze place, if zey veren't left in zis box, you vell know zese haulage lads, zey don't giff a shizen."

"Ja, unt make sure zat you tell ze vinder, zat it's men riding unt not just materials, I can vell do mitt out ze ride of my life just now, sank you werry much," he added as he squeezed into the cage alongside the case, then climbed up and sat on top of the trolley.

The cage came to a stop and, as expected, the Onsetter was not where he should be. *No doubt sitting in ze shtables, reading ze newspaper or maybe even having ein shleep,* he thought.

Kurt lifted the barrier, fixing it up under the holding latch, then proceeded to push the trolley out onto the rails at the pit bottom. He pulled down a lever, moving the points across and pushed it out onto the main line, then went into the stables. Sure enough, the Onsetter was sitting in Ben's office, reading a book.

"Hey, Adolph, I didn't hear any bells. Did you just come down? I thought you'd changed your mind. I was told you would be down ages ago."

"Ze vether is so lousy up zere, it's pissing down cats unt dogs, as you people say, I had to get help to push ze trolley, unt zere aren't too many folk around zis time of ze morning."

"Raining cats and dogs, raining, not pissing, you stupid Kraut dick," he said aloud, as Kurt went past further along the stables. *If his work was as bad as his language, we'd all be in trouble*, he thought to himself.

"Move over Prince, come on, vake up unt move over," Kurt said to the pony as he pushed the stubborn rump of a disinterested, sleepy pony, whose ears went back at the jingling sound of the harness. As he tried to put the bit into the pony's mouth, the animal clenched his teeth shut.

"Aw, come on Prince, none of us really vants to be out of bed at zis time," he added as he forced his thumb into the side of the pony's mouth, pushing down on the rear tooth free part of the gum. The bit slid into place, rattling, as Prince moved his teeth to get comfortable. Kurt slid the bridle over his ears, and then put on the heavy padded collar, as he led the pony out of the stables and past the office.

"What time will you be back?"

"I'm not qvite sure, but you von't be going far, vill you?" he knew that the other man was calculating how long he could sleep. *Cheeky German Git,* the Onsetter thought to himself as he returned to his book.

Man and pony came around the corner; Kurt walked over to a row of wooden shafts. He took a pair and strapped them to Prince's harness, then connected them to the trolley.

Bringing the reins back, he climbed on the front of the trolley, shaking the leather straps and clicking his tongue at the same time. The pony pushed forward into his collar.

As the steel rope was slack and not in the normal place, Kurt decided to walk in front as Prince was having difficulty seeing the rope pulleys.

"How much longer do you think we have to sit here in the dark?" asked Gerald.

"I think I now know what it feels like to be blind," he added. I turned on my dim light and passed him the unlit Davy lamp, pointing to the lighting device, operating it and igniting the flame, then extinguishing it. Then I put the lamp behind him, turning my lamp off.

"See if you can find the Davy lamp and light it in the dark," I said to him.

"What's this, some kind of initiative test?" he asked with some sarcasm.

"I suppose it is, just try." I heard him, as he fumbled around in the dust; actually I'd moved the lamp from where he first saw me put it. Eventually, I heard the rattle as he located it, after a good couple of minutes of fumbling,

"God damn it, I can't find the bloody switch."

"Now use your memory, as well as your fingers." A minute of silence then.

"Got it," the light flickered into life.

"I passed the test, then," he grinned, "but what was the purpose...."

"Shh, listen," I said cutting him short. I could hear a faint grinding noise, as though the rope were moving. I knew that wasn't possible; bending down and putting my ear to the rails, I could not only hear, but could feel the wheels traveling in our direction.

"Put your ear to the rails," I said. After what seemed an age there was still no sign of anyone, so we moved into place as agreed. I took a manhole on the outbound side of the disused tunnel, Gerald on the inbound. As we sat in total darkness, I saw the faint glimmer of light, then after a few more minutes we heard the familiar jingle of a pony harness.

Chapter Nineteen

Back Above Ground

The knocking on the door started as a polite tap, and then it became louder, until it was accompanied by an authoritative loud deep voice.

Bang, bang, the door shook.

"Is anyone there?" Bang, bang. "Hello is anyone there? This is the Police." The lamp room attendant almost fell between the two chairs as he awoke with a start, he saw the beam of a flashlight as louder banging came from the door of the lamp room. *Is there no rest for the wicked?* He thought.

"Coming, I'm coming, hold your horses, what the hell is the big panic?"

He opened the door, looking up into the face of a young Police Constable, water pouring off the peak of his helmet.

"I thought everybody had gone home," said the Constable.

"What's the big panic, Officer?" the lamp man asked.

"There is a strange van parked out on Pit Lane. No parking lights on it, and I can hear a two-way radio going on inside the vehicle. Do you know who the owner might be, sir?"

"I haven't got the faintest idea, how the hell would I know, lad?"

"It's not from this area, it's more like a London number I think," the Constable added as water spilled down over his cape.

"Come inside, lad, don't stand out there in the rain."

"Thanks, sir, I don't mind if I do. That's very kind of you, it's not such a nice night out there." He took off his helmet as more water splashed to the floor.

"I was wondering if you had a phone that I could borrow."

"There's no phone in here, only one that connects to the office, I don't have a key to the main office, I'm sorry, lad, I wish I could be of more help. Wait a minute, they have a direct line in the Ambulance Room, and that's manned twenty-four hours a day. Why not go and ask them, and I'll put the kettle on, we'll have a cup of tea when you get back," the lamp room attendant said smiling.

"Now you're talking," said the Policeman, putting on his helmet, a big grin across his young face. *They say that when the police start to look young you're getting old*, the lamp man thought to himself.

Bang, tap, rap tap, went the door again.

"The door is open, Officer," shouted the lamp man irritably as he poured the hot water into the tea pot. The door opened and a perfect stranger walked into the room.

"How do you know that I am an Officer?" said the stranger, looking surprised.

"Are you a clairvoyant or something?"

"Oh. I'm sorry. No, sir, you see the local Policeman who was here just this minute went out the door to use the phone in the ambulance room. I thought you were him coming back, who are you anyway?" The man reached into his pocket bringing out his credentials.

"I'm captain Hamilton of British Military Special Investigations Branch. We have been conducting enquiries in this area. One of my officers failed to report in before signing off last night. He didn't return to base, and we know that his last radio report was received from here. Just then the Police Constable returned.

"I got a call through to the station. Constable Elis had reported seeing the same vehicle earlier, just before he went off duty; it was driving out of the grounds of the Mansion earlier this evening. Oh, forgive me, I'm sorry if I'm interrupting anything," said the Constable, seeing that the lamp man was speaking with someone else.

"That's alright, young man. This here's Captain Hamilton of Special Investigations Branch. It appears they've lost one of their men somewhere around here last night.

"What kind of vehicle was he driving Captain, is it standard issue Morris van, with London registration tags?"

"Yes, it is young man, a black one." I think maybe you'd better come along with me Captain, if you don't mind, sir," the Constable said as he held open the door.

"Did I hear you say that someone saw the van earlier, Constable?"

"Yes, sir, you did. It was one of our officers. There's a full report at the station, sir." The rain was now coming down in torrents as the two men left the building.

"I'll make that three teas, shall I?" The lamp room attendant said, speaking aloud as the door was closed with a resounding bang.

"I may as well get on with some work, there's no chance of a bloke getting any sleep around here tonight, that's for sure and certain," he said to himself as he went to his workbench littered with pieces of lamps and batteries.

Back Underground

The sounds of the oncoming trolley were much louder now; the light became brighter as I looked out of my hiding place and down along the main road. I had an odd feeling of foreboding, like butterflies in the stomach.

The steady jingle and tinkle of the harness for some silly reason put me in mind of sleigh bells and Christmas. A subject far removed from the current circumstances, the thought seemed so ludicrous that I sniggered aloud at my own stupidity. I thought that I'd only seen the one lamp, checking again there was only the one. I'd had it in my mind that there would be more than one person.

But if so, how would they get other people down the mine without permission, or indeed without anyone else seeing them and what would they use for lamps? I dismissed the thought as the trolley came nearer; we both drew back into our respective manholes and waited as the pony drew closer to us.

I couldn't help thinking about my recent near-entombment; the mere thought of going back down that gate gave me the heebie-jeebies.

I could only imagine that when he got further inside the gate, the German would see the situation and then abandon the whole project, unless he felt inclined to move a few thousand tons of rock. But move it to where? Such an undertaking would need many men, time and equipment. Not to mention that an operation of such magnitude could not be kept secret.

I crouched into the corner of my refuge as the sound of the pony's feet and the grinding of metal on metal came closer. The light was extremely bright as the blacksmith came past my manhole first, leading the animal behind him. I froze, squatting down under an old piece of tarpaulin I'd found there; the trolley went past me without incident.

"Whoa, Prince, zat's fine boy," I heard him say as the pony came to a halt.

I squinted around the corner of the manhole and saw the German unhook the shafts from the trolley; he led the pony into the entrance of the gate, where I heard him tie the animal to a girder.

The German then took out a wrench and proceeded to remove the bolts that held the top of the case shut. He seemed to be talking to himself a lot as he carried out his task. He looked both ways down the road every few seconds, as though half expecting someone to appear. Once he had removed all of the bolts, he started to undo the straps that went around the container.

I could see all of this very clearly in the light of his cap lamp as I was about twenty feet away. I assumed that Gerald was also getting a ringside seat of events, as he was no more than thirty feet inbound.

It seemed as though the man was getting annoyed with himself. I thought that the lid had become stuck as he pushed a bar underneath, and then with a loud creak the lid shot up and fell with a loud clatter to the ground.

Neither Gerald nor I were ready for what took place next. Just like a coffin in a Count Dracula film, a hand came slowly over the side of the case from the inside, then the head and shoulders of a man emerged, followed by a second person, and then a third one.

I was dumbfounded, rooted to the spot, as the three newcomers climbed to the ground it became obvious that the second figure was that of a tall woman.

The first was without doubt the big German with the short hair, the original recipient of the parachuted boxes. I didn't know the third one, but had seen him at the hotel earlier. His steel-rimmed spectacles shone in the light of Kurt's lamp.

They carried flashlights, which were totally illegal down any coalmine as they were capable of making fatal electrical sparks.

The three of them lifted the case from the trolley, which seemed no simple task judging by the grunts and groans, then they replaced the lid; the big man taking one end, the other two opposite, they carried their load into the entrance of the gate and then they returned, tipping the trolley over to the side and leaving the main railway clear.

The Blacksmith then began the task of removing sufficient boards from the barrier to enable entry into the gate. Shortly after, all three of them went through the entrance, carrying picks and shovels and proceeded down the gate, disappearing eventually around the curve, at the same time plunging us back into complete darkness.

I waited maybe thirty seconds.

"Pst pst, Matt you there?" I heard Gerald whisper, a little too loud for my liking.

"Yes," I replied. I came out of the manhole, having put my lamp on dim, half covering the lens with open fingers.

I walked along past the overturned trolley, across the end of the gate and saw Gerald standing a few paces further along.

"What did you think to that lot?" I said in a whisper.

"Gave me quite a shock," he replied.

"A bloody woman too. She must be one tough lady. What next Matt?" Gerald asked. I thought for a moment or two then answered.

"We have to wait here for a short while to see whether they abandon the whole operation once they get to the obstruction in there. If so it will just be a matter of following them back to the pit bottom."

In the meantime I took the Davy lamp, as they rattle when carried, along with our water bottles and my haversack, putting them in Gerald's manhole. Covering them with rocks and stone dust, we went back towards the entrance, standing next to the case we waited, listening intently in the darkness.

Meanwhile Above Ground

The pit yard was by now a scene of total organized chaos. There were two Police cars, a military police van, and a half dozen men wearing gumboots and carrying powerful flashlights, two were leading dogs.

The offices were now open and the lights were on but visibility wasn't good. The relentless rain made all of their tasks that much more difficult. Suddenly all was revealed as the main, rarely used floodlights were turned on; the whole area was bathed in bright light. Another car arrived hurriedly sending a spray of black mud and water splashing over one of the men.

"Found anything yet, Captain?" asked the passenger from the rear seat of the car.

"Only the van so far, sir," replied Captain Hamilton.

"This rain is hampering any real progress, sir," he added.

The only other vehicles on the property, apart from the law, were a number of coal board trucks, an ambulance and several motorcycles. The under-manager's car had only just arrived and right next to that was Gerald's car. One of the investigators was already taking down its number along with those of the motorbikes.

Sergeant Macgregor's van had been put onto the back of a military low loader and covered by a tarpaulin. It was four AM when the other men were called to the offices.

"Ok, men, listen up. So far we have drawn a blank, assuming that Sergeant MacGregor is missing. As you are all aware he is a trained investigator and would not deviate from normal procedures. He did not sign off, nor make any contact in his last hour of duty. We can only assume the worst, and hope for the best. The weather, nor the time of day, has been on our side so far. To date, we have found a piece of rag with bloodstains on it, but the heavy rain hasn't helped us there either.

The local police have been very helpful; they understand that we shall carry on with our own investigations. No complaint has yet been made to them, so until they are notified of a complaint or that a crime has been committed; they have no investigation to carry out.

I want you to continue searching, and don't leave one stone un-turned. Is that clear, any questions?"

Apart from a few nods there were no comments from the group.

"Carry on, Captain Hamilton," the Brigadier added as he walked out of the room.

"I shall expect a full report on my desk by lunchtime tomorrow, er, I mean lunchtime today," he said, pausing to look at his watch as he reached the door, then he strode out of the office.

The Captain pointed to the make-do blackboard, which was the back of an area map, fixed to the wall with thumbtacks.

"O.K., we know that the approximate time of disappearance is between these two times, he pointed to the wall. There's no sign of a struggle near his vehicle, therefore we must assume that any abduction or struggle must have taken place elsewhere in the vicinity. I want this area thoroughly searched; if necessary you'll spread out until you cover the whole damn county, now get to it!

When the men had left the room, Captain Hamilton went into the general office and asked to speak with the manager.

"Unfortunately, he's ill in hospital" said an older looking man.

"I'm the under-manager; can I be of some assistance, Captain?"

"I know it may be an imposition, but do you have an office that we can borrow until this matter is cleared up, sir?"

"Certainly lad, there's a room behind the canteen used for meetings and classes. It doesn't have a direct telephone line out, but you can go through the switchboard.

"Thank you, sir, your assistance is greatly appreciated, we apologize for any inconvenience," the Captain said, as he walked out of the room.

Below Ground

The Germans had been gone for a good five minutes, there were no signs of their coming back out of the gate; we could still hear some faint sounds of their activity from that direction.

"I think it's time to take a look," I said. Just then we both distinctly heard the noise of wheels on metal rails coming from inside the disused road, then we saw the reflection of light, flickering around the curve.

We retreated to our hiding places as the wheels came to a halt at the other side of the barrier. Then I saw Kurt and the big German tip the wooden case on its side, facing into the tunnel. From the sounds I could hear, they part lifted and part dragged its contents through the barrier.

Curiosity took over. I just had to see what was going on. I came out of my manhole and into the road. I was operating from memory now as the only light was the faint glow from their lamps. I felt for the upturned trolley, now, by my reckoning, about ten feet away.

I stumbled on the end of a sleeper, kicking a loose rock, which made a dull thud against the end of the wood. I froze to the spot, knowing if they came out, they would certainly see me……. As luck would have it, they'd not heard me. I moved along the last few feet slowly, feeling each girder cautiously with my hands as I went along.

My hand eventually finding empty space, I saw the lights in the disused road. Crouching down behind the overturned case, I saw two of the men pushing a second trolley, obviously the one I had rested on earlier. I sensed Gerald's presence by my side as they disappeared around the curve.

"I missed that Matt, what happened?" I told him what I had seen.

"Come on, let's take another look," he said. We proceeded slowly past the barrier, along the dark road. It became patently obvious that we weren't going to be able to peer around the corner; the bend was so gradual that we could be spotted at any time.

On the right hand side, was a pile of rocks where a girder had been removed, sufficient to squat down beside, but not high enough to get behind. I motioned Gerald over next to where I knelt.

We could see now quite clearly from the light of the lamp and flashlights; they had also managed to obtain a Davy lamp, which now hung from the center of a girder.

They were close to the rock fall, I could see the great pile of rocks beyond them. Strangely enough they seemed to be concentrating on the right hand side of the tunnel before the fall where they were removing rocks from the side.

In these older working areas, the coal had been taken from both sides of the tunnel, some thirty feet to either side. After its removal, the stone and rocks obtained when extending the tunnel were thrown into the empty space. Then a sort of dry stonewall was built on the outside to retain and support. This area is known as the Gob or 'The Pack.'

I could see the trolley in the center, it was the very same one I'd sat on not so many hours before. They were working like beavers, pulling rock from the pack, knowing full well that time was against them.

"What do you reckon they're up to?" Gerald whispered.

"Obviously they have something hidden in the pack; it can't be those boxes as they were far too large to go under there. If you ask me it must be the contents." I turned my attention to the trolley.

"I wonder what's in the bags on the truck, I'm going to get a little closer and find out," I whispered.

"Be careful, remember these people are not playing games." With Gerald's whispered caution in my ear, I lowered myself to my stomach and began sliding along the top of the right side rail. I pulled myself with each sleeper and at the same time pushed my foot against the sleeper behind.

Slow progress, but this way there was no danger of falling down or walking into something. From where we had been observing to the trolley was about twenty yards, which would amount to the same number of rail sleepers; I counted them as I slid along.

Nearing the trolley I could see the Germans quite clearly, the woman was throwing rocks to the left and right of the now sizeable hole in the pack, the others were underneath throwing debris back to her. I could not see them, but it didn't take a Sherlock Holmes to work that out.

Reaching up, I felt for the edge of the trolley and began carefully to pull myself up onto my knees. As I did so, my hand rested on the Hessian opening of a sack. I began to slide my hand slowly inside its neck.

The next split seconds will be permanently etched on my mind for posterity; I dragged my hand away in absolute revulsion and terror.

I had just put my hand on the head and face of a person, a very cold, clammy, and very dead person! My hand was covered in a thick sticky substance. I felt the bile rise in my mouth and I began to vomit violently and uncontrollably; at the same time I was blinded by white dazzling light, accompanied by a familiar voice.

"Get on your feet, and put your hands on the side of the tunnel."

I was completely blinded and therefore disorientated. I got to my feet, reaching for the side of the tunnel and promptly fell over the rail. I felt my right ankle crack as I twisted round and under the rail, the pain was excruciating.

I thought I was going to pass out. I twisted and writhed in agony, now three lights shone into my face.

"Vere dit he come from?" A highly accented female voice whispered.

"It's ze yung man I haf tolt you about," replied the blacksmith.

"You said he would be no trouble to us, do you think he knows anything about our operation or just wandered in here by accident?" hissed the big man; he spoke in perfect English now. As my eyes became accustomed to the light, I saw the gun in his hand.

"Undo your belt, and give the battery and lamp to me," he ordered. The pain from my ankle was making me feel nauseous.

"I think my ankle is broken," I groaned in as loud a voice as I could, in the hope that Gerald would hear me.

"That, young man, is the very least of your problems," the big man snarled. I looked across at the trolley and could now make out the shadowy shape of a body under the sacking.

"Do you think he's alone?" asked the big man.

"I would think so," replied Kurt. They spoke totally in German now, assuming that I couldn't understand.

"Thinking so is not good enough, go and look around thoroughly and be sure, don't come back until you are certain," the big man commanded.

"While you're doing that, I'll decide what to do with this nosey, interfering young idiot."

When the big man walked over towards the woman, the blacksmith whispered to me in a low voice,

"I dit vorn you tvice before, you ask too many qvestions, now vatch yourself, he vill shoot you as soon as look at you," he finished in a whisper nodding in the direction of the others.

Gerald had watched me crawl along the tunnel, already on his feet should there be a problem. He saw a rapid movement as one of the men moved quickly and quietly to the other side of the tunnel, keeping well behind the lights of the others.

As if he was watching in slow motion and standing there utterly helpless, unable to prevent the inevitable, he watched me fall to the ground, hearing me say I thought my ankle was broken.

Then seeing the gun, Gerald turned and made a speedy exit from the tunnel, with no light he kept to the center, making three foot strides on the sleepers, his feet moving around inside of his uncontrollable footwear, making his progress that much more difficult.

He knew being discovered now could prove fatal to us both. As he neared the barrier he risked a quick flash of his light with fingers over the lens then he was through the boards and standing in the main road, perspiring heavily and appreciating the relatively fresh air. He looked back to where he had just been and saw the flicking of a light as someone followed.

He made a snap decision. Turning towards the pit bottom he switched on his lamp and ran as fast as he could, passing the first and second man holes and diving into the third, then killing his lamp simultaneously.

Breathing heavily he peered around the corner, he saw someone emerge from the tunnel, then turn in his direction and start down the road towards where he hid. The person paused at the first two manholes, and then carried on towards Gerald.

He paused only three feet short, took out a pocket watch, muttered something in German, then turned around and went back in the other direction.

"You're a very lucky man, Mr. German," Gerald said quietly to himself.

Back in the tunnel the big man passed the gun across to the woman.

"Keep an eye on him, if he moves shoot him, another nosey Englishman won't matter one way or the other," he said in perfect English, obviously for my benefit.

He went back to the trolley. I could see from the light of his lamp that he'd lifted the cover and was searching for something; as he did so I could see the shoes and legs, but not enough to identify the body.

"Where are the damn keys, Helga I can't find the keys," he said, again speaking in German.

"Ah here they are, I have them." I heard a clicking sound, at the same time turning my head as light came from the other direction. The air was close to being putrid. I was luckier than the others, lying here on the ground the air was a little clearer, not that much, but better than the air higher up.

Kurt returned breathing heavily and saying there was nobody to be seen, adding that there was nowhere to hide out on the main road. The big man came over to me, bent down and grabbed my right wrist, snapping a handcuff onto it.

"On your feet," he snapped.

"I don't think I can stand," I replied.

"That wasn't a suggestion, it was an order," he yelled as he yanked on the metal bracelet dragging me to my feet, nearly pulling my arm out of its socket in the process.

I was then pulled, hopping on my left leg towards the trolley. He took the other cuff and locked it onto one of the girder tie bars. This bar was about four feet up from the ground and made it impossible for me to sit, so there I stood on one leg totally helpless in the same dreadful place for the second time in hours. They carried on with their task, as though nothing had happened.

Tie bars are fastened to the girders by way of two half-inch bolts at each end. On many occasions the tunnel workers are either short of materials or too lazy, and often use only one bolt in each bar. As I had been tied by the right hand, being right-handed, the removal of these bolts would be a problem. I slid the handcuff to the left of the bar, there were two bolts at that end. *All I need now is to find the only conscientious worker in the coal industry,* I thought, as I slid the cuff to the other end.

Bingo! Only the one bolt there, though it did have a nut on the end, tightened up sufficiently for me to be unable to move it by hand easily.

The Germans were talking in more excitable tones; they began to pass packages out of the hole. These were of different shapes and sizes, wrapped in what looked like oilskin. They stacked them beside the trolley. I could see from the dust and grime caked onto the oilskins that they had been there for some considerable time. Apparently the Germans were now all working under the pack at the same time.

I thought I saw a rapid flash of light out of my right eye, it had seemed so quick that I dismissed it, as my imagination.

"Pst, pst," the welcome sound of Gerald, as he came to my side.

"Sorry I took so long, but I went well down the road when the bloke came out, I just couldn't believe he didn't see me," he whispered.

"He walked within three feet of me." I updated him as quickly as possible.

"Whose is the body?" he asked, looking down at the trolley.

"I've no idea," I replied. While the coast seemed clear, Gerald grabbed the Hessian, pulled it up and made one quick flash of his lamp, revealing the blood covered grey face of Sergeant Donald MacGregor.

"Christ, we have to make a move soon, or we could be next," said Gerald.

"I wonder if they have only the one gun. That black-smith doesn't look like he'll be much of a problem. I must say I've been dying to tangle with that big bastard ever since I set eyes on him." He worked on the bolt holding the tie bar as he talked.

There was a ping as the nut fell to the ground.

"Slide to the other end," he said as he strained to move the bar in an effort to release the bolt.

"It's jammed solid, it'll need a sledge hammer to move that." Then all of a sudden with one final vibrating twang like the string on a taut crossbow, the loose end of bar flew up at the roof, as the whole girder moved a good inch. Small rocks rained down on my safety helmet, I pulled the bar back into place just in time as the big German came running across.

"What's happening here," he yelled, waving the gun in my face.

"This is an old area, the roof is starting to cave in."

He looked at the handcuffs, and then looked up at the roof.

"If it buries you, it'll be one job less for me to do," he smirked maliciously as he walked away, staggering over the rails as he went. Gerald was back in a trice.

"I thought the whole place was going to come crashing down."

"It should be alright, this seems to be one stretch of the tunnel where the demolition men didn't, or maybe couldn't take out every other girder, so it should hold up, with a bit of luck." I winced as I put my foot down by accident.

"I've a plan," whispered Gerald.

"There's now a sizeable pile of rocks either side of the hole they dug. I'm going to try to get to the other side of the furthest pile, then hide behind it. When I do, I want you to keep your eyes peeled, if the big guy comes out first, you shout so that he looks this way towards you.

If they all happen to be in the hole at the same time, then wait till I flash once and then you start to shout and yell. I'll clobber that big-un when he shows his ugly head, got that?"

We agreed, and then waited for an opportunity for Gerald to take up position behind the rocks.

The big man came of out the hole carrying another package, which had the appearance of covered board; it was flat, about two feet by three feet and maybe three inches in thickness. Someone spoke from under the pack, went back down on hands and knees and immediately disappeared into the hole. Gerald was across the space, seeming very agile for a man of his size. From the glow of the Davy lamp hanging above, I saw him as he made it safely behind the pile of rocks on the other side of the hole.

It seemed an age, then Gerald's lamp flashed once in my direction.

"Help me! Come quickly, the whole place is going to cave in at any moment," I yelled so loud that I thought my lungs would burst. A head came out of the pack, it was the blacksmith, and he was starting to stand up when Gerald landed behind him, hitting him hard in the kidneys. Kurt went down as if he'd been pole axed. I yelled as Gerald bent down to grab him, but I was too late.

The pistol smashed into Gerald's ear as he landed on top of the blacksmith, equally unconscious, the big man astride him.

"Take one of the straps from the case, and tie him up, tie him well," the big man growled at the woman. Shortly after tying Gerald up, the woman came past me pushing the trolley nearer to the hole in the pack. Then the body of Sergeant Donald MacGregor was un-ceremoniously rolled from the vehicle and dragged out of sight into the pack.

There was a lot of grunting and groaning noises as the blacksmith managed to squeeze himself out from under the weight of Gerald's still un-conscious body. He stood bent double, his hand behind him holding his kidneys. Meanwhile the others had closed up the pack, whilst the woman came past me pushing the trolley.

She then returned, pushing the trolley with the case on the vehicle, and the packages were loaded into the case. As they passed me again for the third time, the blacksmith, who had joined the other two, gave me what I can only describe as an apologetic look as he went by.

Then, as the big man followed behind them, he paused as he came level with me. I froze as he raised his right arm holding the gun. I saw a bright flash, heard nothing, felt no pain, just nothing but fluffy blackness!

The Pit Bottom Later

At the pit bottom the engineers were finishing their work on the haulage engine. Apart from them, the area was deserted. Kurt the blacksmith came from behind the stables, unhooked the pony from the trolley, took off the shafts, then stood them alongside all the others, leading the pony through to his stall. Passing the sleeping Banksman, he returned to the bottom.

Then he took seven or eight packages that were sitting loose on top of the large packing case, placing them into a separate tub with 'Blacksmith' painted on the side. He threw some broken harnesses over the top to cover up any view of the items, additionally putting on the special fitted lid. Then he pushed each vehicle in turn around to the bottom of the shaft where he lifted up the barrier, first shoving the larger trolley into the cage, followed by the smaller tub, which only just fitted in there.

Once that was completed he phoned to the top, asking the Onsetter to give him enough time to get into the cage below, then signal the winding room for men riding, but stopping at the blacksmith's platform and not the upper level.

The cage took off and whisked up to the surface, he pushed the two vehicles out onto the rails, closed the gate, and then shouted above to the Onsetter that all was clear.

It was dark and still raining heavily; he saw by his watch it was 5:45 AM. He looked across at the large packing case sitting on the trolley, physically shuddering with revulsion.

He looked across the yard, there were people everywhere: strangers, men with dogs, police cars outside the offices. Some of the men were stopping every vehicle as they entered; the busy day shift was about to start, as colliers poured into the mine yard.

Kurt went over to the large packing case and looked around very carefully. After making sure he was unobserved, he whispered into the air vents around the top, and then pushed it around towards the coal hopper, behind the shaft where the large rail freight cars were loaded. Finally, he pushed the trolley and its cargo into the loading bay; he had just closed the big doors.

"Excuse me, do you mind if I have a word with you and take a look in that truck sir?" The man held out his credentials. Sergeant Cyril Smith, Special Investigation Branch. There's been someone reported missing, can you tell me where you've been for the last seven hours.

"Certainly, I haff been down ze mine all night." Smith looked down at the tub with the fitted lid and 'Blacksmith' daubed amateurishly across its side.

"Would you mind the lid," he said curtly.

"Ja be mine guest take a look for yourself," replied the German. The sergeant lifted the lid of the case, saw nothing but a pile of broken pieces of leather harness, thanked the man, and went to leave.

"Oh, for the record, what is your name and position here?" Sergeant Smith took down the details, then went back across the yard.

"Nothing there Captain. Just the blacksmith and he says he was down the mine all night, that's confirmed by the Onsetter. The truck was empty apart from some pony harnesses for repair; he's about ready to go home. We have his address, which agrees with Sergeant MacGregor's reports. He doesn't have a vehicle, lives a short walk up the lane in one of the coal board houses."

"Sergeant, the overriding factor still remains; he was a prime suspect on MacGregor's list. At the moment we can't ask him why, but we do know MacGregor is one of our top investigators, so get back out there and use your considerable powers of deduction to some advantage."

"I want our man found, and I want it like yesterday, is that clear?" Captain Hamilton glared at the man as he spoke.

"Yes sir, Captain, very clear," he replied curtly as he left the room. "Anything new Sarge?" asked another investigator who sat in the canteen next to the temporary incident room, enjoying a well-earned coffee.

"No, there's nothing new Corporal. I reckon the longer that you sit there on your fat ass drinking coffee, the less chance there is of your finding anything new; now move yourself and get on with the job!"

"Yes Sergeant."

"Come with me, Corporal, I want that blacksmith's shop searched thoroughly!" They searched the whole workshop. The small office area was tidy, nothing out of place, *so tidy, particularly for a busy workshop at a coal min,.* the Sergeant thought.

At the rear they opened two large doors which led out to an area overlooking large coal-filled railway freight trucks; parked in the area in front of them was a single, empty, dust-covered flat trolley.

Earlier during the night, they had found tire tracks matching those of Sergeant MacGregor's van; these were at the back of the mine property on the rough road that led to the freight yard. It ran alongside the railway track where the freight trucks were shunted up to the mine head. They were filled from the massive hopper, which was topped up continually on the day shift, as tubs were lifted and emptied into its enormous silo.

Back Underground

The continuous singing noise in my ears seemed to be coming from a motor; the pain from the side of my mouth and up to the side of my ear was unbearable. There was untold agony emanating from my right foot. Furthermore, I was hanging by the right arm that felt like it had come out of its socket, and to add to my misery, I was finding great difficulty breathing. My mouth felt as though it was full of blood, and I could feel with my tongue that my front teeth were splintered and broken.

Combine all that with the pain from my left arm, damaged the previous day, there were few parts of my anatomy left unimpaired.

As my mind began to clear, I looked around urgently for Gerald. Then I saw the glow from the Davy lamp still hanging from the girder, the flame giving off a blue aura. I knew only too well what this could mean.

There was also another source of light coming from the floor, this came from the cap lamp of Gerald who, I assumed, still lay there on the floor, remembering the heavy blow that he had taken.

Turning to the right, my right arm still held above my head by the tie bar, I tried to get onto my right knee, but the pain from the ankle was more than I could bear. Twisting the other way and pushing my head under my right arm pit, I managed to take the weight on my left knee, now pulling the bar with my left arm. I slid the handcuff over the free end as my right arm released, sheer agony at the shoulder, but numb from elbow to the fingers.

I fell onto my backside, trying to force the pain from my body; I rolled over face down trying to lift myself, but could not push my shoulders up, as the pain in my arms was too great. I collapsed face down into the stone dust; excess pain and the lack of air got the better of me.

I awoke with a bright light shining in my face; I could feel cold steel on my left cheek. My face had landed on the rail when I'd collapsed. If my face had landed into the thick stone dust, who knows?

"Come on Matt, you can do it, don't you die on me now." I recognized the voice of Gerald, his voice seemed to be echoing down a long hollow tunnel, and as I tried to answer him, my own voice sounded the same.

"Water, water, I need a drink of water," I heard my own voice sounding as though it were coming from a long way off. Through my blurred vision other lights were coming towards me, I felt myself being lifted up, as pain again seemed to shoot like electric shocks from all areas of my body.

"Get him up and out into the air," someone shouted.

"Did you say there was a body in here?" I recognized the voice of Ralph, my friend, the Overman.

"Yes, over there behind the stones at the side," replied Gerald, pointing to the pack.

"By the look of the flame on the Davy lamp we should all get out of here, until the gas can be cleared," Ralph added with some concern in his voice.

I was carried on a stretcher out into the main road, the smell of fresh air wafting over me was sheer heaven as it began to clear my lines of thinking. There were lights everywhere; I looked around me as I moved along on the stretcher.

"Gerald, Gerald, are you..."

"Don't worry, young Matt, this is me, carrying this end of the stretcher." I looked up, happy to see his face. He seemed relatively unharmed as they set me down on the stretcher by the side of the road. I heard the paddy train as its squeaky wheels pulled up right beside me and a group of men clambered off.

"Gerald Steel, Matt Harper?"

"I'm Gerald Steel, who are you?" asked Gerald.

"Captain Hamilton S.I.B." As they moved away and began talking, I managed with some difficulty to pull myself up by my left arm into a sitting position; then I was soon standing on my left leg. Reaching over, I hopped and dragged myself onto one of the wooden benches of the paddy train.

I heard the whir of an electric motor as they began to pump air into the old gate; one place I really had no desire to set eyes on ever again for as long as I lived.

"Yes, this is Matt Harper over here, on the stretcher Captain," added Gerald, going over to the empty first aid stretcher, and then quickly looking over to where I sat, he grinned.

"You're a stubborn tough young bugger, I've got to give you that," Gerald grinned, his white teeth and eyes contrasting the blackness of his face.

The S.I.B. and police went back into the tunnel. I sat enjoying the relative fresh air, as we headed to the pit bottom, the train rattling along.

I was sure that I was feeling the bumps more than most of the other passengers.

"Those bastard's got out you know," said Gerald punching the air with a look of sheer anger on his face.

"But we'll get 'em, young Matt, of that, you can be sure, I won't rest until that big piece of crap lies down at my feet."

I, more than most, knew that threat should be taken extremely seriously. In some respects I felt sorry for the German, but only ever so slightly!

After I had blacked out back there in the disused road, Gerald had regained consciousness, managed to get free and got out into the main road. He'd made his way back to the telephone I'd used earlier. With assistance he got through to the pit top, alerting the authorities and summoning help.

For the second time in as many days, I came up that shaft physically worse off than when I'd gone down it. After an hour or so in the ambulance room, where the dislocated shoulder was, as they nonchalantly said, '*popped back in'* (which sounded a lot less painful when described than in actuality) and my sprained right ankle was tightly strapped up. Gerald drove me home, where we both had a hot bath and some real food from Mary, who became quite tearful at first sight of me, until I reassured her I felt better than I looked.

Later we had to meet with the police and give statements. Over that splendid breakfast we had discussed our theories as to how they got out of the mine un-detected, and how they may have gotten the packages away from under the very noses of the law.

Apart from a few aches and pains fogging my thinking, I was absolutely certain that this affair was far from over. We still had the chance to have these people put where they belonged; in prison for a very long time or, perhaps, even on the gallows.

I knew for sure that Gerald wouldn't rest until they were apprehended or worse. Neither would the select group of the S. I. B. with a dead colleague to avenge.

We'd heard whilst sitting in the ambulance room that Kurt had cleared off.

He'd gone home as usual, packed his clothes and was driven off in a big black car a few minutes after getting home. Evidently the old lady he lived with told the police he seemed to be going against his will.

Chapter Twenty

The White's Mansion that Same Morning

David awoke feeling on top of the world, the best he'd felt for a very long time. Carl awoke in the hospital, apparently still not knowing who he was. Cheryl awoke wondering if she was doing the right thing. But Donald MacGregor would never wake up again!

David had been out of bed since six-thirty, a quick shower and shave, then he decided to walk around the estate for an hour. Such a long time since he'd appreciated just how magnificent the grounds were: the smell of the morning air was always a delight, birds singing in the trees above, the different noises of the farm animals, somewhere in the distance a tractor working in the fields.

Pausing to pat the nose of one of the horses standing at a fence with its magnificent head in the air, he too was sniffing the delightful fresh morning. As David took a walk into the stables, one of the stable hands looked up.

"Good morning, Master David, this is a pleasant surprise, to what do we owe the pleasure?" he asked. They exchanged pleasantries for a few minutes, and as he went to leave the building, the man said, "Did you here about the murder at the mine last night, Master David?"

"A murder at the mine, who?" he asked. The news came as a great shock. *A murder in the village of Casleton.* What next? The stable hand did not have any other information on the shocking news, other than it was rumored to be a policeman.

Walking back towards the house, he saw his father standing at the top of the stone steps in front of the open door, a newspaper in his hand.

"What got you out so early?" asked his father as David approached.

"I was just thinking how great life was, until I heard the terrible news."

"What news is that?" Once inside the house, they sat down to breakfast, David then passed on the news, both father and son looked at each other, obviously very concerned.

"Where did you here about this murder, David?" Harold asked.

"From one of the stable boys," he replied.

"Do you know who was killed?"

"The stable lad wasn't sure, but believes it was a policeman."

"Good God, not Constable Ellis?"

"I really don't know father, we can soon find out, why don't you call the station?" Harold walked toward the credenza, picked up the phone and dialed the number of the local police station.

"Constable Ellis, what a pleasure it is to hear your voice. No I am not being sarcastic, I just heard that a policeman has been killed at the mine, can you enlighten me on what happened?"

"Thank you, Constable, thank you very much."

"Evidently it's all a bit hush, hush. Apparently a Special Branch officer was shot last night at the mine, he can't give us any more information than that; also asks that we don't repeat this."

"On a much lighter note, it really is good to see you out on a morning, so much like old times, you even seem to be walking a lot better," Harold smiled as he put his nose into the newspaper.

"I lost my walking stick the other night, I don't have a replacement so I've just had to get along as best I could," David replied.

"I've an old one somewhere that belonged to your grandfather, shall I dig it out for you?"

"No, that won't be necessary father. I think that I can manage just fine." David smiled as he tucked into a huge plate of scrambled eggs and bacon.

"I've no doubt you will son, no doubt whatsoever," Harold added peering over the top of his half moon spectacles, nodding with satisfaction. He also had a strong feeling of relief knowing Matt Harper was safe, or at least not involved in any way in this killing, he misguidedly thought to himself.

"Shall we go to the mill together, Dad?" David asked as he moved his chair back to leave the table.

"No, you go on ahead; I have a few calls to make this morning. I might give the office a miss today and pop across to Leeds."

"O.K. Dad, who are you visiting in Leeds at such short notice. Not some new lady friend I don't know about?" asked David, in a semi-jocular manner.

"Take your inquisitive nose and push it into the pile of bills I put on your desk yesterday, find out why those materials have gone up in price so much, then we'll all have a more profitable day," replied Harold with a grin, tapping David affectionately on the shoulder with his rolled newspaper as he left.

A few minutes later when David got into his car, he couldn't help noticing the large bunch of flowers on the rear seat of his Dad's Rover. Maybe his little joke wasn't so far from the truth after all!

Bruce Bell's Office Later that Day in Leeds

"Well, Dad, what do you think for modern day technology?" Bruce pointed to the folder, left by the salesman from Kalamazoo.

"It all seems a bit complicated to me: move up five holes here, insert the carbon there, move over three columns here, I don't think I'll get the hang of this easily."

"Precisely, Dad. You're not going to have to think about it at all and for that matter, neither am I. There are three people downstairs waiting to be interviewed to do that job. The systems manufacturer has already trained them.

We need to see all three and decide who gets the job as our accounts manager; this will free us up so we can spend more time selling, and hopefully counting all the money we'll make," he added, as he led his father by the arm downstairs to begin the interviews.

"Good afternoon," a distinguished looking grey haired man said as he walked across the room towards Bruce, holding out his hand.

"Won't you come this way?" asked Bruce.

"Take a seat, will you," he added directing the grey haired man to a chair. Frank Bell looked up suddenly when Bruce asked the man for his name.

"Good lord. Harold White, what are you doing here, it's been a good couple of years since I saw you. How the hell are you, dear chap?"

"Bruce, you know who this is?" He looked over at his son.

"This is Harold, Harold White, the father of one of your old school chums, David."

"Oh, I'm so sorry Mr. White, we were about to start interviewing some applicants for a job, I thought you were one of them."

"Don't apologize, pleased to meet you," Harold smiled.

"Come on up to my office," Frank said." We have a lot to catch up on." He put his arm around Harold's shoulder as they went up the staircase together.

"OK, so tell me what really brings you to these parts, after all this time?"

"Actually, it's your son Bruce that I need to talk to, but we can catch up with all the news until he gets through his interviews."

"You have me intrigued Harold, but I won't press you, no doubt I'll find out all in good time." They spent about half an hour chatting, then Bruce came into the room.

"Sorry to intrude on you two, but the show has to go on, as they say. Dad, could I prevail on you to go meet the successful applicant, tell him a bit more about the company and how things are run, that sort of thing, I left him in my office."

"Oh, all right, that works out quite well, as it's you that Harold came to see, I'll be downstairs when you are finished." He sounded slightly peeved at not being included.

"Ok, Dad, I won't be too long," replied Bruce. The door of the office closed, and Bruce turned to Harold.

"What can I do for you, Mr. White?"

"I'm not sure where to start," replied Harold. He explained that there was a problem between David and Carl, that they weren't talking to each other and he didn't know why.

Now Carl was in hospital, rather badly hurt, apparently under mysterious circumstances. He said that when he'd challenged David for an explanation, David had said he didn't know what was wrong either.

"I'm on my way to visit Carl now, perhaps he'll talk to me and tell me whatever the problem is. David thought you might hold some of the answers, that there may be more to this situation than just an unfortunate accident with Carl. To add even more trouble to the Armitage family's problems, there was a death at the mine last night, someone was shot dead," Harold said gravely. Bruce immediately jumped to his feet, startled by the last comment, and very obviously concerned.

"Do you know who was killed?" he asked.

"No, I don't believe the police have released the person's identity yet," Harold replied.

"Why are you so concerned?" asked Harold.

"I'll tell you what I know so far: a friend of mine was doing some investigation at the mine last night, along with a young man working in the mine called Matt."

"Hold on there a minute, now you have me worried, too," Harold said to Bruce; at the mention of Matt's name, Harold went cold. *Matt couldn't possibly be involved with any of this,* he thought, *how could he?*

"All I can tell you is that the murdered man was a special branch Police Officer, although as I said they haven't released his name yet," said Harold.

"I was told that in the strictest confidence. Do you think that Carl is somehow mixed up in this business?"

"I'm not sure but it begins to look very much that way," Bruce replied. The ringing of the phone interrupted their conversation.

"You're alright then, Gerald?" Bruce spoke into the phone.

"What happened?" Bruce listened quietly without interruption, as Gerald brought him up-to-date on the events of the previous night.

"Good, then I'll see you later today when you've finished with the police. Did they get away?" after a long pause.

"Was this young lad Matt hurt?" another long pause.

"Give me that address again and I'll keep an eye on it; call me when you're leaving," Bruce added, and then he replaced the receiver.

"Well, it appears you were right about a murder, but the killers got away. My man there received a bang on the head, and the young man Matt, who you seemed mighty concerned about, was hurt but not too bad." Bruce got up from his chair, walked across and held the door open.

"I'm sorry, I hope you'll excuse me, I have to make an urgent call, then I have to leave right away. I would visit Carl if I were you, as you may know he's suffering from amnesia, and any face from the past could jog his memory. Please don't think me rude but I just have to leave now." Bruce shook hands with Harold, and then saw him out the door.

After making a quick call, Bruce also left in a big hurry. Gerald had asked him to put some surveillance on the big German's house.

The Coal Mine Castleton

After almost two hours back at the coalmine offices, the police questioned Gerald and me extensively. Because the incident was now officially murder, they had involved the regional crime squad. Later we also met and were questioned by a member of MI5. We had given them every detail of the events of last night but not a full account leading up to those events.

Of course we had to explain Gerald's presence at the scene, which made it necessary to bring Carl into the picture; though regrettable, it was unavoidable at this stage. At the end of the boring repetitive rounds of questions, I was told in no uncertain terms to stop playing detective and get on with my work-studies.

As the interview progressed, Gerald and I were seen individually; towards the end, we were both sat down in front of a Chief Superintendent, alongside the man from MI5

"I want to make myself abundantly clear to both of you, that's why I'm taking this unusual step of closing this round of interviews with you both together," said the Superintendent.

"First and foremost, you've both interfered with a very important on-going police investigation. Whether by accident or intent, is neither here nor there at this point.

Any further interference will result in your arrest on a charge of obstruction, and maybe even complicity. As this matter is of national importance and involves both war crimes and war criminals, it will be necessary for you both to be sworn under the Government Official Secret's Act not to repeat any matter involved this case.

"Contravention of this will mean a very long time in His Majesty's prison on charges of treason. Do I make myself quite clear? Are you starting to get my point?"

"Now as for you Mr. Steele, you left a distinguished police career behind you. If you desire to pursue your significant investigative talents, perhaps you may wish to re-apply; we can always use men of your caliber and experience. Otherwise leave things to the professionals!"

Then he turned glaring at me.

"Harper, I'm still not clear as to the motivation behind your involvement in these matters. If you wish to become a detective, then either apply for a license or fill out a police application form. My advice to you at present is to continue your academic career as planned."

"To both of you, keep out of matters that don't concern you; if you choose to ignore this warning then I will land on you with all of the power of the law behind me. My colleague here, similarly, but with all the might of His Majesty's Government," he gestured towards the man from MI5.

With that parting threat hanging in the air, he got up and walked out of the room. As he reached the door he turned again.

"One other thing, if any information regarding this case should come into your possession, it's your duty to report it to me." *There goes that phrase again,* I thought.

After he left, the government agent remained seated, then as we stood to leave he said, "Sit down a moment gentlemen please. Although this isn't openly acknowledged, the government isn't quite so hard and fast on its rules in a time of crisis, as the Superintendent would like you to believe."

"I want to talk to you further on this matter, also about your possible continued involvement in this case."

"This is not the place to talk further, added to which, I'm sure that you've both seen quite enough of coal mine surroundings for quite some time to come."

The agent pushed back his chair and stood. "Gentlemen, if you're interested in continued involvement in this matter, meet me in twenty minutes at the Bay Horse Inn, up on the main Leeds Bradford road. If you don't show, I'll take it that you decided against the idea. Talk it over!" He walked straight out of the room without turning.

Gerald and I got up and left, both interested in his offer, but wondering what the hell MI5 could possibly want from us.

Minutes later we climbed into Gerald's car and headed directly for the Bay Horse Inn. Curiosity had got the better of us as we pulled into the parking lot.

Chapter Twenty-One

Harold White was driving into the busy grounds of the Infirmary at Leeds. After parking his car, he made his way into the busy waiting area, walked up to the reception desk, a big bouquet of flowers in his arms.

"Would you kindly direct me to one of your patients, a Mr. Carl Armitage?" he asked, smiling at the pretty receptionist.

"Just a moment sir, please. Leeds Infirmary, may I help you?" she answered the phone.

"Putting you through," she put the receiver down.

"Sorry about that sir, now, who did you say you were looking for?"

"Carl Armitage."

"Armitage, Armitage," she ran her finger down a long list of names.

"Ah yes, here he is in a private room, room 403, on the fourth floor."

He thanked the girl and went off in the direction of the elevators. The receptionist called after him:

"Excuse me sir, excuse me!" Harold turned to see the receptionist beckoning him so he walked back towards her.

"Sorry sir, but the patient was released about a half hour ago, he was returned to his home."

"Mr. White, what brings you here?" Harold turned to see Cheryl standing there.

"Why Cheryl, how nice to see you, I came to see Carl, evidently I've just missed him."

"Yes, he left with Mum and Dad a few minutes earlier, I'm just collecting his few personal effects, how nice of you to take the time to visit Carl."

"I should really have called first," said Harold.

"Here are the things that you required, Doctor Armitage," a white- coated male said, passing a large brown envelope across to Cheryl.

"Have you had lunch yet?" asked Harold.

"No, I really haven't had the time to stop so far today."

"Fine, that settles it then, we shall have lunch together right away, I won't take no for an answer. Oh, you'd better have these," he added, handing her the flowers, then taking her arm.

"Come, we've lot's to talk about," said Harold as they left the hospital building.

Meanwhile, Gerald and I had been sitting in the Bay Horse Inn for about ten minutes thinking that maybe the man had changed his mind, when he walked into the bar.

"What can I get you chaps," he asked. He seemed quite a pleasant man, about the same age as Gerald. In those days I'd some difficulty in assessing the ages of people. I've since learned that, as one becomes a little older oneself, guessing ages becomes easier. As requested, he brought back a pint of bitter for Gerald and a half of mild for yours truly.

"I don't know about you chaps, but I'm damn near starving." He went back to the bar, spoke to the bartender, then returned carrying a glass of what looked like whiskey.

"Now let's get down to brass tacks," he said.

"My name is John Cotes, as you know I'm a special agent with MI5." He went on, "I sat listening to most of what went on this morning, unlike the police I deal in results and not threats. In my profession, without the help of people like you we would get nowhere. Whatever your motivation," he said looking pointedly at me.

"I need to be told what you know and I would like to achieve that without too many problems."

"As we all know, the police got a new murder on their hands today, but I've been on the tracks of these people for some years now." He paused as a lady came over carrying a large plate brim full of freshly made sandwich-es.

"Here you are, gents. An assortment of roast beef, ham, cheese and chicken," she said, placing them down in the center of the table.

"There's more if you need them, mustard anyone?"

"Come on dig into these sandwiches," the agent said.

"I think that we can work together on this. For whatever reasons, you both seem to want these killers brought to justice. Believe me, so do the powers that be in Whitehall."

"I can't be held responsible for the outcome of your disobeying the police, if you should run foul of the law again; I'd have to plead complete ignorance. Therefore I will not give you as my source of any information to anyone. In return I agree to give you what information we possess."

"How do we know that you'll tell us everything?" said Gerald.

"You don't, in the same way that I won't know whether you are telling everything to me." He paused to bite another sandwich.

"What do you think, Matt?" asked Gerald.

"It sounds like a good idea to me," I said.

"What do we have to lose?"

"Do we have a deal then?" asked John Cotes.

"Looks that way," replied Gerald.

The sandwiches by now were all gone; they tasted quite delicious.

"Let's have another round of drinks to seal our agreement. I'd like to meet you both in Leeds tomorrow, first thing in the morning. Here is the address of the office that I'm using temporarily," he gave us both a card.

"See you both at Eight AM, prompt," he said as he left the pub.

I was tired and hurting when Gerald dropped me off at home.

"See you tomorrow," he said. As I opened the front door, Titch was there to greet me, wagging his tail as usual. Dad was home for once, he listened to my tale about the goings on at the mine, told me to keep out of trouble and not to come home like I've just been in world war three. I promised, we had an early dinner, then I crashed for the night.

The Carlton Hotel, Leeds

The headwaiter led Harold and Cheryl to the table.

"Your usual spot, Mr. White?" He held back the chair for Cheryl, unfurled the crisp linen napkins placing them on each lap.

"May I get you something to drink?" Harold looked across to Cheryl.

"I'd love a glass of sherry," she said, "Make that two, please," Harold added.

"Will that be dry sherry, sir?" They nodded in unison.

"What a pleasant surprise to see you today, I've been hoping to bump into you," Harold said with a genuine smile on his face.

Cheryl was sure that she knew what the topic of conversation would be between her and Harold so she had already prepared herself for the event.

"I've been meaning to have a word with you, Mr. White."

"Please, call me Harold, I really would prefer it that way Cheryl. Makes me feel so old the other way," he said. The expression on Harold's face then changed drastically.

"Cheryl, I've never been a man to beat about the bush, so here goes straight from the shoulder." *Here it comes,* she thought.

"Cheryl, do you know why Carl continued to refuse to speak to David for such a long time? I appreciate that he's ill at the moment and I pray that he will soon return to his normal self and continue to enjoy good health. But this question has nagged at me for some long time now. I'm sure you must be aware of the effect his behavior has had on David."

Cheryl was completely taken aback by the subject, she had anticipated questions about her relationship with David, she was not prepared for this, and her reaction must have shown on her face.

"Is something the matter, my dear?" Harold reached across placing his hand on the back of hers.

"No, Harold, nothing at all, I'm fine, just fine," said Cheryl.

The waiter arrived to take their orders for food, this *gives me some time to come up with an answer* she thought. They both chose a mixed salad, followed by a Dover sole. Harold selected a nice light Chablis, then looked across at Cheryl, waiting for her answer. As the waiter left she looked across to Harold.

"David asked me the same question only yesterday, my answer to you is the same. I have a rough idea, but I'm not sure. I don't have all of the answers. I feel it could be as simple as this. Carl was always the leader between the two of them, when it came to physical activities: athletics, rugby, swimming, school fights, arm wrestling, chasing the girls, you name it, he was always up front.

But David carried out most of the planning and thinking; he definitely was the one with the brains. Carl's name may have appeared on most every trophy the school possessed, but as you know he rarely excelled in academia. He did concern himself about this but David would reassure him that he should not expect to be good at everything, and be satisfied to be such a born athlete.

He always built up Carl's ego, and never made him feel lacking in any direction. In short Harold, David was Carl's mentor; without him, Carl was lost. I don't know whether you can remember back to the time when David went to hospital with scarlet fever."

"Yes, I do, David was quite ill," Harold said. Cheryl nodded her head, continuing.

"Carl was in at least six fights during that time, as a result he lost his place in the school rugby team, and did so badly in class that he spent most of his free time carrying out extra studies forced on him by unhappy teachers. Again, without David, Carl was adrift."

The meal arrived at the table; Harold had already tasted the wine whilst Cheryl had been talking, he held up his glass, as she did the same.

"Here's to seeing these two dear young men back together," he said as he touched his glass against Cheryl's.

"I'll drink to that any day, it's one of the dearest wishes of my life," said Cheryl. There was little more talking as they ate their food in comparative silence. Later sipping her coffee, Cheryl went on to say:

"When the war came upon us, that was really the beginning of the end for Carl. It was a great blow to his ego, not to be allowed to enlist because of his deferred occupation working in the mine, and he felt less of a man having to stay at home. Then he sees David, his friend and mentor enter the forces, shortly to be followed by his own sister.

These events were more than he could handle, he felt belittled, and then to see David so highly decorated was almost more than he could take. He knew he would have been right in there too. Cheryl continued:

"His feelings of inadequacy and loss turned into envy, then to hatred. In the meantime, he took to drink in a big way, worrying Mum and Dad half to death. According to Dad, he spends most of his time at a gambling club in Leeds. It appears that he was coming home in the early hours of the morning on many occasions; our parents were staying awake, listening for his return. When they asked him what he was playing, his answers were close to being rude and abusive.

Father believes that he's got himself into a situation that he can't possibly handle involving gambling debts. Evidently, he left some personal stuff around that brought Dad to this conclusion.

His refusal to speak wasn't just confined to David. I was included as well; he's made life quite miserable for me too, you know. It appears that one of their old school pals, Bruce Bell, met Carl and accompanied him to this club in Leeds.

Whatever happened there that night made Bruce suspicious that something wasn't right. Shortly after, Carl was hurt. Since then Bruce and a friend have been trying to obtain any information at all, they are convinced what happened to Carl was no accident."

"Well, my dear, what you've told me answers a lot of questions," Harold said gently.

"All we can do now is pray that Carl regains his memory soon, then maybe he will answer the remainder of the questions himself. We'll just have to wait and see." Harold signed the bill.

"Is your car back at the hospital?" he asked. Cheryl nodded her head.

Later, Cheryl drove home, still wondering why no mention was made about her relationship with David.

Meanwhile, after Gerald had dropped me home, he headed back to Leeds; his head was throbbing badly now, the effect of the pain killers given to him had long since worn off. As he touched the side of his head he thought about the man who'd hit him, and a strong feeling of anger consumed his whole thought process.

Driving through the market, Gerald ignored a friendly wave from a stallholder and finally he parked his car behind the office. Noting that Bruce's car was not in its usual parking spot, he went into the office.

"Hello there, Gerald," said Frank Bell.

"Looking for Bruce?"

"Yes, Frank. Have any idea where he might be?"

"Not the faintest, he went off in a hurry a couple of hours ago. I've collected a whole list of phone messages for him whilst he's been gone."

"Anything I can handle?" Gerald asked.

"I don't think so, but maybe you should take a look to be sure." Gerald went through the list, all seemed to be normal run of the mill stuff, with one exception.

"What's this one here, Frank?" asked Gerald, passing the note to Frank. "Er...oh yes, it was one of those men who've collected bad debts for us in the past, you know the big bald one."

"Yes, Frank, but what's this note about: Tell Bruce to come quickly, I think I've found what he's looking for," Gerald asked.

"Didn't the bald guy say any more, maybe where he was calling from?"

"No, his coins ran out as he was talking and the phone went dead," Frank replied with a resigned shrug of his shoulders.

Gerald went out of the office; he knew that the bald man had been watching the house where the Germans had stayed. He climbed into his car and took off as fast as the traffic would permit.

After driving for ten minutes or so, he parked on a side street and locked the car. Looking round carefully to make sure he wasn't followed, he walked two streets, went into a corner shop and purchased some aspirin, then he looked out of the shop window, double-checking for a tail.

The coast seemed clear, so he walked a further two streets, turning into the same street where he had earlier sat in his car, disguised as the old man.

As he walked along, he noticed Bruce's car parked by the sidewalk; he tried the driver's door, which was unlocked.

That's strange, very unlike Bruce, he thought to himself. *The phone message from the bald guy must have been the second one,* Gerald thought as he saw the scribbled address on the front seat. He assumed that another of Bruce's men had also alerted him to come to this place. *Where is he now*, Gerald asked himself.

He decided to go back to his car and move it near to Bruce's. Once he'd done that, he sat in the car and opened the bottle of aspirin and swallowed three tablets in an attempt to kill the fierce headache. Welcoming the chance to sit quietly and collect his thoughts, he began to feel the effects of a night without sleep and the additional trauma. After a couple of minutes or so, he checked through the car mirrors, everything looked fine.

He left the car and then went to the end of the street walking quickly around to the rear of the houses. He reached the spot where he had seen the German drive off earlier, spotting a garage at the rear of the garden.

The building was made of asbestos panels, with a piece broken out of one of the panels, just about eye level.

A target had been drawn around the hole in chalk by the local kids.

He looked through the hole and to his utter and absolute surprise, he saw the big black Austin inside. There seemed to be no lock on the door, it was held shut by a brick pushed against the bottom. He kicked the brick to one side, and then pulled one of the doors open as it scraped along the ground making far too much noise for his liking.

Reaching behind, he pulled the door closed, then peered into the rear of the car. There in the back, stacked from the floor up, were some of the oilskin-covered parcels from the mine.

He went to the rear of the car and turned the handle of the trunk, only to find that it was securely locked. He looked around the garage for something that would open the trunk lid. The place was purely a shelter, possessing no tools of any shape or form. He went outside and began to search along the fencing he found an old broken part of a stroller, pulled off a piece of the handle, and then went back inside.

He wedged the make-do gemmy under the trunk lid. As he pressed down, it broke in half with a loud crack, at the same time the trunk popped open, revealing yet more oilskin parcels.

One of the smaller parcels caught his attention. He'd guessed it to be about the size of a shoe box, and there were about a half dozen more this size. The weight of the parcel was incredible, he wasn't prepared for it, it was so heavy that it fell right back into the trunk with a thud.

He raised it again, more prepared for the effort. Holding it in his hands, he assessed its weight at around thirty/forty pounds, maybe even more. Gerald placed the package on the floor and closed the trunk. Then he carried it outside, pushing the door closed with his foot and kicking the brick back into place. He then went back to Bruce's car, putting the parcel onto the floor in the rear.

Finally he returned checking that he wasn't followed, the coast was clear.

The backyard of the house was badly overgrown with weeds and shrubs, which of course made an unseen approach that much easier. Gerald skirted round the hedge, coming up to the rear of the building.

As he got closer he noticed the house had a basement, with stone stairs leading down, slippery green moss covered the steps. He went down to the ground as a light came on from below; moving carefully down the treacherous surface of the stairs, he reached the bottom.

A solid old door faced him at the bottom, with a window to the side at waist height, so dirty that it was virtually opaque.

Behind the door he heard voices. Gerald couldn't hear what was being said; he pressed his ear hard against the musty smelling surface of the door, but this was no help either.

He decided to go back up the stairs and around the side of the house, where he spotted a small window with a broken pain of glass. With care, he got his hand through the broken pane and undid the catch. The window was old, it had not been opened for a long time, but eventually it gave way under his pressure. A loose piece of glass fell down, luckily landing on the outside in the long grass without too much noise.

The window was just large enough for Gerald to squeeze through; it led into a small walled-off area. There was an old disused sink under the window, into which he climbed, and then he slid to the floor. He cracked a door open and could see through into a larger area, the staircase from upstairs partially blocking his view.

Opening the door he crept into the room and saw Bruce sitting on a low chair, his hands behind his back threaded through the back supports, then handcuffed together. A medical bandage had been used as a gag on his mouth; blood was running down his face, his ankles were tied to the legs of the chair.

As Gerald got closer, he saw that the only other person in the room was a little man wearing thick spectacles; he recognized him from the mine the night before. His back was turned to the doorway; he was muttering something at Bruce in German.

Gerald hit the man behind the neck with such a forceful blow that his spectacles shot off his face and flew clear across the room, there was a loud clatter as a gun fell to the concrete floor. Gerald looked across at Bruce and couldn't understand the look of despair and terror on his face. He bent down to pick up the gun, when a voice said:

"Leave that right where it is! Well, well! If it isn't the tough, beer- throwing friend from the club and the coal mine. I should have put an end to you down there," the German said. Gerald bent to get the gun as the German was speaking. The big man kicked him in the groin, Gerald went down on one knee, white from pain and temper. He grunted:

"You Bastard," he attempted to stand.

"Don't try anything stupid, you know that I'll use this gun at the slightest provocation."

The little man was groping around blindly on the floor for his spectacles.

"When you've finished making a total fool of yourself groveling around on the floor, go and get something to tie up this interfering lout, will you." He sneered at the little man speaking in German. The man was rubbing the back of his neck not looking exactly in the game yet, as he dragged the wire spectacles over his ears and staggered from the room.

"You never seem to know when you've had enough, do you my interfering friend?" the big man said to Gerald.

"I'd like to see how tough you are without that thing in your hand," Gerald replied, pointing at the gun.

"I really wish I had the time to show you, now put your hand down unless you are feeling extremely lucky," the big man ordered. Bruce saw the hate in Gerald's eyes; he'd seen him furious before, but nothing like he was at that moment.

The little man returned with a piece of thin rope about two feet long, the big man shouted something in German, the door opened and the woman walked into the room.

"Helga, tie this man up will you," he said in English. As the woman came across to Gerald, she went behind him pulling his hands together, then Bruce began to move his head frantically from side to side.

The diversion was sufficient as the big man took his eyes from Gerald for a split second, in which time Gerald pulled his hands free and lunged for the gun. The big German lost his balance as he leaned back to avoid the attack.

Gerald's arm caught the side of the pistol, which fell from the German's grasp, clattering to the ground. At the same time reaching for the throat of the now unarmed man, Gerald pushed upwards; he felt the muscles tighten in the man's neck, as his left hand began to secure its grip. One more step and he would take the German's head clean off his shoulders with his right hand.

In the confines of the cellar below ground, the sudden gun shot was deafening as it echoed round the small room; a burning pain went through Gerald's calf, removing all ideas he may have had, as he fell to the cold concrete floor, grasping his leg, blood oozing through the material of his trousers.

The little man with the thick glasses stood holding the gun, a look of surprised horror on his face as a thin wisp of smoke floated from the barrel of the gun. The big man took the Lugar from him.

"You can't even shoot straight," he snarled as the man began to shake violently.

"But I suppose that you did save me a lot of trouble," he added, looking down at Gerald as the woman tied his hands behind his back.

"Now roll him over and tie his legs to his arms, we have to get moving, it's time to go. Make sure you tie him tighter than you did down the mine." They left the room. Gerald was hog-tied and gagged on the floor, Bruce securely tied to the chair, Gerald's blood slowly staining the floor of the damp dark room.

Chapter Twenty-Two

The Following Morning, Leeds City

I'd decided to go to Leeds by train for my meeting with the agent, which meant I had to walk down to the railway station; it seemed the less agonizing of the two available options. Riding the bike up to West Casleton and catching the bus was completely out of the question.

The walk was slow and painful; I used an old walking stick which had been around the house for years, maybe generations. Last night, I'd gone to sleep as soon as my head hit the pillow, but woke after a couple of hours as a result of the pain and also the turmoil in my mind.

Going over the previous day's events, I wondered how we would ever find the Germans now. I reflected on how this mystery had thickened since that first night which seemed light years ago.

What had started out as a childish schoolboy affair was turning very ugly and nasty. A man had been killed, but for what? What was so valuable that the Germans would kill for it? Then to toss the body into a hole down a mine as though it was just a piece of garbage didn't even bear thinking about.

As the train came to a halt at Leeds Central station, I stayed in my seat, letting the usual mad rush for the exit pass; eventually I climbed onto the platform and casually glanced at a line of mail trolleys. Immediately my mind went back to the day when I had lost my Mum in the crowds.

I wondered if the same ticket collector was still here. Making my way slowly towards the ticket barrier, I noticed the collector, this time a woman; she gave me a big smile.

"My, my, we have been in the wars."

"Does the other feller look as bad as you?" she laughed as she punched a rectangular hole in my ticket.

I must have looked a bit of a wreck: stitches, lots of bruises still on my face, broken teeth, walking with a bad limp to the right leg, using a walking stick, and still tending to hold my left arm to my chest, in that position the bruising was less painful.

Fishing into my pocket with my right hand I found the card given to me by John Cotes. I wanted to check the address before leaving the station. Outside in City Square, the traffic had come to a complete standstill, the statue of the Black Prince, still viewing the confused masses from astride his horse, his head still adorned with pigeon droppings.

I made my way towards Queens Square; it was now seven forty-five. I popped into a corner café, grabbing a newspaper from a street vendor as I went. Armed with a cup of tea and a toasted teacake with lots of real butter, I found an empty table where I carefully lowered my aching carcass.

Searching through the paper, I couldn't find any mention of the murder. I wondered why, *that information would be all over the village by now, so how come it's not in the paper*? Finishing my breakfast I hobbled off to my meeting.

The offices were easy enough to find. John was already sitting at a desk. There was nobody else in the office, no name on the door, only space for one office desk; it looked very temporary and unused.

"Good morning, Matt, how are you feeling? Hope the night's sleep has helped ease some of the aches and pains. Seen Gerald on your way up?"

"No, but to be honest I wasn't really looking," I replied.

"Have a look at some of these photos while we wait for Gerald; let's see if you recognize any of these people." He passed me three large photo albums. I began to look through the array of faces, half an hour passed, still no sign of Gerald.

I had picked out from the photos the big German, a much younger looking blacksmith, and the woman Helga, along with one other face who'd been at the village during the war, as a prisoner, working either on the roads or the farm, I couldn't quite recall which.

"I wonder why your friend Gerald isn't here," John said looking pensively at his watch.

"He doesn't strike me as the sort of guy who would be late for a meeting, without a good reason," I replied.

"Do you have a number for him?" asked the agent.

"No, I don't but surely we can find it easily enough, do you have the local phone book?" He already had the book in his hand.

"Let's see, Frank Bell and Son Ltd. isn't it?" he said with a smile, letting me know that he'd done his homework.

"Here it is," he passed the thick book across to me, his index finger on the number. "I think it will be better if you make the call," he added. "The least number of people that associate either of you with me the better."

The phone only rang twice before it was answered by a gruff voice.

"Is Bruce there?" I asked.

"No I am afraid he's out. Who's calling? Do you want the order department?"

"No thanks," I replied. "Is Gerald Steele around?"

"I haven't seen him this morning either," answered the gruff voice.

"Hang on a minute will you," there was a pause of a couple of minutes, during which I updated John.

"Hello, Frank Bell speaking." I explained who I was, that I was meant to meet Gerald an hour ago. Mr. Bell then said that he was slightly worried, because neither of them had shown up for work and that was very unusual, without phoning in to let him know. He wasn't quite sure what to do.

"Don't do anything. A friend and I will be there right away Mr. Bell, and don't worry," hoping my overt display of confidence had done the trick.

Across the Other Side of the City

Bruce had pulled and twisted all night in an effort to break the backrest of the chair, his wrists felt as though all the skin was torn off, the thing just wouldn't budge. *There comes a time when good workmanship is not such a good thing,* he thought as he continued to strain and pull. He gave one last big wrench, felt the chair wobble, then he fell over sideways, his face hitting the damp floor with a slap.

It was pitch dark in the cellar; he'd lost all sense of time, occasionally he would hear heavy breathing coming from Gerald's direction. The frustration of not being able to see or talk had become over- whelming. Worried about the gunshot wound, he knew only too well how quickly the presence of lead could very easily turn to poison in such a wound.

If only he could get his hands free, *these animals are going to get away scot free. If not,* he thought, w*hat a state to be in, so absolutely helpless*. He thought he heard movement upstairs, then he heard the noise again, it was the sound of the postman pushing mail through the letter box; he recognized the click as the spring-loaded flap closed.

He continued to strain at the chair, when, crack, the wood suddenly gave way, splitting under the pressure. One more strut to go before he could free his arms, but now he had more moving space, so he wrenched and pulled with renewed vigor, then the second obstacle broke away.

He still had problems as his ankles were fastened to the chair legs, his hands still securely tied behind his back, so he decided to roll onto his side and shuffle backwards in Gerald's direction.

Gerald lay on his side, his back towards Bruce, just then he felt a hand moving along his own bound wrists as his friend began to undo his bonds.

Meanwhile across the other side of town, John made short work of the drive from the City Center to the market. He seemed very knowledgeable with the back streets of Leeds for a man from out of town.

"Good morning, Mr. Bell, please?" I asked a cordial looking man sitting behind a desk in the upstairs office.

"Yes, you must be Matt, do come in, you didn't waste any time in getting here," he said gesturing towards two chairs. "This is a friend of mine, John Cotes." We all shook hands, then got down to the matter in hand.

When Bruce's father had gone over his story, John asked for permission to see his son's office. It was a pleasure to see a professional at work; within ten minutes he had covered every area, not a stone was left unturned. Frank Bell watched with interest as John did his job; eventually he held up the large desk blotter to the light at the window, and said:

"Where did your son sit when he took his phone messages?"

"Right at that desk there," replied Mr. Bell. "No, wait a minute; yesterday he sat talking to Harold White, a friend of mine, then he was sitting at my desk, in my office."

My ears shot up at the mention of Harold's name; I wondered what he was doing here in Leeds yesterday.

John went to the next-door office, the desk was immaculate, no scraps of paper or any scribbled notes. He picked up the blotter again, holding it to the light as before.

"Got a soft-leaded pencil there Mr. Bell?" he asked. Frank Bell took a pencil from the top pocket of his jacket, passing it to John, who proceeded to shade over the imprint in a corner of the soft white blotting paper.

"Does this address mean anything to you?" John asked Frank Bell; the writing was now clearly legible on the blotter.

"Doesn't mean a thing to me, but I know where it is."

"How far is it from here?" asked John.

"About ten minutes to a quarter of an hour by car," replied Frank Bell.

We left for the address found on the blotter. John Cotes asked Mr. Bell not to contact anybody until he'd heard from us.

We arrived in the street of the address. It actually took twenty minutes, the traffic had been unbelievable: we parked two streets away. As we walked along together, John said:

"Keep walking, don't turn around, I think we're being followed," he peeled off and across the other side of the street.

I continued on, about a third of the way along, and then stopped dead in my tracks. I was fairly sure that the car I had stopped next to was Gerald's. Bending down, I pretended to adjust my shoelace, looking and recognizing the unmistakable grey black mud caked around its tires. Then straightening up I continued to the end of the street, where I saw John leaning against the wall.

"I must have been imagining things, there was nobody behind, but it's always best to double check," he said in a matter-of-fact resigned way.

I took him back and showed him Gerald's car; he went to a pocket notebook, looking through the pages.

"Yep, that's Gerald car," he said.

"How can you be so sure?" I asked.

"Simple, I have the tag number, what did you think, that I was a clairvoyant?"

We found the house that matched the address and also came upon Bruce's car, which was unlocked. I looked in the car and noticed the package on the floor as being from the mine, but chose to keep that snippet of information to myself for the time being.

We approached the house from the rear, there was some kind of garage at the back, its doors wide open, empty, except for a broken stroller handle and a fresh patch of oil on the earthen floor.

The back yard was more like a jungle than a garden. We stood for a good two minutes, behind a bush, looking for any sign of movement from within the house, but saw none.

"Ok, here's what we do," said John. "We must work on the premise that these Germans are maybe still in the house, they know your face, and not mine so I'm going to knock on the front door. As I do, I want you to simultaneously get through the back entrance. I'll come with you first to find the best entry point. Follow me," he said, moving off into the back garden.

We peered down a miserable dank stairway that looked as though it had been unused for centuries. Moving to the side of the house, manor from heaven, we found an open window, its glass broken. John Cotes indicated I had two minutes, then disappeared.

I'd left my walking stick in the car which I now regretted. Though the window was only waist high, it wasn't going to be easy for me to climb up in my current state and get through the orifice. As the two minutes were now up, I swung my good leg onto the windowsill, pulling myself up with great difficulty. I slipped and then ended up sitting astride the windowsill, one leg outside, one in a sink on the inside, eyes watering. Needless to say which part of my anatomy took the brunt!

As I clambered through the restrictive space, I heard a rending crash from upstairs. I stood perfectly still against the wall holding my breath. After what seemed an age, I ventured through the door and could see an open staircase as I crossed the cellar. I neared the stairs, my heart almost came into my mouth as a hand touched my shoulder, another clamped over my mouth: "Shh, it's me." I assumed the whispered voice was John's. We stood for a second or two, and then heard a movement across the room, which was suddenly bathed in light as John found the light switch.

The sight that met our eyes was not a happy one, both Bruce and Gerald lay on the concrete floor, Bruce tied to a broken chair and my pal Gerald half hog-tied, lying in a pool of blood. Both had been bound and gagged, Gerald looked particularly pale.

Quickly as I could, I untied Gerald's bonds and then took the gag from around his face; he started to breathe in great gulps of air. I heard Bruce doing the same as John untied him, then he said:

"Those bastards shot Gerald in the leg, is he alright?"

"Take it easy, man," John replied. "Everything is going to be alright, by the way, I'm John Cotes MI5, this is Matt Harper, a friend of Gerald, and I suspect about to be a friend of yours, too."

John went over to Gerald, pulled out a knife from somewhere, and cut up the side of the blood-soaked pants, in that dim light the leg really looked quite a gory mess.

"Let's try and get these two upstairs," said John.

"I can manage alright on my own," said Bruce.

"Me too," growled Gerald, speaking for the first time since we'd found them.

Upstairs the house was deserted; we found hot water and cleaned up Gerald's wound. John said that the bullet had gone straight through the fleshy part of the calf, causing no bone damage.

He then poured a little whiskey from a hip flask over the wound, causing Gerald to squirm. Also, we'd found an open box of bandages which the Germans had used to silence the two, along with some antiseptic in the bathroom, so I cleaned and bandaged up the leg.

"Should heal as good as new," said John.

"Thanks doctor," Gerald almost grunted sarcastically, with a nod of his head.

"We're both pleased to see you two," Bruce added, looking across at me. "You must be the young man from the old school," he continued while John cleaned up the back of his head.

"You could use a couple of stitches here," John muttered as he dabbed carefully at the semi-congealed blood patches. "If we're to catch these scum, we don't have time for such luxuries," came a very curt reply.

I'd found some coffee in the kitchen, had got the pot going, and John poured them both a stiff whiskey each from his hip flask.

"Ok, so tell us what happened, and take your time," said John.

"Matt, if there's a phone in here, call Mr. Bell, stop him worrying. Put his mind to rest. Tell him everything is just fine."

"Will do, John," I replied. After he'd debriefed them both, we all sat down together to work on a game plan for the final tracking down of the Germans.

"You really ought go to go to the hospital with that wound Gerald," said John.

"The only problem is that all hospitals must report gunshot wounds automatically. I'm sure you don't need to be reminded about your meeting with the chief superintendent, so you'll need to keep a very close eye on the wound. First sign of any infection, you know the answer!" the agent said, tapping his hand on Gerald's shoulder.

"I'll live," was the curt reply.

Chapter Twenty-Three

The Armitage Residence Later that Morning

Carl's mother walked into the room; her son sat staring out of the window as he had done ever since he came home yesterday. Nothing in the house seemed to have jolted his memory back into action; he appeared oblivious to everything around him.

He turned to his mother.

"I think I'd like to go outside and take a walk," he said in a more assertive tone than she'd heard since his injury. He walked along the hallway to the cloakroom where coats and footwear were kept and he put on his favorite jacket. Astonished, Eve watched him as he put on a tweed flat cap, adjusted it in the hall mirror, then went out the door. He hadn't gone for a walk in years. He stopped outside, looked into the garage, then walked off across the fields towards the village. As Eve turned to go into the sitting room, she saw Cheryl standing at the top of the stairs.

"Did you see that?"

"Yes, I did," Cheryl replied.

"What do you make of that, then?" her mother asked.

"Not sure but it seems a little odd to me. Has he given any indications that his memory may be returning?"

"Nothing that meant anything to me," Eve sighed resignedly as she spoke.

They went into the sitting room where George Armitage sat reading the newspaper; he looked up as they walked in.

"Well ladies, anything new to report on the invalid's recovery?"

"I believe he's starting to recall a little, like knowing his way to the village without asking the directions; also he knew where the coats were kept," Cheryl said to her father as she described what had just happened.

"Which way did he go?" George got up from his chair before they could answer. "Be a love and pass my coat Eve, please. I think I'll take a stroll myself." He placed his book on the coffee table, put on the coat that Eve passed to him, and then strode off out the door.

George could see his son well in front crossing the fields; he followed at a distance, hoping that Cheryl was right, that Carl was improving so that some degree of normality would return to their lives.

His thoughts then turned to the murder at the mine, which hung like a black cloud over the village. *At least my son is not involved with that,* he thought, as he strode across the fields, the black slagheap rising into view as he saw the village in the distance.

George walked along the edge of the ploughed field, its separating hedge ran alongside the railway line towards the coal-loading hopper. He rounded a clump of bushes, realizing his son was nowhere to be seen. Carl had disappeared.

He looked in every direction, obviously he could see clear across the open field, so he went into the bushes where he was confronted by a wooden fence, beyond which was the overgrown embankment down to the rail lines.

Lifting himself up and standing on the bottom bar of the fence, he could see below him that the embankment was a mass of gorse and wild blackberry bushes.

A quarter of a mile along the line the large rail wagons were parked under the towering coal hopper, but no sign of Carl.

He heard a distant steam engine puffing and hissing slowly way in the opposite direction, sooner or later coming to the mine to collect another cargo of coal.

He hadn't realized until that moment just how much he missed the mine, it was in his blood. Feeling dejected and worried, he turned round and started to walk back towards home.

As George Armitage turned and headed for home, Carl came out from his hiding place beneath the bushes, one of his favorite places where they'd all played hide and seek together as kids. He watched his father disappear into the distance, and then carried on walking towards the loader.

During his last days at the hospital, his memory had begun to return slowly; it had started when he remembered his athletic prowess at school, and slowly progressed from there. He believed he'd fooled everyone, with the exception of the psychiatrist, and maybe his sister, though neither had actually said as much.

The bottom had fallen out of his world when he'd overheard his father say there had been a murder at the mine the previous day. Until then, he'd planned out how to put the whole mess to rights; he'd spent a long time thinking matters over, realizing clearly what an absolute self indulgent fool he'd been. He'd hurt many people, in particular his family and close friends.

It was his avowed intention to uncover the German's plans and make a clean breast of things, whatever the consequences were to him personally.

But now, with this latest news he wasn't so sure. Revenge seemed the only thing that came to mind, revenge for the pain, for the heartache. His burning hatred for the big German was beginning to consume his whole thinking.

Carl climbed the fence and slid down the embankment with the agility of a cat, then began walking along the railway line towards the towering hopper that filled the rail wagons.

He noticed the new addition of a small chute that had been made by the blacksmith to unload their packages at ground level, away from the prying eyes of other employees. Though Carl was not used to looking at the hopper from this angle, he'd spotted it right away.

He recalled from an earlier conversation at the night club how the big German had outlined their plan when he had given Carl no choice but to assist them. They were to send packages down a slide to a waiting accomplice, into a marked rail wagon, to be collected at the railhead later.

The German had said that it would be pretty unusual for anyone to climb up and look into a wagonload of coal, so they could safely assume the parcels would remain undiscovered.

Carl realized, since the slide was still there that the transfer might not have happened yet. He walked back along the track, scrambled up the embankment, then sat on the fence. It was now time to work out his game plan, time for some decisive action.

To catch these people he needed the answers to quite a few questions like: Why was the policeman killed at the mine? Who killed him? Where were the parcels now? *Where can I get these answers,* he thought to himself, *who can help me?*

As Carl walked towards home his mind began to formulate a plan that might well provide the answers he so desperately sought. Entering the house he took off his coat and walked into the sitting room, George was sitting in the window seat.

"I've just been thinking son, would you like me to take you to the mine?" asked George.

"Maybe something there will jolt your memory. A name or a face," Cheryl interjected, as he spoke.

"Why don't we go to the pub, or the village club? People are much more relaxed and at ease in that kind of environment, all the faces from the mine are usually in one or the other," said Cheryl, smiling as she walked into the room. Having heard the offer made by his father, her suggestion was exactly what Carl was looking for.

"That sounds like a brilliant idea," he said.

"Good, let's all go this evening. I'll bring David along too. It's such a long time since we all went out together, it'll do us all the world of good.

"Dad why don't you tell mum not to cook tonight, we'll get some sandwiches there. She'll be pleased to go out for a change," added Cheryl with a grin on her face.

"I'll give David a call right now." Hearing Cheryl's comments about David, Carl realized he couldn't continue his subterfuge for much longer and not have to face up to

David. Suddenly he wasn't so sure that this evening out was the good idea it had seemed a minute or two ago.

The Harper Home the Following Morning

I awoke after a night where I'd slept fitfully, my mind seemed to be working overtime. When I did get to sleep eventually, I'd dreamed. I remembered later the recurring theme always surrounded the mystery killing at the mine.

Later, when I attempted to get out of bed, every bone I possessed either ached or creaked or just didn't want to function. I lay back on the bed as Titch licked my hand; my watch showed it was 8.30. I could hear Mary moving around downstairs, and then there was a knock on the bedroom door.

"Fancy a cup of tea, Matt, dear?" Welcome words, as Titch jumped off the bed and ran towards the door. She came into the room with hot tea and toast.

"You didn't look at all well last night, going to bed so early and without food, I thought I'd get up early and make you a big breakfast, what would you like?" I asked for eggs and bacon and the likes, and then pried my aching bones into the bath. I had already decided to make this night my final work night at the mine. Not just as a result of what happened there, but I did have a long report to write on the total time spent there, which would take up at least a whole day.

After a great breakfast, I put all of my papers together neatly in two folders, those that applied to my work-study and the others that were part of our ongoing investigation. I put them all carefully into my music case.

After a quick meeting with myself as to the punishment preferred, considering all the aches and pains, whether walking or riding the bike, I chose the latter as I could walk up the hill leaning on the bike, and then free wheel down to the mine.

Arriving at the mine offices, I told Fred that I had to do my report.

"Why don't you use Master Carl's office, he won't be using it for a while, you'll get some peace and quiet in there. I'm sure he wouldn't mind, you two being from the same school and all," a mild hint of sarcasm in his voice.

I took my case through into Carl's office, out of respect I sat at the other side of his desk, not behind it, and then began to pick up where I'd left off on the work-study.

After working about a half hour or so, I heard a knock on the door. A man entered the room. I thought his face seemed familiar.

"Good morning, I'm George Armitage. I used to own this place before nationalization of the mines.

"Good morning to you Sir, I've heard a lot about you. My name is Matt Harper, my father is Jack Harper from the village, and I've just completed a work-study project here."

"Yes, I remember hearing about that. How are you getting along, have they been giving you all the support you need here?" he asked quite sincerely.

"Everyone without exception has gone out of their way to be helpful," I replied.

"This other matter is a messy affair, the death of the policeman, don't you think?" he looked around the office as he spoke to me.

"I've spent many hours in this room, mostly happy ones," he said reminiscing. "I see that Carl still keeps some of the old pictures around, you've met Carl, I take it?"

"Yes, we met when I first came here, then unfortunately he had his accident; I haven't seen him since. How is he feeling now?" I asked.

"He's at home now, but still suffering from amnesia, I tried to persuade him to come here today, thought it might jog his memory, but he declined. I've been asked by the police to come here today, I don't know why they wish to talk to me, I haven't been here for months."

He went on to tell me the family was going to take Carl to the village club that evening also maybe the pub, hoping somebody or something might jog his memory. He went off to keep his appointment with the police. I felt sorry for him, he had a lot of problems on his mind, all that money and yet so unhappy. Proves the old saying, money doesn't bring happiness.

I finally returned to my report and stuck at it until the mine hooter went off, heralding the end of the day shift. The sharp tone of the telephone bell jarred in my head. I let it ring four or five times then picked it up, not expecting the call to be for me.

"Hello there, young Harper, and how are you today?" it was the voice of John Cotes.

"I'm not feeling too bad, all things considered," I replied.

He told me that he'd been trying to get hold of Gerald all morning, without any success. He wanted to know if I'd spoken with him today.

"No, John I've been here most of the morning. He hasn't contacted me, why, is there a problem?"

"Not a problem exactly, there is a twenty-four hour surveillance on the club and the hotel. We have been through the house they were using with a fine toothcomb, came up with zip. The whole group seems to have disappeared off the face of the earth. Nothing around the mine so far, so we're working on the assumption that they got their parcels away, but how? Judging by yours and Gerald's statements, there was far too much stuff to be carried away under their arms, they must have used some form of transport or other." He went on to say if I heard from Gerald, ask him to contact his office number.

I had hardly put the phone back on the hook when it rang again, this time it was Bruce.

"Hey Matt, Gerald was just on the phone, he wants you to meet him urgently. Didn't say where he was, just that he wanted you to phone him and arrange to meet right away. I have to rush, I'm to take over from one of the boys watching the club." He gave me the number to reach Gerald.

"I've just this minute got off the phone with John Cotes, he told me MI5 has a twenty-four hour watch on the club, and the hotel, but he believes they've flown the coup. Be careful Bruce, what's the point of doubling up on the surveillance anyway?"

"Because Gerald's determined to get there first," he replied in a most serious voice.

Having fully completed my report despite all of the interruptions, I decided to walk across to the canteen to order a mug of tea and a beef sandwich. Taking them back to the office, I spotted the SIB Captain.

"Hello Captain Hamilton, how's your enquiry progressing?" I asked.

"It's not really," he replied. "We think they may have hidden something here, possibly coming back to retrieve it, but that's a long shot." He shrugged his shoulders as he walked to his vehicle.

Back in the office I called the number given to me by Bruce, it was answered after two rings by a stranger. I asked for Gerald, was told to hang on, shortly after Gerald came on the line.

"You took your time, where are you?" he snapped.

"I'm at the mine offices."

"OK, here's what I want you to do Matt: take your bike to the Bay Horse Pub where we met Cotes the other day, leave your bike behind there and be out on the main road. I'll be there in exactly forty-five minutes, be certain that you're not followed."

"Are you onto something?"

"I don't have time to talk right now, just do as I asked." I packed my papers back into my music case, left the desk as I'd found it, then sat down to eat the sandwich and drink my cold tea.

Going through the general office on my way out, I said 'cheerio' to Fred and the rest of the staff, thanking them for their help and support and promising to come back to see them, before I left to return to my studies.

Fastening my case to the handle bars of the bike, I cycled across the yard, then walked up Pit Lane, past the house where the blacksmith had lived. *I wonder where you are right now*, I thought as I looked towards the cottage. I made my way towards the main road with about twenty minutes to spare. At the pub I asked for the landlady, who on approach immediately recognized me from before.

"Yes love, what can I do for you?" she asked with a broad smile on her face.

"My friend is collecting me in his car, may I leave my bike out back until later tonight?"

"No problem, put it inside the bottle shed just in case it rains love, alright?" She whisked off collecting a couple of empty glasses as she went.

After stowing my bike, I went out and stood on the northern side of the road, waiting for Gerald to arrive, making sure I wasn't followed. Gerald arrived within five minutes; he picked me up, drove back some way towards the village, then he turned back.

"I'm feeling a little paranoid about being followed, there are many different people with a vested interest in what's going on, they'll fall over each other if they're not careful," he said. He headed off in the general direction of Leeds. Within fifteen minutes, we were driving around the outskirts of the city.

"Are there any new developments?" I asked.

"Quite a lot has happened since yesterday. Grab that parcel off the back seat," he replied. Turning quickly, I saw one of the parcels from the mine.

The most peculiar sensations passed through me as my hand settled on the object, after all of these years, I was actually touching part of the floating flying boxes. My hands felt the coarse greased material. As I tried to lift the object it felt as though it was bolted to the seat, it was so heavy. I turned around and kneeling up on the seat, before I could exert enough power to lift it, all of my recent injuries complained in unison. At last I sat with the parcel on my lap, someone had already opened it. I pulled back the covering to look inside. The look on my face must have been a sight to behold.

"Yep, that's four blocks of solid gold there!" Gerald said.

"Where on earth did you get these?" Gerald cut short my stuttering disbelief.

"I took the packet from their car in the garage out back of the house and put it into Bruce's car just before that bastard shot me. I should've taken the bloody lot whilst I had the chance."

He told me the back of the German's car was loaded up with the parcels, but felt sure there were more in the packing case than he'd seen in the car. Looking at the gold blocks in awe, I touched their smooth silky surface, wondering how many other people might have died for this, or how many more would do so!

As we drove around the ring road, I took a closer look at the block on my lap.

"I wonder where this came from originally," I asked out loud. There were no official stamps or seals on the block, just some un-decipherable etchings on its surface.

"It's more than likely stolen gold melted down, those blocks are much larger than a normal gold ingot, maybe twice the size," replied Gerald. I turned, knelt on my seat and returned the gold to its place on the rear seat.

"Push it right under your seat, it'd be a shame to have it stolen, wouldn't it?" he said grinning as he spoke.

We drove into an area called Hunslet, an older, very built-up suburb of the city, then on to Armley, location of the Victorian prison, a grim drab area. Row upon row of identically terraced houses; the stonework blackened over the years. There were two enormous gas containers, bigger and higher than all the houses on the two streets. They contained coal gas, piped to the houses for light, heat and cooking.

It is an evil smelling coal-based product often the final solution for the demented or depressed. A way out of life's toils and tribulations.

Man found dead with head in gas-oven was not an unusual newspaper headline in those days.

Gerald pulled up opposite to a large stone-built chapel, its walls black from years of grime, then he pointed to a block of three houses with a corner store on the end, *Lodging House* written over the center door.

"I think this is where our friends are currently staying."

"How on earth did you find them out here?" I asked.

"Friends did the work for me, it's not what you know, it's who you know, especially in this business, friends do come in handy," he added, with a smirk. "Always remember that, young Matt." We both nearly jumped out of our skins at a loud bang outside as something landed with great force on the top of the car. I turned to my left looking into the stern face of John Cotes who was glaring in through the window, and he gestured for me to wind it down.

"Good afternoon gentlemen, though I use that phrase loosely. Do you wish me to call the Chief Super now and get him to read you your rights, or is there something that you two would like to tell me?"

"Get into the back, Matt," Gerald said to me. "Let Mr. Cotes sit in front and talk, make it snappy, we don't want to scare these people away."

"For someone who just rescued your ass yesterday, I'm feeling a little left out of things, wouldn't you agree Gerald? I thought we had an arrangement to share all relevant information, so what's going on?"

Gerald apologized, then he rapidly brought John right up-to-date.

"Pass the parcel over Matt, will you please?" Gerald handed a gold block over to John, who remained silent for a few seconds.

"You both know what this is, don't you?" asked John.

"Yes it's solid gold," I replied.

"Do you have any idea where it might have come from originally?" said John.

"Probably stolen then melted down," Gerald answered. "How about from those inhumane prison camps that we never knew about till after the war. Could be gold teeth fillings, taken from the bodies of dead prisoners; these people we are dealing with could very well be involved with something as gruesome as that.

"Try to mess with me again by not keeping me informed and I'll have you thrown in jail for the rest of your lives, we don't need any heroics; you've already seen what these animals are capable of doing. They'll stop at nothing. "You're pissed off at just a few here. I want the whole damn network, so stop making my life anymore difficult than it already is, do you both understand?"

"I'm sorry, but I just wanted so much to get my hands on that big piece of crap before anyone else. I've got a score to settle with him!" the big man said emotionally.

"Hey, I fully understand, but sometimes we have to put our personal feelings aside, in the interest of others. In this case The National Interest. Where did you get the gold from anyway, Gerald?" Gerald explained.

John Cotes then said he'd need to take the gold with him, as proof to his superiors that we were on the right track. Gerald then went on to explain what he'd discovered regarding this locality. John interrupted him.

"Gerald, I've been trying to get in touch with you unsuccessfully all day. We've had this address watched for the past six months, others within their group have stayed here too. My men reported your car here earlier today, so can we all stop wasting energy unnecessarily. I promise you'll not be left out of anything in the future."

"I need to know more than I do about these wartime parachute drops. They were made in other parts of the country, as well as here. We're slowly placing the pieces together, but it's going to take time so I'm asking for your patience and understanding. If you'd like to go home and rest for a day or so, you may find some serious action starting very soon.

"Matt, I've got to go to the mine, can I drop you off at The Bay Horse to collect your bike?" he said with a knowing grin on his face. *How did he know where I had left my bike*? I thought.

I arrived home early evening. I'd remembered what Mr. Armitage had told me about going to the pub or the village club. I decided to go along there, too. I might hear something of use regarding the Germans' whereabouts. Of course there was another ulterior motive involved, I'd not seen Joan for some time now and it was time to renew our acquaintance.

I walked down to the local phone box and called Joan's number. After a couple of rings the phone was answered by a woman's voice.

"Is Joan there, please?"

"Just a moment, who's calling?" I gave my name.

"Hello Matt, hold on a second, I'll just go and get her." We arranged to meet at the club around seven-thirty. After a quick bath and change of clothes, I cycled to west Casleton having crawled up the hill first. Arriving twenty minutes early, I sat astride my bike at the junction of the main Leeds Bradford road, just watching the traffic go by. I was partially hidden from view by a large white sign on a bed sheet announcing the local Church garden fete that weekend.

"Hello, young Harper, nearly missed you behind that sign, I hear you've been getting in the wars lately then." It was none other than the erstwhile Constable Ellis.

"Apparently you're becoming well known in police circles, your name cropped up in a police memo just yesterday."

As he was talking, I thought I half glimpsed John Cotes drive quickly past on the main road. If it were he, he certainly wouldn't have seen me as I was fairly well hidden by the sheet.

My head almost came off my shoulders as I did a double take, too late as the car sped by. I thought that I'd seen another person sitting in the front of the car with John, there was something eerily familiar about the passenger, but as Constable Ellis had continued talking, he'd diverted my attention, and so the whole experience became rather subliminal.

"Everything alright Matt, you look as though you've just seen a ghost?"

"I'm fine Constable thanks, and you?" The car had been traveling very fast so I dismissed the incident, pushing it to the back of my mind. I didn't give it another thought; besides my mind was turned to more pleasant thoughts, namely my imminent evening with the lovely Joan Waters.

Chapter Twenty-Four

The village club was quite dead in comparison to the weekend, it was Thursday evening. I assumed that most saved their visits until Friday and Saturday evenings. There were a few miners sitting, talking, some were playing dominos and billiards, but not too many with their wives and families.

Joan and I sat in a corner and talked together for thirty minutes or so. We were seated next to the small stage where the entertainers performed. As a result of the last couple of day's events, I was still quite uptight and decided to unwind a little. Leaving my seat, I climbed up onto the stage, sat at the piano, lifted the keyboard lid, and began to play; Joan sat next to me on the piano stool.

"I'd no idea you played, so beautifully too," she said smiling and looking proud of me.

"You are obviously a man of many talents." I turned to see George Armitage with his wife, along with David and a young woman enter the club. I stood up.

"Don't stop, the music is so pleasant," said David. I continued to play for another ten minutes or so, until the club began to get much busier. I closed the piano lid and went across to the bar area where the group was sitting. Carl was standing at the bar talking with a number of miners. Then I heard David calling my name, beckoning me over.

"Matt, I'd like you to meet Cheryl Armitage. Cheryl this is Matthew Harper, the young man I've been telling you about," he said to the attractive woman sitting next to him.

"You look as though you've been having a rough time of it," she said leaning forward, taking my chin in her hand and looking closely at my war-torn features. I'd remembered that she was a doctor, as I gave her the same explanation I'd given to everyone else. Quickly changing the subject:

"David I'd like to introduce Joan Waters, a friend of mine," I said, as he shook hands with Joan. After introductions all the way round, I played darts with David and George, whilst the ladies sat and became acquainted.

Carl seemed well-occupied at the bar, talking with Ralph, the Overman along with Ben from the mine stables. George Armitage must have made quite a few calls during the day to engineer this number of people at the club on a Thursday night.

Earlier when he'd walked into the club, Carl noticed Matt playing the piano, then he spotted David entering the bar with his sister Cheryl on his arm. Ralph was speaking to him.

"I hear that you haven't been feeling too well since your accident." Carl looked at him, then at the barman.

"I haven't been at my best of late, that's for sure," he answered, picking up his pint; he seemed miles away watching as his father played darts with David and the young man Matt, his Mum talking happily with his sister and another pretty girl. *What I'd give for things to be different and not have this terrible cloud hanging over me,* he thought to himself. Then he overheard Ralph talking to the barman.

"Yes, isn't it awful, he was shot outside the blacksmith's shop, yes, I believe he was an officer in the SIB. The authorities have evidently been chasing these people for some years. They got clean away, that Kurt the blacksmith was one of them, and he's disappeared along with them!"

"What were they hiding?" asked the barman.

"Nobody knows exactly, but whatever it was is gone too. It was stashed down one of the old disused gates, we've all gone past it a hundred times, they hid it behind the pack, and that's where the bad buggers put the body afterwards.

"How did they get the body down without somebody seeing it?" asked an inquisitive miner.

"The blacksmith took it down in a big packing case marked "machine parts," and then the others got inside with the body, would you believe that?"

Carl listened with interest, those bastards had got away, but had they taken everything out? If so, how did they get it all away from the mine in one trip? He couldn't understand why they had not removed the temporary chute; the big German was too meticulous to leave it there to be found.

He knew there were two places where they had stashed their packages; the other one was nearer than the other, at the back of the stables at the pit bottom. He played out the charade; eventually when he'd heard all that was to be said, he felt sure there were still packages hidden under the noses of the police.

This made him determined to find them and foil the plans of the arrogant German and his cohorts.

Squaring his shoulders, Carl walked briskly over to his family.

"David, how nice to see you again," he said to the total amazement of his old friend.

"Father, what can I get you to drink? Why is everyone here looking so somber, come on drink up, the next round's on me, give the whole club a drink on me," he shouted to the barman. Sitting down next to his mother, he placed his arm around her shoulder as he saw tears of joy running down her face. "Come on Mum, cheer up, why so glum, why the miserable face?"

The scene that night at the club was strange. It was as though someone had thrown a switch. One minute Carl was standing at the bar in complete silence, the next he was ordering drinks, music and food, almost hysterical in his behavior.

I couldn't help noticing the look on Cheryl's face, also that of total amazement on David's.

Cheryl's look was one of doubt and skepticism, David's was more a look of relief; either way the mood was far more relaxed than when they'd first arrived. As the evening was drawing to a close, I said my goodnights, then Joan and I started to leave the club.

"Don't forget that you're invited for dinner on Saturday evening," shouted David. "Joan, please come, you're invited too," he added, as we reached the door.

Joan and I walked along the footpath, my left arm around her, my right pushing my bike, my mind in turmoil. Nothing I'd like better than to sit and talk with Joan, start to get to know her better, but something was troubling me, something I just couldn't ignore.

When we reached Joan's house, I walked her to the front door, kissed her goodnight, then I cycled towards home.

For some odd reason, I was suddenly drawn inexplicably towards the mine. Turning left, I freewheeled down Pit Lane, stopped before the entrance to the mine, then rode up the lane beside the rail tracks. I turned off the battery lamp on the front and rear of my bike, un-clipped the lamp from its bracket, and hid the bike behind the bushes.

Climbing the fence, I crossed the field leading to the rear of the mine and towards the slagheap. It was pitch black dark, ten o'clock by my illuminated watch face.

I heard the church clock strike the hour. I was almost opposite the mine cottages. I noticed there was a light burning upstairs where the blacksmith had lived. Also I could see activity going on at the mine as the night shift was just starting.

It took some time to accustom my eyes to the darkness. I stumbled once or twice; I had to pause as the pain shot up my leg from my sprained ankle, a swift reminder to play it carefully as my right shoulder throbbed in sympathy.

I went over the path and started to climb up the slagheap, sufficiently high enough to allow me a full view of the loading hopper behind the shaft, getting a good view of the rail track leading to it. I could see the yard lights reflecting off the spinning wheels of the mine shaft, thinking, *business as usual, glad I'm not going down there tonight.* As I adjusted my vision something caught my eye directly below; someone was walking along the path beside the rail track, along my side and keeping close to the bushes, every now and then I caught the flicker of a small flashlight. I couldn't make out the identity of the man; it was too far away from where I squatted.

He got nearer to the hopper then climbed the fence, disappearing for a moment or two, only to re-appear. Now he was walking along the railway sleepers, towards a number of loaded freight wagons; there were three of them.

I kept perfectly still as I watched the flicker of his flashlight, he walked around the coal-laden wagons. My curiosity was beginning to get the better of my common sense. I stayed put, which as it worked out, was the right decision. The man went to the base of the hopper; he seemed to be searching for something on the ground. Then he returned to the rail wagon furthest away from the hopper and began to climb up its side. As he reached the top, he shone his light over into the coal; he leaned forward, dislodging some of the larger pieces.

Suddenly and without warning, I saw a bright yellow flash, no sound, just a flash. The man's head jerked backwards as he fell like stone from the side of the wagon bouncing from the ground then seeming to land on the rails. Had a man just been shot, or was I seeing things?

Though there were flood-lights high on the hopper, I couldn't see sufficiently well in the darkness. I'd seen the flash and indeed where it came from, but I didn't see any more movement. I watched for five more minutes before I ventured to move at all. Then I crept slowly and carefully towards the railway cutting, skirting the bottom of the slagheap. I began crossing an open area to reach the bushes, as quickly as my injuries would allow me.

Chapter Twenty-Five

The Armitage Residence

George and Eve arrived home from the club in good spirit, still puzzled by the quick turn of events earlier.

"I think I'll take a stroll before hitting the sack, I don't feel very sleepy yet," Carl said.

"That's fine son, Mum and I will go up now, we'll see you in the morning."

Carl put on his walking jacket, his tweed cap, then took a small flashlight from the cloakroom shelf and went out of the door. What he'd heard earlier that evening at the club had concerned him greatly, he knew the mind of the big German better than most. He felt sure that time was of the essence. It was now or never to stop him before it was too late.

He went along the same route that he'd taken earlier during the day, keeping close to the hedgerow. After ten minutes walking he could see the hopper behind the shaft; he went through the bushes, climbed up the fence, and then sat there in the darkness, watching for a few moments as his eyes grew accustomed to the darkness. After some minutes, he lowered himself over the fence, then slid quietly down the embankment. He began walking along the track towards the rail wagons that were parked under the hopper. After searching for a while he couldn't find any trace of the make-shift slide, it had been removed recently. *Damn, am I too late, have they beaten me to it?* he thought.

He could see fresh footmarks in the coal dust by the big hopper, he looked around the ground for further evidence and saw at least three different sets of footprints.

Carl walked back towards the parked rail wagons which were already filled. He looked around for signs of any intruders and then stood perfectly silent for a moment or two to listen carefully for any unusual sounds.

All he could hear were the familiar sounds of the cage gates being closed, the rap of the signal bells, and the grinding of metal wheels on rails coming from above.

Reaching the furthest wagon away from the hopper, he put his flashlight into his pocket, and then he began to climb up the side of a coal-laden container. As he neared the top, he got a good foothold on one of the big bars that kept the side closed.

Peering into the truck he pulled his flashlight out and shone it onto the cargo, moving some of the larger pieces of coal to have a better look, and then he saw the canvass wrapped packages beneath the surface.

They say that if someone shoots a firearm at you, if you hear the explosion you're too late. All that Carl heard was the "phut" of a silenced handgun as the lead projectile found its target; he fell from the truck to the ground. Carl Armitage lay dead on the rail tracks, a perfect round hole through the side of his temple, his blood slowly seeping onto the worn wooden sleepers down to the coal dust below.

I'd crept along the edge of the slag heap, keeping clear of some of the larger rocks, just in case I were to trip and fall in the dark. My nerves were jangling, every sound coming from the mine sounded as though it had been amplified twenty times. I knew I was taking a very long time to cover the rough ground; my ankle was really starting to throb.

In the middle of the open area halfway between where I stood and the bushes, there was part of an old farm implement. I ran across, crouching behind it, waited a moment or two longer just to be on the safe side, then I saw him: A squat lean figure, dressed completely in black and wearing a black balaclava over his head and face. He came out of the bushes on the other side of the path holding a gun, he looked both ways; he could only have been twenty feet away from me.

He crouched there for what seemed like ages, he waited, his nose in the air, like a wild animal sniffing for signs of danger. Where I lay quiet and still in the open field was too far away to receive his attention, thank God. Then as quickly as he'd appeared, he moved off with the stealth of a jungle cat, melting into the darkness. Within seconds he was out of my sight. I waited a moment or two longer before leaving the shelter of my hiding place, then I crept very cautiously over the footpath and into the undergrowth, from where the man in black had just exited.

Crawling under the bushes I soon reached the fence, climbing painfully atop, I sat looking down towards the rail wagons. I actually had to pinch myself to be sure that I wasn't in a dream; they were gone! All three of the trucks had completely disappeared, vanished as though into thin air.

I looked around in total amazement, then got down from the fence and slid down the steep embankment, standing where I thought I'd seen the man's body fall.

There was nothing but coal dust two inches deep between the rails. I knew there had been three wagons there earlier. I hadn't been seeing things; I was just about to pinch myself again to see if this was all one big nightmare.

Then I remembered having seen the shunters in the big rail yard in Leeds, how they rode on the back of the rail wagons that freewheeled down the inclines without the aid of steam engines.

They would down stand on the long brake levers bringing the trucks to a halt. I looked down the track away from the hopper; there was a definite down gradient. I followed the direction of the track; I'd never been that way before. Walking carefully I had to hop every other step as my ankle was giving me a lot of pain now. The rails curved to the right running alongside a lane on the opposite side of the track, two hundred yards further along I spotted the rear of a stationary coal wagon. I moved up the embankment, which was less steep than before. I saw that the fence had been broken allowing me to walk straight through and out into the open lane.

It was quite narrow with high grass on both sides, which would prove to be a mixed blessing. I saw the big black Austin car parked there in the lane unattended. I moved quickly back into the long grass stopping at the fence.

Now some hundred yards from both the car and the trucks, first checking my rear, I crept back along the lane. I was determined that nobody was going to surprise me from behind this time. After double-checking in both directions, I returned to the fence. The wagons were now in full view. Standing on top of one was the little man with the thick spectacles. He was passing packages down to the woman.

I heard the sound of an approaching car engine, at the same time the black Austin was driven away. Moving in the direction I'd just come from, I saw the flicker of headlights, so I kept my head well down in the long grass as a Royal Mail van swept by.

I decided to go back, cross the track and move along the other side so that I could get level with the truck. Maybe I'd hear what was going on and perhaps find out to which destination they were taking their cargo. I assumed this was the last of the stuff from underground.

More importantly I wanted to find out the identity of the man who'd fallen from the wagon earlier.

I crossed the track and climbed the embankment on the other side. This time the boundary was a barbed wire fence. Luckily the bottom run of wire was missing, the next one only a foot off the ground. I crawled under it, the wire missed the seat of my pants by just a fraction. Memories came flooding back from the night of the parachutes as I saw cattle in the adjoining field. I thought of John's torn pants back then.

Moving along the hedge I came level with the three rail wagons, where the track had come to a hollow they'd obviously just let them run free until they had settled into the dip, one behind the other.

The little man was still on top of the coal, having some physical difficulties judging by the grunts and groans. I hoped his kidneys still pained him. *Whether my choice of languages at school included German by accident or choice was immaterial,* I thought. *Fortunately I'd excelled in the Aryan tongue, and now was the time to benefit.*

The woman hissed in German, telling the little man not to worry about the body now, but to dig out the remaining packages from the coal before their car returned. They couldn't park for too long in the lane, it was wide enough for only the one vehicle, or in case someone saw them.

My mind was in turmoil, should I go to get help now, and run the risk of having them disappear before I got back, or stay put and try to learn of their plans?

The sound of an approaching vehicle coming down the lane made the decision for me. The car approached coming in the same direction the Mail Van had traveled. It slowed down considerably. As the woman identified the car, she'd gone out into the lane signaling with a flashlight that the coast was clear.

The car engine stopped, the lights were extinguished, I heard the thud of a door being closed, then the face of the big German appeared through the hedge. Immediately the woman began to pass packages to him. For the next half hour, they worked like beavers, talking very little. I lost count of the large parcels carried up the embankment, but I did manage to count the small heavy ones, they had numbered thirty.

"That is the last one," the small man shouted in German, sounding relieved that they'd finished.

"Helga, come up here and keep an eye on the road, I'll put the body inside the truck," the big man shouted.

"If a vehicle comes from your rear, you'll have to drive to the village then come back around, remember not to stop until you get my signal." He then clambered down the well-worn embankment with the agility of a cat and swung up onto the top of the truck.

The law won't find this character for some time, nobody looks into a full freight wagon, he won't be discovered until the coal reaches its destination, by which time we will be long gone, the big man thought arrogantly to himself.

"Quickly, we have to finish loading the car, then go to meet the others. We will meet the truck from Scotland tomorrow morning, at a transport cafe on the A1 at..........."

Damn and blast! His last words were drowned by the sound of an oncoming lorry as its brakes squealed around the bend; men in the back were singing, obviously quite inebriated. The truck swayed from side to side, by the time it drew level, the woman and the Austin were gone. *Damn it! I missed hearing the meeting place, it could be anywhere. The A1 stretches from Scotland to London. How shall we find them now*? I whispered to myself.

Within minutes the woman returned in the car, pausing only for a very short while. I heard the triple thuds of three doors closing, then the sounds of the exhaust as it disappeared into the distance.

Now what? Should I call Gerald, John Cotes or the police? I still don't know the identity of the body buried under the coal. I left the scene quickly, or at least as fast as my ankle would allow. I retrieved my bike and went off to the mine offices.

There was a solitary light burning in the general office, the door was unlocked, so I went through and saw the Assistant Manager sitting down completing his report for the night.

"What brings you out at this time of night, Matt?" he asked.

"I had a couple of beers at the club, then remembered that I'd left some of my papers in the manager's office earlier today," I replied

"All of the police seem to have gone then," I added rhetorically, fishing for the latest news.

"When I got here at seven this evening, there were just the two of them; bad business, that killing," he sighed without looking up from his writing.

I went through to Carl's office. Picking up his direct line I called the number Gerald had given me earlier, last Tuesday. It was a long shot as the number had been a pub in Leeds. The number was answered after about ten rings.

I couldn't hear the reply once again for the background noise.

"Is Gerald Steele there"? I asked, as the noise seemed to abate.

"Gerald here, who is it?" Relieved, I explained as briefly as I could what had taken place; there was a pregnant pause, then he said,

"Here's what we do. You must go back and make sure that nobody goes near that rail wagon; we're going to have to let John Cotes in on this one. I'll contact him right away, I've got a number where he can be reached twenty-four hours." Gerald then asked for my exact location.

"I'll be with you in less than forty-five minutes, keep well hidden, just in case they decide to come back. As I approach I'll open the window and whistle the tune Yankee Doodle, Cotes will do the same if he gets there before me. Now you get back there quickly, and Matt, be careful, keep your eyes peeled."

Gerald was off the phone and gone. I returned to the scene and took up my place under the bushes. It felt quite eerie to know there was a corpse only a matter of feet away from me. I was about to see my second body in as many days.

I crouched down letting my imagination run wild, then I heard someone whistling, but not Yankee Doodle, it was the night constable, doing his rounds. I hoped I'd hidden my bike sufficiently well, I would soon find out; he went past without incident.

Within twenty more minutes I heard the approach of a motor vehicle, as its engine slowed down there was a poor rendition of the required tune. I emerged from under the hedge to greet the whistler with my lamp; it was in fact John Cotes, very closely followed by a second car with Gerald at the wheel and Bruce as passenger.

All four of us scrambled down the embankment, John and Gerald then climbed up the sides of the coal-laden rail wagon.

Within a short time they both descended looking very grim faced indeed.

"Its Carl Armitage, they've killed Carl; the bastards!" Bruce roared at the top of his voice as though in agony.

George and Eve Armitage had gone to bed both feeling worn out after a fairly traumatic night. Sleep didn't come easily. They both lay awake looking at the ever-changing light patterns on the ceiling, not talking to each other but both with the same thoughts in mind.

As far as George was concerned, he wondered if Carl did have any knowledge of the recent events or maybe even have some involvement; why was he keeping quiet about the whole thing, even pretending not to remember.

He'd been behaving very strangely during the last few months before the incident at that club. George turned over in his bed for the twentieth time, realizing he'd have to wait and see what tomorrow brought. Turning he looked at Eve who had just fallen asleep. George hoped his suspicions were wrong. It would break Eve's heart if he turned out to be right.

Meanwhile, John Cotes told us to make ourselves scarce. He would contact the police and lead them to believe he'd discovered the body of Carl Armitage. He pointed out that although the police had no reason to doubt my word, this would save me a lot of needless questions, although he himself would want to debrief me thoroughly tomorrow. Gerald and I arranged to be at his office at seven-thirty the following morning.

Chapter Twenty-Six

The Mansion, Early the Following Morning

David woke to the distant ringing of a telephone, which then stopped after a couple of rings. Maybe he was hearing things or perhaps dreaming, then he sat bolt upright, a voice shouting, then a loud knocking on his bedroom door.

"Master David, there's an urgent phone call for you, it's Miss Cheryl, she sounds very upset, will you come right away?" It was the voice of the family cook.

"I'll be there right away; tell her I'll call back." David scrambled into his clothes and was downstairs and dialing Cheryl's number all within the space of five minutes.

"Oh God, David, come quickly please, Carl's been shot, he's dead," Cheryl sobbed hysterically into the phone as she spoke.

"What!"

"Someone's killed my brother, who would want to do such a thing?" David was in his car, speeding down the long drive from the Mansion, his mind in complete turmoil. *Carl dead, how could that be? I was with him only last night. Who were these people he'd been involved with, what could be so important that they would take his life? They'd almost killed him before. Maybe they're the same people who killed the policeman.* He pulled up at the Armitage residence, there were cars everywhere. As he went to enter the house, George Armitage waved him through the door.

"Where's Cheryl?" David shouted.

"She's with her mother in the kitchen, my God David, what are we going to do?" said the distraught man. There were ten or more strangers inside the house. After trying to console the women, David went back outside and walked up to the man who seemed to be in control of things

"Can someone tell me what happened exactly?" he asked the tall distinguished man, who was speaking into a squelching, squawking car radio.

"I'm the Chief Superintendent in charge of this enquiry," replied the man, passing the radio handset back to an officer inside the car.

"Would you mind telling me who you are and what your business is here?" he added. David answered the questions, then was told what had been discovered so far. The death was being treated as murder and unfortunately they had very few leads thus far.

The body had been discovered partially buried, in a coal-loaded rail wagon, they hadn't found any spent shells from the firearm.

Another man came across, who was introduced as John Cotes, evidently an agent with MI5.

Apparently, he'd discovered Carl's body last night. John told David that the murder had taken place behind the mineshaft, where the wagons were loaded from the mine. *Why would Carl be there at that time of night, and what would an MI5 agent be doing there at all?* David thought to himself.

He went back inside the house just as his father was arriving, pushing past a group of persistent reporters, then being stopped and questioned by the police before being allowed through.

Cheryl had managed to calm her mother with a mild sedative; George sat on the couch with Eve, holding her hand and trying to give her some sort of comfort. David had his arm around Cheryl as Harold came into the room.

"These people won't tell me anything" he said.

"There is something going on here that I don't understand, something of national importance, mark my words."

Train Journey to Leeds the Following Morning

I was on the train making my way to Leeds to meet with John Cotes still thinking over the dreadful events of last night. Before boarding the train I had picked up the early morning edition of the Daily Herald. Right across the front page was the heading: **Second Slaying At Village Coal Mine.** No names had been printed yet and not much detail had been given on either murder, I assumed because they really didn't have a lot of information. As usual the newspapers tend to deal in sensationalism particularly when short of facts.

The train pulled into the station, at 6:45 am there weren't so many passengers and the station looked fairly deserted compared to normal. Much to my relief a cafe was open just outside the station. I went inside. To my surprise, Gerald and Bruce were sitting at a table.

"Morning, Bruce. Morning, Gerald, fancy seeing you two in here," I smiled at them both.

"This happens to be the only cafe near to Cote's office so we assumed that you wouldn't walk half way across the city from the bus station to get a cup of tea. Perception, I think you would call it," said Gerald with a grin.

"Another cuppa luv, please," he called to the lady behind the counter.

"Listen Matt, Bruce here is going off in a minute. He's taking a few of our boys from the market with him. They are going to check all the transport cafes on the A1 starting slightly north of Leeds in search of those Krauts. All we need to know is the type of vehicles and the tag numbers, then we'll be able follow them later.

It's a bit of a long shot, I grant you, but this way we'll have about five different cars on the lookout. They will all phone into the market on progress and once we get mobile we'll do the same. Now let's you and I go get this meeting over and done with."

"See you later," he said to Bruce, "let's go get these murdering rats."

Gerald and I stood up to leave; Bruce waved his hand as a car came across from an adjacent side street, pulling up at the curbside. As we were walking away, I saw Bruce leave the cafe and climb into the waiting car as two more vehicles pulled up behind and the convoy drove off.

Gerald and I walked towards the offices of the MI5 agent.

"What do you make of this John Cotes fellow?" I asked Gerald.

"Don't know for sure, he must be who he says he is, there aren't too many people going around impersonating secret service agents, unless they're agents of some other Government, why do you ask?"

"Don't know, there's something that I can't put my finger on, I get the feeling he knows a hell of a lot more than he's letting us in on. Maybe we should challenge him on our agreement, just like he did with us the other day." I looked pensively into a shop window as we walked past.

"Got something on your mind young 'en?" Gerald asked, as I came back from my thoughts.

"Funny you should say what you just did about Cotes. Yesterday I thought that I saw him driving down the main road at the village. He was moving very quickly. It was a bit like one of those out-of-body experiences that scientists talk about. I thought there was somebody else with him, somebody sort of familiar, just can't put my finger on it." I stopped talking just as we approached the offices of John Cotes.

We got there with a few minutes to spare. John was already sitting at his desk.

"Morning chaps," he said with a smile.

"I suppose that you've both seen the headlines today." We nodded in unison.

"Now tell me, what were you doing at the mine last night, Matt?"

"I really can't give you a satisfactory answer to that question, it may seem strange, but it was as though a sixth sense drew me there," I replied.

"Tell me exactly what you remember." I went through the events of the previous night step by step, taking care to cover each point. As I spoke, I was also reading my notes, which I'd completed on my return home last night. After he'd taken me through the whole process twice, we all came to the same conclusions:

The coal dust had been put down after the shooting to cover up any blood stains. The shell from the bullet was probably in the bushes, not on or around the track, as the shot had been fired from there. I had not seen the shooter at all from my position, just the muzzle flash over in that direction.

"Still the most intriguing question, why was Carl there anyway?" John said: "I think that Carl was somehow involved in part of this affair. Maybe he was blackmailed into letting the Germans use the mine as a stash for their loot. Perhaps he'd tried to back out of the deal, hence the first accident, a kind of warning."

I said to John: "Whether his amnesia was genuine or not, we'll never know now. Perhaps after he met with the people at the club last night and heard what had taken place, he realized that maybe there was more loot to be moved. So he went to the mine last night in the hope of seeing them and perhaps spoiling their game. For the second and last time he underestimated their determination and ruthlessness." I went on to say that I did indeed have all of his diaries and some notes that were now beginning to make sense.

"Do you have them with you now?" asked John.

"As a matter of fact I do, they're right here in my music case."

"May I take a look," he asked.

"I don't really want to part with them," I added.

"Matt, these documents are now evidence in a murder case. If you're going to withhold such evidence, perhaps you'd like to explain to the Superintendent just how you came by these items. I'll give you a receipt, look them over, and then give them back, how's that?" John went on: "All I want to see is just how much he knew."

His request seemed perfectly acceptable to me, besides what other choice did I have; at least this way I would be able to retain them. Though, I was starting to get heartily sick of the repeated threat of the police superintendent being held over our heads like the sword of Damocles.

As I saw the situation, there were three different groups chasing the same goal: the SIB, the police, whether they be local or Special Branch, and us, or if you like, a combination of MI5 and us.

It didn't matter to me who was able to stop and capture these killers, as long as they were put away for life or better still, hung for murder.

Though I was slightly biased because I believed we had more information than all the other groups put together, somewhat reluctantly I handed over Carl's belongings. As I did so I looked across at Gerald whose look was a little doubtful, he also seemed to be boiling on the inside. Suddenly he leapt to his feet, knocking his chair to the ground with a clatter.

"And while we're here Cotes, we were talking earlier amongst ourselves, we believe that you're only telling us what you want us to know. This comment is based on nothing other than a gut feeling but is general amongst the three of us. So far, you have threatened me personally twice for not keeping you in the picture, so what gives here?" said Gerald his voice beginning to raise with anger.

"Let me tell you something Mr. MI5, if I find out that you are reneging on your word, I will personally kick the living shit out of you, MI5, MI6 or whoever the hell you are. To coin your phrase, am I making myself quite clear?" Then as though he had read my mind he added: "The next time you use that bloody Superintendent as a threat to either of us, my old son, I'm going to break your bloody neck, agent or no agent, you got that, have you, Mr. Cotes?"

"Well, well, unrest in the ranks," Cotes replied facetiously.

"Just get one thing clear, Mr. Cotes, I've beaten better men than you. When I make a promise or a threat, you can take it to the bank. Now just tell us everything that you know."

John then took us into his confidence and told us what he knew, there was obviously a lot more to the case than even we'd imagined. Gerald's threat had done the trick, the agent's attitude was decidedly and apparently more respectful. *I have to say that so would yours and mine have been, given the same circumstances looking into Gerald Steel's sincere but angry eyes.*

In his own inimitable manner, John went on to say:

"I suppose that we'll be sharing the resources of your small army of trackers that left for the A1 a half hour ago," then he smiled holding up the palms of both hands in a gesture of surrender.

"We don't miss a lot at MI5! These people are making their move at last. Four other parts of the organization are carrying out similar operations in different areas of Great Britain. As far as I am aware there have been no other killings, or at least none have been reported yet."

"We don't know how they intend to leave the country, but we're sure that they do intend to depart soon and with their loot. So first we have to get onto their trail, as quickly as possible. I have men in position at every airport, and every sea port.

"It's unlikely that they'll try to go by air, due to the weight and bulk of the loot. The police will pass on surveillance from one city to another as the targets are spotted, so we have to put a game plan together in order to keep in touch with each other at all times."

Bruce's Office Later that Morning

"Frank Bell was speaking. Yes, Bruce, what's happening out there?"

"Nothing at the moment Dad, between us we've checked all cafes on the main AI from as far north as Weatherby right down to the outskirts of Leeds. Please make a note on the chart to that effect, along with the time and date.

Gerald and another man will call, and Cotes will be on with similar reports for you, keep them informed of any progress. By the way, Dad, you're doing a great job. Make sure that the phone is manned all day or until you hear from me to the contrary, I'll talk to you soon." As he'd put the phone down it rang once again.

"Hey, Frank, Gerald here, did you hear from anybody yet?"

"Yes, just heard from Bruce, he's covered from the north to the outskirts of the city, nothing to report." Frank began to feel like the Field Marshall in a military operations room.

"O.K. Frank, we've nothing to report from here. We're headed well south as agreed; I'll talk to you soon." Gerald replaced the receiver in a phone box, just as an Army truck pulled into the parking area next to the transport café, followed by a second military truck which pulled in behind the first.

Two soldiers in uniform jumped down from their respective cabs, each walking round the vehicles checking their loads, then went towards the cafe together.

Gerald entered the cafe, wearing a knitted cap pulled well down over his ears, and went up to the counter where he ordered a mug of tea with an egg sandwich. While waiting for his food he checked that there was no one in the café that he knew, and then he went over and sat down next to the window, making sure that he had full view of the parking lot. Just then a third military truck pulled into the area, parking next to the other two.

He looked across the cafe at the soldiers who were sitting together talking in whispers. *Most unlike the Army,* thought Gerald. They're normally a rowdy bunch, not quiet like these guys; there's something very odd going on here!

Moving across to where the soldiers were seated, he noticed that they all wore different shoulder patches.

One wore The Royal Tank Regiment, another The Royal Marines, and a third The Staffordshire Regiment.

As he sat listening they spoke in secretive whispers, the juke box was playing at full throttle. It was impossible to overhear their conversation, then to make matters worse the man sitting right next to him struck up a conversation.

"I don't know if these unions are all they're cracked up to be, I'd no choice when I took this job. If I didn't join, I didn't get the job, it was as simple as that."

Gerald nodded his head a few times as though in sympathy, then went back to the counter and ordered a second cup of tea.

He went back across the busy café, then sat on the other side of the soldiers, this time at an empty table. He glanced underneath the table, noticing immediately that one of the soldiers wore a pair of light brown civilian shoes with patterned socks. Closer scrutiny showed that the berets worn by the men were new and ill fitting.

He was just about to go to the telephone and call in this information when he recognized one of the men from the market walk through the doorway.

He walked towards Gerald, who looked across giving a slight shake of his head, which was sufficient warning that the other man should not show any sign of recognition. He took a seat next to Gerald.

"You gotta light there, me old cocker?" he asked, holding out an unlit cigarette.

"Sure," replied Gerald pulling a lighter from his pocket and lighting the man's Woodbine.

"Cum far, ave yer?" the newcomer asked.

"Came down from Leeds, I'm on my way to London," Gerald replied. He winked nodding in the direction of the army uniforms, then put his forefinger to his lips.

"Stay here and pay attention to what they say, I'll be back in a minute," he whispered, holding his mug of tea in front of his face as he spoke. He went outside to the pay phone and called in to control and spoke to Frank Bell.

"When Bruce calls in, tell him I'm sure I've got some of the people under surveillance. Ask him to round up the other two and meet me here. I'm at the Target Transport Cafe on the main A1 at Grantham. I think we can call off all of the other lads, get them back to work, the three of us can manage from here on in.

When they arrive, if they've any doubts whether it's the right place, there are three Army trucks in the parking area. Tell them not to show they recognize me. I'll approach them when the time is right. Frank, you're doing a great job. Thanks very much indeed. I'll be in touch."

The other helper from the market told Gerald that nothing of any consequence had been said in his absence. Gerald then passed the man sitting next to him a note telling him he could go back to work.

The man got up to leave.

"It was a pleasure to meet you, hope you have a safe journey." Gerald pulled out a bunch of papers and feigned reading them, after some minutes the obvious leader of the group stood.

"Come on you lot, we have to get to the next meeting point within two hours. Those old army trucks aren't exactly the fastest things on four wheels." They paid at the cashier's desk and went to leave.

Bruce came through the doors just as the soldiers left. He went to sit at a table across the other side of the cafe where a waitress arrived and took his order.

Gerald remained where he was, watching everyone very closely. He'd noticed a blonde woman sitting in the far corner; she'd been there since Gerald had first arrived. As tall blonde women were not at the top of his favorites, he paid her more attention than he would normally. He had certainly never seen her before. If she was a part of the setup then she was extremely clever. Never once had she averted her eyes from the newspaper she had in front of her. He'd watched her visit the toilet twice, each time she'd given herself adequate opportunity to glance surreptitiously around the café on her return.

Looking further around the room he saw an older man sitting near the exit, he had been there the whole time the soldiers had stayed, he too spent time looking around the room continuously.

Gerald felt uncomfortable but didn't know why, he knew by now to trust his instincts. He felt sure that someone was in there watching, he couldn't afford for them to spot him or Bruce. He paid his bill and left. Starting the car, he drove out of the parking area, turned left and headed north.

Bruce had put two and two together as he ate his sandwich and swallowed his tea at record speed, hardly looking up as he saw Gerald leave the premises. His thoughts were confirmed when he saw Gerald's car drive off in a northerly direction, a bluff, and a message to Bruce that they were certainly being watched.

He finished his food, settled his bill and walked slowly towards his car. He got into the front seat, picked up a wad of papers from the other seat and began to read, though he was actually paying strict attention to those leaving the café, in particular the blonde woman who came out soon after he did. She, too, sat in her car for a few minutes, and then drove out of the parking area turning south.

Following the meeting earlier that day in Leeds with John Cotes, we decided that I would ride with him as I hadn't yet learned to drive. Gerald and Bruce would travel in their own cars. There were also five other vehicles keeping surveillance on the regular transport, stopping places along the main A1 road.

We stopped at a couple of places, then after calling in to Frank's office, we learned that Gerald had possibly spotted a group of the crooks, evidently they were traveling in three army vehicles. This was rather like looking for a needle in a hay stack as there were plenty of military vehicles on the roads in the years after the war.

On our last check-in with Frank, we learned that Grantham was the place. We drove past a road sign indicating the borough border of Grantham, spotting a transport cafe in the distance. As we approached I noticed a car traveling in the opposite direction flashing its headlamps.

"That was Gerald's car," I grinned at John.

"I do believe you're right there, Matt," he pulled into a convenient lay-by. Shortly after, Gerald's car came up behind us. He climbed into the rear of our car and briefly explained what had taken place and what he'd seen. We then decided to leave Gerald's car in the lay-by, all three of us would now travel together. Evidently Bruce had remained at the truck stop and would keep up with the military vehicles.

As we approached, we saw Bruce about to leave, trying unsuccessfully to get into the busy southbound traffic. John flashed his lights and slowed down, waving him on in front then overtook him, indicating that he should follow us.

John drove along until there were no cars close behind, and then turned off into a side road. We pulled into the rear car park of a quaint thatch-roofed country pub. Inside the bar John ordered beers all round and portions of pork pie and pickles. Rather poetic, as we were in the area of Melton Mowbray, an area famous for its pork pies and sausages. We set about the task at hand.

.It seemed the crooks were, as expected, probably collecting more packages on their way down to the south. Gerald was convinced that the soldiers he'd seen were bogus and wearing borrowed, stolen or hired uniforms. He also believed he was on fairly firm ground assuming that the army trucks were being used by the Germans. In fact the four of us agreed, but we needed to be certain. The only way to achieve that was to find the trucks and take a look inside.

We finished our brunch, decided to split up and take only two cars, we would collect Gerald's later. We set off on our southerly trip. I rode with Bruce as I really hadn't spent much time in his company; we seemed to have a lot to talk about, particularly the old school, but Carl's murder was the main topic. By the time we'd driven for about forty-five minutes, I had brought him completely up-to-date, including telling him of Gerald's sincere threat to John Cotes earlier that day.

Another half hour more and we drove past the signs for the town limits of Peterborough. A few miles further south and we spotted a large roadside cafe with a motor repair center. Amongst the parked trucks were a number of military vehicles.

We followed John's car at a discreet distance as he drove on past the cafe. He pulled into a petrol station a mile or so further south, we drew in behind. This provided a good opportunity to replenish both fuel tanks, as we followed our agreed plan.

John was less familiar to the Germans so it was agreed that he would go back alone to the truck stop, see what he could find out about these military vehicles.

Meanwhile the three of us would sit it out and wait.

Chapter Twenty-Seven

Back at Casleton Village

The scene at the Armitage household was one of complete bewilderment, distress and sadness. The reality had finally hit Eve and she'd broken down completely.

As for George, he displayed an attitude of ambivalence, whether this was his way of covering up his feelings was difficult to decipher; he'd always been quite an insular man.

The one bonus, if there could be such in these circumstances, the crime scene was not in the home.

Although, that area was still being gone over by the metaphoric 'fine tooth comb'. There were people in authority everywhere. The crime scene had been roped off; as usual word had got to the village. You can't keep a secret in Casleton, at least not one of such magnitude.

Uniformed police were keeping back the ghoulish onlookers as best they could. What were they expecting to see? Something quite horrific no doubt, instead of a number of forensic types searching the ground and shrubbery, inch by inch.

Down at the mine and further along the rail line, the coal in the leading wagon was being emptied by hand into another wagon nearby. The regional crime squad had taken over the case, they now controlled the investigation.

This was cause of much territorial argument between the different police authorities. In this case there was the added complication of the S I B. involvement, particularly strong as the first killed was one of their own.

"But Mr. Armitage, do you have any idea why your son would go out at that time of night? Was he inebriated? We're informed that he'd been drinking at the Village Club. Did he say anything before he left?" Just then a short man, his hair neatly plastered down with Brylcream, came striding across the room in the Armitage residence.

"Alright that's enough if you don't mind, officer," he passed a card to the Chief Superintendent. I'm Mr. Armitage's solicitor, no more questions for the time being. As this is not the scene of the crime, I'm asking you to leave these good people in peace for awhile, please leave now."

The village had never received such attention; there were reporters from as far away as London, Glasgow and Birmingham. All drivers of vehicles entering and leaving the village were being stopped and questioned. People who would normally pass through the village on the buses were getting off and heading to the scene of the murder. At lunch break most of the staff from the mill headed in that direction to catch up on the latest news.

A man from Wakefield was cashing in on the unfortunate state of affairs; he was selling sandwiches and tea from the rear of a van. The gossip amongst both villagers and strangers alike was being escalated into mammoth proportions. *International Nazi Crime* and *Espionage* were some of the emotive words being bantered around by reporters using the two telephone boxes in the village. Many more of them were lining up outside, waiting to phone through their reports.

The two pubs nearest to the scene were doing a brisk trade, as more sightseers kept pouring in on cycles, motor bikes, cars and on foot. Some even arrived on horseback.

At one point a fight broke out near the entrance to the mine as a man shouted out 'pickpocket,' then proceeded to beat up another man he said had stolen his wallet. The loud bell of an ambulance rang above the noisy scene. The vehicle made slow progress through the crowds. A police 'Black Maria' followed close behind, stopping as the doors burst open and police officers poured out from its rear.

The ambulance continued up the lane alongside the track to collect its sad cargo as the police from the van began to disperse the onlookers and to clear the area.

"A second slaying at the coal mining village of Casleton, and the killers are still on the loose," came the voice of a radio commentator.

"Nobody knows who or why."

The newly arrived police kept the sightseers back as the ambulance pushed its way slowly through the throngs of people. The onlookers pushed and shouted, standing on tiptoe trying to see through the opaque windows of the ambulance.

"Come on, tell us who's been killed now, what's the big secret?" a voice shouted from the crowd. A police sergeant came up to the Chief Superintendent.

"The crowds are starting to get a bit ugly sir; they're demanding some answers, they want to know who's been killed."

"OK. I'll come out and talk to them in a minute, Sergeant, though what the hell I'm going to tell them, God alone knows!" answered the senior officer.

Back on the A1 South

We sat waiting for John's return from the transport cafe area; he seemed to have been gone for ages. The proprietor of the petrol station grew suspicious and came out wanting to know what we were waiting for. I suppose it must have seemed a little disconcerting to have three grown men sitting outside your premises, we just hoped he hadn't called the police.

The last thing we needed was to be pulled over for questioning at this precise moment, so we decided to vacate that particular venue, post haste, which left us with the problem of meeting up with John. Fortunately, the problem became purely academic. As we neared the main road, he turned into the lane and opened his window.

"I think they're at that last stop," he shouted.

"We need to check their trucks. There are at least six of them with three trucks that I can see. There's no telling what other spotters are with them, but you can rest assured there will be others up front along with them; they won't let that cargo out of their sight for one minute." We all piled into the one car for an update.

"Here's what I think we should do next........" As John talked we put together our plan. Then three canvas-covered Army trucks went by, the high-pitched whine of the special military all-terrain tires setting them apart from other traffic. Getting back into our respective cars after a suitable wait we followed, one car first, then the other further behind.

I sat next to John Cotes in the lead car, bringing my notes up to date as we drove south. I reflected on the way things had multiplied and increased in their complexity since that evening in the fields.

There was the sound of a horn behind us. I looked round to see the flashing of the headlights from a vehicle behind; John drove on a little way, then he pulled into a side road. The van behind followed, then drove past us stopping up front. 'Hertfordshire Electricity Company' was painted on its rear; John said that this was to be our new transport, delivered by one of John's men!

After exchanging vehicles, John and I drove down the road in the electricity company van, I in the rear putting on the company overalls and the safety hat which had been supplied with the van. We drove along for some twenty miles or so, eventually catching up with Gerald and Bruce. Soon we approached the town of Hatfield, coming up on a very large rest area with restaurant, fuel station and store.

We parked in an area where we couldn't be seen from the main buildings. John went across and brought Bruce and Gerald over. They clambered into the back of our undercover van, they changed into the clothes provided, which included hard hats, as well as the knitted variety.

Eventually we drove over to the main building, parking by the side of the three Army vehicles, hoping they were the ones we were looking for.

We went into the cafe and saw the soldiers talking and drinking tea. Gerald was left inside the van, after a few minutes John sent me to join him.

He and I had sat there for a good twenty minutes or so, when another plain truck drew up behind us, parking across the rear of our van and the Army trucks. There were no windows in the back of our van, only some small ventilation slits, through which I heard a voice speaking in German. The hairs on the back of my neck were instantly standing on end.

I'd recognized the voice instantly, luckily Gerald was at the other end of the van and therefore he didn't hear who it was.

I put my finger to my lips and gestured for him not to move and to be quiet, then heard ropes being unfastened, the unmistakable scraping of boxes being slid along the wooden floor of a truck, followed by the shuffling of feet on the ground, then a heavy thud of something landing in the back of the truck next to us.

This operation was repeated many times before ropes were fastened midst garbled conversation. Doors thudded closed and we heard the roar of the engine as they drove away.

"Was that those Krauts?" Gerald shouted from the front of the van.

"Yes it was, and it was your friend and mine, the big one." I had all I could do to restrain Gerald from flying through the door.

"I want that bastard," he snarled.

I pulled on my knitted hat. Gerald, once he'd calmed down, donned a safety helmet, then we went inside to join the others.

The café was very busy, spotting someone or indeed being spotted would not be the easiest of tasks. Looking around without being obvious, I went to the counter and collected two teas, taking a different route back to the table. I couldn't see anyone that I'd ever seen before, but of course they, too, could be in disguise.

I explained to John about the events that had taken place in the lorry park, which strangely neither seemed to excite him nor to interest him unduly. I followed as two of the soldiers went towards the toilets, but all they were discussing was last weekend's soccer game. They made no reference to any other subject until they were leaving, then typically their topic changed to the large-breasted girl behind the counter.

Whether it was the pickled onions that I had eaten earlier or the pork pie, I'd more than a sudden urge to remove myself from the urinal and into a toilet, which I achieved with much rapidity. I'd sat there for a couple of minutes when I heard the restroom door open and close twice.

"How many more stops have we to do yet? Frankly, I'm getting fed up with drinking semi-cold tea; I don't think I could look another sausage roll in the face," a voice moaned.

"Don't complain, we're being well-paid aren't we?"

"What do they keep putting into the trucks?"

"Don't know and don't care," was the snappy reply.

"What if the police pull us over, then what?"

"That's unlikely, the only ones who would possibly do that would be the military police, and I have all of the paperwork needed for them. Now come on, leave the brainwork to me, I'm the only genuine soldier here anyway. MPs don't spend much time on this road. Oh, by the way, change your civvy socks when you get back into the truck, wear the ones provided, that's the sort of thing an Army cop would spot in an instant."

"Now, I have a phone call to make, get the others ready to leave. We have to be at Luton in one hour. That gives us plenty of time. Thirty miles an hour is standard military convoy speed, make sure you don't exceed it. It's the last leg of the run to the port at Dover that will take the time," said the authoritative voice as they left the room. I followed them back into the cafe and reported the conversation to John and the other two. We had no need to rush now we knew exactly where they were going.

"We have the time to go back and pick up the other two cars, maybe you and Bruce and Matt want to go back to Leeds now, and let us conclude this affair," John said to Gerald.

"Not on your life," replied Gerald.

"You can say that again," Bruce added.

"If you think that we would drop out now, you have another think coming."

"I could make you go back."

"Don't put money on it," Gerald snarled, with a very serious look on his face.

"As I've already told you very clearly once before, don't push your luck, we are partners until those bastards are caught or dead. So resign yourself to that fact, what I've just said goes for these two as well." He gestured towards Bruce and me as we nodded steadily in agreement.

With that settled we left the café, then climbed into the van and set off driving back north. We were all returning to Leeds, taking some of the transport back, picking up fresh clothes, and then heading down to the port of Dover.

"Where did you get this van?" Gerald asked as we bounced around the uncomfortable interior of the electricity company vehicle.

"Oh, didn't I tell you, we stole it from the electricity compound."

"We?" Gerald exclaimed.

"There are one or two other people at MI5 you know," said John with a grin. I never go anywhere without backup. Apparently we do have a bit of a problem though. Evidently someone else is on the same track as we are."

The woman sitting in the Morris car watched the departure of the electricity company van without suspicion and then she drove across the parking area. Passing the café, she pulled up outside the restaurant. Inside at the rear, she joined a group of three people sitting at a table, one was the big German.

"Is everything in order, Helga?" he asked her.

"I haven't seen anything to worry about so far; nobody followed the trucks when they left; there is only one face I remember having seen at two of the stops so far. If it's not a coincidence then I will have to deal with him, he's the one who drives a vehicle with the long antenna," she replied smugly.

"Possibly S.I.B., same as the interfering pig at the mine, I think." They finished their meal, went outside and climbed into a car with a caravan trailer big enough to sleep at least four people attached.

Once out onto the main road they headed towards London and the south. After a pause of about two minutes, a small black car with a long antenna crept out onto the A1 and drove off towards the south, and London.

On the way north we collected the other two cars and went back into Leeds, where Bruce had a number of things to do in the office. Gerald also had some chores to take care of while John went back to his office to check in with his superiors and tell them what we had learned so far.

Meanwhile, I called the mill and asked to speak with David but was put through to Harold instead.

"What's been happening with you, where have you been? Mary and your Dad have been driven sick with worry."

"We've been trying to find Carl's killers," I replied.

"We, who's we?" he asked.

"We, Gerald, Bruce and I have tried to get onto the trail of these people, but to no avail," I lied uncomfortably, and felt that Harold had perceived as much.

"Isn't this really a job for the law? What is going to happen now as far as you vigilantes are concerned, may I ask?" he added somewhat sarcastically.

"That's why I wanted to speak with David."

"Go on," he added.

"We've some ideas that may amount to something, so I'd like to postpone my work-study at the mill and continue these investigations along with Bruce and Gerald," I blurted out.

"You would, would you? In which case it's me you should be talking to and not to my son David. Matt, you'll never make a good liar, you're on to something I'm sure; so don't you go trying to pull the wool over my eyes. I gathered from Bruce's father that you've had this bee in your bonnet for some years, something to do with Germans and parachutes. Though I firmly believe that this is a matter for the police, I, for one won't get in your way, on one strict proviso. I go to your home right away to let them know you are all right, OK?"

"Thanks Harold, thank you very much."

"Don't thank me, just be extra careful, you have come close to total disaster on more than one occasion during this affair so be ultra cautious, do you hear me, Matt?"

"Yes, Harold, I'll take care. Please tell David what's happening. If you should be asked any questions about me by the police, I'm sure that you know how to handle them."

"Where are you now?" Harold asked. I told him that I was back in Leeds but wanted to leave for Dover straight away, after a trip to the hospital to have the stitches taken out.

"How are you for money?" he asked.

"Not too good, I left my savings book at school."

"Here's what you are to do: go into Midland Bank off City Square and ask for Mr. Bingham, I'll make sure there's some money waiting for you."

"Thanks, Harold, you're a gem."

"You take care remember, and keep me posted from time to time."

Meanwhile, back at the market, Bruce had finished all his duties. As I walked in, Bruce's dad was asking how long he intended to be away.

"Come on in, Matt," said Mr. Bell with a smile. It seems you were all taught to be foolhardy at that school. Makes me wonder what I spent all my money on!" He spoke to neither of us in particular. Bruce grinned.

"You'll be alright, Dad, I'll phone on a regular basis. The new man has the accounts perfectly under control, just pretend that I'm still at school and that you're the boss man again, with no interference from me, won't that be great, eh?"

Our conversation was interrupted by the ringing of the phone.

"It's for you," Frank Bell said to me.

"Matt, the police have just been round here snooping, asking when you start your work-study program," Harold said.

"I told them I'd sent you on a short holiday, after the recent hectic spell at the mine."

"Harold, you shouldn't lie on my behalf."

"I didn't lie, I told them I gave you twenty pounds and sent you down south, which is precisely what I've done. Just wanted you to know that they're on the war path, so be careful and take care." With that, he rang off.

As I'd put the phone down, it rang again. Bruce picked up the receiver.

"Hang on a minute and I'll see if he's here. It's the police wanting to talk to Gerald." As if by telepathy, Gerald walked through the doorway with a big smile on his face, which soon disappeared when he heard who was on the phone.

"Hello, Steel here, yes Superintendent, and what can I do for you?" there was a long pause, during which Gerald made faces at the phone.

"Of course I would tell you, absolutely, sure I don't want to go to prison," then his voice increased in volume.

"Neither do I take kindly to harassing threats, particularly from a bloody Superintendent of police who should know better. If you have nothing more to say I will bid you good day, Sir." He slammed down the phone grinning from ear to ear. Frank Bell raised his eyes heavenwards.

"I've always wanted to do that to a Superintendent," he said smiling and rubbing his hands with glee.

"Cotes was on the phone a short while ago, he wants to see us within the hour, not at his office…says the police are watching his premises, and ours too.

He suggested that we leave both our cars outside the office here, get a cab to the rear of City Station. "Evidently, somebody else is missing now," said Bruce.

We dismissed the idea of a cab; instead, we got one of Bruce's drivers to take us round in one of the company vans, equally as inconspicuous as any taxi cab, in fact more so. As City Station was off City Square, my trip to the bank was facilitated. I could collect the funds Harold had promised. To describe my funds as depleted would amount to the understatement of the century as the last two cups of tea I purchased had cleaned me out completely.

I was in the bank for less than five minutes, I'd asked for Mr. Bingham, given my name. Almost as if by magic, a thin, sad-faced man came out, asked me who'd organized the envelope in his hand, and then said:

"Sign here, Mr. Harper." I took the packet and left the bank.

Rounding the corner to the rear of City Station, I spotted John Cotes sitting in his car. I was about to cross the street when I stopped suddenly, seeing a car that looked vaguely familiar. The rear door window was wide open, the car seemed unoccupied. I crossed the street, walked past John's car, pointing as I headed for the black Austin.

I almost tripped over my own feet as I stared into the dark interior of the car.

There, slumped across the rear seat was the body of a man. I could see blood behind his ear as I ran back quickly towards the others, or as quickly as my recent disabilities would permit. Feeling rather sick, I opened John's car door and jumped onto the back seat.

"Christ, what's up Matt, you near made me jump out of my skin, you look as though you've seen a ghost!" exclaimed Bruce.

"You're not far out, that car over there belongs to the Germans, it's their Austin and there's the body of a man slumped over on the rear seat, that or someone's fast asleep in there with blood running down his ear."

John Cotes went immediately across to where the Austin was parked, checking the surrounding area carefully he opened the door, holding the handle with his handkerchief. He came back with a grim look on his face, he got into our car, then told us to drive away from the street as quickly as possible.

"It's the body of Sergeant Cockerham, SIB," he announced with anger in his voice.

"He went missing last night, our people last saw him at Hatfield."

"Those shits have killed him and brought him back up here to keep everyone off their scent," Bruce replied in amazement.

"Yes, and by the smell of the cigarette smoke in the car and the heat coming up from the engine, the driver who left the car here went very recently. It certainly wasn't Cockerham. He was already dead. I would guess they left some time in the last half hour."

"We must make an anonymous call to the police to let them know about Cockerham," Gerald added.

"Look, John, we know where these bastards are heading, why don't we follow them? We could probably bag them all and bring this thing to an end?" Gerald added.

"There's a lot more to this case than you comprehend, Gerald," said John.

"Try me," said Gerald.

"All in good time, my friend, then you'll understand. You forced me into letting you come along, just be patient. Soon all, I hope, will be revealed."

We pulled up at a phone box on the outskirts of Leeds. John left the car but returned quickly, cursing vandalism. We stopped a little later at a phone that evidently the vandals had missed, so he went into the box, we assumed to call the police.

As we drove towards the south, John began to outline a plan for the next stage of the chase. He believed that we should be following the Germans and not the soldiers in the military trucks.

We knew the trucks contained the loot, so surely the Germans wouldn't be too far away from their packages.

"The killing of Cockerham indicates they are very much alert and aware as to who's following them, so we need to tail them from a distance. If we become repetitious or careless, they'll spot us immediately.

"Really, we can't take the risk of them seeing us by going directly to Dover. They may even change their mode of transport for the channel crossing: there are just too many variables for us to become complacent," said John.

That evening we stayed at a cheap and cheerful, but clean bed and breakfast house just south of Luton. Luckily we'd seen the car and van trailer at a roadside lay-by north of the town.

I managed to make two phone calls, one to Harold to thank him for the money, also I'd promised to keep him up-to-date with any new developments. He then told me that the murder of Sergeant Cockerham was not yet in the newspapers.

Finally, I asked him to give my apologies to David; I didn't think I would be able to keep the dinner date on Saturday as arranged. Harold said that occasion had already been postponed because of Carl's unfortunate death. My second call was to Joan.

"I'm so pleased to hear from you, Matt," she said with obvious concern in her voice.

"I was very worried when I heard the sad news of Carl Armitage this morning. The village has gone mad, it's been packed with reporters and sightseers all day.

"I went to your house to see you but nobody was at home, so I phoned Harold White. He told me you'd gone away for a few days rest after your accident in the mines, apart from that, you were fine. Also the police were around here asking me if I knew where you'd gone, so I told them what Harold told me. They seemed quite happy with that, but where are you and what's going on, Matt?"

"I can't go into it right now, but I'm fine, don't worry, if the police come back don't refer to this conversation. I hope to be back real soon, I'll see you then. I just wanted you to know how much I enjoyed your company at the club. Oh, just to let you know, dinner at the Mansion has been postponed due to Carl's death. I'll be back before you know it and I'll try to call you again, maybe tomorrow around the same time."

"I miss you, Matt, take care of yourself," she added with a sad note in her voice.

"I will, and I'm beginning to miss you too, Joan."

I must have slept like a log all night. I awoke with a start, as stiff as a board, the sound of many toilets being flushed, along with the banging of many doors, the clatter of dishes, and the unmistakable smell of eggs and bacon cooking somewhere close.

Crawling out of bed, I put on my trousers, went along the corridor to a door with 'Bath' written on it, my towel over my shoulder, the 'Occupied' sign showing. Eventually, a man opened the door and came out.

"Morning, the water's cold," he said with an irritated look on his face, two small pieces of toilet paper stuck over bloody razor patches on the side of his chin. I washed quickly in the cold water, went down to the dining area where the others were already eating.

"Good afternoon, you must have slept like the dead," said John grinning.

"Some of us have been up for hours." Over a huge breakfast it was decided that Bruce and Gerald would catch a train to Dover and do a bit of reconnaissance work there while John and I would keep track of the Germans from a distance.

Communicating would present a problem, so John had obtained the number of a pay phone in the passenger terminal of the cross channel ferry boat company.

Bruce and Gerald were to stand beside that phone at four o'clock that evening for a debrief update and further plans.

"You'll have to catch a train from Luton to Kings Cross, London, get the underground to Victoria Station where you'll board the boat train to Dover. The train goes directly into the Port.

Find yourselves a guest house that gives a good view of the actual boats and loading areas and particularly the parking area.

"Here, take these," he passed a pair of binoculars to Gerald.

"Do you have sufficient money with you?"

"I raided petty cash," Bruce replied with a guilty tone in his voice.

"Oops, so did I," said Gerald, a broad grin across his face.

"I left the cupboard bare." He stood gesturing with both hands apart in a sort of weak apology.

"The new accounts manager will be pleased. I assume you put a chit in the petty cash box?"

"No," Gerald replied.

"Me, neither." They both roared with laughter like two naughty schoolboys.

After breakfast John Cotes and I hit the road again, first dropping the other two at Luton railway station. I managed to grab a morning newspaper and we were on our way.

After some many miles we approached the outskirts of London and the start of the north circular road, which I learned describes a semi-circle around the Greater London area, eventually meeting up with the self-explanatory south circular, where we would subsequently join the A 25 road going south to the coast and Dover.

The press had plenty to say about the small mining village of Casleton that morning, but nothing new had been added to yesterday's news. No suspects had been found, no motive had been uncovered. There were pictures of some of the crowd scenes, a photograph of Carl in which he appeared much younger, alongside another photograph of a covered body being carried on a stretcher by two uniformed policemen; so, no startling new clues or revelations so far. No mention of the body in Leeds.

The north circular was a busy road, about half way around it I pointed out the sign of a transport café coming up on our side of the road. We were both feeling a bit sluggish, so we turned left into the large busy parking area, primarily to get something to eat. The cafe was set well back from the busy road and could hardly be seen from the entrance because of the many trees surrounding it.

A bakery delivery van had pulled in behind us. John stopped the car rather quickly, much to the annoyance of the van driver who hit his horn and shouted some choice words through the open window; his whole conversation was leaning towards the vernacular. John got out of the car, went back to the van and leaned through the window of the vehicle. The van driver pulled over to the side, John came back and got into the car and moved it over to the side.

"What's going on?" I asked feeling somewhat mystified.

"I've decided to have a change of job, I'm going to be a bread delivery man for a while," he replied with a smirk across his face.

"You wait here until I get back, don't show yourself, these people know your face. I'll bring something back for you to eat. John then went behind the van and put on a white coat that the driver passed to him. The driver opened the rear doors of the van, pointing to various trays stacked on the sliding shelves. To my amazement they both climbed into the van and drove off towards the café.

The London to Dover Express

The train journey into London's Kings Cross station was slow and torturous; on arrival they ended up in the usual commuter rush hour madness.

"Sit down, let's wait until they've all gone, we're in no specific hurry," Gerald said.

Once the crowds had thinned out sufficiently, they went off towards the underground station. Here they were packed like sardines in a can, except sardines don't have to stand up. After what seemed like an eternity, hanging onto a strap and trying to keep their balance, they left the thoroughly unpleasant environment of the underground system, surfacing at Victoria Station like rabbits being pursued by a hungry ferret.

The Boat Train was due to leave the station in just twenty minutes time, traveling non-stop through to Dover. They boarded the train and found themselves two seats together, and then went to find the refreshment coach where they sat down with a bottle of beer each. They'd hardly got settled into their seats when Gerald shot his head in the opposite direction to the bustling platform.

"Quick, turn this way," Gerald said, hastily pointing at the window opposite the platform.

"Don't look back," he added, "whatever you do." He held a tight grip on Bruce's arm.

"OK, it's alright now, you can turn."

"What the hell was that all about?"

"It's our friend, the little Kraut with the thick lenses; the bastard that put a hole in my leg!" Gerald said, gritting his teeth as he spoke the words. "He just went along the platform, looks like he's damn well traveling on this train, too."

"Was he alone?" Bruce asked.

"I don't know, I'm not sure, maybe it was him that drove the body back to Leeds," said Gerald.

"We'll need to find out, and that's for sure."

The train began to pull out of the station as they spoke, gradually gathering speed as it went on its way. They had decided to split up to check if any of the other Germans were on the train. Gerald headed towards the front of the train, Bruce walked towards the rear.

As usual, the train service to the southern port was packed. A mixture of tourists on holiday, foreigners, Naval personnel returning to ships and the Royal Marines going back to their base at Deal in Kent.

Chapter Twenty-Eight

The Transport Café South of London

John walked into the café behind the bread delivery man carrying a packed tray of loaves on his shoulder, the place was packed. As he returned through the kitchen doors to fetch another tray, he scanned the room but couldn't see any soldiers in the dining area. He went out of the door, and from the vantage point on the top of the steps he had a good look around, but couldn't see any military trucks in the surrounding parking area.

He took another full tray of cakes and pies from the van, walking back inside the café, through to the kitchen.

"Finding the work so hard that you need an extra pair of hands, are you?" said a white-coated cook to the deliveryman.

"No, he's just in training to take over his own route," said John's new partner to the cook. John looked through the round window of the door leading from the kitchen to the dining room. He was pretty sure that he had seen none of the Germans or bogus soldiers there.

After they delivered the last tray he said to the deliveryman,

"OK let me buy you a nice cup of tea to thank you for all your help, it's the least I can do."

They sat down with their tea while John positioned himself so he had a full view of the room. He remained inconspicuous in his white coat and had plenty of time to take a good look around the tables, but didn't see anyone whom he remotely recognized. Leaving the café they drove back towards John's car.

"Are you really MI5?" asked the driver. John opened his I.D. to show him.

"Bloody hell, you are! Wait till I tell the wife when I get home tonight, she won't believe a word of it." The driver parked the van next to John's car and yours truly.

They got out of the van and John went to the rear to return the coat.

"Here, take a couple of these, one for you and one for your mate in the car, it's not every day I gets the chance to play at being a spy," the driver grinned, giving John two cream cakes.

"Why, thanks very much and thanks again for all your help today, you've been of great assistance." John got back into the car. He'd been gone quite some time so I'd catnapped for a while.

"Here you are, wrap yourself around this," he grinned, passing me a fresh cream cake.

"Oh, thanks, custard slices are my favorite."

"It's about the only good that came out of that little escapade," John laughed.

"Not so, when you were in the café, the car and trailer drove in, look they're parked just over there, so it's not been an entirely fruitless exercise!" I said, wiping the cream from my face as I dug enthusiastically into the delicious delicacy.

Meanwhile on the London to Dover Express, Gerald had drawn a blank on his foray to the front of the train. He was just getting into his seat as Bruce returned. He came through the door from the rear of the train looking like the cat that got the cream.

"He's in the last coach before the guard's station, in the first compartment, facing front. The only other people in the compartment are sailors, and a pretty rowdy lot they are, too. The corridors are full of the Navy and Marines, you can hardly get through there," Bruce said.

"Let's have a spot of fun then," Gerald replied with a fiendish grin across his face.

"What do you mean by 'fun'?" Bruce asked.

"Follow me, you're just about to find out," Gerald replied as he strode quickly towards the rear of the train.

They entered the last carriage and stood in the packed corridor alongside a number of Royal Marines. The whole area was a cacophony of sound: singing, shouting, joke-telling, arguing, you name it. As they stood there, a sailor came out from the first compartment to use the toilet, which was, as usual, occupied.

"How's it going?" Gerald asked.

"I'm returning to my ship," the sailor replied.

"We're heading for the Suez area, they are predicting trouble there," he added. Gerald told the marine that he was a former 'Bootneck,' then he added:

"See that bloke in your compartment, the little one with the glasses, well I think he's a bloody German spy!" exclaimed Gerald in a voice loud enough for the whole corridor to hear.

"I heard him speaking to the ticket collector at the ticket desk, he has a very strong German accent, hardly speaks a bloody word of English. We've been watching him ever since! Can't stand those krauts," Gerald shrugged his shoulders, a totally innocent look on his face.

"I wouldn't have thought that His Majesty's Royal Navy would let a potential Kraut spy have a very pleasant trip."

"I can't believe that your Brother Marines here would think much of your lot if you did," Gerald said in an even louder voice, turning as he spoke towards a Marine with a 42 commando patch on his arm. As an ex-Marine, Gerald knew well the ongoing tussles between the Navy and Marine corps. He'd placed the charges and he'd lit the fuse, now it was time to retire.

As Gerald and Bruce made their way back to their own compartment, to coin a phrase, "the shit had hit the fan," a full carriage length away they could hear men shouting:

"Heil, Hitler."

"Ve haff vays uff making you talk."

"Let's see him goose step."

"Here let me take a look at those spectacles, Adolf."

"They should keep him busy for the remainder of his journey, that's if he gets to finish it." Gerald said, as he grinned from ear to ear.

"You're a wicked bugger," Bruce said, with a note of admiring pleasure in his voice.

Back on the Road South of London

John and I decided to leave the Germans at the café and continue driving south. We knew they were heading for Dover anyway so we could afford to take off and be in front of them for a while.

Driving along the road, I bit into the last bit of my cream horn and was suddenly reminded very effectively of the damage I'd sustained to my teeth. A piece of the creamed horn hit the raw nerve end of my broken front tooth. I gave John a perfect exhibition of spontaneous levitation, as the pain shot through my nervous system. When my backside returned to the seat, I groaned in agony.

"You really need to get those teeth seen to pretty soon," John said, twisting his face into a sympathetic wince.

"Those stitches need to come out of your face, too," he added. I nodded in agreement as I reluctantly tossed the remains of the source of my agony through the open window of the car. The toothache was to persecute me for most of the day.

John seemed to be driving slower than usual, we'd covered the North Circular and were traveling the southern orbit of the Metropolis; this part was less industrial, offering more of an urban scene. A little further along we came to a tree lined lay-by which offered seclusion from the road but allowed us to see passing traffic. We pulled in, then placed ourselves at a good vantage point to see the oncoming traffic.

After waiting there for at least an hour, we'd just decided to move on when the car and trailer went past. We still hadn't seen any of the military trucks go by.

"They may have changed the vehicles," John mused.

"Maybe the pickup collections are finished, they could well be using just one large vehicle now." he added looking concerned. After a suitable pause we followed the car and trailer, but kept a fair distance between them and us. By now we'd left the South Circular and were on the A25 having crossed the outskirts of Croydon and entered the County of Kent. Passing a sign for the town of Sevenoaks, we saw the car and trailer parked outside a small hotel called The Grange, which seemed to be a combination of bar, hotel and restaurant.

We drove about a mile past this hotel and came upon another transport café, the parking area packed with heavy goods vehicles. A sign outside read: 'Good clean, inexpensive accommodations.'

"This looks like the place for us," said John. We drove around to the rear of the building, parked the car, then secured two rooms for the night, or should I say two cubicles, a more apt description as how small they turned out to be.

John then drove us back to the Grange, where we had seen the Germans parked earlier. He stopped outside the main entrance and told me to stay in the car as he went inside. He was back out within five minutes.

"There are four of them in there: the big man, two other shorter and very fit looking individuals, and the woman. At the moment they're all eating together in the restaurant. I find it hard to believe there'll be many more of them around, but we can never be too careful. There must be at least one guy keeping an eye on things."

Cotes climbed back into the car and we drove over to the transport area where we were staying.

There were two parts to the building, well three, if you count the sleeping quarters. We could see one big dining area, then leading off was a smaller recreation area with a bar and pool tables, along with the inevitable juke box. I put on a jacket and went into the dining area, taking a seat to the right of the entrance, behind an area where clothes were hanging. John passed by and went into the bar, but he was back within seconds, beckoning me to follow him.

The bar was packed with the usual array of customers; over in the corner was our man, the big soldier surrounded by the other three I'd overheard in the men's room earlier.

Last time we saw them they were in army uniform, now they were wearing civilian attire.

We left the building, both with the strong feeling that someone was keeping a close watch on us, although we hadn't noticed anyone paying particular attention. Outside it was dark as we looked around at all the vehicles in the parking area.

"Lets get to it, then. We need to find their transport. Are they still using the military trucks, or have they switched to other vehicles by now? I hope they're still with the trucks or this could prove to be a very busy night for us," the agent moaned.

The Ferry Port, Dover

Gerald and Bruce had been lucky in finding the Kentish Arms, a small inn set on the street above the port. It was a small local pub that had five letting rooms, a small dining area and a busy bar. The room that Gerald and Bruce were given looked directly down over the ferry port. With the help of the binoculars, all the parked vehicles and the gangways onto the boats were clearly visible.

They sat in the passenger lounge area of the ferry service, having purchased open tickets for one car and four occupants, useable on any day, given that space was available. Also, they had obtained schedules on all the ferry crossings.

"The weather is not at its best just at the moment," the booking clerk had told them.

"But you know what the English Channel is like. It's the most un-predictable stretch of water in the world, one minute calm, the next, the ships rocking and rolling all over the place." It was ten minutes past the time John should have called them at the terminal. They were standing by the kiosks when the phone rang, Gerald grabbed it quickly.

"Anything to report," asked John.

"No, everything's quiet here. We've done all that can be done. It's just a matter of waiting now."

"Well, we're just past Sevenoaks, close to Maidestone. We thought it made sense to stay with these people; we're here for the night. We'll make an early start, we should be with you first thing tomorrow. Give me the number of the pub where you're staying, if there is any change I'll call you there."

"At the moment we don't know what transport they're using for their cargo. We think they've dispensed with the military trucks. Those soldiers are staying at the same place as us, but now they're wearing civilian clothes; we hope to find the vehicles shortly. The big guy and the woman are driving a car pulling a caravan trailer."

"Keep your eyes peeled, just in case they leave here before we establish what trucks they're driving. Check every vehicle that arrives at the port, don't miss any. Remember being one step ahead is what's kept these buggers in business for so long. I'll sign off now, I won't contact you again unless it's an emergency." The phone went dead.

Gerald and Bruce had just finished eating sandwiches in their room. Between them, over the last three hours, they hadn't taken their eyes off the ferry terminal for one split second. As Gerald continued to look through the glasses yet again, he was having some difficulty seeing clearly, the port lights reflected on the lenses. He sat up abruptly. He thought his eyes were playing tricks on him. He took the binoculars away from his face, cleaned the lenses, rubbed his eyes, and looked again.

"Shit, it's them; they're here, look Bruce, quick, take a look," he said passing the glasses to Bruce. "Over there by the fire station, you can just see their trailer sticking out from behind the building."

While Bruce was looking through the binoculars, Gerald was busy looking at the ferry time table on the bed. The next sailing was at midnight, the one after that was at seven o'clock the following morning.

Thoughts raced through Gerald's mind, he wondered how he could possibly contact John. What a shame John hadn't given a phone number for the place where they were staying.

He felt sure that Maidstone or Sevenoaks probably had lots of transport stops and guest houses.

"You stay here," he said to Bruce. If John calls tell him what's happening, then come out and find me." With that, he disappeared out the door.

As Gerald left, Bruce had a horrible thought. He knew his temperament, *if he sets eyes on the big German, heaven only knows what might happen*, he thought. Gerald was already out of the pub, down the steep embankment in no time at all, then swiftly but cautiously he moved around the perimeter of the port area. As he neared the place where he'd seen the trailer, he peered from behind a parked furniture removal van with no printing on its sides. He looked across and saw the trailer, which had been disconnected from the car, its tow bar resting on a concrete block.

He approached the trailer with caution, seeing the curtains were drawn shut. There were no lights on inside, he tried the door handle which turned with a resounding click, then swung open. His nerves began to jangle as he entered the vehicle, it was deserted. It was as though it had never been occupied, nothing of any real interest. After a quick search he left rapidly.

Gerald ran steadily from vehicle to vehicle for at least a half mile, though not quite sure what he was looking for. As he approached the booking offices, he donned his knitted cap, pulling it well down over his ears, then strolled through the building, hands in his pockets, his jacket collar pulled up around his face, trying to look as casual as possible. The room was packed full of people.

It was then that he saw both the big German and the woman standing together, talking to a booking clerk. Getting as close as possible, he took a seat near the desk, hoping to hear their conversation.

He picked up an evening newspaper and pulled it close in front of his face, so as not to be noticed, but not before he'd seen the headlines.

Another Yorkshire Coal Mine Killing. The German was beginning to raise his voice in anger.

"We have to catch the midnight boat! It is vitally important to us."

"That may be sir, but I say, again: we will accommodate all the passengers and the car, but we cannot possibly get the truck on this crossing. That's a very large vehicle, sir. We just don't have the room until the first crossing tomorrow, there's no more to be said on the matter."

"That is just not good enough," snapped the German angrily.

"I'm afraid that's the way it has to be. What do you want me to do, manufacture space for you? Not only don't we have the space, but we also have very strict rules regarding weight on the ferries. Now do you want to book the passengers and the car or not? There are other passengers waiting to purchase tickets."

The German stomped off angrily, in such a hurry that he only missed stumbling over Gerald's foot by the merest fraction of an inch. The German went across the room to get into a huddle with the others.

Gerald moved as close as he dared without drawing attention to himself. As he went past he heard them speaking in their native tongue, *where are you when we need you, young Matt*, he thought to himself.

He went back to where he'd been sitting and waited for the inevitable return of the big German who was back within minutes.

"We will book now for the crossing tomorrow morning, the big truck, the car and seven passengers."

"I'll need the names and passports of all of the passengers," the clerk replied.

Back at the transport stop, the agent and I had searched the whole area for over an hour; we couldn't find a trace of the vehicles anywhere.

On returning to the bar, our soldiers were not to be seen anywhere either.

Back at the reception desk, John asked for the manager. When he arrived John showed him his I.D., then asked to see the register. Evidently only six rooms of the twenty available were occupied. Two by drivers from British Steel, the other two were traveling salesmen, and of course, us.

We took a note of the registration numbers of all four vehicles, thanked the manager, before we went out to check each one individually. Two were open trucks; the others, a car and a station wagon.

"Let's go back and check the Grange," said John. We got into the car, driving back the few miles to the hotel; there was no car and trailer caravan in the car park, everyone had left.

After a very short discussion we decided to leave and head south, try and catch up with them on the road. As we set off for the port of Dover, I turned on the radio.

"I wouldn't hold your breath, Matt. I haven't had a peep out of that bloody thing for weeks. I fiddled with the dials to no avail; we heard the crackle of static, then surprise, surprise.......

"Good evening, this is the nine o'clock news from the studios of the BBC. On Satur," sssqqqqshsh. The crackling and squelch killed the remainder of the introduction, then: "There are still no clues in the Yorkshire coal mine murders. A spokesman for the police said that no stone was being left unturned in their investigations.

"The body of another S.I.B. officer was found in a car in Leeds, bringing the total to three killings in the space of one week. One source of information even suggested international connections.

"On a slightly more amusing note, earlier today a small man was found stripped of his outer clothing, wearing only his undergarments. He had been bound, gagged and tied to the overhead luggage rack of the Dover to London express train. Pinned to the front of his under vest was a note which read: 'I'm a German Spy.' The man, a German national who wore spectacles which rather oddly contained no lenses, spoke very little English. He was detained for questioning by Scotland Yard's Special Branch……. The prime minister today opened a".........sssqqqqqqhhhh.

"What the hell was all that about? I bet you that bloody Gerald Steele's involved somewhere there," exclaimed John shaking his head in disbelief.

"That description fits the little German with the thick glasses, except the glasses weren't thick" he said smirking.

"I guess you're probably right, don't forget he's the one who shot Gerald in the leg," I replied to John, smiling despite the toothache at the thought of the man's clothes and lenses being removed.

"He must have driven that body to Leeds, caught the train to London and Dover," said John. *I wonder what the news report would say if ever Gerald got hold of the big German,* I thought.

"Do you think that Special Branch will tie this German in with the Yorkshire affair?" I asked John.

"They will after they receive an anonymous phone call from me, telling them to check his prints with any in the car containing Cockerham's body." The remainder of the journey passed uneventfully, until eventually I saw the welcome lights of Dover.

The Mansion at Casleton Village

Harold White sat listening to the evening news on BBC radio. He had heard the sad report of yet another killing in Leeds. Like many others, he wondered when this whole mess was going to end. He reflected on how things had changed of late, in particular how events had altered his own life over the past few years.

It had all started with a seemingly innocent soccer match, back in the war years. He'd met this young lad Matt, quite by accident, in fact, due to an accident.

There was something about the boy that he couldn't explain, maybe in his eyes or the way that he spoke, the way that he carried himself, he wasn't sure what it was. After speaking with the boy's mother on the way back to the hospital that day, he learned that the boy was an adopted orphan, the mother died giving birth, there was no record of the father. He'd overheard the boy's date of birth as forms were completed at the hospital.

Weeks later, a letter had arrived on Harold's desk marked "private and confidential," the postmark was London E1. It contained a detailed report from a private detection agency in London. After reading the report for the second time, Harold had laid the papers on his desk and staring at the back of his trembling hands, he couldn't believe what he had just read; a large lump formed in his throat.

His mind went back all those years ago. His wife had died tragically of the dreaded scourge tuberculosis. He'd been distraught and started to drink his sorrows away.

During those few lost months he'd sought solace in the arms of a chambermaid at the mansion who unfortunately had fallen pregnant. Harold paid the woman money to go away to have the child adopted. Still in the strong grips of alcohol, he'd enforced his cruel decision only to regret it for the rest of his miserable guilty life.

Years later, and a small fortune spent on private detectives, he had given up his futile search for information on the woman or the child. Harold carried an irreparable, invisible scar on his mind.

There in front of him lay the irrefutable evidence. The young man, Matthew Harper, was the lost child. This young man was the second son of Harold White.

The report contained a copy of the original birth certificate, sadly accompanied by a copy of the death certificate of the mother bearing the same date stamp.

Harold remembered receiving the news in stunned silence, but he quietly thanked God that he'd be able to make some amends for his unforgivable actions those many years before, amends to this young man, amends to his son.

He held the papers, stared down and read the detective's report again, even after these many years later his hands still shook with gratitude. He was jolted back to the present as David knocked on the door of his study.

"Father, when did you say that young Matt Harper was to start his work-study at the mill?"

You mean, when is your brother to start his work-study? Harold thought to himself.

"I'm not sure of the exact date David, but it will be within the next few days," Harold answered.

A twinge of concern, nay worry, crossed his mind, as the report of the recent murder was fresh in his mind. He wondered what Matt was doing, and most of all he hoped that he would remain safe.

The Ferry Port, Dover

Meanwhile, down at the port, Gerald went across to the pay phone in the terminal as the Germans left the building. He called the pub and asked to speak to Bruce, who after a short while came to the phone.

"Hear anything from the others?"

"Not a peep," Bruce replied.

"I think all the people that we're looking for are already here except the weird little man from the train. He cleared his throat twice, sarcastically, "I'll try to find their vehicle," he added.

"You stay put, if John or Matt come on the phone, tell them to get here as soon as possible. Keep a lookout with the glasses."

Bruce chose to ignore Gerald's instructions to stay put as he went outside and made his way towards the port to see what assistance he could offer Gerald at the terminal.

Outside in the badly lit parking area, Gerald was going from truck to truck looking for some sign that would connect any vehicle to the Germans. He came up to the large van he'd noticed previously. It was the size of a large furniture removal van, the cab was unoccupied, he tried the door. It came open easily; he looked around before climbing up onto the passenger seat.

The steering wheel was on the left side of the vehicle, obviously it wasn't intended for English roads. He was looking around for any kind of identification papers when, without warning, the passenger door burst open. A bright light flooded the cab as someone shone a torch directly into Gerald's face.

Chapter Twenty-Nine

"Don't make a move," it was the German woman's voice. Gerald tried adjusting his eyes to the glare of the light in his face, he noticed the dark blue sheen of the silencer on the end of the Lugar barrel, pointing at his head.

"If you should be so foolish as to try anything, we both know that you won't be the first to die this week," at that point the driver side door was wrenched open.

"Hello again," it was the familiar voice of the big German.

"Well, we meet again, but this time will be our last meeting, let me assure you of that.

"Helga, fasten his hands and arms securely, then be absolutely sure that he's tied firmly to the inside framework of the truck and be certain that he cannot move or shout for assistance."

"I'll take care of this English pig once and for all as soon as we set sail."

He had a look of anticipation and sheer pleasure on his face as he spoke.

Bruce, in the meantime, had skirted the area; he'd got as far as the terminal building, then he'd doubled back towards the heavy goods parking area. He still hadn't seen anything of Gerald, but then if Gerald was checking all the vehicles, he wouldn't exactly be walking down the center of each lane for everyone to see what he was doing.

Finally, he gave up looking for Gerald and decided to go back to their room and watch. He would take up his position again and watch the terminal with the help of the binoculars.

Back at the terminal Gerald was pulled out of the cab by two men that he'd never seen before; the woman, Helga, kept the gun trained on him, watching him closely.

He'd thought about trying to escape but a picture of Carl's body came quickly to mind and he thought better of it.

He was unceremoniously bundled into the rear of the big van. As the two men pushed him towards the dark interior, he noticed the inside was huge, at least two thirds of the area filled to capacity with packages reaching almost to the roof. They strapped him to the staunch metal framework of the van, a gag was stuffed into his mouth, then tied behind his head. Then he was tied spread eagle, hands and feet, with his face hard up against the framework of the side of the vehicle.

Throughout these proceedings the woman stood at the back of the vehicle holding a flashlight in her left hand, the gun in her right. She never took her eyes off Gerald until he was securely tied to the framework of the vehicle.

She then climbed into the van and checked each of his bonds, grunting with satisfaction as she jumped down to the deck below.

Back at the pub, Bruce's attention was attracted by the flicker of a flashlight at the rear of a large closed van in the terminal, parked across from the trailer. He saw the large doors reflect the light as they were pushed shut. At the same time there was a loud knocking on the door, Bruce thought that Gerald had come back. He remembered Gerald had taken the room key in his own pocket when he went out.

"Coming Gerald, hang on a second," he strode across the room, opened the door, and came face to face with John and me.

"Hello, you two. You must have flown to get here so quickly," he exclaimed.

"All the Germans are here, also the car and trailer; we're just in the process of identifying their other vehicle. They've obviously dumped the military trucks and are using something else."

"Yes, we already guessed they were here, we didn't see any signs of them on the road coming down.

"Where's Gerald?" John asked.

"He's out there somewhere amongst those trucks, looking for their new mode of transport," Bruce answered, gesturing towards the docks, passing the glasses for John to take a look.

"You're quiet, Matt, cat got your tongue?" Bruce asked me as John scanned the mass of vehicles at the terminal.

"No, I've got a raging toothache from damaging my teeth down the mine the other night; you wouldn't have any aspirin, would you?"

"Yes, I do, actually they belong to Gerald. They're over there on the dresser."

I tore four tablets from the paper strip and scooped some water from the washbasin in the palms of my hands. Bruce offered me a small bottle.

"Put some of this in your mouth and hold it on the offending tooth," he advised. I opened the half bottle of whisky and did as he had suggested. The initial surge of pain was inexplicable; then, just as quickly, it subsided into a welcome numbness, a sort of pleasant tingle to my gums. The experience put me in mind of the football match, when Harold had given me some brandy to revive me after my mishap. God, it seemed a lifetime away.

"I don't see any movement at all down there," said John. "I'm none too happy having Gerald down there on his own, he's capable of losing his temper. I wish you had kept him here until we'd arrived."

"You should try stopping him when he's got a bee in his bonnet," said Bruce. John let the comment go over his head.

"We'll have to go down to the terminal and look more thoroughly. I hope he hasn't run into any kind of trouble. By the way, you weren't totally correct when you said that all the Germans were here. Thanks to you two, I believe, one of them is missing, or should I say apprehended."

"Thanks to us, what do you mean?" I related the content of the evening BBC news. "Wow," Bruce said feigning innocence and surprise, then laughing as he informed us of the mischief Gerald had got up to on the train.

"Which reminds me," said Cotes.

"I have a phone call to make on that score. Let's all go down to the bar and work out the best way we can systematically check each vehicle. Remember the next sailing is at midnight. Do we know what bookings the Germans made?"

"I don't think so," replied Bruce.

"Gerald never mentioned it when he phoned me."

We left the room. Heading down to the bar John went into the hallway, he picked up the phone to make his call. I decided not to drink anything, the pain in my gums had subsided, no point in tempting fate.

A couple of minutes later John joined us in the bar. As agreed when we arrived at the terminal, we needed to check the vehicles that were already lined up ready to board the ferry. One of us would keep watch, while the other two checked either side of each truck.

At the terminal ten minutes later, I'd been the designated spotter, to keep watch for any signs of trouble. Our MI5 man gave us both a pocket-size flashlight for signaling purposes.

We went through the agreed drill, John and Bruce checked each line of vehicles, I stayed at the rear watching for any sign of trouble. Later, the other two came back to where I was and by then we all agreed we were pretty sure that so far we'd missed nothing unusual. No sign of Gerald anywhere.

Finally we decided to investigate the big van which had aroused Bruce's interest earlier along with the trailer. John warned us that we must be prepared for the worst.

"If they have Gerald now, chances are he's probably dead." Chills went down my spine as he spoke those words; I looked across at Bruce, his face had turned ashen.

"We all know what these people are capable of doing, so don't try anything heroic, you'll just end up very dead."

He then scratched out our new plan in the dust on the ground.

The big van was at the end of a row of some twenty vehicles, crossing in front of it was a one way road, directly across that road was the trailer, parked up against the perimeter fence.

The plan was for me to crawl under the truck parked immediately behind the removal van. Then John would position himself underneath the truck with the tarpaulin cover, which was parked next to the big van.

Bruce was to go over to the perimeter hedge, the other side of the trailer keeping watch from there. We had the trailer covered from front rear and right.

One flash of the torch meant something was happening, two that trouble is coming your way, three abort and get out.

"If they do have Gerald still alive, I believe he must be in one of these vehicles. Remember this is now a cat and mouse game, they are possibly doing exactly the same thing, trying to find us.

"We don't know exactly how many there are or how well-trained, so let's assume the answer to those two questions is more than us, and extremely well; that should keep us on our toes. They're armed, so be very careful. Remember, thirty minutes exactly, then we regroup here. Check your watches, lets get to it," the agent said as he walked off first.

We moved into our positions. I was still suffering from the abuse my body had taken over the past few days, crawling around underneath trucks wasn't that easy at the moment. Stretched horizontally under the lorry between the front wheels allowed me to look to the front and the rear but remain unseen from the sides. I felt liquid dripping down the back of my neck; engine oil, it felt very sticky and it must have been old, too, judging by the burnt smell. I could see the rear of the big van clearly, also the shape of the wheels of the trailer at the perimeter side.

We had been there about ten minutes, nothing, not a sound. My right leg began to cramp up on me, the air was becoming decidedly damp. I was brought abruptly to attention by the distinct click of a door handle, my nerves rattled, then followed the sound of footwear scraping on the dry gravely surface of the ground. I could just make out the dim shapes of two pairs of shoes next to the trailer, then the glow of a cigarette butt as it was dropped to the ground and stomped out as the owners of the shoes walked away.

Looking towards the rear of the big van I thought my vision was failing me, I could just barely make out its shape at the back, everything was becoming blurred. I couldn't even see the truck next to me that was John's hiding place.

I began to feel a sense of panic, my eyesight was failing. I looked down at my watch, the luminous face was as clear as a whistle, so was the ever-increasing oil patch near my elbow.

The rear of the lorry was almost gone from my vision, then it dawned on me. Fog!

This area of is England was well known for it, almost instant blankets of fog that could drop without warning. This was a real pea soup, nearly the color of sulphur.

I looked at my watch again, there were two more minutes to go before the half hour was up. It was at this point things started to happen, in fact, all hell let loose.

Footsteps came running past the side of the lorry above me as headlights came on. Simultaneously, at the other side a car engine started up. A red glow appeared as the rear lights of the big van were switched on, its engine roared to life as the rich fumes nearly suffocated me. More running footsteps, the door above me opened, and then it was slammed back into place as the engine touching my head shook violently, screaming to life. I rolled towards the rear of the lorry, assuming that the driver would go forward rather than reverse in the foggy conditions. I twisted around, then rolled over and over, finally out to the left of the vehicle. A very close shave, as the truck lurched forwards.

I lay there still somewhat shocked as the tail lights of a car followed the big removal van. The fog had by now completely enveloped the whole area. *Later I wondered what Vera Lynn would have made of that strange evening scene, she wouldn't be singing 'Blue skies over the white cliffs of Dover,' that's for sure!*

As the small convoy disappeared into the fog, I moved towards the trailer the Germans had left behind. At the same time I saw a figure approaching from the left, holding a small flashlight, then another figure coming from the right. I flashed my light, receiving an affirmative signal from both figures, we met up together near the trailer.

"Well that was quite exciting whilst it lasted," John Cotes said with a grin.

"You speak for yourself, I found it quite a hair-raising experience myself," I replied.

"Well I don't think their moving off was a result of anyone spotting us. Maybe one or two passengers didn't like the look of the fog, choosing to cancel the midnight crossing. Our friends must have grabbed the vacated spaces.

"Gerald, what about Gerald?" I asked, as the sudden thought grabbed at my stomach, we looked at each other and with one accord, moved cautiously towards the trailer. I noticed that Bruce held an ugly piece of wood in his right hand, the look on his face left no doubt that he intended to use it.

"Both of you keep either side of the door," whispered John, it was then that I spotted the gun in his hand. I took the door handle as it turned with a nerve-jangling click.

John wrenched the door open with his left hand in one movement, literally sprung through the opening, landing on his side on the floor. We waited for the sound of gunfire but nothing happened.

"You two can come in now," John growled from his position on the floor. The trailer was deserted, except for a couple of dirty glasses and the evening newspaper, it could have been empty for years.

We all sat down, the adrenalin had stopped racing, leaving a temporary hiatus in my energy supply. John Cotes looked thwarted as he sat staring into space.

"Our priority now is to get onto that boat with the Germans. Also we have to locate Gerald. I really wish he hadn't gone off on his own like that. To be honest with you, I think he's in that big van being held captive by the Germans. Let's give this area another quick search, say within a radius of a hundred yards, but be back here as quick as you can," John's voice snapped out the order as we dispersed and searched, but still to no avail; no Gerald.

When we met up again, John asked what arrangement had been made regarding the channel crossing. Bruce replied he thought Gerald had made some open bookings for the four of us and the car.

"There is one big problem, John," said Bruce.

"What's that?"

"Gerald has the damn tickets with him," he replied with a sheepish look on his face.

"What now?" I asked of no one in particular.

"Whatever happens, we have to get on that ferry as soon as possible," said John.

"It's absolutely imperative," he added. I'm the least familiar to the Germans, so I'll go and buy four tickets and one for the car.

If the car can't go, then I'll just get the passenger tickets, we're bound to get those. Bruce, you go and fetch the car with whatever's left in your room at the pub; I'll meet you back at the terminal. Matt, come with me and keep a close watch outside the terminal. Keep your face out of the way, wait outside the terminal until I come out.

"I'll see what can be done about the tickets Gerald bought previously."

Bruce ran off towards the car, John Cotes and I strode off in the direction of the terminal. The fog was really thick now, down to about three feet, visibility at this stage of the game an absolute bonus, helping us to stay under cover. *But what about the sea crossing, that could be another story!* I'd heard they were forecasting rough weather as well! I stood waiting in the damp foggy shadows outside the terminal.

Apart from John and one other person in front of him talking to the booking clerk, I could see another man sitting on a bench who seemed to be fast asleep. I was tempted to venture inside the terminal away from the damp fog, when I saw the sleeping man lift up the hat that was pulled down over his face. He was totally wide awake and listening very intently to the conversation going on at the reservation desk. I looked around me on the ground at the edge of the terminal, found a rock the size of a tennis ball and threw it with force at the metal siding of the buildings construction.

The resounding bang had the desired effect. The fake sleeper jumped about six inches up off his seat, the booking clerk jumped bolt upright, John Cotes turned round with a surprised look on his face. I made myself scarce, but I had achieved the desired effect. The sleeper rushed out of the building, running off quickly toward the line of vehicles, all of their engines running and ready to board the boat; smelly exhaust fumes added to the already oppressive atmosphere. I nearly jumped out of my shoes as a hand landed on my shoulder, at the same time a voice whispered in my ear; "What the hell's going on, Matt?"

I too must have gone six inches off the ground as I turned looking into the face of Bruce.

"Don't do that." I replied. It looks as though Mr. Cotes is going to have to pay again. I'm no lip reader, but the way the reservation clerk keeps shaking his head, it looks very much that way," I added with resignation.

"I think not, I'll take these to John right now," Bruce exclaimed, showing me an envelope.

"They're the original tickets, I found them in the room after all," he added as he patted my shoulder. I watched as he took the envelope to John, then came back to join me in the shadows. John followed shortly after.

"The passenger part is ok, but no space for the car. The sailing has just been delayed for three hours due to rough seas, not the fog mind you, but very squally water conditions. The clerk told me there are bound to be some no shows, especially in this weather," agent Cotes said confidently.

We returned to John's car and headed back towards the pub on the off-chance the room might still be available. Unfortunately, when we arrived the place was in darkness, so we resigned ourselves to sleeping in the car. We returned to the terminal.

As things turned out, not much sleeping was done; after nodding off a couple of times between aches and pains, then only sleeping fitfully. The noise of truck engines startled the three of us back to the land of the living, as the ferry began to load its cargo of vehicles.

John drove across, following the sign marked 'passengers with cars'. Bruce went into the office to see if there had been any cancellations, but came back looking decidedly glum.

"Still passenger only space, as yet they can't take the car," he explained. Evidently there was still a chance that there would be space for the car but the actual sailing was not scheduled for another hour and a half. So we sat in the line-up and waited, the fog seemed to be thicker than ever, I could hear the sea in the distance angrily crashing against the sea wall.

"Bruce, go up front and see where that big van is; also see if the German's car is in this lane," said John.

"I've a feeling that they managed to get their car cleared to cross," he added. Just then a uniformed official came up to the side of the car, tapped on the window, shining his flashlight through the window.

"There's a cancellation Sir, if you'd like to go back to the booking clerk, he's reserving a space for your car. We shall be boarding you shortly; even though the weather is still rough, we need to get everyone aboard in readiness for the crossing," he said to John. Bruce returned and climbed into the front seat.

"Their van is just being taken aboard though I can't see their car in this line. Maybe it's already onboard. They expect to sail in one hour. Evidently there's no fog in Calais but they are talking of seas, eight to ten feet in mid-channel, and that's big!"

Within the next thirty minutes we were onboard, our car was stowed below as the ferry was ready to leave. Fortunately, we had been able to secure a double cabin which had twin bunks and a semi-comfortable chair. Our MI5 man thought it would be better if we stayed out of sight in the cabin; he would do whatever watching was necessary, or until such time as we were needed in the vehicle hold below.

I climbed onto the top bunk and was asleep almost as soon as my head hit the pillow. Bruce did exactly the same below me.

I was awakened abruptly by a bang to the side of my head as it hit the wall of the cabin. I was then thrown violently in the opposite direction against the safety rail. The boat was underway, and as predicted, the seas were very rough judging by the motion of the room we were in.

Poor old Bruce awoke to find himself on the floor of the cabin, where the movement of the boat had unceremoniously dumped him. The cabin was on the inside of the ferry, thus there were no portholes so we were unable to see exactly what the weather was like, or indeed how big the seas were.

The agent arrived back in the cabin, looking very wet and windswept.

"I've found both vehicles, there is one person sitting in the cab of the big van, the car is unattended. I managed to bribe the assistant Mate who let me look at the cabin plan. It looks like our friends may have a cabin on the deck above this one.

I noticed that the bar and adjacent cafeteria are totally deserted. Most people seem to be sitting in the main salon, many of them looking very green and sea-sick."

He explained that our car was in front of the German's van; therefore it would be a good plan to make our way below decks, and sit in our car. From there we could watch the big van, awaiting our chances to look inside it for Gerald. We anticipated that the man in the van would need to leave the cab sooner or later.

"With a bit of luck, the guy in the cab may get seasick and need a toilet in a hurry, leaving the way clear for us to sneak into the rear of the van," John said rather gleefully

We left our cabin but had to go up on deck in order to go down again by a separate stairway to the vehicle deck.

Passing by the deserted salon and bar area, we could see many of the other passengers on the top deck with their heads over the side, throwing up; not a very pleasant sight, one which can be quite infectious.

Getting myself orientated I realized we were at the rear end of the vessel.

Way up front I could see massive waves crashing over the bow of the boat as the nose went up in the air, then smashed back down into the waves. When I'd first seen the boat at the dock it had looked gigantic, but now, being thrown around like a rubber duck in a bath tub, it looked minuscule in comparison to the mighty ocean.

Making very slow progress, we walked along the deck, one hand over the other along the handrails until we reached the steel door leading to the stairwell. Just as Cotes pulled the door open, the boat lurched to the left, tearing the handle from his grasp. The door swung out fiercely and hit Bruce full in the chest, hurling him bodily along the flooded deck towards the stern of the ferry, nothing but the post and wire rail to stop him going into the water.

It all seemed to happen so fast. I clung to the rail on the bulkhead of the boat for dear life. As I did so, Bruce's body hit the post, he managed to grab the side of a life boat, hanging on to the canvas covering. The ferry swayed in the opposite direction, giving Bruce the chance to crawl back towards where we were clinging for dear life to the rail.

"Christ, that was a close shave," he shouted above the wind, as blood mixed with sea water ran from his grazed knuckles. Somehow we managed to get through the door, securing it shut.

Next was an equally daunting and perilous task of descending the violently moving metal staircase, now wet, slippery and very badly illuminated.

The movement of the boat was fore and aft, as she went into a head sea; the staircase faced aft as the steps seemed to move up and down like a fairground ride, our downward progress slow and precarious.

Decidedly much the worse for wear, we eventually opened the door into the cavernous vehicle deck, so dimly lit that the vehicles housed there were barely visible. We made our way slowly to the front of the floating parking lot, passing the big long van on our way. The man was still sitting in the driving seat, so we cautiously crept around and behind an adjacent truck, moving further up front to find John's car, unseen by the van's occupant.

When we'd located the car, I sat in the front passenger seat next to John who adjusted the interior mirror, allowing him a view of the big van's radiator behind us. After about five minutes John suddenly announced:

"I'm going to have a scout around, I'll leave by this forward staircase," he indicated towards another exit, similar to the one we'd entered by.

"Unfortunately, I'll have to repeat the procedure we've just been through to re-enter the parking area at the other end and come up behind the van.

"Try to adjust both wing mirrors so that you can see behind the car and down both sides of the big van. I'm going to try to get into the big truck's rear doors. If you should see any danger, hit the horn on the car. Let's just hope I'll hear it above all this noise," he said, gesticulating to the area in general.

He left saying he would be behind the truck as quickly as it took him to complete the perilous round trip again. Certainly we didn't envy him the trip along that moving deck above, but then sitting there in the dark tossing and rolling in a car wasn't much of an improvement.

Inside the big vehicle, Gerald had regained consciousness. He was bound, gagged and tied very securely to the strong inside metal framework of the vehicle with his face towards the wall. The interior of the vehicle was in total darkness, with the exception of a chink of light coming in through the crack between the two rear doors. Earlier he had heard some muffled conversations in English, from which he understood they had obtained tickets for both the car and the truck.

Eventually he felt the vehicle moving, he assumed to board the ferry, accompanied by much shouting from the parking loaders.

Once the big van's engine stopped, he heard the hammering home of the chocks that would keep it secure during the crossing. After what seemed an age, he felt deep vibrations as the ferry's engines started up. At first a gentle moving sensation, then as he assumed that they'd moved away from the dock and shoreline, the increasing rolling and pitching began.

Steadily and rhythmically from his left to his right at first, then increasing to such a violent crescendo that he felt bilious and totally disoriented in the darkness.

The direction of the boat's movement changed, so that now his face was being banged up against the side of the vehicle's interior, his neck muscles nearly bursting as he pushed against the retraining bonds in an effort to keep his face from the sharp, metal-reinforced structure.

He began to lose all track of time; it seemed he had spent hours trying to free himself with little or no success.

Apart from removing most of the skin from his wrists, he'd made little progress, until suddenly with a resounding crack, the metal cross member holding his left hand came away from the side of the truck.

Although it had come away at ceiling height, he was able to bend it down and eventually release his hand, after an extended struggle he managed to release the other hand.

It took ten minutes of massaging to bring his numbed hands back to life sufficiently enough to undo the gag around his mouth. This task was further hindered by the constant movement of the boat, the total darkness, and still having both of his knees and ankles tied to the side.

Earlier, he'd had to exert immense mental control to avoid the ever- present desire to vomit, the rocking and rolling of the ferry had made him feel very sea-sick. If he had allowed himself to do so, he would surely have choked and died, as a result of the gag in his mouth.

Now with both hands free, he removed the gag first and immediately began to feel better. Eventually he started working on his numbed legs once they were freed. At the same time, his mind was already racing; he wondered where the others were. *Had they managed to get onto the boat for this sailing?*

But foremost in Gerald's mind was the threat issued by the big German, along with the subsequent hate that welled up inside him, urging and motivating him into undoing the bonds that much quicker. He was just getting the feeling back in his legs when suddenly he thought he heard someone ever so gently and quietly moving the door handles on the truck's doors, followed by a louder metallic crack.

Meanwhile, sitting in the car, I began to feel the effects of the everlasting movement of the boat as she was continuously lifted and dropped by the power of the ocean. When John had left earlier, I'd moved into the driver seat so I had a clear view from of the mirrors.

Looking out at the mirror, I saw to my horror the driver getting out of the cab of the lorry and walking cautiously to the rear of the vehicle as though trying to creep up on someone stealthily. I hit the horn button but nothing happened; then it dawned on me, the ignition needed to be turned on first. I could see no key, so I quickly abandoned that idea.

I turned to Bruce and told him what was happening, at the same time I was rushing out of the car and moving swiftly towards the big truck behind. As I moved along the side of the vehicle, the driver, with his back to me, was waving his left hand in the air. He was shouting at John Cotes to turn around, his right hand was still, I assumed he was holding a weapon.

Having very little time to think as I closed in on him, I delivered a blow to his kidneys with all the might I could muster. He slid to his knees with a groan, which in turn produced a broad smile on the face of a very relieved John Cotes. Just then Bruce came around the other side of the vehicle wielding an evil looking tire lever.

"We don't have a lot of time Bruce, force the lock will you," Cotes hissed his instruction.

"Matt, go and see what you can find in the cab to tie this character up with," he whispered to me. I heard a loud snap as I returned and the lock broke under the strain of Bruce's tire lever, the door swung open.

The three of us peered expectantly into the darkness of the big cavernous interior. John shone his flashlight, we could vaguely make out the shapes of the packages, but there was no sign of Gerald. I was the first to speak.

"Oh my God, it looks like maybe they've killed Gerald, too!"

"Don't be in such a hurry to see me dead, young Harper," a voice came from somewhere inside the dark interior of the vehicle as a head came up from behind the packages.

Gerald staggered over the packages towards the back of the vehicle looking white and drawn, but otherwise apparently OK. As speedily as possible we threw the tied and gagged driver into the back of the truck, fastening him firmly to the side structures. Finally we replaced the broken lock, it would look alright at a glance, but wouldn't pass close scrutiny.

We returned to our cabin using the rear stairwell. Judging from the movement of the boat, the sea seemed to be calming some. Back in the cabin, we got Gerald into the bottom bunk so he could stretch out and relax.

Our MI5 man became a waiter; he'd been out and returned from the cafeteria with some hot coffee and sandwiches which seemed to touch the spot. Within twenty minutes of being back in the cabin, Gerald was sitting in the chair; he said he felt, and he certainly looked, a hundred percent better.

He passed on to John any relevant information he'd been able to hear whilst he'd been held captive in the truck. There were two voices he hadn't heard before, both English, apparently they were talking about heading to Austria and Bavaria once the ferry docked. John interrupted him.

"When I went to the cafeteria, I asked some of the crew when they expect to dock. They reckon, due to the head seas they've been battling, it could take as much as another hour before we get to France," he added with a note of gloom in his voice.

"You lot had better stay put, let's have no more unnecessary mishaps or heroics, at least until we reach the other side," he added, to which we all readily agreed.

Apart from the continued rough weather, the remainder of the crossing was, by comparison, uneventful.

If, as Gerald had inferred from his eavesdropping, the Germans were headed for Austria and Bavaria, we were in for a long ride.

We agreed that on arrival Bruce would drive the car off the ferry; the three of us were going to walk off. Pedestrians get off long before vehicles do, so this would give us the opportunity to watch the Germans disembark. But, as John pointed out, they were just as likely to have someone doing exactly the same thing, looking for us.

"Don't underestimate the master race," he added somewhat sarcastically.

The sea had definitely calmed by the time we docked. I looked at my watch, it was five-thirty in the morning as

John, Gerald and I walked off the ferry and into the main building.

Two men approached us making themselves known to agent Cotes. We followed them through a side door and into a small room. The greetings were friendly as they all spoke in French; obviously from the way he communicated, John was absolutely fluent.

Our papers were taken away, brought back, duly stamped. We were given coffee and croissants, afterwards taken outside and shown our latest mode of transport, a small Renault van. John told us to put our things in the rear, then get seated and ready to leave.

After thanking the French Secret Service for their help, John drove the van around to the passport and customs checkpoint for vehicles, where we sat and waited for Bruce and the Germans to disembark the ferry.

Most of the commercial vehicles were being checked by the officials, their loads against their manifests, maybe one in four were let through without being checked.

Some of the cars were given a cursory check while others were made to pull round to the side for further scrutiny. We saw Bruce approach the checkpoint, he was asked to take it around the side of the building; John Cotes smiled knowingly, as though all was going according to plan.

Eventually we saw the big truck come off the boat and lumber towards the check point where it was stopped. The papers were scrutinized by officials, the interior checked, then to my surprise it was waved on. A large Mercedes came next in the car lane.

"It's them!" I shouted out loud to the others. "It's the Germans."

The Mercedes had French number plates. The official looked at the papers, then they came to the car making all four occupants get out. The car was searched as the Germans were taken into the building. Bruce appeared from around the side of the checkpoint and then he got into the front of the Renault.

"That's what you call international cooperation," said a grinning agent. He explained that the Renault had been supplied by the French authorities; they'd even added two seats in the rear of the van which could have been described as being mildly uncomfortable. Within ten minutes the Germans had exited the building, settled into the Mercedes and driven off.

"Right," said John, "here's what has just happened. The French are working with us on this part of our journey. They supplied the transport along with any other vehicles we may require en-route between here to the German or Austrian borders, wherever the Germans choose to cross.

"They also made everyone get out of the Mercedes so that we could see exactly who was in there. We know that they found the man we left in the back of the big van, as the two English men were in the front. We also know that they are aware of our presence, as we rescued Gerald from the vehicle.

"Hopefully, we'll have very little surveillance to do in France as the French authorities will watch them, reporting back to us. We'll stay with the Germans, but at a discreet distance until they leave France. It's a fair ride to either border, I guess around two hundred fifty to three hundred miles. Any questions?" he asked. "Yes, why didn't the French search the van, confiscate the cargo and lock them all up?" I asked.

"Good question," replied the agent.

"The reason being, that neither the French nor us want to spoil the plan; as I've already told you we've been on this trail for years. Our aim is to catch the men at the top of this organization. We assume they'll be at the final destination of the cargo."

"Bruce, Gerald, Matt, you don't really need to stay here any longer unless you wish. I want to thank you for all the help you've given me, I do appreciate you have a business to run. You, Matt, have your studies to attend. You can take the car and go back on the next ferry if you like," he turned towards the back seat as he spoke.

"You must be joking, if you think for one minute that I'm going to miss out on the capture of those German bastards. Though I'd like to have a word with Dad, let him know that we're alright," Bruce said.

"That apart, wild horses wouldn't get me out of here. I'm here to the end."

"Me, too, as I'm sure you expected Mr. bloody MI5," Gerald growled from the rear, his right hand on the back of John Cotes neck, I assumed rather painfully.

"Same goes here," I replied.

As we crossed to France, the results of wartime artillery activity was clearly evident, some areas worse than others, though certainly nothing like the devastation in England. But then, the French had surrendered themselves to be occupied by the Germans, had they not?

Our quarry had made good time since leaving the ferry. We stopped at a place called Hirston, and stayed overnight; we had traveled about a hundred miles from Calais. We motored all of the following day. It was Monday evening when we eventually pulled into the town of Montimend, which was some hundred miles from Strasbourg at the German border.

The big white van was parked outside a pension, a little further down the road the Mercedes was outside the Hotel Montmart. We had booked into another small boarding house on the outskirts of the town and planned to go out and have a light meal downtown.

We'd seen little of our quarry since arriving on French soil. John continued to made regular contact with the French secret service, who seemed to be keeping us well informed of events.

That particular evening, we'd decided to make sure that all of the villains who'd arrived on the boat were still present.

As we passed the pension where the van had been parked, it was no longer there and nowhere to be seen. We drove hot-foot to the Hotel Montmart; the Mercedes was not there either. We traversed the town thoroughly, then around the outskirts, but came up with a big zero, nothing.

Back at the Hotel Montmart, John ran into the reception area then came back to the Renault.

"Damn it, they've checked out," he shouted as he climbed back into the Renault.

"I assume the same applies at the pension, too," he added angrily.

As we sat, somewhat irritated, discussing the situation and planning what we should do next, a big white vehicle with a blue cross on its side went by us at high speed.

"What was written on the side of that truck?" John asked me.

"It's a German vehicle with 'Urgent Medical Supplies' written on the side in German," I replied.

"Of course, follow it, John," I added hurriedly, as the significance of what I'd said suddenly hit me. A German truck, German writing on the sides close to the German border. It was purely a spontaneous reaction.

We took off after the truck, making sure we didn't get close enough to attract their attention. The vehicle went through the town at a fair speed, then as it reached the outskirts it turned into a lane on the left side of the road.

We followed with caution; there, sure enough, was the big removal van parked along the lane. We drove straight past as the Medical vehicle slowed down behind the white van.

Our cheap little Renault at that time was such a common sight in France that in these circumstances it was almost invisible. Driving on to the end of the lane, we turned around and drove back past the two trucks, now parked along side of each other. The task of transferring the cargo was already underway. The packages were being moved to the German Medical truck.

Positioning ourselves across from the lane on the main road, we saw the big van leave the lane; there was no evidence of the car but we assumed it was still around somewhere.

Within the hour the medical truck emerged from the lane, heading off in the direction of the main route towards the German border. The removal van was taken back towards the center of the town where we followed at a safe distance.

It pulled up outside the Hotel Montmart, the big German and the woman climbed down from the big truck, which then headed back into France, we assumed, on its return journey to England. The couple went to the rear parking lot, climbed into the Mercedes, driving off in the direction of the main route to the border. We followed at a discreet distance. Shortly after that, the Mercedes caught up and overtook the medical truck, as we all made our way to the border and Germany.

Chapter Thirty

Tuesday Morning, Casleton Village

David awoke routinely at six, the sky was dark and the morning gloomy. The village had been in total uproar since the report of Carl's death. The front pages of the newspapers seemed to have nothing else to write about. Another body had been found in a car at Leeds, this sad event was also being connected with the two murders in the village.

Though Cheryl had seemed to handle the situation well, David knew that she'd soon have to let her feelings show. She hadn't shed a tear since her brother's death, which wasn't natural. Conversely, George Armitage had taken the death of his only son very badly. He would go out for long walks not telling anyone where he was headed, returning home late in the evening; his behavior was adding to the stress that his wife was already bearing.

In the bathroom about to have a shave, David turned the radio on to the news station.

"Good morning, this is the BBC news at six-thirty on this Tuesday morning, the seventh of September. Yet another body was discovered last night in the village of Castleton, Yorkshire, which police have connected with the other recent murders at the village. This brings the mysterious death toll to four. The body found in a car parked near Leeds Central station two days ago has also been linked to this strange set of events.

"The latest body discovered last night was that of a German ex-prisoner of war, who'd worked as a black-smith at the local coal mine for many years. He was found in an old garden shed behind where he lived as a tenant in one of the coal mine cottages.

"According to the police, he'd been shot through the head at close range, his body had been there for some days.

"The German male taken from the London to Dover express is still being questioned by members of Scotland Yard's Special Branch."

"There has been no explanation as to why he was found tied to the luggage rack of the train, wearing only his underclothes.

"A police source suggests there may be some connection with the Casleton murders, as traces of coal dust were found on him by forensic specialists; there is some suggestion that his fingerprints were found in the car at the murder scene in Leeds.

"If anyone has any information regarding this matter, please contact your local police station."

David limped out of the bathroom across the landing to his father's room, wiping shaving soap from his face as he went to the door of the room, which was slightly ajar.

"Father, did you hear that report on the news?" he shouted through the door.

"Which report was that, David?"

"Apparently there's been another murder, this time in Pit Lane. The police have found another body, an ex-prisoner of war, a German who'd worked at the mine as a blacksmith."

"Good Lord, is this mess ever going to end?" *I haven't heard from Matt for a couple of days, I hope he's still alright,* Harold worried in silence.

"I'm taking George Armitage out for the day, see if I can help him to come to terms with what has happened to Carl," he said to David. "I won't be in the office at all today."

As David sat eating breakfast he saw the same shocking news across the front page of the newspaper, except this time there was mention of a spy ring and possible Nazi involvement.

Later, when David arrived at his office, his first call was to the offices of Frank Bell and Son. The phone was answered promptly by a young lady, who couldn't say whether Bruce would be in that day; instead she put the call through to Frank Bell, himself. He too seemed unable to give an answer, other than to say that Bruce wasn't expected back for a couple of days or so. His answers seemed evasive.

David then decided he would drive around to my home and ask Mary if she knew of my whereabouts. His phone rang, it was Cheryl, who wanted to meet him for lunch. She'd sounded very low and depressed; she told him that Special Branch wanted to ask her some further questions. Please could he be there when they arrived as she just couldn't face much more of the everlasting questioning.

As David drove to see Mary, on his way to see Cheryl, he wondered what else could happen. It seemed unbelievable how his life and the lives of many others around him had changed so drastically in such a short space of time. He'd lost an old friend in Carl, or had he already lost him a long time ago?

Would they ever have been friends again like they used to be? David already knew the answer. Deep down he knew that whatever had happened to Carl, things would never have been the same as they were before. At least Cheryl was back in his life, an answer to his deepest wish, but for how long he wondered?

Saverne France, Tuesday Evening

We'd driven hard through the night and most of the following day making only a couple of stops for essential food and toiletries. Along the way we'd managed to get some short naps, me more than the others; not having a license I couldn't do my share of driving.

At the town of Saverne, John said we were about fifty miles from Strasbourg and the border. We'd found a small pension, all feeling absolutely exhausted, prepared to bed down for the night.

"Not so fast," Cotes said.

"We've come this far, we can't afford to lose them now. We'll take shifts watching them until the morning. Matt, you got more sleep than then rest of us in the car, so you can take first watch from ten till two, then we will split the rest up between us," he added.

"First, I need to get a change of transport. I'll make phone contact, change the Renault, then we can eat and get some sleep."

Within the hour I was sitting in an all-night café opposite a small French roadhouse. I could see the large medical truck, but so far we hadn't seen the Mercedes since they changed the big van.

As I sat there, my eyelids getting heavier, a car pulled up outside of the roadhouse opposite. There were only two other people sitting in the café. I watched one of them who made notes in a book as the car pulled into the parking lot across the other side of the road.

I was slightly puzzled as the man across the café nodded his head when I'd looked at him, then smiled beckoning me to join him at the table. At first I didn't like the idea one little bit, with that pause he got up and came over towards my table. As he passed the counter he spoke in French to the patron, then came and sat opposite me.

"Bonjour, monsieur," he said smiling,

"I am Jacques Montande, of the French Special Branch," as he spoke two coffees arrived at the table.

"I don't understand why John Cotes would send you here tonight to keep watch, but there really is no need for you to be here. I'll be around until my relief arrives at six in the morning," he added with a resigned shrug.

"Thanks all the same but I think I'd better do as I was told," I said.

"As you wish."

As we spoke a stranger walked into the café. I turned to look but I didn't recognize the newcomer so I turned back to my table companion; he'd disappeared, he was nowhere to be seen.

I sat for a while longer, or for as long as it took to drink the coffee he'd bought me; deciding to take a stroll, I left the café and walked along the main road for a few hundred yards and then turned around intending to retrace my steps. I could see the white medical van clearly from the lights of the café.

Then I saw, not too clearly in the darkness, the figure of a man move down the shadow-cast side of the vehicle, the door of the cab was opened. An obvious struggle was taking place between two people, as they disappeared from view into the darkness.

I moved quickly towards the scene without really thinking of the consequences. Getting my brain back into gear, I realized that I was in full view, rushing off into the darkness was foolhardy. I turned to my left, went past a hedgerow and came up behind the roadhouse, intending to approach the two figures from their rear while under cover of darkness. I heard the shuffling of feet on the gravel surface, followed by grunts of exertion, then everything seemed to lapse into deathly quiet.

I'd learned some pretty salutary lessons of late; I reflected, as I froze and held my breath, waiting for the next sound to break the eerie silence.

The only noise I heard was the throbbing of my own racing heartbeat, hissing loudly in my ears, as it pumped away. I waited for what seemed an age, not moving a muscle, rooted to the spot. I covered my wrist as I saw the glow from my luminous watch face, as it moved up to my eye level then back again. Then there was the briefest burst of light as a rear door to the road house was opened, then, just as quickly, closed again. *Did someone come out then, or did someone go in?* I asked myself. I heard footsteps in the distance and could just make out the shape of a man walking away from me towards the front of the building. He appeared to be moving with some difficulty.

When I could no longer hear the sound of his feet on the gravel, I waited a moment or two. I felt into my pocket for the flashlight that John Cotes had given me in Dover.

Not knowing whether there was a second person present, with baited breath I turned on the flashlight. Nothing, there was nobody; down on the ground a few feet away I could see the signs of a recent struggle. I extinguished the lamp and moved cautiously in the direction of the rear door to the building.

Standing back I waited again, then after hearing no further movement I gently pushed open the unlatched door. It was the entrance to a rear staircase. The floor was covered in cheap linoleum on which some dark fluid had been spilled. I turned my flashlight on which enabled me to see clearly that the fluid was blood, the drops went on up the stairs. I turned out the lamp and quickly beat a hasty retreat.

Making my way back towards the café, I searched the area with my flashlight; I found no traces of blood drops so I assumed that the injured party had retreated into the building, maybe the other combatant was still outside there somewhere.

The lights of the café came into view, at the same time the white van became visible. I could see that the cab was unoccupied, but gave the vehicle a wide berth, just in case. The time was now a little after twelve-thirty. The all night café was deserted with the exception of the patron behind the counter. I crossed the road, deciding to go to the side of the café and watch the roadhouse from the cover of darkness. I found an old barrel to sit on, and got myself reasonably comfortable; then every nerve in my body tingled in unison as I heard a muffled sound coming from the darkness behind.

My nerves jangled so much I swear that they made an actual flash across my vision when I heard the sound of someone expelling air, breathing heavily, followed by a definite wince of pain. Turning on the flashlight again, I saw the figure of a man on his hands and knees doubled up in obvious agony, with his head touching the ground. As the agonized face came up into the beam of my light, I saw that it was the French Special Branch man Jacques Montande. He was clutching his stomach.

"Are you alright?" I asked, with hindsight what a damn brilliant question that was!

"I got into a tussle with a man who came out of the truck," he gasped in strongly accented English.

"I need to be taken to a doctor quickly!" He tried to point feebly in the direction of the parking lot.

"My car is the black Renault," then he passed out, rolling over on the ground.

Examining him quickly I found a profuse amount of blood around his mid-section. I assumed he'd been stabbed in the stomach, he appeared to continue losing a lot of blood.

I realized I was left with only one option, so I hurriedly searched his pockets to find his car keys. Taking care to gently roll him over onto his side, I then went in search of his black Renault. I went to the only black Renault in the car park, and opened the door.

With much trepidation I commenced the first practical driving session of my entire life. I located the ignition key slot along with the light switches, then finally turned the key and pressed the starter button. It hadn't been noticed by the others that I'd been paying close attention to their driving techniques over the last few days.

I'd done this in preparation for the inevitable driving lessons necessary for me to get a license. Coordination has never been one of my weak points, but it has to be said that driving a manual car can only come with a certain amount of learning and much practice.

On my first clutch depression, and selection of first gear, I released the pedal too quickly and the car shot forward and stalled instantly. On the second attempt, the vehicle kangaroo jumped towards the injured man, almost putting him out of his pain and misery on a permanent basis.

Stopping the car I opened the rear door, then went across to him. Raising him into a sitting position from his rear, putting my hands under his armpits, I then dragged him on his backside to the side of the car. Crawling onto the back seat I somehow managed to manipulate him in there, but what a struggle; all of the time aware that whoever did this, might return to the scene at any moment.

I thought I could remember the location of the guest house so I put the car into gear and this time it took off with one massive jerk. At this juncture I really didn't fancy changing gear; later the others told me, I'd probably tried to take off in third gear, causing the jumping and stalling.

There was no time to waste. I went towards the guest house at a rather rapid pace, knowing that I had to find John Cotes quickly. After a mile or so I recognized the building, took the turn into the forecourt, and only then realized that I'd been driving down the wrong side of the road! Luckily it was so late that there was no other traffic on the road. I drove into the car park, checked that the Frenchman was still breathing, found the key, and raced into the guest house.

I could see light coming from under the door that Gerald and John were sharing. I tapped lightly on the door, which was opened very cautiously by John holding a gun.

"That's the right way to get yourself shot, you young idiot! You should have said who you were when you knocked. Aren't you a bit early anyway, it's another hour before two o'clock?" he asked.

"Come quickly," I said, almost out of breath and bringing them both up-to-date. We, all three, then left the building. When we reached the car, the Frenchman had regained consciousness. He gave a telephone number and address to John, who jumped quickly into the driving seat.

"Gerald, here's the keys to our new transport, it's a large milk tanker parked round the corner. Follow me will you, we've got to get him to a doctor as quickly as possible," he said throwing the keys across to Gerald. Around the corner I got into the tanker with Gerald, thanking God that I wasn't going to take lesson number two in that monster.

After we deposited Jacques Montande and his car at the address of his doctor, we drove back to the pension in the cab of the milk tanker. I admitted that I wouldn't be able to sleep now, I was definitely too wound up. Gerald drove into the car park where I gave John a run down in full detail of my earlier duty. There was no further movement from the Germans, so eventually we all had a very early breakfast at around four-thirty.

As we were about to leave the cafe, a lone driver arrived in a black Renault, taking a seat in the far corner of the room. He ordered food and drink and sat reading his newspaper. John stayed on for awhile; Gerald and I were feeling tired by then so we went back to the pension and had a couple of hours shuteye. We decided not to disturb Bruce, letting him have as long a sleep as possible. We had no idea just how much he was going to need it.

We had also acquired a second addition to our transport fleet, a German motor bike complete with two leather helmets and two pairs of goggles. Bruce evidently had previous experience; Gerald and John were both fairly experienced.

On the next leg of our journey I rode pillion with Gerald, the cab in the tanker would have been a little overcrowded with more than two people.

It was around seven o'clock that morning before we departed. The tanker was parked outside the café with the bike behind. The Medical truck left shortly after, followed by the Mercedes with only a driver in the truck and three people in the car.

John and Bruce followed them in the tanker, we held back behind the café as other vehicles left.

"Come with me, Matt, we ought to check this place out," Gerald said. I followed him across the street and into the rear of the Roadhouse, its entrance somewhat familiar to me after last night's episode. As we climbed the stairs, I noticed that the blood had been cleaned up. At the top was a door which led into long a corridor. Bedroom doors led off on both sides, most of these doors were wide open, their rooms vacated untidily as is the norm.

"You check the left, I'll do the right," Gerald said.

"What am I looking for?" I asked him.

"I want to find the rooms occupied by the Krauts," he said.

"Just knock on each closed door, if you get no reply, go in and take a look around.

I did as he asked. I had checked at least five of them, and on entering the sixth I smelled some sort of perfume, and another unpleasant sickly smell that I couldn't quite recognize.

I checked under the bed as I'd done in the other rooms before, then I opened the old wooden wardrobe. I got the shock of my life as the body of a man literally fell on top of me. I let out a shout of horror as Gerald came rushing into the room.

"Just as I thought," he said as he carefully examined the body. There was a severe cut across the side of the neck, a massive cut across the palm of the right hand, and a neat bullet hole between the eyes.

"He's the man your Frenchman fought with last night, but those German bastards shot and killed him anyway, those bastards finished off one of their own, eh?"

We searched the room thoroughly. Gerald checked the man's pockets and found an address on a small piece of paper screwed up in the man's shirt pocket. It was covered in blood, he'd said, difficult to decipher. Gerald put it into his pocket, saying that I could look at it later. The body, like the room, had been carefully checked leaving not a clue.

Just before leaving we shoved the corpse under the bed, checking that we'd left the room as we found it. I opened the door to come face to face with a chamber maid about to commence her duties. I think she apologized in French, and then she ambled off down the corridor. We made ourselves scarce and left the roadhouse, jumped on the motor bike, then sped off in the direction of the main route to the German border.

Within half an hour we saw the milk tanker ahead, slowed down keeping a good mile between us. About twenty miles further down the road, we approached a hold-up in the traffic due to road works. The line of waiting vehicles must have been at least a half mile long; fortunately, being on the motor bike allowed us to creep along on the curbside until we were three or four vehicles behind our milk tanker.

Unfortunately, the repair crew was working on the bend of the road which made controlling traffic more difficult. Much the same in any country, there was a man at each end of the workings with a double- sided sign, red on one side, the other green.

The traffic on our side of the road was moving slowly when the man holding the sign spun the red side around at the car directly in front of us. Traffic began to come from the opposite direction, as a farm truck broke down in the middle of the road, bringing everything to a total standstill.

It seemed ages until eventually they pushed the fully laden vehicle to the side of the road, onto a grass verge. At last, the sign was spun to green on our side and we were waved along. As soon as we rounded the bend, we began to speed away from the road works. We started to overtake most of the traffic, but there was no sign of John's milk tanker.

"I seem to have lost John," Gerald shouted over his shoulder.

"It looks like we have lost the medical truck, too," I shouted back, as Gerald nodded in agreement. We drove a few miles further until the traffic had thinned out, the road was relatively clear, we pulled over to the side, puzzled. The milk truck didn't have anywhere near the speed of the bike.

"Where in the hell did they go?" I asked looking round in every direction.

"We're going to have to go back and check every turn off, Gerald," I replied.

"OK, let's get started," he said kicking the bike back into life. It seemed like a lost cause, there were so many small lanes off the main route; eventually we conceded defeat. Somehow we'd lost them. We set off rather dejectedly in the direction of the border City of Strasbourg.

Chapter Thirty-One

Earlier, as John and Bruce had driven away from the café, they saw Gerald and I walking across to the road-house. Once out on the main highway, they kept a discreet distance behind the medical supplies van. After some twenty miles or so into the journey, the traffic began to slow down until it was almost a snails pace; ahead John could see the cause of the delay as workers were repairing the road.

"Here comes Gerald, I can see him about two or three vehicles behind," John told Bruce. When he looked up front he couldn't see the Germans ahead.

"Come on, come on," John said impatiently to the unhearing traffic controller with the stop/go sign. As his line of traffic began to move, the milk truck just got through, as the sign was changed back to red for the car behind him.

A bit further on through the workings, a man stepped out signaling him to stop as two men carried a huge road drill from one side to the other, only to be followed by a tractor carrying earth. After at least a four minute hold-up, he was finally waved on, by which time the road ahead was clear, not a vehicle in sight.

At last they were able to get a move on to catch up on the lost time. The road took a turn to the right, as they came around a very sharp bend they were faced with a diversion ahead. Large arrows on a notice were directing them to a right hand turn.

Following the directions they rounded another bend in the lane, but immediately ahead was a barrier completely blocking the road. At that precise moment the tanker brushed tightly against a patch of dense bushes at the side of the road, Bruce saw two men at the barrier holding guns; instantly he flung the door open diving headlong into the thick bushes.

The medical supplies truck had somehow managed to get behind them; it came up on the rear of the tanker. As John was forced to a stop at the barrier, the two armed men then went to either side of the cab, pulling open both doors. They appeared surprised to see John sitting there alone, immediately shouting to the woman to look around for the other Englander. After a brief search they gave up. Taking the agent back to their truck, they proceeded to set the milk tanker on fire.

Bruce looked down from his hiding place up in the trees as the stench of the acrid black smoke began to billow towards him.

He heard the German truck drive off, tires skidding and screaming in reverse down the lane, and then the tree in which he'd hidden shook from the force of the explosion as the fuel tank of the milk container blew the vehicle airborne, then over on it's side.

Once the Germans had disappeared from sight, Bruce was down the tree and running for the main road. As he reached the main thoroughfare he saw that there was no sign for the diversion; the Germans had them high and dry, completely taken by surprise.

Now that John was captured, Bruce began to wonder where we had traveled with the motor bike, had we already gone past there or not? He had to make a quick decision on what to do next. He hoped he'd made the right one as he stood on the roadside thumbing the passing traffic, desperately wanting a lift to Strasbourg and the border.

Meanwhile, inside the medical supplies truck, the MI5 agent had been handcuffed, bound and gagged, then strapped and spread-eagled face down to anchor hooks on the floor of the vehicle. He was surrounded by the packages that had been the cause of so much suffering and death. Whatever his captors had in store for him, he knew he was of value to them or he would have been dead by now, if the past few days were anything to go by.

At least Bruce had escaped; he couldn't believe the speed and agility with which Bruce had left the milk tanker at the road block. It was a pretty impressive exit. As the truck rumbled on towards its destination, John worked frantically to free himself but without any success.

That same moment at the roadside Bruce stood holding out his thumb, the international sign for a free ride. Eventually a motorist pulled over, then stopped, much to Bruce's surprise the car bore the front number plate of a London registration. As the car came to a halt, a voice said;

"I don't speak a word of French young man, but you're welcome to a lift, I'm going as far as the German border."

"That suits me just fine," said Bruce, a smile stretching from ear to ear.

"I'm heading for Strasbourg."

"Hop in then lad, it's your lucky day." As they drove along Bruce told of a story sufficient to convince the man that he was a reliable and honest passenger. About an hour or so along the road, right out of the blue, Bruce saw the motor bike parked near a roadside café.

"Fancy a nice cuppa? It's the least I can offer in return for your kindness."

"That motor bike over there belongs to friends of mine, the ones I told you that went ahead to get help."

"That's fine with me, young fella. I'd like to meet these friends of yours," he replied.

Gerald and I were sitting in the café having a cup of tea as we saw the car pull up.

"That's an English car, has British plates on it, too, a London number if I'm not mistaken," I said to Gerald as we watched it being parked. Once parked the doors opened; you can imagine our utter amazement as we saw Bruce and a perfect stranger get out then walk towards the café. Bruce's face showed relief to see us sitting there. The look on our faces must have shown our surprise to see Bruce with a perfect stranger, and in a different car, minus John.

"Where's John?" Gerald asked. Bruce sat down and told us his story. The stranger sat and listened with utter disbelief written all over his face.

"Sorry, Matt," Bruce said turning to his transport benefactor, "if I had told you the truth, you'd most likely have thrown me out of the car."

Though our new-found friend was driving a car with London plates, he actually came from Wakefield in Yorkshire, and was fully aware of the current situation at the village of Casleton, so luckily we didn't have to reveal too much. We all hurriedly left the café, almost as soon as it took to drink a cup of coffee and eat a roll.

Gerald went off on the bike, and our newfound friend agreed to drive Bruce and I on towards the German border town of Strasbourg.

The remainder of the journey was uneventful as we drove into Strasbourg. There had been no trace of the medical supplies truck during our journey. We thanked our English friend for the ride, said goodbye, and then sat wondering what the hell our next move should be.

We discussed our options over a late lunch and agreed that finding John Cotes was the top priority, but just where to start was the problem. The Germans obviously were well ahead by now and, unlike us, they were on their own turf. If they'd left Strasbourg already, then we were in serious trouble; we would have to return home, defeated.

Sitting at the table in the small café, tired and dejected, almost ready to give in, we were awaiting our coffee, when a stranger approached us.

"Bonjour, do you mind if I join you?" he asked in highly accented English.

"You are all looking as though your world has come to an end, I recognized the motorbike," he continued.

"I am a friend of John Cotes, also a colleague of Jacques Montande, who has asked me to pass on his sincere gratitude to you all. Which one of you is called Matt?" I put up my hand.

"He is still in intensive care, but thanks to you, monsieur Matt, he is expected to make a full recovery. Is John

Cotes here?" He listened carefully as we explained the situation to him then he gave us his advice.

His assessment of the situation was that Germany was now under the complete control of Britain, America, and a separate Russian sector; we had entered the British sector, it should be a matter of record as to vehicles entering or leaving the country. He went on;

"Admittedly there are two pre-suppositions here: one, they are still using the same vehicles, and two, they have entered at an official check point rather than crossing illegally at some remote place," said the Frenchman. We had the third problem of not having John with us; therefore we did not have the ability to ask questions of the authorities.

Our most urgent problem was the serious lack of transport as we only had the one motor bike left between the three of us. The agent quickly solved that situation by telling us he'd brought along an exchange vehicle for the tanker anyway, so we could use that. He advised us to hang onto the bike as it might prove invaluable in certain situations. In addition, he threw down a small package, explaining it contained some much-needed French and German currency. This would certainly help our situation as we continued the journey.

"If you would care to wait here for a while, I'll try to get more information regarding the Germans' whereabouts now." He slid the financial package across the table, tipped his cap and went out the door.

We sat drinking hot chocolate and planning our next move, most definitely feeling happier than we had a half-hour earlier, anticipating the French agent would return with the vital information that we so badly needed.

In this semi-relaxed state, none of us noticed a man sitting at the other side of the room reading his newspaper, then making notes in a small book. The French agent returned with the news that the medical supply truck along with the Mercedes had passed through the checkpoint two hours before, supposedly heading for the Bavarian town of Ingolstadt.

He gave us documents for our new transport, and we all went outside. Just around the corner from the café, we saw our new mode of transport; we were staring at a ten-ton NAAFI truck (Navy Army Air Force Institute.)

The NAAFI was well known to all British servicemen anywhere in the world. They were military base stores where most requirements could be bought *(A similar organization to the US Military PX).* Inside the truck were sufficient canned goods to keep us alive for years; also soap, toothpaste and other toiletries sufficient to clean up a battalion.

After voicing much appreciation to the Frenchman, we were back on track once more. We passed through a checkpoint with little or no trouble, leaving a case of tinned salmon for the Military Police there. When we departed earlier we'd put the motor bike in the back of the truck, giving Gerald the chance to have a break. Then off we went in hot pursuit of the Germans, the packages, and of course, John Cotes.

As we passed through small towns and villages, we noticed that both military and local police would wave, or totally disregard us, NAAFI vehicles were obviously a common sight.

From what we could see by looking at the map, the journey to Ingolstatd was upwards of a hundred miles. So we settled down to the prospect of a fairly long and none-too comfortable journey; it was now late afternoon on Wednesday.

Chapter Thirty-Two

Casleton Village, Thursday

Cheryl woke to the sound of rain beating incessantly on her bedroom window. She drew back the curtains to see outside that it was still dark. Today was the day of Carl's funeral; yesterday the Coroner had released the body after holding a post-mortem. He'd solemnly pronounced his verdict as "Death at the hands of persons unknown."

Cheryl decided to go for a walk. The events of the past few days had taken their toll, leaving her feeling absolutely drained of energy physically, spiritually and emotionally. She'd watched her father age considerably in the space of only a few days. Her mother had lost the shine in her eyes, she'd become very withdrawn, Cheryl had even overheard her talking to herself.

David had been a continued tower of strength, but over the last couple of days she had found his touch and attempted embraces somewhat unwelcome.

Putting on her raincoat and rubber boots, she picked up an umbrella from the stand in the hallway and went outside into the driving rain. She walked for some considerable time, her mind a complete blank. She eventually found herself standing by the side of the hedgerow close to the point where Carl had met his untimely death. The area was still roped off with official police signs warning trespassers to keep out of the crime scene area. This was a place where they'd played as children. She crouched down looking under the bushes.

Usually this was the very spot where Carl could be found as a youngster when they played hide and seek, or if he wanted to be left alone.

The rain was still pouring down as she closed the umbrella and went into the bushes. The tin cover he'd put there for shelter all those years ago still remained intact.

Cheryl crouched under its cover as the noisy rain rattled mercilessly on the old rusty metal.

As she sat down on Carl's up-ended log, at first small tears slowly began to trickle down her cheeks, welling up in her eyes. Then she began to sob uncontrollably, her whole body shaking with spasms. After a while, when the tears began to subside and her vision slowly cleared, something caught her eye, something shining in the rotted vegetation on the ground below where she sat.

Wiping away her tears with the back of her hand, her eyes began to focus, and she stooped down to pick up a bunch of keys. They didn't look as though they'd been there very long, they'd remained dry and clean under the make-do shelter. She shook off the dead leaves and put the keys into her pocket.

Going through the bushes, she stood at the fence looking down at the railway lines; to her horror she saw a cardboard cut-out in the shape of a body put there by the police. It lay between the rails now soaked by the driving rains, a sad and pathetic sight; her only brother, Carl's epitaph. As the tears began to flow again, she heard a rustle in the bushes.

"Cheryl, is that you Cheryl?" It was the voice of her father. She turned and looked at the figure in front of her, a sad old man looking lost and so alone. Rushing to him, she threw her arms around his neck. They stood locked in that embrace for some time, father and daughter united in grief. There they both stood holding hands, looking at the pathetic cardboard effigy below them.

"May his soul rest in peace," George Armitage sighed deeply, his voice shaking, his lined tear-stained face looking towards the heavens.

"God bless you my son. I'll always miss you. This war continues to take its prisoners."

They walked back towards home, holding hands in silence, her umbrella still furled; both were oblivious to the driving rains soaking through to their very bones.

Once back at the house, Cheryl's mother came rushing across to them and all three stood in a tearful embrace, experiencing at last the blessed release of their pent-up grief.

Later, as the rains continued to rattle on her bedroom windows, Cheryl sat on her bed looking at the keys she had found. She had instantly recognized the lucky charm rabbit's foot; she'd given it to Carl many years ago. W*hat good luck had it brought him?*

She left her room, and then walked along the landing to her brother's room. Opening the door quietly she went in, they had always kept their own space private and even now she felt like an intruder as she walked across the room and sat on the bed. Carl's room looked very different from the last time she had been invited in there.

Gone were all the trophies of bygone victories, gone were the cricket bats, golf clubs and school memorabilia.

The room was bare with the exception of a photograph of David White alongside a framed newspaper cutting of His Majesty the King decorating David after the war. Close by was a photo of Cheryl.

She opened the wardrobe, in the top corner she saw a metal box on the shelf above. Reaching up she brought it down, carefully placing it on the bed. Cheryl tried to open it but the box was securely locked.

Looking for something that would bring back pleasant memories, she found Carl's old school scarf, which she held closely to her face, and then wrapped it around her neck. She left the room, quietly closing the door and taking the locked metal box with her.

Back in her room she placed the security box on her dressing table. After trying a number of the keys she had found, the lid eventually popped open. Inside were four sealed envelopes with other pieces of paper.

Later that same day, two big black limousines stood waiting outside the house. George Armitage and his wife Eve left their home and climbed into the back of one of the cars, followed by Cheryl and David; other close relatives filled the second car.

The hearse was standing further along the drive bedecked with beautiful wreaths of flowers. Eight coal miners stood, four on each side of the hearse to act as pall bearers at the church, they wore coalminer black protective helmets. The entourage moved off slowly, the procession left the grounds turning onto the road. There was an unusually large crowd of people along the roadside.

Men were doffing their caps, which they held to their hearts in respect, some were making the sign of the cross, others bowing their heads in silence. The event seemed to have attracted many press photographers.

Outside, the church was crowded. Many were miners; as a mark of respect the mine had been closed for the day, the mill also. In the distance, the sound of the mine siren could be heard as it went off every minute marking the death of one of their own.

It seemed that the whole village was in mourning. The eight pall bearers carried the coffin into the Church; after a short service, Carl's remains were carried to his final resting place in the grave yard.

"In the midst of life we are in death," the voice of the village vicar seemed distant to Cheryl.

"We commit the body of Carl George Armitage ...In the sure and certain knowledge ...Dust to dust, ashes to ashes."

Eve Armitage began to shake uncontrollably as George tried to console her. She dropped a handful of earth, which clattered noisily on the top of the polished wooden coffin.

"Goodbye, my son" she sobbed. Finally, the service over, they walked back to the car.

"I've really lost my son now, you know," sounding like a little girl, as she spoke to no one in particular. Cheryl supported her left arm.

"I know, Mum, I know, but whatever his troubles were, they are over now, he'll be able to rest in peace at last."

Chapter Thirty-Three

Ingolstadt Bavaria

The NAAFI truck lumbered into the old Bavarian town, most local inhabitants were still fast asleep. It was dark outside and we'd been traveling for almost twelve hours; Gerald and Bruce had taken turns at the wheel. I'd managed to get some sleep in the back, though the rattling of cans and bottles and the oily smell of the motor bike had made extended sleep somewhat impossible. I was nodding off once again, just as the vehicle came to a halt. My luminous time piece told me it was four-thirty AM. Bruce opened the rear door.

"Wakey, wakey, rise and shine," he shouted. I collected my aching bones together, made worse by the hard wooden floor. I slid down from the back, my rear end numbed and limped around to the cab.

"I thought we'd park up here for a while as we've made good timing. Maybe get a spot of shuteye in the back of the truck. I think I noticed some bedding supplies in there. While we sleep you check around to see what you can find out; after all, you're the one who speaks the lingo. Also, look for a place where we can eat when we wake up," said Gerald. With that they both disappeared into the back of the truck. *Bedding supplies in there? I never saw any and I slept on the boards!* I thought.

As the doors of the truck were closed, a German policeman appeared out of thin air. He stood at the front of the vehicle, asking what we were doing there at that time of the morning. He was looking at me and my facial damages with a fair amount of suspicion on his own face. I explained that we'd been traveling all night, that the other two were sleeping in the back. He began to ask even more questions as two MPs drove up in a jeep.

"He giving you trouble, Mate?" asked the sergeant. Before I could answer, he gestured with his thumb to the police officer, basically telling him to get on his bike, so to speak. I watched as the local cop walked away, the MPs drove slowly looking around as they watched him leave, then sped away.

Meanwhile, in the back of the German's medical supplies truck, John Cotes was in absolute agony; he was still staked out and spread- eagled on the floor like some prisoner in a western cowboy and Indian film.

Such a long time had gone by, he'd lost track, surely at least twenty-four hours had passed by now.

Suddenly he felt the smooth road change to more uneven terrain, then the vehicle came to a halt. There was total peace as the engine stopped. Voices could be heard approaching the rear of the truck. With a click of the locks the door was thrown open and the agent was temporarily blinded by the bright daylight.

Looking beyond the two men standing there, he could see that they were parked in a thickly wooded area. The sun was shining and sparkling through the trees, giving an overpowering smell of pine needles. The first man climbed up onto the truck and clambered over the packages, making his way towards John. He began to cut the bonds free. His legs were cut free as he was unceremoniously dragged to the rear of the truck.

"When you're ready, give him to me," the agent heard the voice of the big German.

"I want to handle this one personally. Tie his hands up again, this time behind his back, and blindfold him. Hurry, we don't have all day to waste, get a move on; we have to get through the town and onto our final destination before nightfall." Once John was tied up and blindfolded again, the two men pushed him from the truck to the ground, where his legs would not hold him and he fell.

"Come on, Mr. MI5; get up on your feet. You've been a thorn in my side for far too long," the big man snarled in English, as he prodded John forward with the barrel of the Lugar.

John stumbled and nearly fell again as he was continually pushed along the ground, he could smell the fresh air and the damp odor of peat underfoot. After they had gone quite some distance, during which time he had walked into a number of trees and stumbled over numerous roots, the German spoke at the top of his voice.

"That's far enough." John tightened every muscle in his body as he heard the metallic click of a safety catch, then he saw a bright flash across his eyes; then total oblivion.

The others back at the truck, by now used to death, heard the shouted instruction, then one single shot. Seconds later the big German came strolling out of the trees displaying his usual arrogant gait along with a look of satisfaction across his Aryan face.

Back in the town of Ingolstadt, I'd found the local military police base, which was manned by both Army Red Caps and Royal Air Force Police; none of them had seen the white medical supply truck pass through the town. The good news was that there were only two main roads leading out of town. As we were now in Bavaria, most of the surrounding area seemed to consist of dense forest.

I'd walked through the town and found a number of places to eat. One of the better ones seemed totally frequented by the richer locals, though quite expensive; the remaining venues were all pretty average. I was told by the cops at the base we were most welcome to use the mess at their station if we wished.

I continued on my way around the old town, the whole area seemed to have escaped the ravages of war. All of the buildings were clean-looking, as though they'd been there forever. I passed a bakery. The aroma of freshly baked bread was irresistible. A bell tinkled cheerfully as I walked into the small shop. I bought a bag of fresh rolls, a small pumpernickel loaf and a pack of butter. I ate one of the rolls, buttered it with my pen knife as I walked back to the truck, breaking the pieces off by hand, making sure not to chew with my damaged front teeth.

By the time I returned from my jaunt, Gerald was awake and sitting in the cab. I gave him the bread and rolls, which he dove into hungrily. Bruce came out of the truck ten minutes later. He, too, attacked the food with vigor until there was none left.

Leaving the truck, we went to the large Germanic hotel frequented by the wealthy, an ancient monument of a building, where we ordered coffee in the lounge area.

After coffee, we took turns using the bathroom and had a good clean up, our pockets well-supplied with soap, tooth brushes and tooth paste, courtesy of the N.A.F.F.I, but sadly, no razors.

We decided on an early lunch at the restaurant in the hotel. After lunch, Gerald brought out the blood stained piece of paper from the murdered German, smoothing it out carefully on the table. The only distinguishable words that had not been erased by the blood were........ '….oss' and '….erg'. Both sets of three letters had dark brown patches of blood in front of them, which really didn't make a whole lot of sense to us at the time. Later, we drove out of the town at around two o'clock, feeling rested and clean, our appetites sated.

Approaching the outskirts of town, we noted that one road seemed to lead in the direction of continued civilization, the other would take us up into the forest area. We decided that the truck could be taken on the lower route, the bike was to explore the upper forest area. I would stay with Gerald in the truck, while Bruce would take the bike into the forest. We would meet at exactly five o'clock back at the main junction.

As we lifted the bike down to the road with much difficulty, Bruce put on the leather helmet and goggles, then off he went along the road as we drove in the other direction.

The motor bike chugged along the narrow tree-lined road, sometimes the forest opened up into large clearings, but most of the time it appeared to be dense and solid with trees.

Later, as Bruce rounded a sharp bend in the road, he saw a smaller lane to the right. As he shot past it he caught a brief glimpse of sunlight reflecting off a vehicle. Going further along the road he pulled into a very small clearing, put the bike behind some foliage and then hid himself under the bushes and waited. Before very long he heard the sounds of an oncoming vehicle.

He almost jumped up and did a jig as he saw the white medical supplies truck, followed by another identical vehicle; bringing up the rear was the Mercedes. *If only I had radio contact*, he thought to himself.

He knew that he didn't have time to go and find the others. The only avenue open to him was to follow the Germans alone. Pushing the bike out of the hiding place, he donned his helmet and goggles, kicked the bike into life and then took off after the killers. The two vehicles were in his sights within a few minutes, but the Mercedes was no longer behind them. For one horrible moment he looked in the rear view mirror, half expecting to see the grill of big car behind him. He turned his head fully and sighed with relief to see the road behind was clear of any traffic.

Back on the Low Road

We had driven for about thirty miles, at least that's what the gauge said, though the road markers suggested more like fifty kilometers. Thirty or fifty kilometers, it made no difference, we'd seen nothing. I had talked to a number of people on the way, giving a full description of the vehicles and their occupants, but they'd not been seen, not even at the gas stations we passed.

Glancing at my watch, I suggested to Gerald that we needed to turn around if we were to be at our rendezvous on time. He complied, turning around at the last gas station where we needed topping up. We returned at last to the junction, fifteen minutes late; there was no sign of Bruce or the motor bike. After waiting around for thirty-five minutes with still no sign of Bruce, we decided to head out along the road he'd taken earlier.

The road was narrower than the one we had traveled earlier and we made slow progress. As there were so many small roads leading off, it would have been impossible to cover them all. We worked on the principle that the unmade roads would be too small for the large German truck. Gerald checked the roads off to his right, and I scouted the ones to the left-hand side.

The road began to get steeper as Bruce followed the white trucks. He kept the bike at a discreet distance at the same time keeping his eye on the rear view mirror. The light was beginning to fail and he knew that soon he'd need lights to see where he was going. He hoped we two would anticipate that he was on to something, or maybe that he was in some kind of trouble.

Hopefully we would come along this road looking for him. It was over an hour since he had been scheduled to meet with us. *They are probably coming up behind me right this minute,* he thought.

Ahead, the two vehicles began to slow down, the gradient was now very steep, then he saw them turn off to the right. He chose to drive past the turn and then he saw the sign 'Schloss Indberg, five kilometers.'

Bruce turned the bike around and went back along the road past the sign, which he believed to mean Indberg Castle. He hid the motor bike in the undergrowth as before, took off the leather helmet, and then settled down to wait for our arrival.

Eventually, he heard the sound of an approaching car from the opposite direction. It slowed down to a halt and turned into the entrance of the road to the Castle. Shortly after, he heard another, then another. He looked out from his hiding place; all of these cars were very large Daimler Benz convertibles of differing colors. Within the next ten minutes he had counted ten such big cars, all heading in the direction the trucks had taken.

After waiting a few minutes and seeing no further activity, he stood up to stretch his limbs to rid himself of the pins and needles sensation creeping up his leg. As he stood he heard a crack of twigs underfoot, at the same time Bruce felt the jab of something hard against his kidneys. A German voice snapped what was obviously a command as he was pushed from his hiding place out onto the road. There, another two armed men stood, wearing some sort of military uniform. Handcuffs were fastened to his wrists, an open military vehicle drove up swiftly and he was un-ceremoniously bundled into the rear. The scout car was driven off at speed up the narrow lane past the sign to the Castle.

Meanwhile, Gerald and I seemed to have driven for miles, without sight nor sound of Bruce, or any other vehicle, not even another human being. I had just commented on the fact when a car came in the opposite direction, it was a particularly large coach-built Daimler-Benz, the type that was used by the very wealthy, or as Gerald said, by the senior military types during the war.

A couple of miles behind it we saw a similar vehicle. Then strangely within the space of ten miles there were at least seven more of the same type.

"Let's find somewhere to turn round," said Gerald, "there's something very odd going on here."

"Got it, I've got it," I yelled with excitement.

"Got what?" Gerald asked, near jumping out of his skin as I'd shouted.

"I saw a sign back there; that's it, the note, the note with the blood stains, the Castle!" I continued to talk in riddles.

"Slow down," said Gerald, "what are you getting so damned excited about? What castle are you going on about, and what does it have to do with the note?" he asked, looking totally perplexed.

"There's a sign back there, Schloss Indberg, take the first four letters off the first word, and the first four letters off the second one, you have the letters on the blood-stained note exactly, and that's where they are!" I added excitedly.

"Schloss Indberg in German means Indberg Castle." While I was giving forth, Gerald had the truck turned around and we were already headed in the opposite direction towards the road sign.

Chapter Thirty-Four

Casleton Village, Thursday Evening

The reception following the funeral was over, it had been held at the village club where over fifty people had been in attendance mainly family, friends and some workers.

George Armitage had asked that the club be opened to the village and he put fifty pounds behind the bar for the villagers to have a drink. He had gone through to the bar where he'd received many respectful nods, also many heartfelt condolences, some accompanied by real tears.

As the family prepared to leave, David went across to Cheryl.

"I'll be happy to drive you all home."

"That's kind of you David," she replied, then they left to get into David's car. They drove home in absolute silence, everyone drained of energy and emotion. George and Eve thanked David, and then went into the house. Cheryl put her hand on David's arm.

"Thank you for everything today, David," she patted his hand gently and left the car. As he drove away he couldn't help feeling how cold and distant Cheryl seemed. He had a really awful feeling of finality, a sort of unsaid goodbye; maybe it was the result of such a traumatic day. He only hoped that's all it was. He could only wait and see what tomorrow would bring.

Cheryl went straight upstairs to her room. She lay on the bed for a few minutes, then got up and went over to the dressing table. Taking Carl's locked box, she went back over to her bed and by using the keys, she unlocked it and tipped the contents on the counterpane.

There were the four handwritten envelopes sealed and addressed to Dad, Mum, Cheryl and David, along with a list of detailed gambling debts.

Cheryl went downstairs and made herself a hot cup of chocolate then returned to her room. She settled down in the chair, turned on her reading lamp and opened the letter bearing her name.

It felt most peculiar reading words and recognizing the handwriting of the man she had just buried today.

She went on to read the words:

My dear Cheryl

If you are reading this letter, then I'm either dead or in such a state that I'm not responsible for my actions. I'm feeling very unhappy and have been so for some years now.

I assume that you found my box. You always were the resourceful one. When you have read this letter, please distribute the other letters for me.

When the war came and David was conscripted, the bottom fell out of my world. I tried to volunteer for military service, but Dad along with Government legislation put paid to that. Then you, yourself went to the war. It was all more than I could bear. I felt so unwanted and useless.

I tried to carry on with my job at the mine. I tried to believe that my efforts would help the war, but it was no substitute for an active man like me, who should really have been fighting the enemy.

After a while I took to drinking heavily, and then began to gamble. All the way through school I had my friend David to lean on and get me out of trouble; now he was gone.

One thing led to another, I was up to my ears in gambling debts at a club in Leeds. This club, as I eventually found out was run by a German spy ring. They then started to put pressure on me to assist them in some of their endeavors. They threatened to go to Dad if I refused; I couldn't face the shame, so I reluctantly went along with their dastardly demands.

They have been stashing millions of pounds worth of priceless treasures around our country throughout the war, some were hidden down our mine. I think that they are currently moving the stuff out. Believe me they are fanatical. They will stop at nothing, evidenced by the murder of that young police officer. Also they were responsible for my recent hospitalization, that was just a warning though. Forgive me for the fake amnesia, I know you, for one, weren't fooled.

By the time you read this I will have failed in my attempts to foil their plans, maybe I've been killed. But believe me I have no desire to live anymore, anyway.

Dear Cheryl, please don't hate me. Sometimes life deals us a good hand and sometimes not, but we're all obliged to play the hand we're dealt. I obviously didn't get a good one. Remember I love you; please show this to the police.

Cheryl, please try to get Mum and Dad to understand, I'm sure that David will never understand. I know that you do. Be happy, I have always loved and respected you. Think of me sometimes.

Your devoted brother,

Carl

Cheryl put the two pages on the bed and prayed for her brother's soul.

What agony he must have gone through, what suffering his tortured mind must have endured, she thought as she jumped up from the chair.

"I won't discuss this with a living soul," she said aloud.

"It's too late now, nothing can be gained by damaging your name, your secret is safe with me, Carl," she said as she very deliberately tore up the letter into very small pieces, and then she repeated the process with the other three letters. Cheryl then systematically destroyed the list of gambling debts. Then she began to pack her suitcase.

Chapter Thirty-Five

Schloss Indberg, Bavaria

We began to retrace our steps, we'd traveled about three miles or so when we came upon the area I thought we were looking for.

"Slow down, Gerald, it's somewhere here." Just then, another large car coming from the other direction slowed down and turned off to our left.

"Keep on going past the turn, maybe a half mile or so, we have to find somewhere to leave this truck, we can't possibly take it in there." As luck would have it, we came across a small unmade lane, just a few hundred yards along on the same side of the road. Gerald turned into the lane to discover it wasn't really a lane, but a small clearing with a wood-cutter's hut, stacked high with piles of logs along with long trees cut for telegraph poles.

The area was dense enough for our truck to be unseen from the road or from the forest. We parked the truck and set off through the undergrowth toward the lane where the car had turned just a moment ago.

"I think we should walk through the trees to this castle entrance, just in case any other vehicles come along," Gerald said wisely. We struggled through the thick, heavy undergrowth.

"What's that over there?" Gerald pointed as he spoke, I couldn't see anything other than trees; after a pause he leaned backwards.

"There it is again, there is something shining in the undergrowth, over there, in the ferns, I swear." I followed as he took off, then he turned crouching down quickly, signaling that I should do the same.

Gerald put his index finger to his lips, at the same time I smelled the cigarette smoke, as it drifted on the air past my nose. There, leaning against a tree, was the figure of a man in a German uniform with a rifle slung over his shoulder, smoking a cigarette. Gerald signaled for me to stay put, and then he disappeared from view.

The next time I saw him, he was coming up behind the tree where the unfortunate soldier was leaning. He tapped the man on the shoulder, who turned round instantly to receive the full power of Gerald's right fist in the solar plexus, followed by a slumber-creating uppercut to the jaw. The German slumped over as Gerald bent down.

Seconds later he beckoned me across. I looked down at the still crumpled figure as we tied him securely, and then gagged him.

"This is what I saw before," he said pointing to something shining in the undergrowth.

"It's our motor bike." Sure enough hidden by ferns was our bike, there on the seat was the leather helmet and goggles that Bruce had worn when he left us.

"What a blessing," said Gerald.

"In one respect, yes, at least we know Bruce is here somewhere," I replied.

"But where, why would he leave the bike here and go on foot?" I asked.

"Good question, maybe for the same reason that we decided to walk through the undergrowth," he replied, looking concerned. We moved the bike back onto the road, he kick started it and drove into the lane, the sign said five kilometers to the castle. On reflection, I was sure that Bruce would not have opted to walk that far, *if he had a choice*, that is.

The one bonus the Germans had unwittingly given us was a motor bike with an extremely quiet engine; it made more of a rumble than a crackle, if driven gently, as Gerald did. It would not be easily heard as we made our way towards our destination, Schloss Indberg.

"What will happen if the soldier wakes up and gives the alarm?" I shouted in Gerald's ear as we headed towards the castle.

"Don't worry, he's well tied up," he answered. Further along, the terrain seemed to be thinning out. They say that great minds think alike. I was about to ask Gerald to stop the bike, as he pulled over, then the castle came into view.

On any other occasion, one would have stopped to look in absolute awe. It truly was a magnificent building, tall turrets around the top half covered in mist and surrounded by a water-filled moat, green growth covering its walls, like something out of a Count Dracula film set.

"Jesus!" Gerald exclaimed.

"What an eerie place, you'd half expect Bela Lugossi to answer the door." *Worse than that maybe*, I thought.

The castle appeared to have a fully operable draw bridge as no vehicles were in evidence, leading us to believe the cars we'd seen were safely parked inside the confines of the castle. As we looked at the barred windows so high above the water along with the massive stone ramparts, the impregnability of the place seemed overwhelming.

The sound of an approaching vehicle jolted us back into action. We literally threw the bike into an available ditch by the side of the approach, then we dived for cover ourselves, as an open topped camouflaged military truck swept past us. It continued until reaching the edge of the moat. Then as if by magic the great drawbridge began to groan and creak as it lowered slowly, like some medieval ritual; we half expected a fanfare of trumpets to accompany its descent. As the bridge became level with the ground, the truck crossed and we could see many vehicles inside, two of which were the white medical supplies trucks. We watched as the bridge was raised back into position; though we didn't say anything, I felt sure that we were both of one accord. *How in the hell were we going to get into the castle unobserved and were John and Bruce in there?* Two minds, one single set of thoughts.

The Armitage Home, England

Cheryl finished her packing, then she went downstairs, her father was reading and her mother working on her embroidery as she walked into the room.

"Hello, dear," said her father peering over the top of his spectacles, looking up from his book.

"Dad, I've decided to go back to my own place," she said in a decisive manner.

"Well, I'm sure you need a break from all of this," he replied.

"No, you don't understand, I'm going back to re-organize my life. I've packed my things, and I'll be leaving in a minute."

"So soon?" asked her Mother.

"Yes, Mum, if I don't leave now, perhaps I never will. I really feel the urge to get away. Of course, I'll be back. I'll give you a call tonight to let you know I arrived safely. God bless you both." She leaned down, kissing them in turn.

"I'll borrow Carl's car if that's OK with you, Dad, it'll only be in the way here now, and it's not quite so old as my jalopy."

George and Eve went to the door and waved goodbye as she drove off, then they both went back into the house and sat down, a sense of loneliness and emptiness had settled on the house.

Cheryl drove into Leeds, going straight to the offices of Frank Bell and Sons. As she entered the office, she saw an older man sitting at a desk.

"May I speak with Bruce Bell please?"

"I am afraid he's not here at the moment, Miss," Frank Bell replied.

"I'm not really sure when he'll be back either," he added.

"I am Frank Bell, his father. May I help you in any way, or perhaps take a message?"

"I'm Cheryl Armitage, my late brother Carl went to school with your son."

"I was so sorry to hear about your loss, my dear, please accept my deepest condolences. I know the same would be said by Bruce," Frank held out his hand as he spoke.

"Thank you, that's very kind of you, I wonder if you would see that Bruce gets this letter on his return." She passed him a sealed envelope written in her own hand.

"I'm sorry, but I must be on my way, I have quite a long drive ahead of me. Please give my best wishes to Bruce," Cheryl smiled, said goodbye then left the office and drove off towards the City.

Leeds City Police Headquarters

The door to the Chief Superintendents office was closed, he was sitting at his desk pouring over the latest reports from his officers, when there was a knock on the door.

"Come," he snapped officiously in his usual curt manner, the door was opened by his sergeant.

"What is it?" he asked testily without bothering to look up.

There's a young lady here to see you Sir, Doctor Armitage, she's the sister of Carl Armitage, the second murder victim at Castleton."

"Well, don't just stand there man, show her in."

"Yes, Sir."

"Doctor Armitage, please take a seat." He walked around his desk and pulled back the chair for her to sit.

"How may I be of assistance?" he asked sitting back behind his desk.

"Actually, I came to give you some pertinent information. Just before my brother died, he spoke to me in confidence."

"Why didn't you tell us about this when we interviewed you after his death," he said cutting her short.

"If you'll allow me the courtesy of finishing what I have to say, then perhaps you will understand. May I continue Chief Inspector?" she added facetiously.

"Yes, please do Doctor, and by the way it's Chief Superintendent, if you don't mind."

Cheryl jumped up from the seat, walking towards the door.

"I'm not here to bolster your stupid ego," she snapped.

"I really don't care if you're a General or Corporal you silly man!"

"Please sit down, I'm sorry if I appear insensitive, I'm afraid this case is wearing us all a little thin, do go on, please." She explained to him most of the contents of Carl's letter. The reason she hadn't mentioned it before was because she was hoping to keep such facts from the press.

"Frankly, Dr. Armitage, we had pieced together much of what you've just told me anyway, you have confirmed our suspicions. What we really need to know is, where are these people with the contraband now?" he added.

"Did you read about the half-clothed German found on the London to Dover boat train? Well, his finger prints matched those found in the car of the second murdered S.I.B. officer. He's now in London being interviewed by Scotland Yard. They have taken over the case now, I will pass on what you've just told me to Special Branch." He offered her a card.

"Here's the name of the officer in charge, if anything else crops up, please contact him."

As Cheryl drove away from the police station, she didn't know whether she'd made the right decision about so many things. Telling the police of Carl's involvement with the Germans, also destroying the letters, and finally leaving home without seeing David. Maybe she should have stayed and faced him.

She'd decided to call him tomorrow anyway and voice her feelings. Sometimes it is easier to discuss a problem when there's some distance between you, rather than face-to-face. She felt confident she would be able to make the right decision regarding her future once she was alone and without any other distractions.

Chapter Thirty-Six

Schloss Indberg, The Final Onslaught

Gerald and I hid in the bushes for the best part of half an hour, watching and waiting intently for any sign of activity, wishing that the others were with us. We had to assume they were both prisoners, more than likely inside the castle somewhere. The main challenges that faced us were how to get in there undetected, then once inside, how to find them; and more importantly, how to get all of us out alive.

It was now rapidly getting darker as dusk turned to night. The plan we'd settled on eventually was to swim across the moat. In order to accomplish this and end up with dry clothes on the other side, we would have to swim across in the nude, somehow managing to keep our clothes above the water.

We didn't think that they would be keeping such a diligent watch on the moat, having in mind that these ramparts had kept back hoards of better-equipped people than we two; maybe they were expecting more visitors, in which case they would be watching the drawbridge approach area.

Once successfully across the other side, we would have to climb up the side of the drawbridge, get up onto the parapet, and then find our way down inside. By any stretch of the imagination an ambitious and daunting plan.

We crept gingerly across the surface of the road our nerves and senses on edge half expecting to be seen at any moment, when suddenly my foot struck a metal object which tinkled noisily, its sounds exaggerated by the deathly silence as it rolled and sparkled in the fading light of the moon, like a small wheel. I stooped down and quickly grabbed the offending object. We both looked down in amazement, at the Mercedes hood emblem in my hand.

At the water's edge, we moved around its perimeter, and out of sight of any erstwhile sentry. Then we stripped, floating our clothes on a large flat board that we had found by the ditch.

Neither of us were ready for the next move, the eventual shock to the system was indescribable, it was absolutely freezing, our audible gasps could surely be heard had anyone been paying the slightest attention. The thought of any unfriendly creatures in the depths of the moat was quickly dismissed, for it would need to be a polar bear to have stayed alive in there.

We swam quickly, both pushing our make-do raft in front of us, the distance across was about sixty to seventy yards, far enough to feel our body heat dropping rapidly, limbs shaking uncontrollably.

We reached the other side with no problems other than potential hypothermia and pneumonia, most likely both; very wide awake and paying full attention after the icy dip.

Then the troubles started: at the other side there was no bank to climb onto, the walls of the castle were actually in the water and covered in a very slippery green slime. There was a slight ledge just above the water line, but it meant having to hang on with one hand and get dressed with the other.

Our teeth physically chattered loudly as we began to realize that the task was impossible, then suddenly:

"Psst, Hey Matt, over here quickly," Gerald spotted a small boat, which hadn't been visible from across the water, it was hidden by reeds. Anyway, we swam eagerly across to it.

Then the fun started. We had to get from the water, into the long thin row boat, without overturning the vessel; naked and half-frozen to death, in full view of anyone who cared to look over the wall.

We eventually sat facing each other, shivering violently. I lifted the oars from the bottom of the boat, fitted them into the rowlocks and then we went across and retrieved our floating wardrobe. After we'd dressed we continued to shake as we took the boat on a circumference of the Castle, keeping very close to the walls.

We rowed around to the other side of the castle where to our utmost delight, we found a tunnel through which we could take the boat, but for the staunch iron gates in the water! We could see that they had not been opened for an age and were securely fastened in position by a very large and very old lock.

"We need something to break that lock open," Gerald said adding:

"It looks pretty old so there's a chance it'll give way under pressure."

The rowlocks on the boat were made of solid brass so I pulled at the U-shaped bracket, which came out of the transom easily, having a nine to ten-inch rod on its end. I held the boat against the gate by the ledge, while Gerald forced the rod into the asp of the lock.

As he exerted pressure, the boat moved, then the brazed joint between the U and the rod snapped clean off, accompanied by an unrepeatable oath. We were luckier using the second rowlock, as the old lock gave up the battle and flew open, splashing into the moat.

It took us another ten minutes to move the gate sufficiently to pass through because the bottom was well and truly fastened by many years of growth at the base. We slid silently into the unknown blackness of the tunnel, only to come up against a similar set of gates at the other end.

Luckily the chain on this one was so badly rusted that it fell apart as Gerald pulled it. Also, as these gates were internal, no sunlight had encouraged the growth of underwater algae and other vegetation, so the gates opened with comparative ease.

Passing through the dank tunnel, we found ourselves at a very damp and slippery stone boat landing, some twenty feet long, with a big iron-clad hinged door at the rear. I had still managed to retain the small flashlight given to me by John Cotes, which I shone around this ancient and eerie dock. We tied the boat to one of the old mooring posts, and then we slithered carefully across its hazardous green slippery surface towards the door; it was locked solid!

"Now what?" he asked, showing signs of serious irritation. We looked around. I found a long iron bar, which once had probably formed part of the old gate. This we forced into the crack of the door, and after much sweating and swearing the door gave way under the pressure; we were at about to enter Schloss Indberg.

Behind the creaking door was a vestibule with a stone spiral staircase leading clockwise upwards. In the vestibule there were a number of items lying around on the floor; one was a good solid pick handle along with two long lengths of stout rope. We took these welcome items and then began to climb the old worn steps with caution and trepidation.

After about twenty or thirty steps, we came to a door on the left- hand side of the steps which on inspection was locked solid, and so we continued on upwards reaching yet another door. This one opened easily for us. I was the first to crack open the door, peering out cautiously with some reluctance. We were looking out on the actual ramparts of the castle; the area seemed totally deserted as we very cautiously exited the stairs.

Looking down on the inside was a different matter. The larger area below was vast, with at least ten large gleaming Mercedes cars parked in a line, each with their long hoods facing castle walls, the nearest two to the arched entrance were a deep red in color, the others a shiny black. A group of jack booted drivers stood around chatting. Two large white medical supply trucks were parked opposite, along with a number of military vehicles including a few motorcycles. An archway led off into an area that seemed deserted.

We needed to find a way down and hoped that the solid locked door that we'd passed on the way up was not the only way out. After thoroughly reconnoitering the whole of the upper ramparts, sadly that door at the bottom of the stone stairs was indeed the only way down to the courtyard, other than a wide open set of steps leading directly down into the courtyard below, and in full view of all.

We moved cautiously around the ramparts, until we were above the deserted area below where we fastened two pieces of rope together, and then around the stone turrets. We prepared to drop them over the side, but not before deciding where to meet after a hopefully successful descent.

Over the wall went the ropes, we slid cautiously down, and I earned a couple of rope burns on the inside of my thigh to add to my earlier collection. We met as arranged behind the trash bins we'd spotted in a dark corner; ready to plan the next move.

I nearly jumped clear out of my skin as someone shouted at me in German, demanding to know what I was doing there. I looked around for Gerald, but he'd disappeared too. I turned back towards the German, fishing mentally for an answer to his question, possibly one of the only times in my life when I didn't have an answer; then I saw a large hand appear from behind my challenger's head, then it snaked around his mouth.

A look of surprise mixed with terror crossed his eyes as he slowly sank to the floor in front of me, blood seeping slightly from the corner of his mouth; he was dead, still twitching slightly, but very dead.

"The third body in just a few days," I whispered nervously to Gerald.

"No time to start getting squeamish now, but its better his body than yours, don't you think, young Matt?" he hissed in a whisper.

"Here, help me put this chap in the trash bin over there," he said, grabbing the dead man's shoulders. We dragged the body over to the bin, lifted him up and deposited him unceremoniously inside amongst cabbage leaves and potato peelings. Gerald replaced the lid, a satisfied look on his face

"Stay here, Matt. I'll be back in a minute." With that he was gone. I moved further into the darkness, away from the trash, in case someone came to dispose of any rubbish, or worse still, if they came looking for the dead man. *Hurry up and get back for God's sake, Gerald,* I thought. It seemed an age before he returned. As usual he was so quiet he frightened the living daylights out of me when he tapped me on the shoulder.

"Come with me, quickly," he whispered.

"There's some kind of high-powered meeting going on in a big hall, problem is I can't understand a bloody word they're saying." I followed him, keeping in the shadows of the building. We went through a door, along a corridor where a German soldier appeared to be asleep on the floor. On closer inspection he was bound and gagged and unconscious, *at least I hoped that he was!* I thought to myself as we climbed up a small staircase.

Once we reached the top he whispered, "Follow me slowly on your stomach." I complied and we slid out onto a sort of minstrel's gallery above what must have been the main banquet hall. I heard the powerful voice of a man speaking in a very motivational and Germanic way, reminiscent of some of the German wartime speeches I'd heard at the cinemas after the war.

He was obviously a trained orator. I peered over the edge through the balustrade to see a large gold emblazoned banner over the stage. A big man stood at the podium, addressing his audience.

He was dressed in the uniform of a Gestapo General with lots of gold and red emblazoned across his shoulders, a large iron cross on a gold ribbon around his neck, a wide red stripe down the sides of his tight pants, tightly fitting into his gleaming black knee boots.

There in the body of the hall, sitting around a vast table, were over twenty military officers. All of senior rank, their gold braided caps in front of them on the tables, these must have been the occupants of the cars we had seen arriving earlier. The banner above the speaker's head read: **The Fourth Reich**. There was a large ominous black eagle emblazoned there, and black and red swastikas were at each end.

"Gentlemen, Officers of the Fourth Reich, the time has come for us to rejoice, the day we have waited for will soon be here. The funds we need and have awaited for so long to achieve our goals are here in this historic castle at last."

"All of our careful planning has come to fruition. The gold will be deposited in our Banks in Switzerland. We already have the buyers for the works of art which will be sold around the world. Within a year we will be ready. We will rise and be powerful once again." His voice had increased in crescendo, until the man almost screamed.

"We will build the super race, this time we shall succeed. Nothing will get in our way. Gentlemen, raise your glasses in a toast to my Father Adolf Hitler. Heil, Hitler, Heil, the Fourth Reich!" The shouting was ear-splitting.

The noise was almost sickly overpowering as glasses were thrown across the room, smashing on the stone floor of the massive fireplace.

The German National Anthem was then played as each man stood to attention, right arms at an angle to the sky, giving the Nazi salute.

"Shit, did you see that?" I whispered to Gerald.

"Jesus Christ," Gerald whispered," now I understand why John Cotes is so determined, the guy there is actually the son of Adolph Hitler!"

"What do we do now?" I asked.

"We have to find the others, and get the hell out of here before they discover those bodies," replied Gerald. *Bodies, I thought, doesn't he mean body?*

The meeting in the great hall continued as they began to discuss the detailed value of the gold and artifacts they'd stolen. We crept back down the staircase out of the great hall and along the corridor. I explained what the General had said, while we moved the unconscious soldier into a large alcove under the stairs, away from prying eyes. I followed Gerald along into another corridor, down another stone staircase; he turned sharply holding up his right hand, indicating silence. The steps were slippery, the air smelled damp and repugnant.

I felt a chill go down my spine like an electric shock as we heard the loud screams of a man in pain, then a sharp voice yelling in accented English:

"Unless you tell us where your friends are, you will die. It won't be a quick death either." Carefully following behind Gerald, I peered through the open door, taking care not to be seen. It was a prison chamber and very dimly lit, apart from a bright light shining on the head of the figure of a man tied to a chair. Another man in Nazi uniform was standing over him holding a wood handled metal rod, with an electric cable leading from it.

I recognized the figure in the chair, it was Bruce. Unfortunately at the same moment, so had Gerald, who rushed through the door at a terrific speed, like a bull in a china shop. Left with no other choice I followed blindly.

As we entered the chamber, I noticed there were two other people in the room as well. In the far corner a second person was fastened to a chair, another inquisitor leaning over him.

Gerald with total disregard for his own safety had gone for the one leaning over Bruce. I rushed across to the other man, as he turned with a complete look of amazement, I hit him full in the face.

The punch was enhanced by the speed of my own momentum, he'd hit the wall hard, his head making a nasty dull thudding sound as it connected with the stone surface, then he slid to the floor, out like a light. My hand hurt like hell but he would certainly have a good headache later.

I could see across the room that Bruce's inquisitor was also feeling no pain, Gerald astride the unconscious body.

Then came a massive shock, the most staggering twist to this whole Castleton affair. I looked down at the man tied to the chair next to me, fully expecting to see the face of John Cotes.

"Thank God, the cavalry is here at last old chap, thought you'd never make it," said a perfectly educated English accent. I froze in horror, for there, with blood pouring down the side of his head, and a broad beaming smirk on his face, was none other than our friend the big German!

The same man we'd been chasing half way across Europe for the last few days; the face I'd originally seen in those fields the night of the parachutes all those years before. I just could not believe my eyes, I was once again speechless.

He, too, had been interrogated heavily by his German captors, very seriously, by the look of his bloody face and busted hands. My mind shot back to the day when I'd thought I'd seen him in Cote's car, back in the village, though I'd still remained doubtful and quite confused.

Just as I was about to ask some serious questions, I heard a commotion; the sound of many voices and heavy footsteps running towards us along the tunnel.

"God dammit!" Gerald shouted, he swung around and rushed to position himself behind the door to accost and tackle anyone who entered. I grabbed the pistol from the belt of the man on the floor next to me, crouching down in readiness, the gun pointing at the doorway, as the approaching sounds became louder.

Out of the corner of my eye, I saw Gerald relax, and heard a familiar voice shout;

"Put the gun down, young Harper, you wouldn't shoot an old friend would you?" John Cotes came running into the chamber, looking across at me, then he said:

"I'll bet you've still got the safety catch on that thing, anyway."

"Don't bet on it," I replied, still feeling in a total state of shock, but I had to admit to myself I'd never before been so relieved to see any one in my life, it must have showed on my face.

He went across the room and began to undo the ropes that tied the big German who, once set free, began feverishly to work the circulation back into his hands and arms.

John continued to undo the ropes around the man's legs and then turned towards us as the big man staggered to his feet exercising his knees and legs.

Then as John Cotes turned to speak, I saw a look of absolute hatred and horror on the face of Gerald as I looked across towards him.

"Matt, Gerald, I'd like you to meet a very good friend and an old colleague of mine, this is Mark Strange," he added holding the palm of his hand out towards the big German, in a gesture of introduction. The big German walked towards me holding out his hand. Gerald and Bruce looked on in absolute disbelief.

"Was I ever pleased to see you two today, you appear to be quite a remarkable and tenacious young man, Matt," the German or whoever he was said. I refused his outstretched hand still not comprehending what on earth was happening or believing what I was hearing.

Gerald too, stood rooted to the ground, a look of total disbelief on his face, as Bruce staggered to his feet next to him.

"What the bloody hell's going on?" Gerald literally screamed across the dungeon.

"Mark, here, is an MI6 colleague, he's been working as a double agent for years during and after the war. Thanks to him, the possibility of a third world war has been averted, and a number of ambitious and dangerous people upstairs are just now being arrested by a special task force.

This force has been set up specifically to capture them red-handed with all of their merchandise, which we've done today. Until today, they've never allowed themselves to be seen in public as a group, to avoid being recognized and subsequently captured.

"We've been after them for years. Thanks to your invaluable help over the last few days, they won't be a threat to peace and world stability any more.

"Oh, the gold and priceless works of art they were going to collect so much money for? Well, once they tried to sell them to their buyers, it wouldn't have taken very long for them to be discovered as fakes; we systematically changed most them for the originals years ago.

"Gentlemen, today is a turning point in the history of mankind, a final nail in the coffin of Fascism and Nazism as we know it."

Gerald walked slowly across towards where Mark Strange was standing and held out his hand. The other man reciprocated.

Quick as a flash with no warning whatsoever, Gerald pulled back and hit him in the solar plexus with such force that he doubled forwards, then Gerald followed with a mighty uppercut to the chin that virtually lifted the big man clean off his feet, his head flew back with a nasty resounding crack. Gerald then followed through and hit him on the side of the neck with a right hand rabbit punch that came clear up and across from his left hip. The man collapsed in a noisy heap onto the cold floor.

"That's for Carl, Bruce, me, and anyone else you double-crossed, you two-timing bastard," said Gerald in a growl, building into a mighty roar.

"Oh no, God, no Gerald!" Cotes almost screamed, looking on at the scene of destruction.

The big man lay on the floor not stirring as we walked quietly from the room. Outside was a scene of much wild activity. All of the senior Nazis had been handcuffed and were being hustled into the back of the two white trucks by men wearing pale colored berets and some kind of combat uniform.

The three of us leaned against the ancient wall of the castle, watching the scene unfold before our eyes, totally and absolutely drained of all energy.

Then I began to shake violently, suddenly it had dawned on me that I could have killed that German inside the castle today. John Cotes came out into the courtyard.

"Gerald, Strange is hurt pretty bad, you could have broken his neck there," he said.

"It wasn't for want of trying," said my big friend, "just thank your lucky stars it's him and not you, Mr. bloody MI5," Gerald snarled as he walked away supporting his pal Bruce as he went.

In the courtyard of the castle Gerald climbed into one of the big Daimler Benz cars with the top down. Looking across at us he grinned. Bruce now leaned on me for support.

"Bruce get into this car next to me." Finally he gestured across at me and shouted:

"Now come on, young Harper, let's see how much you remember from your driving lesson the other night!" as he pointed towards a third car, a deep red one.

"We're taking these cars as payment for our services, you sort out the details Mr. Cotes," He looked hard at the agent, challenging John to argue as he started the engine then began to drive slowly towards the drawbridge. John Cotes came across to me.

"That safety catch was off, Matt!" he said to me with a sheepish grin across his face.

"Now you take good care of yourself, Matt Harper, I have the strangest of feelings that we'll meet again in the future," he shouted, waving as I pulled away a tad jerkily. Gerald had overheard John Cotes' comments and shouted back in reply.

"Not if we see you first, Mr. MI5, go take care of your friend, I think he's going to need a lot of tender loving care. And make sure we have clearance all the way through to home, will you?"

With that roughish grin on his face, he gave the final insult; he stood bolt upright in the open-top car and gave a German salute as we drove out to the road.

I realized that I had a considerably long journey in front of me, giving me plenty of time to reflect on all that had happened since the night of the parachutes all those years ago.

Before I could give this any serious reflection, Gerald turned round in the lead car with a big grin on his face.

"Convoy Ho!" he shouted militarily, waving his arm in a circle, and then pointing forward. The most unusual convoy took off down the road on the long journey home. As the others drove past me I saw the emblems on the front of their vehicles, as they shone in the early morning sunlight. It was only then; I noticed that mine was missing!

John Cotes stood in the middle of the road, his hands on his hips, shaking his head from side to side in disbelief, a broad grin across his face. Then suddenly he waved his hands in the air and raised his right hand in a military salute.

"God bless you, blokes, you're the salt of the earth. I'm grateful for all of your help. So is the whole world," he shouted after the fast disappearing trio of cars, hardly distinguishable now through a heavy cloud of dust.

He turned to see his opposite number from MI6, leaving the castle supported between two burly men. You're right Gerald. I do thank my lucky stars, sooner him than me! Mark, here isn't going to feel good for quite some time, if ever. He shuddered as the thought went through his mind, then he walked past the badly beaten man.

As I drove, perhaps more correctly described, *aimed* tentatively along that tree-lined forest road in the strange long car which felt more like Captain Pete's fishing boat than a motor vehicle, I thought of those people who had died, and especially of Carl Armitage.

I wondered: If I had told the police what John and I had witnessed that night back in the war, would it have changed events? I'll never know the answer now, but you can rest assured, that question will remain with me forever.

Some would say that the deaths of five people was quite a small price to pay to avert another world war, perhaps saving the lives of millions in the process. Particularly if their life wasn't one of the five who'd paid the ultimate sacrifice!

Enjoy other mystery novels by Mike Rollin.

Royal Di-lemma
Mayhem in Paradise
Vengeance

Read a synopsis of each of these thrillers on the web site.: **mrlproductions.net**

Book reviews from professionals and book buyers alike are raving about Mike Rollin's first mystery novel 'Royal Di-lemma.'

In their own words:

Mike Rollin has used the premise of a well-known tale to create a fast-moving story of romance between a People's Princess and the son of a powerful, wealthy man determined to gain British citizenship - at any cost. The short chapters and crisp writing keep the story moving along in what feels like real time. With active point of view shifts, the reader is able to glean the entire story from every imaginable angle which makes the tale ever more compelling.

Mike Rollin's *Royal Di-lemma* is a behind the scenes glimpse of a monarchy determined to retain its power and government agencies determined to control destiny. It is a great, engaging quick read with an ending that does not disappoint. **Professional Reviewer: Lisa Haselton**

Shirley Roe, All Books Review states: A princess and the son of a wealthy international businessman meet at a party and have an instant connection. While security is high and privacy is low, the two fall in love and envision a future together, knowing there are large obstacles to overcome. Together, they are determined to make their future a reality.

Various people in powerful positions want the relationship to end—at any cost. *Royal Di-lemma* is a roller coaster thrill ride through streets, on water, and in the air. You may think you know what is coming as you turn the page, but what you find will surprise you.

"What a spoof of the firm (Royal Family)! I thank you for entertaining reading! 5*" **Colorado reader / Laura**, a recent buyer, had a simpler review: **"I Love It!"**

Get your copy today for a really great read.